THE BRASS GOD

First published 2018 by Solaris
an imprint of Rebellion Publishing Ltd,
Riverside House, Osney Mead,
Oxford, OX2 0ES, UK

www.solarisbooks.com

ISBN: 978 1 78108 507 3

10 9 8 7 6 5 4 3 2 1

A CIP catalogue record for this book is available
from the British Library.

Designed & typeset by Rebellion Publishing

Printed in Denmark

The BRASS GOD

The GATES of the WORLD Book Three

K. M. McKINLEY

SOLARIS

A Political Map *of the*
HUNDRED KINGDOMS
of RUTHNIA

IRRICA

CORREADOS

THREE
LANDS

GALLONIA

QUIREADOS

WEST
FARTHI

MUSRA

SOUTH WE
FARTHIA

MARCENY

Perus

MACER
LESSER

MACERIYA

Stoncastrum

KARSA

Karsa
City

CORREND

GIRARSA

HERRING
STATES

BIFESTINIA

TULCVA

S

CHAPTER ONE

An Unwelcome Recovery

A HARD LURCH startled Tuvacs to consciousness. Dark dreams chased him from a black hell. He scrabbled for purchase on the waking world. Tuvacs' hands pressed against wood. He tried to sit, but his movements were restricted and sharp pain tore across his back. Muscles spasmed all over his body in a storm of cramps. His eyes were so dry his eyelids would not part, and when they did they scraped mercilessly. When finally he struggled his eyes open, he was forced to shut them against the sky. Weight dragged at his arms as he shielded his face. He wanted to vomit. Dazzled, his head spinning, he fell back onto the wood, his skull glancing on metal bars on the way. He lay on his side and waited for his senses to return, panting lightly to lessen his nausea. Rallying what few resources his body had to offer, he propped himself up on his elbows, and rested the back of his head against the bars to stop it falling down. The effort made him shake. The bars juddered with motion, each start bounced him against iron, but he was too dazed to move again. All that effort and he had not even managed to sit.

7

"You're awake, welcome back from the halls of the dead," said someone in accented Low Maceriyan.

Tuvacs squinted. After a time, his situation came into focus. From harsh daylight, a miserable scene resolved. Dejected prisoners sat shackled against iron bars in a cage mounted upon the back of a wagon, and he realised for the first time that his hands were manacled to a short chain like theirs. The uneven rocking called forth a harsh music of grinding wood and metal. The prisoners were silent. A light breeze could not overcome the hard, animal stink of the cage, made worse by the reek of the giant beast hauling the wagon. A boy, a young man he supposed, not much younger than himself, stared at him expectantly. Tuvacs stared back.

"Wagon," said Tuvacs. His voice came out a croak. "We're on a wagon." Figuring that out felt like a small triumph. He wanted to share. It was all he could do. Tuvacs closed his eyes. His head was full of wool and his thoughts struggled to fight their way through.

A thin blanket half-covered him. He plucked at it with feeble fingers, pulling it further over his legs. It did little to keep off the freshness of the breeze. "I was warm in my sleep," he said. He shivered. "I'm cold. Cold. I am so hungry."

"Yeah. We all are," said the young man. "It's freezing in this wagon at night, and what they do feed us you don't want to eat. You're one of the lucky ones. You were dying. Now you are not. There were dozens of men in this caravan who were in better shape than you, but who are dead now."

The light, filtered pinkly through Tuvac's eyelids, went dark. He must have fallen asleep. When he opened them again he found the youth staring down at him, curly hair made a halo by the sun behind it. He shook Tuvacs' shoulder. His chains rattled.

"You must wake now. They didn't kill you. They might if you don't show some strength."

"Who are they?" said Tuvacs, sincerely wishing the youth would leave him alone. "I feel like I'm dead anyway," he said miserably.

"You are not dead, not yet, though you nearly were." The youth was angry. "I've seen lots of people die. Be grateful you're not among them."

"Where am I?"

"You are a prisoner of the modalmen."

The youth helped Tuvacs up into a sitting position. The skin on his back stretched painfully, like it might tear.

"Gods." He couldn't suppress a whimper.

"Your back was hurt. The wounds were deep, they got infected. You have been locked in a fever. None of us thought you would survive." The young man spoke at a normal volume, but with the others being silent it sounded dangerously loud. Their fellow prisoners gave them looks that held more than a modicum of fear. The young man ignored them.

Tuvacs screwed his eyes up and looked past the bars.

Under skies of perfect blue, a caravan rolled across the Black Sands. Ahead and behind, cage wagons moved steadily in single file. Some were furnished with bars made of bone instead of metal. Each was pulled by a massive creature. Reddish manes crowned their long necks, spines and shoulders, elsewhere their skin was bare and the colour of cooling charcoal. Grooves and whorls marked their flesh, glimmering faintly with an inner light that could not compete with the sun. They plodded with their wide heads low, eyes and nostrils half-shut against the blowing sand. High shoulders over long forelimbs sloped down to massively muscled hindquarters, where two further pairs of legs were grouped apart from the fore pair.

"How long?" croaked Tuvacs.

The young man shrugged despondently. His attitude was an odd mix of defiance and resignation. "Weeks, definitely. Months, maybe. I've lost track of time. Got worse things to think about, like who is going to get eaten next. You should have died a while ago. They ate most of the rest of the injured. Beats me why they kept you alive. There's something going on here with you. Some of the others think they're testing us, keeping you alive."

"Do you think so?"

"I think a man will say anything to remove the randomness from his life. The worst seems a little better when there's a reason behind it."

Tuvacs pushed himself more upright. Pain raced across his back, hammered behind his temples. Everything hurt.

"You nearly died," said the young man again.

"I'm thirsty."

"I would give you water, but there is none."

"Who treated me?" asked Tuvacs.

"Me, mostly. But that one there saved your life." The youth nodded toward an old man sleeping against the bars. Tuvacs recognised Metruzzo. He didn't know him well, but he had been on the railhead staff manifest, a minor magister with the profession of surgeon-barber and an unfortunate gambling habit.

Tuvacs rolled up the arms of a shirt he didn't recognise. Sure enough, magisters marks had been painted onto his skin, in his own blood, by the looks of it.

"It was just you two?"

The young man shrugged. "No one else helped. No one cares. This is a cage full of islands of misery, every one alone. I fed you. Cleaned you, gave you water when we had it. The modalmen insisted. We were starving. The others hate you for the waste. You were raving at times. You kept us from sleeping."

The other prisoners watched him in silent hostility.

Tuvacs examined what he was wearing. Patches of his britches were thick with dried blood, and his jacket and shirt had gone. The shirt was two sizes too big with a hole punched through over the heart. He didn't have to ask where it had come from.

"Your clothes were ruined, the back was all ripped open, stiff with dried blood. Metruzzo had to cut them away."

"It doesn't matter," said Tuvacs. "They are just clothes, and this shirt is better than my old one."

"Don't you remember what happened? We've been in here together for a long time. Sometimes, you seemed lucid."

Tuvacs shook his head. All his body was wasted. His neck felt as thin and brittle as a chicken bone. "Thank you."

"I had no choice," said the young man. "They wanted you alive. They made that clear to me. It would have been my head if you died. Somebody would have been made to, if it weren't me. The modalmen would have made it happen. Their leader speaks a bit of Maceriyan. Brauctha. Nasty bastard." The boy rolled his 'r's heavily; he was Mohaca like Tuvacs, but not from the city. A country boy.

Tuvacs looked around at the others in the cage. He thought it likely most of them would have let him die even if forced to care. There were easy ways to finish a dying man. He would have been disgusted, but he honestly didn't know if he would have done better.

There was no way out. Either side of the caravan went the modalmen themselves. Most were mounted on the same breed of beast as pulled the carriages. From poles attached to the back of their high saddles, pennants decorated with barbarous writing snapped in the breeze. A few of the modalmen walked alongside the cages, massive weapons cradled in their four arms. They wore heavy boots and thick trousers. Their heads were covered against the sun with scarves, and so Tuvacs could not see how their faces were, but their torsos were naked, covered in the same grooved spirals as those on their beasts, and their skin was grey-black also. One trudged past, inches away, head bowed in thought, covering the ground easily despite the slowness of his stride. Tuvacs was astounded by the modalman's size. He was bigger than a Torosan godling and more heavily muscled. Another kind of six-legged creature walked obediently at the warrior's side, head broad and short like that of a hunting dracon, but the snout was capped with a horny beak from which protruded glaring fangs. It had none of the reddish fur of its cousin species, but its skin was the same black, and also deeply carved with spirals. The modalman ignored the prisoners, but the eyes of the hunting creature fixed themselves on Tuvacs. It bared the full length of its teeth, showing bright pink gums, and let out a deep growl.

"By the gods," Tuvacs said.

"It does no good to pray to them," said the youth. "I've tried."

Tuvacs managed a smile. His lips cracked. "The bastards wouldn't listen even had old Iapetus not kicked them out."

The boy grinned at him. "You are Karsan? You spoke mostly that while you were ill. I do not know much of the language."

Tuvacs shook his head. "Mohaca."

The boy sat up, eyes bright with pleasure. "Then that is something good. I am pleased to meet you, my fellow countryman!" said the boy, switching from Low Maceriyan to Mohacin. "What is your name?'

"Alovo Tuvacs," said Tuvacs.

"I am Rafozak, friends call me Rafozo."

"As they might call me Tuvaco."

They touched their hearts and shook hands in the way of their people. Tuvac's hand felt heavy on the end of his arm. He was alarmed at how feeble he had become.

"It always pays to have a friend, Rafozo, especially in bad times like these." Tuvacs affected a calm he did not feel.

"Metruzzo said you came from Railhead," said Rafozo.

"From the rail head. The end of the line, not the town," said Tuvacs. "Stupid name to call the town, though I suppose Railhead was at the head of the rails once." In the cage wagon talking of towns, places where people went freely about their lives, seemed ridiculous. The boy was impressed nevertheless. A new light came into his eyes.

"So you've been out here working?"

"Yes." Tuvacs frowned. "You weren't taken from the desert?"

Rafozo smiled shyly. "My life was very boring. Always, I said to my father that I wished to work the glimmer, but he said no, and I was a dutiful son. Now I have my wish for adventure, and I regret it. I was taken from a caravan headed out from Horoecz over the Kulzanki Pass to Farside to trade. We were attacked as we came down to the grasslands from the mountains. My father sold grain to the farmers that way. He's dead," said the boy matter-of-factly. "He died defending our drays."

"Kulzanki Pass?" said Tuvacs. "That's nearly two thousand miles from the Gates of the World, and far from the desert too."

"Farside is broad there," Rafozo nodded, and lowered his voice. "Some of the others here are from even further afield. Modalmen have been raiding over the mountains, sometimes deep into Farside, always in small groups."

"They'd be seeking to avoid retaliation by attacking at once," said Tuvacs tiredly. His throat burned with thirst. "Small groups move quickly."

"Do you remember what happened to you?" asked Rafozo.

"I was at the edge of camp when they attacked," said Tuvacs quietly. "I got away, on the back of a dray. Something caught us."

"Your back was torn up by one of their hounds. I am amazed you survived."

"I was alone?"

"You were alone."

Images flashed into Tuvacs' mind. Julion, speared like a lizard. A burst of flame from the construction camp, and Boskovin, stupid Boskovin making a pass at him and getting riled when Tuvacs did not respond favourably. Boskovin was pitiable, and had otherwise been good to him. The modalmen had killed him. Tuvacs' face fell.

"I am sorry," said Rafozo.

Tuvacs looked away. The images lingered in his mind. He was glad his voice was already a wreck, it covered its breaking.

"Remind me to thank Metruzzo," said Tuvacs. From the relatively clean state of his clothing, Tuvacs guessed Rafozo had helped him relieve himself. Sitting in his own shit until they got to wherever they were going would have been unbearable. He was more grateful for this preservation of his dignity than anything else.

Thinking about toileting brought on an urgency to Tuvacs' bladder. "I need to piss." He stood gingerly, wincing as he hooked his braces over his shoulders—at least he still had those.

"Your strength returns!" said Rafozo.

"Not really," said Tuvacs. He gripped the bars. Black spots danced across his vision, and he had to close his eyes for a moment. The rocking of the wagon made the weakness of his legs worse. It took a few minutes before he trusted them with his weight.

"I suppose I just point it out into the air?"

"That's the way. We made a space for those who need to crap." Tuvacs pointed out the one spot at the back of the wagon where no one was sitting. The bars were too tightly spaced to stick a backside through, and the boards there were thick with matter.

"We shovel it out after—"

"I understand," said Tuvacs. He took several attempts to unbutton his britches flap. He aimed out between the bars and let out a long stream of dark urine that splattered loudly on the sand. The modalmen ranged alongside glanced at him, then went back to staring at the ground.

"The modalmen don't seem very interested in us," said Tuvacs, doing himself up again.

"Most aren't," said Rafozo. He became wary, and dropped his voice. "There's one who is the most dangerous, worse even than Brauctha, and he is interested in us, but only for hurting. We call him Golden Rings, for the jewellery he wears in his face. He hurts men for pleasure. It is his job to select the ones who will be taken out, and they do not return. Mostly they take the weak, but some they let live that you'd think they'd kill, like you, no offence."

"There is none to be taken," said Tuvacs.

"They've killed some strong men too, and..." he became downcast. "And there were a few women and children. They were the first to go, along with the old. There were fifty of us in here to begin with. Those that showed their fear openly were taken early on, after the women and the children. Those that go mad are carried off. Men go mad all the time in the cages. It is impossible to predict who will break next. The hardest of men fail under such pressure. When I was taken, there was so little space in the cage we could barely breathe. Several men died from thirst and exhaustion in those awful first weeks, until the choosing began." He sat back. "Now we all have plenty of room."

"I survived that?" said Tuvacs.

"Yes." Rafozo dropped his voice. "They are eaten, the ones they take. They eat them, and they also feed them to us. I warn you, Tuvaco. Check your food. The modalmen's broth is not always made of good meat."

Rafozo looked frightened.

Tuvacs glanced out at the modalmen trudging alongside the cage. "Is it safe to talk?"

"The rest of the modalmen do not care as long as we make little noise in the day. Not many of them know the tongues of the west. At night it is different, then they do not allow a single word."

"Nobody else is speaking," said Tuvacs. Eerie silence punctuated his and Rafozo's conversation. The modalmen and their beasts were quiet, and the desert was empty of life beside the caravan.

"They are in despair, and most do not speak Maceriyan. Karsarin is unknown to them," said Rafozo. "Two are our countrymen." He jerked his head down toward the front of the cage. "I talk with them, but they are frightened, and will not speak much. The rest are from everywhere, up and down the mountains. They won't talk anyway. Golden Rings has snatched out men who speak overmuch, or laugh. He hates laughter. Fulx there, he is Marovesi." He nodded at a sleeping man. "He used to talk. He doesn't any more. Dunets is the only one who says much, but he's a shithead, a bully who will steal your shirt if you let him. He talked one man into biting out his own wrists because Dunets wanted his boots," he said, pointing at a second sleeping man, better fed and dressed than the others. "The rest are the same as you find anywhere, some good, some bad."

Tuvacs took a closer look at his fellow prisoners. He counted twenty-three, many with facial features and modes of dress unfamiliar to him.

Despite the disappearance of the weakest, the people in the cage appeared well fed, if dirty. His own thinness was unusual.

"What do they want us for?"

"I can't say," said Rafozo.

"Where are we going?" said Tuvacs.

"North," said Rafozo. "The desert plays tricks on us. The sun does not always move as it should across the southern sky, but I'm sure we're going north"

"How many cages like this are there?"

"Many," said Rafozo. "I haven't been able to count them all. There are hundreds of modalmen here. An army goes ahead of us, and a rearguard some miles behind. I think they are being followed. I will not hope it is men who come after them to save us."

Tuvacs fought back dizziness to crane his neck and get a better view past the draft beast to the front, then past the wagon behind. He counted five further wagons. The dust in the air suggested many more.

The caravan started to climb the side of a low ridge that ran to the horizon. The land here was rockier than the site of the massacre, but the black sand of the desert was ubiquitous and coated the ground thickly. The formations of red stone rising from it looked like the hairy backs of the creatures. Tuvacs looked back as they went up, the elevation allowing him to count a dozen more cages.

The wagon crested the ridge, and began to descend to a plain free of rocks, dominated by black sand alone. The cages made a long line winding across the desert, flanked by lines of dispersed modalmen riders and infantry. Fifty or so cage wagons down the line, other carts and wagons bunched together at the head of the convoy, beyond that was the modalman horde, huge shapes shrouded in the dust of their marching.

"Why are they going north?" Tuvacs asked. "There's nothing north; only desert, then the High Spine."

"What are you thinking?" said Rafozo. A few of the others were looking at him now, woken by their talking.

"That none of it will matter if we end up on a modalman's plate." Tuvacs gripped the bars tighter, watching the vast cloud of dust kicked up by the modalmen.

"Are you proposing escape?" when Rafozo said this, a couple of the prisoners who knew Mohacin looked at Tuvacs expectantly. Their interest spread further. The prisoners leaned in to listen.

Tuvacs' legs had used up their little strength and he sank to a painful crouch. "Maybe. It would be better than sitting around waiting to see in whose gut we end up, don't you think?"

Rafozo shrugged. "I do not want to stay here and find out."

Tuvacs thought about Suala, carrying his child back at the camp, and about his sister Lavinia, whom he had been forced to abandon in Karsa. Not once in his life had he sat back and taken what life had thrown at him, not when their parents died, not when he was struggling to survive as a gleaner in Mohacs-Gravo, not when he had fled with his sister to the faraway Karsan isles.

And not when the modalmen had attacked. Not even then.

Tuvacs felt behind himself, brushing his fingers against the bar he rested against. It was a thick piece of iron set directly into a socket in the wood without screws or other fastenings. He grasped it and tugged. It jiggled a little in its hole. He turned to face the bar. The wood's grain was exposed by erosion and desiccation. He picked a few splinters out with his fingernail from around the bar's base.

"This will come out, if we have enough time," Tuvacs said.

CHAPTER TWO
Unholy Alliance

AGE WAS PAIN. Adamanka Shrane got up from her morning prayers grimacing at the throb in her limbs. Her muscles creaked. Her knuckles ached. Her knees required a certain effort to straighten, and they did so to a fusillade of popping cartilage.

She hobbled from her prayer mat to her bed and sat with a groan.

Summer was only halfway through; the hottest time of the year had yet to come. Already the morning's sun beat on the lead roof of the Pantheon Maximale. Her quarters in the tower would be stifling by noon. Rain fell rarely that year, and only the times when the Godhome shaded the city provided respite from the heat. Nevertheless, she was always cold. Age came on her faster and harder than it ever had. Shrane turned her hands this way and that. A mere two years since her last rejuvenation and she was already ancient. Her skin was wrinkling, thinning to the point of translucency. The faint outlines of emerging liver spots dotted the back of her right hand. The marks were the first to appear. This time they had come quickly. She frowned at their unwelcome return.

When she had been young—not truly young, but after the first couple of rejuvenations in the pool of the Iron Fane she still regarded herself so—she had been vain. The gift had gladdened her. Back then she lived for years between immersions, but the effect of youth now lasted such a short time, and each expenditure of magic she made to hurry the Iron Gods' return aged her faster.

There were other, new hurts she had never experienced before. An ache so persistent it took on solidity; the invisible wound where the Iron Gods' king had split her in twain. There had been no pain until her other self's death in the Sotherwinter ice, where she was slain by the Goddriver's scion, Vols Iapetus. Only then had the sting of the king's sword returned, never to leave again.

With the death of her magical duplicate, much of Shrane's power had consolidated itself in this single body, along with the memories and experience her other self had gathered. But by no means everything had come back, and the sense of something lacking gnawed at her in the night. Most unsettling of all was the uncertainty of who had been the real Shrane; her, in Perus, or the one who had gone south. She feared that she didn't exist at all any more, but was a copy of herself.

"I live to serve," she whispered, and made the sign of the Iron Church, a loosely curled fist placed on her stomach. Her mouth was gummy. Her lips were slack over her teeth, and never properly closed. Still she was glad. Vols Iapetus died defeating her. She had served well. The Iron Gods had arrived at the city of their ancient enemy, the Morfaan, and mustered a huge army there. Had she been of one body, she did not doubt that she would have survived her confrontation. Empowered by her masters, she would have smashed down Iapetus without injury.

That was not to be, so she put it from her mind. Shrane had an uncommon focus. She did not allow regret or pride to distract her.

She stood stiffly, but as she crossed the floor to the round window she grew stronger. She opened the slatted blinds fully and pushed open the single-hinged pane, allowing the smoky air of Perus into her rooms. The sun was still climbing. It was an hour or so until it would be blocked out by the looming disc of the Godhome whose edge rested on the hills of the Royal Park like a lid half-lifted from a pot. Warm peach sunshine sliced through the slats, dividing up her room into narrow lanes of light and dark.

She began the day's tasks. Her night robe dropped to the floor. She took toilet and cleaned herself with water and cloths. She looked in her mirror sparingly, so as not to see that her body had lost its voluptuousness. She dressed hastily.

Once her iron staff was in her hand she felt powerful again, though her palm tingled at its touch. She gave a quiet gasp of pleasure as its magic washed through her, driving out aches and pains, straightening her posture. For the time being age was a fleeting visitor. It came in as surely as the tides of the Earth, and receded with the sun's rising. However, at the close of each passing day she was a little older. She wondered if the pool of the Iron Fane would regenerate her at all next time she visited it. For every one of her predecessors there had come an occasion when it had ceased to work.

She stood taller, and took in a deep, resolute breath.

Only then did she notice the man standing in the doorway leading into the dark attic over the Pantheon's knave. He lurked outside the rule-straight beams of sunlight where velvety blackness clung to exposed stone and wood. He was hardly there, just a glimmer of eyes in the shadow. He only assumed a solid shape as he stepped forward; a shadow seeming to detach from the darkness into fully rounded life.

She gasped at being caught unawares, and levelled her staff at him.

"A little alarmed to have a strange man watching you dress?" said the stranger. He smiled insinuatingly.

"You are no man," said Shrane. There was strength in her words. A shiver of magic passed over the stranger. He made an admonishing face and waved his hand, as if shooing away an insect.

Shrane flinched as her spell was dismissed. The end of her staff jerked up a half inch, momentarily out of her control. She pushed it back down and kept the top trained on him.

"There is no need to attack me in that way. You could simply ask me what I want," he said. He stepped closer, emerging further into the fuzzy light, though he avoided the stark slices of sunlight pouring through the blind.

He was unhealthy. His skin was pallid, with a greasy sheen, with red patches around his mouth and nostrils in bright contrast. He had shoulder length hair, very dirty. Missing hanks exposed his scalp. His teeth were rotting in his head, and his breath reeked so strongly

Shrane smelled it across the room. His clothes were Karsan, finely cut, but threadbare and caked in filth.

"I am not fit for court, I realise. This shell takes badly to my presence. It appears both you and I suffer a regrettable degeneration of physique. Such is the burden of power."

"Who are you?"

The stranger held up a finger. "It must be very unnerving for such a grand puppeteer like yourself to be so ambushed. I have been watching you for a few weeks. You use others." He looked down. Beneath the planks of wood and stone under his feet, the cathedral was full of the devout. He smiled a brown smile, as if he could see the congregation of the Church of the Returned running about like ants in the hall below. "I will not be used."

Shrane followed the man with the head of her staff as he paced around the pool of patterned light. She had little affection for her accommodation. She had laired here out of necessity, if with a certain ironic glee at skulking in the church of the false gods, but having this thing in there with her was a violation.

Shrane forced back panic, and appraised her foe. He was not human, but wore a man's body. There was something else inside the cloak of flesh, something wicked.

"You are of the Y Dvar," she said.

The man dipped his head. "That is so."

"Are you one of the false gods?" Her grip tightened on her staff. This was an unwelcome development. A god, even a false god, she could not stand against, not with all the power her masters had invested her with. One of their servants she might best. She wracked her memory, looking for signs that would help her discern what order of being he was. She had been a young woman when the gods and their ilk were driven away. They were unimportant to her church, and she had been taught to disdain them. Facing one in person was another matter.

"You are asking yourself, now how can that be, when Res Iapetus banished them?' said the man. He was enjoying himself. His rotten smile made her heart pound with fear.

"You have got back into the world."

"Or I never left."

"The numbers of the remaining gods are but two."

"Not true," he said. He trailed his filthy fingers curiously along Shrane's few possessions. He came close to touching the cloth bound sacred book of her church. She was the last of its adherents. The book was all she had of her people. She tensed. He paused before touching it, then withdrew his hand carefully with a knowing smile. If he was vulnerable to its sacred nature, that was something. She shifted her stance. There was a scent of corruption to him beneath his body's stink.

"Reveal yourself," she said, putting a touch of magic into her voice. Her veins burned. Her sorcery was a poisonous sort wedded to iron, powerful but deadly to its user.

The Y Dvar grimaced, and again brushed her power away. "I told you not to do that. The wards of the ancient gates are weakening, a situation you and your masters are abusing. You know this. There is no need for enchantment."

"Then speak freely!" she said, suffusing her utterance with more power. The being flinched.

"You do have some ability. Very well, I said I would say! Really." He tutted, then he bowed. "I am no god, but merely a servant of the Dark Lady, ostensibly anyway. I serve myself in the main. You have been using the lure of the gods to make men do your bidding." He wagged his finger and shook his head. "Very naughty."

"You cannot stop me. Your gods are not gods. I commit no blasphemy."

"I have no intention of stopping you," he said. "And, for the record, your gods are not gods either. It just so happens the aims of these gods who are not gods concord. I come to you in the spirit of alliance. We should work together. You wish to allow the Draathis back onto this Earth, I would allow the return of my mistress's pantheon to their home. These desires are not mutually exclusive."

"The gods of men are irrelevant to the Draathis."

The being shrugged. "Maybe they were once. Times change."

"And if I refuse?"

"Ah, well," he ran his hand along a shelf, holding it up to inspect for dust. He frowned at the grime he found, and wiped it on his dirty clothes. "Then I will have to stop you."

"You cannot," she said.

"Do really want to risk that? You are close to success. I understand you are the last of your kind. If you fail, then your entire line will have wasted several thousand years of their time. Think! An entire culture dedicated to one cause, pursuing it doggedly, and you come within a hair's breadth only to throw it away by making the wrong decision." He looked at her sharply. "So I advise you, don't make the wrong decision. Come now, you and I are only servants. We can work together. Our respective masters can resolve any problems they may have with each other once they are all safely back upon this world."

She hesitated, then put up her staff and let its butt slide to the floor with a clank. A choir had begun practicing in the cathedral. Since the incident on the Godhome and the lights seen there, the numbers of worshippers coming to the Pantheon had increased sharply

"Perhaps," she said. "Give me your name."

He smiled. "I never had one until recently."

"So you are of the lesser Y Dvar, and not of the benevolent kind."

"How can you tell?" said the thing with mock hurt.

"The stench gives you away."

"Oh very good," he chortled softly. "Yes, I am, well, I *was* Y Dvar. At the moment I am not. I am here because I have found someone whose testimony will aid you in your aims, if you will but choose to ally yourself with me."

"Then, goodfellow," she said levelly, "who are you at the moment, until your stolen body falls apart? Reveal your name to me, and we might bargain."

"I have nothing to lose by giving you my name, and everything to gain. All you had to do was ask." The being made a deep, elaborate bow. "My name is Guis Kressind," it said, with genuine relish.

"And who is this other you speak of?"

"Ah, I think you know him. In fact, if I'm correct, you're the one that sent him and his lady friend off on their perilous little jaunt."

"That boy," she said. "Harafan. You found him?" This was bad news. She had been looking for the Harafan herself.

"Harafan, yes, that's the chap. I found him before you could, you see. A handsome young fellow, and as I see it, an important part of your schemes. I am sure Comte Raganse will be intrigued to know that he was recently on the Godhome. I think that was your intention for him, wasn't it?"

"What is the bargain you offer?"

"Cooperation, a pooling of resources. We work together to bring the Draathis to Perus, and the gods also."

"If I refuse?"

He grinned evilly. "My dear goodlady, either Harafan can come with both of us to see the comte, or he won't be coming at all."

CHAPTER THREE
Bad Tidings

ARKADIAN VAND WAS not accustomed to silence. For days he had been rushing from one factory to another. All his world had been constructed of noise. His affairs in Maceriya in particular concerned him greatly; all this nonsense about the gods' return had the lands of the old Maceriyan septet in uproar. Revolution was in the air, and such political upheavals had a tendency to divest men like Vand unfairly of their assets. Meetings with his agents and the grandees of various governments had taken him across nine lands in as many days. To add to the upheaval on the continent, Katriona Kressinda-Morthrocksa had been agitating for greater rights for the workers of Karsa, and the movement was gaining traction there. If it took root in the heartlands of industrialisation, it would be but a matter of time until it spread across the continent. Vand had barely slept, barely eaten and his clothes smelled of spent glimmer from the many trains he had ridden. A week and a half had whirled away, the passing of the days marked by the clatter of train wheels, the roaring of engines, and the shouting of stressed men.

Then there was discovery at the dig at the Three Sisters and that, above all other things, required his attention.

Now this.

His office in Karsa City was unbearably quiet. Three clocks ticked loudly. Some city noise worked its way in through the tall windows. Vand heard none of it. A bowl of apples, his favourite fruit, sat untouched on his desk.

The report held his attention in a trap. His clenched hands stretched the paper until it was taut as a drum skin. One more tug would take it past the point of failure. Vand understood material tolerance better than any man alive, and held it there purposefully.

The cords on his neck stood out hard. Men of vast wealth were often fat. Vand would have hated to be thought so. Persin, his rival, was fat. Vand worked hard to keep his body trim.

Arkadian Vand was a man who liked to know everything about everything, but he did not know how he felt about this news. Not exactly. What was better: absolute knowledge that Trassan Kressind was gone, a cruel blow which could be absorbed and dealt with, or fretful uncertainty, which at least had the benefit of hope but which bred anxiety?

His breath through his nostrils, when he finally exhaled, was acid. Vand despised anxiety even more than inexactitude. At that moment, therefore, he despised himself the most.

"You say he is probably dead." Vand pulled the paper tighter, reading the short report on it again. "You are not certain he *is* dead."

Two men were in front of his desk. Goodman Robar Filden stood ramrod straight. The man had never shaken off his military past. Such habits as the army had drummed into him were both useful and irritating to Vand. Filden kept his gaze fixed over Vand's head, as if he were permanently waiting for a dressing down from a superior officer. His pale, scarred face was studiously blank. He looked old and weak, but Filden was anything but. Magister Hissenwar was forged from different steel, and managed to look simultaneously sympathetic and nervous. He had a broad, worrisome prospect, like an owl, features that were uncanny despite their complete blandness. He annoyed Vand more than Filden, although they were in good company. Nearly everyone and everything annoyed Vand. Nothing went fast or far enough for him.

"Convinced he is dead, yes," said Hissenwar. "Certain, no. Two scheduled sendings from the mage on the *Prince Alfra* have come and gone without word. We cannot find his etheric signature, which suggests that he is dead, which suggests..." He shrugged, and let the sentence hang.

How on earth this miserable piss streak had gathered the funds to attend the magister's college confounded Vand. Hissenwar was from the impoverished Three Lands. Two sun scorched islands and a scrubby peninsula in the Ellosantin Sea comprised their territorial extent. A sleepy backwater of goats and smug idiots who prattled on all day about how nice it was.

Hissenwar redeemed himself by being an unusually talented magister. Vand's temper made no allowance for that.

"What by all the hells does that mean?" demanded Vand.

"We cannot read the ship. We cannot even find it. The ship is a needle. The Southern Ocean enormous. You might as well ask me and my comrades to find a particular goat in Khushashia."

"There are many goats in Khushashia, but there is only one iron ship, Hissenwar," snorted Vand.

"There are many hundreds of thousands of square leagues of water," explained Hissenwar patiently.

Vand felt ashamed. Another emotion he hid. Hissenwar was handling this well. Vand was not. What could he expect? Trassan Kressind was... He was...

He is dead, thought Vand. *That is what he is*. The report was clear on the page before him. Hope tormented him; he turned it upon his men as anger.

The only outward sign of Vand's upset was a slight lessening of the deep frown. Too subtle for his employees to notice.

"Have you tried the site of the city?" he asked gruffly.

"Achieving an accurate sending to the Morfaan city before was hard, Goodman Vand. You will recollect that we could never approach too closely in spirit form." Hissenwar spread his hands. His fingers were stained with ink. "And regrettably, something has occurred there. Our rituals can no longer summon sufficient energy to get us close."

"What about your machines?"

"They are no help. It has become harder."

"How much harder?"

"Harder, as in impossible," said the magister apologetically.

"So," said Vand, laying the message upon his blotter and smoothing it flat. "You extrapolate, without evidence, from this phenomenon that you cannot descry correctly, that Trassan Kressind is dead."

"My lord," said Hissenwar more forcefully. "The *Prince Alfra* is missing. For all we know it is at the bottom of the sea. There is an enormous amount of magical flux present on the Sotherwinter continent that simply was not there before. From the distance we could astrally approach to, we see an immense column of steam rising from the city's site. In my opinion, Goodfellow Kressind attempted to activate the machines there without proper precautions. He was a fine engineer, but he had no magisterial training, and he was impetuous. I—"

"How dare you!" Vand shot to his feet, his face flushing red. He held out an accusatory finger. Filden arched an eyebrow at him. Vand took breath, and reigned in his rage. "How dare you," he repeated without shouting. "Trassan Kressind may not have your particular, limited gifts, but he is a thousand times the engineer you will ever be. Do you hear me?"

"Goodman, you must appreciate—"

Vand's fragile hold on his emotions broke. "I said, do you hear me?" he bellowed. A delayed warmth followed by a throbbing pain informed him he was pounding his fist upon the table so hard it hurt. So this is grief. The analytical part of Vand that never slept, that was both his curse and his genius, catalogued his pain, pinning it down like an entomologist's sample.

Damn you, Vand thought. "I pay you for facts, not opinions. Get me more facts. Approach this like the rationalist you proclaim yourself to be. No more witch's mumblings about bad portents or shrouding veils."

"Goodman, I assure you our machines are built to the most stringent rationalist principles. We are empiricists, not witch doctors. We operate at the limit of their—"

"One day, goodmagister," Vand interrupted again, "I am going to examine your machines. I am sure I shall uncover their numerous weaknesses in short order. After improving them, I am going to put you out of a job. Do you hear? What am I paying you for?"

"Magical engineering is not as straightforward as what you may think," said Hissenwar.

"Permit me to disagree with you," said Vand. "Trassan Kressind could manage it despite his supposed lack of talents," he finished pointedly.

Hissenwar blinked at him.

"I don't care how much money you have to spend fixing your gods-damned remote sending apparatus, or how many lesser magisters you exhaust operating them, find me Trassan Kressind!"

"Goodman," said Hissenwar, whose shell of confidence had been stripped away to nothing by Vand's verbal assault. "You must understand—"

"No goodmagister, *you* must understand," said Vand, stabbing his finger at Hissenwar. "That I am paying you to do a very specific task for me. If you cannot, then I will be forced to replace you."

"Goodman—"

"Out!" roared Vand.

Hissenwar bobbed his head submissively, nearly tripping on his robes as he left the room. Vand glared hard at the door after it had shut.

"Incompetent. What am I paying these fools for?"

"Goodman," said Filden, who expected Vand's robust admonishment every day, and was therefore better placed to take it. "This whole venture was a risk. We were prepared for failure. This outcome was foreseen."

For failure, yes, thought Vand. *But to lose Trassan. I have no sons,* he nearly confessed. *He was my successor. Can't you see? My son is dead!*

If he spoke aloud he would have spat those words like bullets, but thinking them weakened his rage immensely, and he sat heavily into his chair, diminished by loss, wrung out by despair.

"This is a damned catastrophe, Filden," he said quietly. There was a bowl full of Morfaan silver beads on his desk next to the apples. Vand picked one up and rolled it between thumb and forefinger, letting its grooves rub upon the ridges of his fingerprints.

Filden saw this moment of introspection, and made an error. "Goodman, if we had a mage on the staff rather than only magisters—"

"Very good!" barked Vand. "We do not have a mage on the staff, do we? Despite my repeated orders that you, Filden, should find one for me!"

Filden's aquiline features did not shift. He kept his eyes fixed on the painted ceiling of the office throughout. It was a good survival mechanism. "Goodman Vand, as you are aware—"

"I am aware I have asked you to do something for me, and you have not done it! Trassan secured himself one, Persin has one, and yet I, the greatest living engineer in Ruthnia, must do without! Fucking hells, Filden! Our best magister, our only mage, the gods-damned scion of Iapetus, and the chiefs of our damned Tyn all on the same boat, and you tell me you've lost them? Where does this leave our magical capabilities?" His hand tightened suddenly around the silver ball. His fingers stood out white.

Filden sighed coolly. Vand read him easily. He had no gift of magic, but he was a fine judge of men. Filden was thinking it was he, Vand, who had lost them, his gamble; that Vand had indulged Trassan's plan from greed. He had exploited his protégé's knowledge, given him all the risk and taken more than his share of the credit. All this was true. Vand could not deny it.

Vand waited while Filden calculated whether to tell the truth and potentially lose his job, or be the lickspittle Vand paid him to be. It was all so despicable, this relationship of master and servant. Vand couldn't help but abuse it. He tested his men as much as his machines, and always to destruction.

Filden opted for honesty. Vand admired him for that.

"They are lost, Goodman Vand. I am sorry."

"Then make sure Hissenwar finds them," hissed Vand. The wave of anger past, the deeps of grief beckoned again. More waves would come, until then, there were long moments of cold despair ahead. He uncurled his fingers. The Morfaan silver gleamed insolently at him, revelling in its secrets.

A half-minute went by. Filden cleared his throat. "What about your trip to the Sisters' Barrens, Goodman?"

Vand sighed deeply. "I am not four hours off the train from Macer Lesser, Filden. I have been harried from land to land by the necessities of business, and now you give me this fine news."

"You are not going then, Goodman Vand?"

"No, no. I am. You see, I can handle this amount of responsibility, Filden. It is only when I am let down by the likes of you that I find myself under intolerable pressures. I may delay a week or two, but I will be heading north soon. Guider Zeruvias is still agreeable to accompanying me?"

Filden nodded. "He is."

"Good. Pay him half his fee up front. He is beginning to get cold feet about it, I can tell."

"He has made no representation to us about his unwillingness to travel, Goodman."

"I am Arkadian Vand. I know, Filden. Give the man his money. One disaster cannot be allowed to unsettle all one's enterprises. If the debacle at the Thrusean steelworks taught me anything, it taught me that."

I let Trassan have his own way too much. I should have reigned him in. He thought I indulged him to exploit him, thought Vand. *It was more than that.*

"Should we inform the Kressinds of this incident?" asked Filden.

Vand shook his head. "Having Gelbion Kressind breathing down my neck right now would be inconvenient."

"The news will out eventually."

"I'll prepare something," said Vand. "But let's try to avoid telling them until we are sure."

Vand lapsed into silence, hypnotised by the silver.

"Goodman?" Filden risked a glance at his employer. "Is there anything else?"

I almost loved him, thought Vand. *He reminded me of myself.*

Vand shook his head slowly, his reddening eyes still fixed upon the silent silver ball. Just do your job. All of you, do your damned jobs." Vand dropped the ball of Morfaan silver into a glass vase where it rattled hollowly. He had been certain Trassan would find a reader at the city. Now he was no closer to unlocking the mysteries of the damned things than he was before. Back to square one. "Send Veridy in on your way out. She's been waiting long enough."

Filden bowed his way out of the door.

Vand snatched up a decanter of fortified Correndian wine.

"Curse you Trassan, and your inability to keep yourself alive," he said, and poured himself two days' worth of wine into one goblet. Vand was not a bibulous man, measuring out each drink with an engineer's precision. There were always exceptional days.

He pushed the message under a stack of paper. His daughter must hear the news from his mouth, and not read it before he had chance to speak. She would have to be lied to. He had to give her some hope, or the Kressinds would be banging on his gate.

The door was opened by one of his servants. Veridy was outside. Her eyes and nostrils were red with weeping. Vand could have stood, and held her, and told her how much her fiancé had meant to him, and that he felt that he had lost a son, but he did not. Arkadian Vand did not show weakness.

Instead he put on his most sincere and stern fatherly expression and laced his fingers together. Let her weep for them both when he could not.

Veridy came forward with the leaden step of the condemned. Her expression broadcast her foreknowledge. If misery were personified, it would have had her face.

"Sit down my dear," Vand said gently. "I am afraid I have some very bad news."

CHAPTER FOUR
Another Breakfast at the Morthrocks

DEMION MORTHROCK CAME to breakfast a happy man.

Contrast the situation of eight months previously, when there was *froideur* at the table, as the Maceriyans say. And now, there are flowers and open curtains through which streams golden sunshine.

He smiled broadly and sat himself at the table. Mornings brought him pleasure. Katriona was still dressing, and he looked forward to their morning talk. She had such passion for the things he did not. He found everything about her adorable, but he had surprised himself by how much he respected her fervour for industry. Despite his father's lifelong efforts, he had no interest in engines, manufacturing or economics. Katriona did. He had thought, when she took over his factory, that he would let her get on with it, but her being interested had made him interested, and for the first time in his life.

"Love is as strange thing," he said, and unfolded the broadsheet.

"I'm sorry, goodfellow?" said the maid, Laisa, who was setting out breakfast on the sideboard.

"Nothing, nothing, my dear. Only that the day is a good one. Karsa's smogs have been blown away to sea, and the sun is shining!"

The maid laughed at his gaiety. The Morthrock house had become a much happier place since Katriona arrived. Laisa left with a smile, and he stood to choose his meal.

Demion's cook had prepared a fine spread. Of all the things his father had left him, the cook was his favourite. He had little time for factories, but food—Demion hungrily surveyed the silver bowls of scrambled eggs, sausage, devilled kidneys and fried bread— Demion liked food. Almost as much as he liked wine, though not quite so much as he liked gambling.

However, what he loved the most in the world was Katriona, and to his great joy, she had taken to him. He had proposed to her not expecting her to say yes; when she had, he had expected a satisfactory life as a martyred husband, quietly adoring his wife at a remove. He did not deserve what he had. She gave him her heart, and he could not quite believe his luck.

There was no point in judging himself harshly. The world had given him all he wished for. Whether he deserved it or not, he intended to enjoy it before it was taken away (a fear that plagued him in the small hours, as it does all men approaching their middle years). He dug his spoon into the dish of eggs, then slowed. He looked at his belly. Katriona had taken to patting it teasingly. He supposed he had become a little fat. Reluctantly, he let half the food slip back into the bowl.

"This won't do," he sighed. "I will have to tell the cook to cut down on the portions." He thought a moment. "Which I shall. Until then, it would be a shame to let all this go to waste." He spooned the eggs back onto his plate, and after another moment of thought, added a spoonful more.

He ate the eggs quickly, before Katriona arrived. By the time she entered the breakfast room, he had polished off eggs, kidney, sausage and sweet cake, and was well engrossed in the racing pages of the broadsheet.

Katriona came in quietly and greeted him with a kiss upon his head that made him shiver. She smelled delightful, like freshly pressed cotton.

"You really are the most beautiful woman in all the Hundred," he said.

She swatted him on the shoulder. "Thank you, but less of that. If I wished for a puppy I'd go to the dray master."

"Of course," he said bashfully. He removed all but the sporting pages of his paper, folded them, and held them up to her.

Taking them, she sat with a small sigh and the rustle of skirts. She appeared more tired than usual. Demion wished she would take things a little easier.

"You have your meeting this evening?" he said carefully, so as not to appear judgemental. Any suggestion from him that she slow down would be harshly received.

"Mmm hm," she said distractedly. "I have a few more manufacturers to see. I have high hopes for Bwidlen, he seems such a warm-hearted fellow. He cares for his workforce, he really does." She bit into a crust of toast, brushing the crumbs that pattered onto the broadsheet away. "It really is quite outrageous, this whole affair. The truths of my opinion are self-evident. If we do not afford better rights to the workers, then they will stop working. We have been on the sharp end of that at the Morthrocksey Mill. It would be best if the labour movement is given proper leadership from the beginning, so that it can grow to the mutual benefit of employer and employee. Who knows where it will end if we are not involved? Riot, misery, and worse! I do not see how the others miss it. They are greedy, blinded by money." She stuffed the remainder of the toast into her mouth. "Speaking of greedy, I am famished today." She lifted the lid of the silver bowl containing the kidneys, a bowl Demion Morthrock had assiduously covered to hide the amount he had consumed. Strongly scented steam billowed from them. "Are these goat kidneys?" she asked.

Demion frowned. "They are. You do not like them my dear. You do not like the smell."

She smiled at him and said with mock seriousness, "Then maybe it is time I tried them. If I cannot bring myself to sample a new food every day, how am I to convince the other captains of industry to change their entire way of doing things? Besides, today they smell delicious." She ladled a good portion onto her plate and set to work with relish.

Only last week, Katriona had protested that Demion keep the lid on the bowl, she so loathed the food. He admitted that, as perfect as she was, she could be quite ferocious in the morning.

He looked at her in concern. "Are you well my dear?"

She waved her fork over the paper while she finished her mouthful. "Never better!" she exclaimed. She flicked over the page, and stopped speaking for a long while. Demion went back to his reading.

"I don't believe it!" she said quietly, setting down her fork with a click.

Demion, who was thoroughly absorbed in the other particulars—to whit the racing times and participants at the next Royal Karsan dracon steeplechase—looked up distractedly. "Hmm?"

"Oh do pay attention my dear! Have you not read the business pages?"

Demion looked askance. He never did read the business pages. "Well, not quite yet."

Katriona slid the paper across the top of the racing gazette and stabbed at an advertisement.

He leaned in obligingly.

"'For sale'," he read, "'by public auction to be held upon 31ᵘ Seventh at the offices of Gerwin, Fael and Runcor, the Lemio Clothing and Shoddy Factory, in whole or in part lots.'" He scanned through the rest of the details: public viewing dates, highlighted items, and an address to which one could apply for a full catalogue of particulars of the sale.

"A sale of a business? I don't—"

She interrupted him again. "It is the mill, *the mill!* That scoundrel Grostiman is selling his bloody business!"

"My dear," admonished Demion. "Please, at breakfast."

Her anger vanished. "Are you going to raise your eyebrows at me for swearing, husband?" she challenged him playfully.

He smiled at her. He rather liked it when she swore. "Not at all."

"Good," she reread the advertisement, and her annoyance returned. "Oh, I don't know! He's sly. I will admit. I... Do we have cheese? I suddenly have a yearning for cheese."

Demion pointed his knife at the end of the sideboard where cold food was arrayed.

"One cannot intimidate these people easily, my love," said Demion haltingly. Katriona was heaping slices of cheese onto her plate. She stopped, then picked up a brace of bread rolls.

"They do not always get their power handed to them with their father's inheritances. Those that fight for their position are not to be underestimated. Grostiman is of good, old blood, but he won what he has himself. His father left him nothing, he was quite poor. You have picked a fight, challenging him." He looked back at the broadsheet. "I say. There is a note here for an article on page twelve. Perhaps that will set the matter to rest in your mind."

Katriona came back to the table and plucked up the paper again. She seemed more short-tempered than usual. Demion Morthrock loved her anyway. Let her rant, let her rage. Her fury was as sweet as her smile to him.

"What? Where?" She crammed in a piece of cheese and rushed to the marked page. "There's a story here," she paused to read. "What? He has issued a statement to say that the conditions of the children at his family's factory were unknown to him! The dog! He reported and closed down his own mill. Well, I am sure his cousin has probably been arrested. How could he? Has he no loyalty? Or perhaps some other has been made out as the guilty one."

Demion went back to the food, where he speared a sausage, then, as an afterthought, took his own serving of cheese; Katriona's had enticed him. "He is a clever one. I'd be wary of him, if I were you."

"Rot and more rot!" said Katriona. She slapped the broadsheet onto the table. "I'll not let him get away with this. What the hells has he done with the orphans in his charge?" She scanned quickly. "It does not say! Here, he's quoted!" She rapped article with her knife. "'Generous benefactors', 'properly cared for.' I'd wager he's turfed them out onto the damned streets!" she shouted.

Demion set his fork down carefully. Regrettably, the racing pages would have to wait. "My dear, please. Be careful with Grostiman."

"It's him that's going to have to be careful." Her eyes narrowed in a calculating way. "I've got an idea that will greatly displease him. I'll—"

She stopped dead, her eyes wide with surprise.

"My dear, are sure you are well?" Demion's concern grew at his wife's suddenly pale features.

"I am terribly sorry," she said breathily. "I have come over quite nauseous. It must be the kidneys."

She stood hurriedly. Her eyes rolled back into her head, her legs folded under her and she span around, knocking her breakfast plate to the floor as she fell. At the clatter Laisa rushed in and stopped uselessly in the doorway, her hands over her mouth. Demion thrust himself to his feet, knocking his chair over.

"Damn it girl!" he shouted at the maid. "The goodlady is taken ill! Do something! Get some smelling vapours, get some water!"

The maid stared back in shock; Demion Morthrock never shouted at anyone.

"Quickly!" he roared.

Laisa ran from the room. Demion mopped his brow shakily. He rang for his butler and knelt by his wife. Her hand felt clammy in his.

"My dear, my dearest dear!" He patted her face. "Oh, confound these female garments!" he said, struggling to loosen her corset.

When his man eventually arrived, Demion had her corset off. She was breathing more easily, but still Katriona had not come around.

"About time!" he snapped at his butler. "Send for the physic. My wife is sick."

CHAPTER FIVE
In the Company of Giants

THAT WIND SPEAKS is not commonly known in civilised lands. Where brick and stone hold sway, the wind is mute. To hear its voice one must travel far from multitudinous humanity. The wilder the country, the better, for it is in the most isolate landscapes that the wind speaks loudest.

At the heart of the Black Sands the winds howls in pain. Its voice is wordless, but its anguish clear. Why it cried so, Rel Kressind did not know, but its misery battered at him as hard as the cargo of sand it carried.

Rel leaned over the neck of his dracon, his face turned from the wind. Scarfs wrapped tightly about his head protected him from the worst of the sandstorm. It was a lifetime since Zhalak Zhinsky had laughed at Rel's ineptitude with nomad's robes. Since then they had become as a second skin to him, donned without conscious effort. Suffering is a good school. Sore eyes, sunburned skin, and sand in every crevice of his body had been his tutors. Rel had learned a great deal about surviving the wilderness.

The biggest lesson, he reflected, was not to go into the damn desert in the first place. Propelled from a comfortable life in the Isles of Karsa by a chain of events he could scarcely credit any more, Rel found himself travelling in the company of giants, the modalmen of legend, in pursuit of a rail gang enslaved by others of the giants' kind.

Rel's companions were by far the least of his worries. They were dangerous, but they sheltered him. If he strayed from the march or fell from his mount, one of them would patiently fetch him back, like he was an errant toddler, and save him from the hungry ghosts, uncanny beasts, and other terrible things that infested the Black Sands.

The desert was full of glimmer, the crystallised stuff of raw magic. All manner of curious phenomenon were conjured by it. Time ran in strange loops. Windows to other worlds opened in the night. Out in the rolling black dunes, following a light in the night could kill you as surely as thirst. Phantoms came from the darkness, and wicked things lurked in the deep, stony, waterless places where nothing ought to live.

Though the Black Sands exceeded the wildest tales, the modalmen proved to be far from the monsters of fable. They were as huge and as terrifying as expected, but though possessed of four arms and covered in glowing patterns, in spirit they did not seem so different to other men.

There were three with Rel: Drauthek, Ger, and their leader Shkarauthir. Drauthek rode behind Rel on his massive garau, a great beast, charcoal skinned and patterned with light like its rider. Ger and Shkarauthir rode ahead, their huge shapes ships in the driving sand.

Since Rel's rescue, he had spent a great deal of unwelcome time trekking north, following the trail of the kidnapped rail gang. For all his efforts to learn the ways of the desert, the modalmen regarded him as an amusing, if ill-informed, novelty.

The stories told in the Kingdoms suggested the modalmen would eat him. This was not untrue, for there were modalmen that would have devoured Rel; Shkarauthir made that clear to him at the start. Maybe the greatest lesson he had learned was that all men were individuals no matter their type, and nations were rarely as homogenous in thought as they looked from the outside. The modalmen were as divided in motive and temperament as other people. The group that had attacked the rail gang were of the Giev En, a man-eater clan. Shkarauthir's group were of the Gulu Thek, and they did not eat human flesh. The Gulu Thek were the enemies of the Giev En, and their philosophies were opposed, principally on the matter of whether or not Rel was acceptable as food. Division was the lot of every human group, no matter appearances to the contrary.

The older Rel got, the more certainties seemed anything but certain. Simple concepts of good and evil failed to capture truth's nuances. Archetypes were often stereotypes, and stereotypes could be based on the flimsiest information. He supposed this was the first flowering of wisdom in his callow brain. He hoped he lived long enough to employ it.

He had a lot of time to think, most of it while bent double over his dracon's neck with the sand blasting at his head. Not that any of the profundities he dwelled on made his journey easier.

Shkarauthir's group rode a day behind the caravan the Giev En had joined, so their dust trails would not give them away, though they had no need to worry about that in the middle of the sandstorm.

"Brauctha's scouts are not so good as those of the Gulu Thek," Shkarauthir had told Rel in his musical, if flat, Maceriyan on a day when the weather permitted conversation, "but they are adequate in skill enough to see us."

Now they were on the way to the Fallen Citadel of the Brass God, and Shkarauthir's men followed.

Whoever the hells the Brass God is, thought Rel. Shkarauthir was being predictably evasive about that, or why the Giev En had raided the camp in the first place, after so long a time of peace. The modalmen were intensely frustrating beings. They refused to explain, and expected Rel to know things he clearly could not know.

Rel's own plan had been to find the modalmen who had taken the workers, and guide in a rescue party. He had been staggeringly naïve.

Instead I find myself at the arse end of the world, going to tea with monsters who would likely murder me for supper, in the company of other monsters who can't give a straight answer to a question.

"Wonder of wonders, my life never fails to get worse," muttered Rel to himself, and was rewarded with a mouthful of sand. He had little choice but to go with them. Death was everywhere in the sands. Only the modalmen knew its every face.

The bass blast of Ger's horn halted the line of riders. The huge shapes of the modalmen on their six-legged beasts turned to the left. The line became a huddle.

Rel rode into the middle, grateful for the shelter the giants provided.

They passed through humps in the sand that grew in number and regularity, and the wind's assault was curtailed a little more. After a few moments, they emerged onto a wide space, flat as a city square.

Rel sat up in Aramaz's saddle. More modalmen appeared from the storm's shroud. Gathered in the centre of the space were dozens of them, their garau herded together, and campfires already established. Through the dusty air, the colour of this new group's marks was obscured.

"Hey!" Rel shouted. The modalmen saw excellently in the dark, but their daylight vision was not as good as a Kingdoms man's. Bright light dazzled them, haze like this was impenetrable to their eyes, though surely they should be able to see this other group. They did not react as if they had. "Hey!"

Shkarauthir's modalmen circled about and stopped, Rel in the middle. Shkarauthir leapt down from the back of his mount. In one of his four hands he held a spear as long as a human's pike.

A warrior came sauntering out from a guttering campfire while the rest of the encamped modalmen got to their feet and set up a fearsome hooting. Whether of challenge or of greeting Rel had no clue. He tensed. Drauthek and Ger sat placidly as their leader alone faced the crowd of bellowing giants. Rel slipped his carbine off his back and undid the fastenings on its oilcloth cover.

Drauthek look over at him and made a small hand gesture for him to desist. Rel ignored him and slipped the rifle free.

The hooting continued as Shkarauthir and the modalman stared at each other.

The display went on too long. By the time the modalmen leaders performed a complex handshake involving all their arms, Rel had a bullet in his gun and his heart in his mouth. He wished he had one of the modern repeater carbines. One bullet would not be enough.

He breathed out shakily as the two modalmen embraced. The hooting calls got louder.

Shkarauthir returned to his companions, where he had words in his own tongue with Ger and Drauthek before speaking with Rel. Dismounted, Shkarauthir was still taller than Rel was upon the back of his dracon. His face was swaddled in a headdress much like Rel's, but his chest was naked. In the grooves in his bare skin, red light shifted to blue and back again.

"We camp here tonight, small one," said Shkarauthir.

"Do you know these... people?" said Rel. "Are they dangerous?" *To me,* he added to himself.

Shkarauthir looked at Rel in that way he often did, which is to say, like Rel was mentally impaired. "They are my people. They are of the Gulu Thek."

"Did you know they would be here?"

"I did not know but I expected." Again he gave that look, though it was changing to one of amusement.

"What are they doing here?" said Rel. He had given up on politeness weeks ago. It did not bother the modalmen if he shouted or asked his questions with meek circumspection. They needed prompting on every point. Allowing himself to be irritable helped decrease Rel's frustration with their obtuseness. The modalmen did not care for Kingdoms manners.

"There is to be a moot," said Shkarauthir.

Rel prepared to ask the inevitable follow up question, but Shkarauthir had evidently learned something of non-modalmen during their association, and offered an explanation.

"My people have been looking for us. A summons came to our god-talkers not long after Ger, Drauthek and I committed ourselves to the hunt." He nodded to himself. "The news clarifies matters for me. It is not unusual for the man-eaters to take small people to the Brass God as gifts, but why in this number and why before the summons were given, I do not know. We will learn at the moot."

"Did you know this already?" asked Rel.

"No, not know. Suspected," said Shkarauthir.

"How did they know to find you here in all this desert?"

Shkarauthir shrugged his upper shoulders. "That is the will of the One. Here is an important place. Much magic is here. It draws us together, maybe. Maybe it is chance. Maybe more of my kind will come. Maybe they will not. The One will decide. Many Gulu Thek wait for us at the mooting ground. All is the One's will. We pursue no longer, we go to talk."

He left it at that and wandered away.

"Hey!" shouted Rel after the modalman. He tugged his scarfs away from his eyes and mouth so he could shout louder. "Hey!"

Shkarauthir turned back patiently. "Yes, small person?"

"Where the hells is *here*?"

Shkarauthir held up his four arms to encompass the flat area and its surrounding mounds. "These are the barracks of our ancestors, in the once-city of Losirna."

With this explanation, the nature of the mounds emerged suddenly, like an image from a trick picture.

Rel was surrounded by ruins.

THE WIND DROPPED, its dying dumping curling waves of sand upon the desert. The moons came up before the sun set. The red emerged before the white, rushing up so quickly that the pair of them were together in the sky for only the briefest time. Between the lunar siblings the looming Twin glowered down at the Earth, pale blue in the evening, rapidly turning black as night drew in. Sparks of light flickered in clusters around its equator. Rel watched awhile. The storms of sparks were something new, something forbidding, and growing more numerous every night.

Little mesas of broken stone surrounded their campsite. Sand banked up against the rubble in line with the prevailing wind, elongating them into shapes like sleeping dracons. Rel inspected the remains as the modalmen threw up their simple camp. He didn't help. The giants were so much stronger than he that he was a hindrance to their efforts. After the fourth time of nearly being trodden on, he had given up. That had been some time ago.

He was also wary of the newcomers. Despite belonging to Shkarauthir's clan, they looked at him strangely. Busying himself elsewhere seemed prudent.

Away from the bustle of the camp, Rel knelt on the ground and brushed black sand away from a door stoop sized for modalmen. Low walls persisted either side. Years of exposure to the pitiless wind had scoured the polished stone rough. Though the seamlessness of the masonry concealed its artificial origins, in many places the eroded details of nooks, carvings and windows could be made out. If it had not been for these surviving outlines of figures and other decorative embellishments, Rel would have taken the mounds for natural outcrops. There were no individual blocks in the wall, and no lines of mortar.

He fished a chunk of rubble from the sand. Although it too was worn, in crevices it retained a little of the glasslike qualities found in many Morfaan remains. He let it thump down to the sand, wondering what could have broken the walls so comprehensively. Very little in the arsenal of the Hundred could so much as scratch Morfaan building glass. On the opposite side of the Gates of the World to the Glass Fort was a ruinous fortification, the twin of the Glass Fort. The manner of its destruction was a fearful mystery. Here was a whole city broken down to dust.

Rel squatted in the sand and poked about for a while, unearthing a few fragments of rustless Morfaan steel. There was little else to find, so he dusted his hands off and clambered up onto one of the taller wall remnants to look around the area. From his new vantage he realised the mounds were the remains of a massive building that had at its centre a square two hundred yards across. The layout fitted Shkarauthir's explanation that this was a barracks, with a parade ground surrounded by armouries, sleeping quarters and stables, only it was far bigger than that of the Third Karsan Dragoons back home. Humps in the sand were the lower parts of rooms. In a few places outcrops of sandblasted building glass poked free of their shrouds. An almost complete archway stood over a roadway of sand to the east. Hummocks suggested three further gates at the other cardinal points of the compass. Very little taller than Rel survived.

Beyond the barracks the setting sun cast deep shadows on the desert. The layout of the streets was easy to see when the sun's rays shone nearly parallel to the ground, but without the sunset the city had been virtually invisible. It would be easy to see it as an accident of geology.

Rel surveyed the city awhile from the mound. The anonymous lumps of the vast ruins spread out for miles. Their camp was on the edge, outside a thick band Rel took to be a city wall.

The Red Moon fled over the horizon and the sun lowered itself after. The White Moon went from the orange of sunset to its pallid, nighttime hue. The Twin became ever more solid, turning from an ethereal vagueness into a circular hole in the sky, neat as a coin and dark as a threat, sparkling with its ominous fires.

With the draining of the light the temperature dropped rapidly. They were far north, closer to the equator, so the nights should have been getting warmer, not colder. He supposed they must be gradually gaining altitude as they approached the mountains of the High Spine, slowly enough that the slope in the land wasn't noticeable. Either that or some magical effect altered the climate. That was perfectly feasible, and would not be the strangest thing he had encountered in the Black Sands.

He shivered, drawing his scarves tight against the chill.

Behind him was thousands of miles of desert. Not all of the Black Sands was covered in the black, glimmer-rich sand, but there was sufficient for the desert to deserve its name. They had crossed thirty leagues of sand as black as the night sky in three days. The broad dark line of the High Spine at the northern horizon grew a little taller with every mile. A ragged line of snow glowed softly across the tops, separating mountains from sky. The rest of their details remained indistinct.

"Hey! Small!" bellowed Drauthek. Drauthek spoke terrible Maceriyan, but he knew enough to make unwelcome comments about eating Rel, and Rel wasn't entirely sure he was joking. "Food time. Come eat. Do not be skinny!"

He flashed a frightening white smile at Rel.

"Wouldn't want to be skinny now, would I?" said Rel. "I would make a poor meal."

"Ha! Yes!" said Drauthek. "No good. Make modalman hungry."

Rel slid down the side of the wall to join Drauthek. The modalman made no effort to shorten his stride, forcing Rel to jog. On the way back to the camp they crossed places where the sand had blown away, uncovering mosaics of roughened glass.

Modalmen went about their business quickly. Garaus snorted and lowed, collapsing to their knees once unladen and rolling gratefully onto their sides. The warriors spoke in their bone-shaking voices quietly, as their rumbling speech carried far over the empty lands. They travelled light, and wore little, although the newcomers were better provisioned than Shkarauthir's hunting band. Over the shoulders of the newcomers' six-limbed mounts were huge water skins big enough for Rel to bathe in. Bedrolls cushioned the back of their saddles. Pouches and baskets held a surprising variety of dried fruits and meat. Shkarauthir said the modalmen spent most of their time in the east where the conditions were kinder. The new band brought pack garau with more comprehensive supplies, notably fodder for the beasts that they freely shared out. Even so, compared to a Kingdoms man's kit they carried little.

One thing they did have in abundance was weaponry. Bows taller than a man, swords Rel could not lift, spears longer than Olbish pikes, arrows like javelins. And though they did not wear it while travelling, all of the modalmen carried armour bundled up in linen behind their saddles.

The newcomers stared at Rel with open curiosity. They had no concept of human manners, being shockingly unbothered by nakedness and bodily functions, often openly toileting right in front of him. Drauthek especially asked Rel questions that were breathtakingly rude. In the Isles Rel counted himself as a man with little time for social convention, and brazenly offended it for his own entertainment; it turned out he was far more prudish than he thought.

The modalmen were not what he expected in many ways, but they were every bit as savage as the stories told, and far stranger.

There was their affinity for one another, for example. When Drauthek, Ger and Shkarauthir spoke with the newcomers, the spirals carved into their flesh pulsed patterns back and forth. Though Rel knew only a few words of the modalmen speech, he could infer a lot from their body language; for all their anatomical differences it was similar to a human's. But in the lights there was another layer of communication that Rel had no insight to at all.

The new group swelled Shkarauthir's band to twenty-seven. Familiarity with the three modalmen did not prepare Rel for being among so many.

"When I was very young," said Rel. "My father took me to Karsa City fair. It's the big agricultural show out on the high moors between Karsa and the Mesus river valley. You won't know it."

Drauthek looked at him quizzically, but did not interrupt.

"I became separated from my nurse while my father admired the livestock; big bull dracons, almost as large as garau."

"Garau big," said Drauthek. Rel doubted he understood more than half of what he was saying, but he needed to talk.

"I spent several minutes in a panic amid them. They did me no harm, but watched me with sad, green eyes. They were a sorry sight, with their horns sawn down, their legs hobbled and necks yoked. They could not move much, but I was terrified."

"Scared?" said Drauthek.

"Very scared. It is how I feel now." He looked around the camp. "You people don't bother me, nor your garau, but I don't like your hounds."

The hounds watched him with hungry eyes set deep over their beaklike mouths. Shkarauthir had had a half dozen with him. There were three times as many now. Rel felt no safer around them than he would have in a stable full of starving dracons.

"At the fair, once my nurse had found me, father scolded me for fear," said Rel, eyeing them warily. "'A goodfellow never shows weakness,' he said. I always try to keep that in mind."

"Weakness bad," said Drauthek. He patted Rel's head with a heavy hand. "You weak. I protect."

Shkarauthir was speaking with several modalmen. By their deference, Rel saw that Shkarauthir was no simple warrior, but a man of high station. The modalman had no badges, markings or anything of that sort to indicate their social degree, at least not so a Kingdoms man could tell, but the others obeyed Shkarauthir unquestioningly, and were actively seeking his counsel.

There were six campfires in the camp. Shkarauthir's small original group had been given the central one, another indication of his standing. Ger greeted Rel and motioned for him to sit down and get warm. He said something incomprehensible. Ger spoke no language Rel knew. They got by on nods and smiles.

The fires burned garau dung. What little moisture there was in the dung dried quickly in the desert, and it smelled a lot better than it should.

Shkarauthir finished his conversation and took his place at the fire. Once he sat, no other modalman would approach him. Ger served up the same evening meal they ate every day: a spicy stew made from dried fruits and meat. Rel had grown to like it, and no longer felt self-conscious eating out of the salt container the modalmen had spared him. Their own bowls were the size of basins.

The modalmen sat cross-legged by their fires to rest, but squatted to eat, and would not start their meal until everyone was in their set place. They had a particular way of doing for every activity. Now there were more of them, their rituals became more apparent. Shkarauthir and his warriors waited until all the modalmen in the camp were ready before commencing their supper, the pulsing of their markings signalling the others to do the same.

When they were done, Shkarauthir wiped his bowl clean with his fingers, licked them, and set the bowl aside.

"Now small person, I tell you why we come north. I have a story for you, for all." He said something to Ger.

Ger translated loudly. Heads came up at that. The modalmen set down their empty bowls and came to Shkarauthir's fire.

Before Shkarauthir began his story, he slipped fluidly into a kneel and prostrated himself toward the fire. The others followed suit. They rose together, then knelt again, all facing Shkarauthir's fire in silence.

A gust of wind tugged the flames into streamers. It was dark, and the million stars of the desert shone in the sky. The luminous ribbon of the God's Road cut the heavens in half.

The modalmen sat up, then crossed their legs, all of them with the left under the right.

"So," began Shkarauthir, "let us start with the beginning."

Rel settled in to listen. He had liked the modalman's stories the few times Shkarauthir had told them in Maceriyan, though he had no faith in his promise of revelation whatsoever.

CHAPTER SIX
In The Beginning

"THIS IS THE Story of the One and the Void, and how it came to be that the world was begun, and the first thinking beings were made," Shkarauthir said.

"In the beginning, there was only the One. It was he who made this world," Shkarauthir gestured to the ground, then pointed at the Twin, "and the dark world as well, he made them both. He made the stars and the moons, and the other worlds around our sun, and all other things that can be seen, and many things that cannot be seen. Where he came from will never be known. We do not speculate, it is not the modalman way."

Rel suspected this interjection was for his benefit, although it could as easily have been a part of the ritual of the story.

"Among the Forgetful, the small people who think themselves true men but are not," continued Shkarauthir, "are those who follow the One, our supreme god, and their priests say many different things about the One. They say perhaps the One came here to see what was underneath his own world, or that he fled a war, or that he was young among his people and recently come into his power, or that he was a being alone, and made the worlds to be his friends. Who knows? The Forgetful do not. We true men do not. Only this is known, and this is true, that the One came into this place in a blaze of light and a fire that rocked all things, bringing something out of nothing.

"The something was the void," said Shkarauthir. "Now, a void is a nothing, but before the void the nothingness was absolute. The void has potential, it can be made and changed. The void was the One's first creation."

The modalmen listened intently. Rel had no idea how many spoke Maceriyan. He thought only a few, if Ger and Drauthek were typical, but they nodded in parts, and hooted in others, and made other signs of understanding with their four hands that confounded Rel. Did they, after all, understand? Or was the story so ingrained in their culture that they knew it no matter the tongue it was told in? Shkarauthir's clan marks moved differently while he told his stories, turning to a bright pulse that ran quick then slow, or chased itself over his arms and body. Maybe they could read that. He wished his brothers were there; Guis, or perhaps Aarin. They had a better intuition of how such things worked. Rel had never been particularly academic.

"The One desired to fill the void. So he made the twin worlds," Shkarauthir went on. "One world was of Form, a perfect unchanging paradise of stone and still fire. The other was of Will, the mutable, thinking spirit that energises all life, and so was always in flux. Because it never stayed the same, sometimes it was a heaven, and sometimes it was a hell.

"The One delighted in their opposition, in the changelessness of Form and the chaotic impermanence of Will. For a time, he was happy, going from one world to the next, marvelling at his cleverness. He would rejoice at the infinite changes of Will for a while, returning to the certainty of Form when he tired of it, and then back and forth, until one day, the One became confused. The void had grown around the worlds, so that their dance about one another no longer filled it. He was shocked! Desiring to fill this emptiness also, he planted a garden of stars to prettify his worlds. Such a difference this setting made, that for a time again he was delighted, and he forgot his worry at the growing of the void. After a time, his delight turned again to despair. The void grew again. So, he made more stars. But again the void grew. For no matter how many stars he made, still they did not fill the oceans of the sky, for as the void was filled it grew again. It grew so quickly that the One's own light was no longer enough to drive away the dark, and Form and Will grew cold. They had voices then, and they cried to their father, so he made the sun to shine on the worlds so that they might enjoy the day and stay warm, and the nights when they might sleep, and he set the other worlds to dance around the sun, and the moons to herald the twin worlds' coming as they swam the void.

"Time rushed by as time does. The void grew ever bigger. The One spent more time away from the worlds of Form and of Will. Into the growing spaces of being he desired to set other spheres, for he could not abide the void's emptiness, although it was his first child, and so he took up grains of sand from his twin planets, and from them made other worlds, and from the diamonds of the stars he grew other suns, and other wondrous things.

"But despite his toil, the One could not fill everything. He worked and he worked and the void continued to grow. No matter how many things he put into the sky, still there was more space to fill, and he came no more to these worlds. His struggle with the void absorbed him. The void had grown so huge and hungry he feared if he ever stopped, it would devour all he had built. The void never spoke, and never showed any sign of thought, but it became a thing in the One's mind of cold will that desired to grow forever, and swamp what little the One had made in unending chill. And so, as he thought it, it came to be. The One's desire to fill the void grew to a hard hatred of his first child, and his struggle took on the nature of a war.

"After many long ages he realised he was not there to love his Twins. Their spirits cried out to him at his inattention. His struggles with the void had made a universe filled with many wonders, but glorious as his creation was, it was nothing without someone to love it. None felt this more keenly than the world of Will and the world of Form.

"'Who will admire our beauty?' they said. 'You are away so often,' and they wept.

"Although the One's heart ached to hear such wailing, he could not love the worlds as he had. He realised his work would never end, and he had many children that distracted him from his Twins. So he promised Form and Will other things to love them in his stead. To accomplish this, he made life, creating first the plants and then the creatures and all things that move and breed. For each world he made a different kind. Life on the dark world of Form was never changing. Life on the light world of Will scarcely could hold its shape before it took on a new form. Both these types were true to the characters of each child. He was well pleased.

"For the Twins, it was not enough. Life was astonishing, that rock and dust and fire could become things that breathed, but as life did not think it could not love. Life did not see the glory around it, it simply was. Life did not worship the Twins as they desired, so again they called for their father, and again the One returned.

"'These things that walk upon us, their feet tickle, they drink our rivers, they sleep on our faces and they piss on us. They make our skin itch, and they do not love us! Please come home forever,' they said. 'Love us, our father.'

"The One thought long and hard. He could not stay to love his worlds. Remaining was impossible but he could not abandon his children either. The void would forever grow. It would not be fair to have his children face eternity with only his new creations flashing into being far away to comfort them.

"So the One set upon his greatest task." Shkarauthir leaned over the fire. The light dancing on his skin cast shadows dark as midnight. "He made things that could think. Before, he had exerted his mind, and so things had been. This great power would not be enough, not this time. Taking up a sharp stone knife, he cut strips from his celestial flesh. The pain was so intense his agonies rocked the sky. His blood was light and it flashed across the heavens, and rained as glowing waters on many worlds. The Twins cried anew to see their father bleed for them, their tears and blood mingled. In this way the thunder, the lightning and the rain were born.

"When at last the agony was done, the One chewed his flesh until it was soft, and moulded it into beings like himself. They were perfect images of him, but he could not give them his power, and though he used the smallest element of his being to make their souls, even this shard of his essence was too much for one body, so the portion of his soul he intended to animate them he split, and made one to be female, and the other to be male. To we modalmen, this is the greatest mystery, but it was so. He breathed these fragments of his spirit into the creatures, diminishing himself forever.

"When the creatures opened their eyes and looked back at him, he felt the most profound love he ever had. He was pleased with his latest endeavour. And so were Form and Will, for his new children looked upon the beauty of the Twins and adored them. Form and Will talked, and after much discussion it was decided the One would set the First Born upon the world of Form, for Will was frightened she might hurt them with her ceaseless changing, these delicate creatures with the power to love and to dream like the One.

"The creations of the One were the gods of our masters. Long before they came to this Earth, they dwelled up there." Shkarauthir pointed his finger toward the Twin. "There they lived for untold years. The One was pleased with his creatures. They could talk, and make music, and they danced and played in the changeless forests of that world. Their antics delighted him and the Twins, causing the One to dally while the void grew and the sky became dangerously empty. The creatures took pleasure in all they did, and most especially in the creations of the One. But their words were those of children, and though charming to begin with, after a time their prattle annoyed him, and their doings he found foolish.

"Dismayed, he withdrew, and wandered the garden of stars awhile, wondering what he could do. He had made the beings exactly as he had planned, and they loved all he made as he so desired. As he looked at all the beauty he had created, and the void that wanted to engulf it that he also had made, a thought struck him. His children had no power of their own to make things with their hands or their minds. They would never appreciate his work truly, until they could do work of their own. Furthermore, should they create, then the ever-growing void might be more quickly filled. The One was a being that transcended the division between Will and Form, being of neither, and greater than both. But his creatures were wholly begat from this creation's duality. Though they were of his flesh, he could not invest them with his own ability, for that is a power from beyond this place. He thought and thought on what he might do, and saw that if he gave them a little of Will's being to complement their hands and minds, they might change the universe. They could never make something from nothing as he had, only change what was already there, but it would be enough.

"In great excitement, he returned to his worlds, and bargained with Will that she might give up a part of herself, so that the First Born could know change too, and truly love; for love transforms, and without love there can be no change. With that understanding of the universe they might make and help fill the void, for making is but changing by another name.

"When the One returned he had been gone for aeons, and the two First Born had become hundreds. In a clearing in a forest of still flame trees, to the greatest five of the First Born he granted Will's gift. Fearing ill effect, he used but a little Will at first. He stepped back to watch his efforts. To his disappointment things went on as before. The Five sang the songs he taught them, and danced their little dances, and spoke the words he put into their mouths. Nothing new, however, did they make. No change could they affect. They made no tools, nor homes, or clothes.

"So the One took them up into his arms, and into them he breathed a little more Will, and the same result he obtained. Then a little more, until finally, frustrated that his own desires not be realised and fearing the hunger of the void, he steeped these Five in so much Will there was little else to them but Will, and the divine flesh that came from himself was greatly diluted by the stuff of Will. The creatures cried out, and fell down still, and he thought them dead. Exhausted and woeful he went away to fill the sky. The Twins cried for him as he left, reminding him of his failure. He grew irritable with them, and he ignored them.

"The next day or century, or aeon, for these measurements of time are man things and not applicable to the likes of the all-encompassing One, the One returned to his world of Form and found its timeless situation altered. The groves of ever burning trees of shiftless fire had become of wood and leaves, and they grew and died. Form had changed, and that, in that changeless place, was not possible. As for his five First Born infused with Will, well, they were nowhere to be seen. He marvelled at this turn of events, and hurried from the clearing where he had changed the Five, and into a whole new world.

"The Five had become many, for the One had been gone far longer than he intended. They harvested the last forests of fire, and refashioned them into cities made of sparks. Everything they looked upon they remade into something new. They made art and music and works of Will that he had not taught them. So amazed was he, he did not stop to reflect on the absence of Form's voice, or how it had begun to lose its eternal aspect, and change. He went among these Children of the Five with great joy, meaning to embrace them and love them, but they scattered from him, and were afraid. His light was greater than their light, and he hurt them, for he comes from without, and there was so little of his flesh remaining in the Children of the Five that his touch burned them. As they fled in terror it was then he realised he could no longer hear the voice of Will either. Once again he withdrew. His new children had changed his old, but how?

"The next time he returned, he found temples and statues. The Children of the Five had come to worship him as a god, and this he did not want. He had made all, and though he desired love and appreciation of his art, he did not wish for blind devotion. So he donned a form of flesh like theirs, and came to them disguised as a teacher. During this life he instructed them in many arts, and laid down the Rule of Twenty, but his attempts to dissuade the people from his worship came to nought, and the many corruptions of his teachings filled him with anguish.

"In the end, the One saw that he spent too much time upon the Twins. They lived, but differently, without voice or thought, they were dumb orbs fit only to house other creatures. Form had lost its changelessness. Will, though no Child of the Five had yet set foot upon it, was changed too, and become more stable in shape. So did the natures of the two worlds begin their long convergence, until there is today little difference between them.

"Cruelly, he blamed the Twins' predicament on their own selfish need for love. The One could not conceive of a mistake on his part. The void continued to grow, and he had abandoned his self-appointed duty to fill it, all because his world children required constant attention! So he spurned them, and loved them less. One last time he went back into the world in the teacher's guise to speak with the Children of the Five, and though for him it seemed but a few minutes had gone, in truth several hundred years had passed while he thought angrily upon the Twins' downfall.

"With a heavy heart, he called the lords and the prophets of the Children of the Five together, and for the last time he spoke with them, and there was now scorn in his voice to embitter his love. At first they did not hear his new teachings, for in their minds they contradicted the old, though they did not realise that was their error, for they had misinterpreted much of what the One had taught them. So much time had passed, they said he could not be who he said he was, and they doubted him. Angered, he cast off his teacher's guise, and stood before them in the full raiment of his glory. They fell to their faces, not daring to look up. Those that were slow were burned by his brilliance, and many were struck blind.

"'My children,' he said to them, 'the time has come for me to leave you. My presence hurts you more than it helps, and this sorrows me. In recompense I leave this world to you to do with as you please. I offer one last warning before I go, and I plead with you that this lesson, unlike so many others that I have given, shall be heeded. You are invested with the power to create. Exercise it well but in caution, for the act of creation changes the creator. The effects of your gifts go further than you can conceive. The worlds of Will and Form have lost their voices and their purity already because of you. I am changed because of you. And so you will also change yourselves. Those that can change may change themselves without intention, for this universe I have made is altered by your presence alone.

"His light grew brighter in preparation for his final departure.

"'Prosper, my children, but never look to the skies and expect my return, for it shall never come.' And with that, he disappeared forever." Shkarauthir nodded in satisfaction. "Some believe the One will relent and return. Some do not. What is true and known is that he never has."

Rel waited expectantly for the next revelation.

Shkarauthir shut his eyes and hummed deeply. "This is why we go north."

The Modalmen stood, and went to their fires in total silence.

Rel looked about in astonishment. He fixed narrowed eyes upon Shkarauthir. "That's it? That tells me nothing about why you are going north!"

Shkarauthir's nostrils flexed. "That is because you do not listen."

"Really? Do you really believe that?"

Shkarauthir shook his head sadly. "So impatient. A true man would hear the wisdom I have just spoken, and, if he did not think himself properly informed, would wait for further enlightenment."

"How long would that take?"

"As long as it takes. A year, a thousand years."

"I do not know how long you live, but I do not have a thousand years," said Rel.

The huge modalman began unwrapping his blanket.

"Come on," said Rel. "There must be more you can tell me."

Shkarauthir sighed. "Though you are as impetuous for knowledge as the Twin worlds were in their desire to be loved, I will offer you this. Creation begets creation. It is easy. Wisdom, however, must be learned, and the Twins and the Children of the Five were poor students. They did not see that one solution can create more problems. The One was a god to his children. In their turn they had children of their own, who worshipped them as gods as the Children of the Five worshipped the One. They were of two kinds, for they were of iron and they were of flesh. Divided from the start, they knew little but war. The urge to create is strong. The children of flesh, the grandsons of the One, could make no children like the One or the Y Dvar. So they stole their own. We are their foundlings, we are their warriors. War comes to our masters' door again, the war of iron against flesh, the war of Form against Will, and that is but the latest campaign in the ageless struggle between being and void. That is why we go north."

"Well," said Rel grudgingly. "Thank you." He unstrapped his bedroll and shook it out. "I still do not think you are telling me the whole of it."

"No story is ever the whole of anything," said Shkarauthir. "No man can ever know all the story. Though there are many themes and many plots, there is only one story, the tale of the One and the void. We come and go into this great story, ignorant of the beginning before us, and dead well before the end. What you heard is enough. Be satisfied."

Rel laid his bedroll. "There would be answers in this city for me. My people have learned a lot digging up places like this."

"Then they are foolhardy. These places are graves, traps for the unwary." Shkarauthir settled himself into his blankets. "Be careful, small one. Stay close by the fire and sleep. It is only safe in the barracks, where my people lived when we served our masters. This was our domain, and it remains so. There is protection here still that is lacking outside these walls."

The modalmen fell asleep quickly and so Rel seized the chance for one last question.

"Shkarauthir?" asked Rel.

"Mmm?" said the great chieftain.

"How is it you speak Maceriyan so well?"

"The One," sighed Shkarauthir. "He put the words into my mouth, as he put the pebbles of words into the mouths of the first people, all blessings be upon him."

With that typically obtuse answer, Shkarauthir was suddenly asleep, as were the rest of his kind, leaving Rel awake alone.

CHAPTER SEVEN
A Cold Fate

THEY BURIED TRASSAN Kressind on a promontory overlooking the shelves of stacked ice that clung to the shores of the Sotherwinter. Little more than a knoll that jutted out over the snow, the hill was high enough that the indigo sea could be seen surging impatiently a mile away.

Though the knoll's rock was free of snow, in its vicinity there were few places uncovered by the gathering thaw. Where the soil was exposed it was loose and moist on the surface, permanently frozen a foot down, so they laid Trassan to rest in a cairn of stones, trusting that the weight of rock would keep his body free from the attentions of the birds and the dracon-skuas that swarmed and dove at the foot of the ice cliffs.

Ilona sat alone upon the stone, listening to the screeching of the seabirds. A final chance to say goodbye, and she had no words to give. It was late, nearly midnight, but still bright as day. A strange clarity was upon a landscape lit by light the colour of pale summer wine.

The service was short. Few words were said. Not for lack of respect, Ilona thought, but from sorrow. After it was done, and Trassan's cold body interred, the others left her alone with her grief. She was grateful for that. Only Tyn Rulsy waited for her, perched on a swelling in the rock. She looked to be staring at Ilona's ironlock propped against the cairn— Bannord had insisted Ilona have one of their remaining guns—though whatever she actually saw with her button black eyes, it was far away from their physical location.

Winter grudgingly relaxed its grip on the Sotherwinter, but it did not rule uncontested. Under the midnight sun the snow crept away from the black dome of the stone inch by inch. Clear patches of ice showed at the fringes where water had melted and frozen again in the brief nights. It was only days after midsummer's eve, so Ilona supposed the process would continue a while, uncovering a little more of the rock before the cold of the polar winter returned and the rock was buried again.

Even at the height of summer her breath clouded the evening air, but there was life there upon the narrow bit of land sandwiched between the ice of the interior and the ice of the littoral. Small flies warmed themselves on the rock, stealing energy for their desperate mating flights. Grasses grew in a crack across the top of the crag, bearing delicate purple flowers. The cairn holding Trassan's body was built over the grass. She stared at the plants, feeling sorry for burying them; their life was hard enough. Right by the lowest stone in the pile, three blooms bobbed madly in the sea breeze. It was so alive, a flash of colour in a monochrome wasteland.

Ilona faced out to sea and wept, crying as she could not in front of the others. The frigid winds dried her tears as quickly as they fell.

"Ilona."

Tullian Ardovani spoke behind her softly. She rubbed her eyes with the cuff of her parka before facing him.

"I'm sorry," she said, feeling the need to apologise, as if sorrow would kill them all in that deadly place.

"Don't be," he said. "How are you?" The magister's expression was all so puppyish in his solicitude that she wanted to slap him.

Nobody knew the angry Ilona of Karsa City. They had seen her once, when she kicked Trassan. After that Ilona had clamped down on her spirit so hard she felt smothered. But it had worked. They all saw her as dutiful and willing to learn. Except, perhaps, Bannord. He could see her true self, she could tell from the way he smiled when she lost her temper and just as quickly reeled it in. Nobody else glimpsed the effort it took not to let her irritation get the better of her.

"As good as can be," she said.

"Trassan was a good man," he said.

"He was."

He came to her and rested a hand on her shoulder. He didn't have his gloves on, and his fingers were red as mince with the cold. It was an awkward gesture. A more confident man would have taken her in his arms, and held her tight, and let her weep. Ardovani was a picture of self-assurance compared to the expedition mage, the deceased Vols Iapetus. He greeted every new experience with a joyous enthusiasm that was lifting to the spirits. But when around her he had the withdrawn timidity that academic men suffer in the company of women. It was a shame. If only she could crush him and Bannord together and make them one, she might have the perfect man.

"If there is anything I can do..." he said.

"Can you bring Trassan back from the dead?" she said, regretting her mocking tone the instant she had spoken.

He shook his head in genuine sorrow. "Only the very greatest necromancers, the Mage-Guiders of old, could do that, and in truth I am not sure they are anything more than stories. I have a small talent for directed glimmer machines," he said modestly. "I am no mage."

"I am sorry. I am prone to making light at inappropriate moments."

"I had not noticed that."

"There is a lot you don't know about me." She sighed. "You are a very trusting man, magister."

He looked a little uncomfortable. She was toying with him, she knew, but the effect she had on him made her feel better.

"I can't bring him back, but I did see him go," he said.

"What, into the...?" she pointed upward, then laughed through her tears. "I'm sorry. I shouldn't laugh. It's mostly relief."

"Really!" he said, sharing her unexpected laughter. "I've never seen a ghost depart before. I mean, all mageborn theoretically *can*, but I suppose back home there is too much noise. Too many other wills pushing at reality. Here, in this place, anything feels possible." He lapsed into thought.

"What was it like?" she asked quietly.

"Beautiful and terrifying. As you might expect. I could not see into the next world, but he was heading there with purpose, and he looked at peace."

"He got through, even without a Guider?"

"I believe he did."

Neither of them spoke of the fates of those who were lost after death, the tormented souls that roamed the Earth, or worse, vanished altogether. There was no Guider in the ship's crew. All souls lost at sea were the property of the Drowned King, excepting those that belonged to the One.

"They say the strong willed find their way, no matter what," he said.

She closed her eyes, to better feel the wind on her face and hide her grief. "I was in love with him when we were children. I had no real friends of my own. My mother's behaviour drove people away, but not family. Aarin was closer to me in years, but Trassan and I loved the same things. He was always more interested in engineering than I was, but we shared a passion for faraway places, and tall tales. He was quite the romantic." She looked down on the stone bed her cousin would sleep in forever. "We were very close. I hated him when he used me to get my father's money. I provoked him, I suppose. I knew he'd never marry me, I didn't want him to, but I couldn't forgive him for making a child's promise he could not keep. And then he broke his other promise, to take me into the crew. I blame myself. If I had not been so forward with him, then perhaps he would not have left me behind like he did, and I would not have had to smuggle myself aboard the ship. Now he's dead. I wish we had parted on better terms."

"I think things were fine between you. There was nothing to forgive," said Ardovani boldly, although in Ilona's opinion he had no basis for the statement.

"I didn't know him for very long, only the voyage. I suppose it was only last year that I met him for the first time. I admit, he was not a happy man when you popped up out of the hold, but he seemed proud of you, and of what you achieved."

The tears came again, and she scrubbed at her face. She nodded. "His father hates women, but his sister is strong. I admire her. I admire them all. I wanted so much to be like them. I wanted to be with them, away from my awful mother. I could not. I was always on the outside."

"You're not on the outside now." Ardovani grasped both her shoulders this time. He looked into her eyes. "You are a soldier, and an important part of this expedition." His gesture was spoiled when his gun slipped off his shoulder. He smiled apologetically as he fumbled for it. The physical contact broken between them, he stepped back.

She wished he would hold her properly. She needed it. "Until I freeze to death."

"That won't happen," he said.

"So sure of yourself. We could all die here."

"I won't allow it to happen to you. I am not a powerful man, Ilona, but I do have talents. I put them all at your service. I couldn't bear it... I mean, such a beautiful... It would be..." He came to an embarrassed halt and looked at the ground.

She smiled at him. "That's sweet, really."

By the colour of his cheeks sweet was more than he hoped for, but less than he wanted. He looked lost. At that moment, he was behaving more like Vols. His confidence was foundering. Ilona was so not unworldly as to be unaware why.

Ardovani suddenly switched topic. "And how are you, Tyn Rulsy?" he said to the Tyn, with something approaching his usual agreeableness. "Are you not in danger? I know the water clans must return to their home springs often, or they are in danger of death. I assume that, as you wear a collar, you are not a free Tyn?"

Rulsy stared at him from the depths of her parka for a long few seconds. She was like a tiny mummy, or a hideous doll. She blew a raspberry at him.

"Are you always so free with questions, goodmagister?" she said. "I am Tyn, but I still like manners. Rudely probing! Tsk."

Ardovani bobbed his head nervously. Ilona smiled to herself. She could not imagine him reacting that way a few weeks ago. He was in trouble. He recovered quickly, however.

"I am sorry," said Ardovani with a bow. "There are no Greater Tyn outside the isles. When I came to Karsa from Cullosanti, I had never seen your kind before. I apologise for my curiosity."

Rulsy grinned wolfishly. "S'alright. I tease you. I get sick of the puppy eyes you make at the mistress here all the time," she said, putting on a lovestruck expression that, on her wrinkled, ancient child's face, was disturbing.

Ardovani's blush deepened.

Rulsy jumped off the rock and patted his arm with an earth-brown hand. "I am Water Tyn. Most Greater Tyn are Water Tyn," she shrugged. "Probably all now, not so many Tyn left any more. But I am also Ocean Tyn, of the Sea Clans. I go anywhere, where there are currents to feed me." She waved her hand around vaguely at the ocean. "I am freer, but I am weaker. Ocean currents are spread thin, magic on them thin too. River Tyn clans get lot of strength from their rivers, but they less free. It is the bargain we make with the Earth."

"What about the Free Tyn?" asked Ilona, curious despite herself.

"Don't ask about them," Rulsy said warningly. "Never about them." She walked off, then turned back. "Not too many questions now, goodmagister," she said. "I have a bucket full of geas on me. Upset me, and I'll sing them all to you in your sleep, then you be bound too." She winked, and descended the side of the knoll.

"You know, from behind, she looks just like a child," said Ardovani. "It gives me the terrors when she turns around, especially at night."

Ilona smiled through her sadness. "What, a magister? A big brave magician like you, scared of a Tyn?"

"We should all be scared of them," said Ardovani, watching Rulsy as she disappeared from sight. "If only half of what I have read about them is true, they are exceptionally dangerous. On the continent, we call you Karsans mad for living on the Isles. We say King Brannon was deluded."

"Well, we say we are as brave as King Brannon. You don't want to know what we say about you people on the other side of the neck."

"I have been in the fortunate position of hearing some of it," said Ardovani. He watched Tyn Rulsy go below. "Be careful of her. Where did she come from? She wasn't in the Morfaan storehouse when Shrane opened the gate. I don't recall her arriving at the sledges."

"She just seemed to be there," said Ilona. She frowned. "She's never been anything but kind to me."

"Even so, be careful," said Ardovani. "Anyway, I came up here to fetch you. The inventory is nearly done. Antoninan wants to be off." Ardovani looked to the northwest, the way they had come. Far, far away in the cold blue skies, a thin column of steam rose up high, flattening itself out against some invisible boundary. "I'll leave you alone for a bit, but you best come soon. I'll see you down there."

He was already leaving as Bannord's head emerged over the edge of the rock. Ilona saw Ardovani wanted to stay with her when he saw the marine arrive, but he had no good excuse.

"First Lieutenant," he said.

"Magister," said Bannord with a cocky grin. Unlike Ardovani, Bannord had no problem being around pretty girls. Nevertheless, there was a little strain in his smile when he jerked his thumb over his shoulder at the departing magister, so slight it was only just noticeable. Ilona was annoyed at his jealousy. She was grieving, couldn't he see that? Although a more wanton part of her was flattered.

"What did he want?" asked Bannord.

"He wanted to see how I was feeling, and he wanted to fetch me for the meeting."

"Well, so do I. I trust you are alright? You Kressinds are a tough bunch."

"I am fine, thank you," she said, though she was not.

He glanced sideways at her gun, propped up against Trassan's grave, and frowned.

"You shouldn't leave that lying about like that," he said.

"I am not on duty, lieutenant."

"Even so... If you get it too cold, it won't work. There's plenty out here beside those iron monsters that would love to kill us. This is unknown country, goodlady, so pick it up."

She sighed at him.

"And less of that, soldier," he said.

"I'm not on duty," she repeated. She picked up the gun anyway, and shouldered it.

Bannord slapped his gloved hands together and made a face. "We're all on duty, all of the time out here, my goodlady," he said. "Now, you're wanted in camp, so double march. Enough of this mournfulness." Bannord's beard was growing in. She preferred it that way, it added to his massive physical presence. He was so much more of a man than Ardovani, who was fine featured and aesthetic in appearance and tastes. Ardovani could do things Bannord could not, feats of magic and engineering that were as practical as they were amazing, and the weapon he carried was the most powerful device she had ever seen. But she still felt safer with Bannord. His smell calmed her. His presence enveloped her in a cocoon that kept her warm.

"Ardovani told me to take my time," she said.

"I'm ordering you not to."

"You're an arse. Sir."

"Don't I know it. Now get a move on."

"Do you know," she said, still not moving, "a beard suits you."

"Do you think? I had one for years; I only shaved it off for the voyage." He stroked his moustaches and ran his hand down onto his beard. "I feel like me again, if that makes sense. You're changing the subject. Down the hill, marine. Chop chop."

They left the knoll, their feet skidding on the short, steep slope of rock as they descended.

By the grave, the flowers danced in the wind.

TYN GELVEN WAS the only other Tyn in the party, and Rulsy knew he was about to leave her behind. She could smell the magic he was gathering from up on the knoll, and sought him out before he set it free. Once out of sight of Ilona and Ardovani, she hurried. No Tyn wished to reveal their urgency to a human being, it undermined the stolid impression people had of them. Managing how they were perceived was all that kept them alive, but Tyn Rulsy was so concerned that she would be left alone without others of her kind that she risked being observed and ran like a serving girl late to attend her mistress.

She ran into a pocket of the world where time went slow. Sounds died. The wind dropped. It was like she had run onto a stage set, or a museum display; some dusty space decorated to appear as the Sotherwinter.

Within it, Tyn Gelven was preparing to depart. A heavy cloud of Tyn magic, invisible to most mortal eyes but clearer to Tyn Rulsy than the light of the sun, surrounded the old Tyn. He had removed the colourful scarf he wore over his iron collar to prevent it scorching, for the collar already was heating in opposition to his magic. As he paced and gestured, looking for all the world like an old man wrestling with a moral dilemma, his form skipped and blurred, and there appeared bright shafts of white light that stabbed out from his body, hinting at a greater being within his wrinkled skin. Then he was only an old, worn out half-man again, and could not possibly have ever been anything else. Only the collar retained its shape through his strange distortions, growing hotter all the while.

"You'll burn yourself!" said Rulsy.

Tyn Gelven stopped pacing, and ran a flat, labourer's finger around the inside of the collar. About his neck was a perfectly circular track of smooth skin, evidence of previous magical workings.

"Ah, that I might," he said. "Could happen." He used the secret speech of the Tyn. To humans it sounded as a rhythmic babble. Unintelligible by the Tyn's design, beneath the glamour was a language of words like any other.

"You could..." Tyn Rulsy paused. "You could take it off."

"Only the Wild Tyn or the Free Tyn dare do such a thing. One lot's mad and faded into sprites, the other lot's wickeder than the lowest demon. I don't want to behave like either."

"That's not true!" said Rulsy. "The oldest and wisest of the Greater Tyn can. I heard tell the Morthrocksey Tyn did it to make the ship. You're old and wise, Tyn Gelven. You can do it."

"Maybe I can," he shrugged. "But I won't."

"How will you go then?"

"Aha, you are right when you say I'm an old Tyn. I've seen a few things. Don't need to take my collar off to do what I'm going to do."

"You'll walk the Road of Fire?" Rulsy said breathlessly.

"Aye, I'll walk the Road of Fire, it's been a while but it's still there, you can be sure of that." Gelven's eyes gleamed.

Rulsy's mouth widened. "You can do that?"

"I forget how young you are, sometimes. Yes, I can."

"The Road of Fire is unsafe. That's what mother told me."

"Well, there's safe and safe. Is it without risk, well I'd have to say no. Is it free of Draathis? The answer right there is yes. The old road's only good for travelling to points on this sphere. It's no world gate, but it'll suit my purposes. Draathis can't walk there. Not yet, anyway. It'll get me back to the ship."

"I never saw the road," she said miserably. "Best I can manage is a bit of glamour, or a tiny hop from here to there, like I did from the ship. I never saw anything, I never lived in the light, just this drabness. Being born, then the fire and the iron," she lifted up her parka's skirt and let it drop. "That's what I got, I a few years of glory. So little I don't remember."

"Better than none, my dear. It's best you don't remember too much. Our children were unkind to us."

"You shouldn't do it," said Rulsy. "There's all that iron in that ship. It's not good for us. If you have to walk the road at all, you could just go home, back to the refuge of the Isles. You'll live."

"One never walks the road," he said, "one always has to run, and I'm running with magic burning off me right into the belly of an iron beast. But to go home now and leave these poor things to their fate, would you really do that? They are your friends."

"We are two beings born of light, rooted in earth and water forevermore," said Rulsy sadly. "Broken. Why help them, when the way we are is their fault?"

"Come now, it's not their fault, not most of it anyway," smiled Gelven, "and if they're so bad, why help Goodlady Ilona?"

Rulsy pulled a face. "She's different. I like her. It's not the same."

"It is the same, and they're all different, not only her," he said. "People are complicated creatures. The worst of them have some good in them. They're like us in that regard, but better and worse at the same time."

"So you are going."

"I am."

"Take me with you," she said in a small voice. "It's cold here. I don't like it."

"You know I can't do that."

"Please!"

"Tyn Rulsy! You left the ship to follow the goodlady, you know your heart's not in your pleading," he sniffed. "Only got it in me to take myself. My, if you saw me fifty centuries ago, I could lead an army down the Road of Fire, then out through a world gate and conquer the sphere beyond." He waved his hand across the sky. "But that was then, and things are different now." Gelven took her hand into his own and patted it. Their leathery, dry skin rasped together.

"It's not fair."

"There, there, Tyn Rulsy," he said. "We're here for good reasons, as the elders always say. It won't forever be like this."

"It will be worse."

"Doubtlessly," he said with a sad smile. "Things can always be worse. I prefer to dwell on the now and what is, not the might be or the what was. Dwelling on the what was brings despair, and that's killed more of our people than any Draathis ever did. Dwelling on the might be leads you further from the path. You don't want to be a Free Tyn now, do you?"

She shuddered. "Ugh, no."

"Well then. Fight your way out of the hell of today before you worry about the one of tomorrow. Who knows? Maybe one day, perhaps a day like this where everything you care for is in danger and there is no light on the horizon, maybe the One will return, and he will forgive us."

Rulsy was dismayed. Tyn did not name the One ever. Not unless they thought they were close to death.

"Don't go!" she said.

He stood up straight. "Now, young lady, tell Ilona and the rest that I have gone to carry a message to the Ishmalani captain. They never had the eye of the One at the start, but they won it. They are good people. He will do what is right. I will inform him that these folk here still live. Best I go. Old sins cannot be undone, but new sins can be avoided. I will not have the deaths of any of them on my conscience if it can be helped."

"Not even that fatty Persin? He made all this happen. He brought the Iron Children back," said Rulsy.

"Not even him. We lost the right to judge folks a long time ago, Tyn Rulsy. Don't forget that, or you'll make mistakes. You'd think our kind can err no more. If only that were the case."

"Wait at least until they have talked. How will you know where they are going? You won't help anyone."

"They will head for Sea Drays Bay. They have no other choice."

"The bay is blocked!"

"Still they'll go. I don't need to be a seer to foretell that."

"You don't know that."

"Oh you know I do." He held up his hands to calm her. "I would stay if I could. The road comes when it will, not when I will it. Not now, not like it was in the old days." He closed his eyes and sniffed the air. "Righty-ho. It has to be now or not at all." He snapped his fingers. Time slowed further. Light ran like treacle, sweet and soft and gentle. Nothing else seemed to change, but Tyn Gelven stepped out of that place and into another, like a paper shape pushed through a slit in a card.

Time ran back to its normal speed with such force Tyn Rulsy fell backward, plopping onto her behind with a squeak.

"Not fair," she said. The magic faded. The human world intruded again. The wind blew cold. The dogs were howling. In the camp, men were leaving behind their tasks and making their way to the tent for a meeting that would decide whether they lived or died, ignorant of the great magic worked in their midst.

Tyn Rulsy picked herself up and grumbled her way to the centre of the camp.

CHAPTER EIGHT
A Question of Priorities

THE CAMP WAS hardly worthy of the name. In the books on polar exploration Ilona had read, a camp meant a well-ordered collection of tents, stacks of equipment, areas for dogs and wood-sided cabins with canvas roofs. There were maps in some of the works she'd studied. They were all very organised. Their camp was chaos, a collection of boxes and sleds scattered at random around a single tent.

Snow patches turned a vibrant orange in the last light of day. It was by then past midnight, and the sun was finally setting. When it dipped below the horizon it would stay there only briefly before rising again.

Days that long affected the body. Ilona felt giddy the whole time, caught in a state partway between exhaustion and elation. Before the events at the city she had struggled to sleep. Since the opening of the gate and their escape there had been no chance to. The truth was she didn't feel tired. At home long winter nights made her sleepy. Bright summer days energised her. This nervous energy must have the same effect at its source, only intensified greatly. She wondered how long someone could go without sleep. She supposed it must be necessary, or why would people do it at all? The light was constant, and though her thoughts seemed estranged from her body, and her perceptions skewed, she could not rest. The days might drive them all mad before winter. She imagined the six months of night that would follow. At the pole the sun was not supposed to rise at all.

The Sotherwinter was as beautiful as she had imagined it, but it was no land for humanity.

The dogs barked. Ilona and Bannord walked a path of dirty ice toward the camp's single tent. The dogs were divided into their teams, tied to iron pickets; those that had come with Trassan on one side of the path, and those that had come with Persin on the other. Piles of supplies were heaped alongside the path between them to help screen them from each other.

Persin had his own Sorkosan leader dogs, of the rare talking breed. Despite Valatrice's fame, Persin's dogs had yet to submit to his authority, and the two leaders, one male and one female, stared at Valatrice in open challenge. Valatrice regally ignored them, chewing upon the frozen carcass of an animal he had found upon the ice. Its skin was twisted and black, its bones white as snow. It looked disgusting, but Valatrice gnawed on it with relish.

"Good evening, little stowaway," he said as Ilona passed him. He had a rich voice, almost like a man's, full of knowing humour.

His lesser kin could not speak, but howled their challenges loudly. The drays were enormous things that weighed as much as three grown men, with withers that came level with Ilona's shoulders. Broad forequarters gave them immense power to pull. Beasts like that seemed too big to prance and snarl. The drays at homes waited patiently in their kennels for work, but these were as full of nervous energy as Ilona, and paced back and forth, despite their efforts in the long cold flight from the city. Out there in the wilderness they wanted to be off and running.

Ilona had no fear of them, so long as Valatrice was there. She smiled at them, and trailed her fingers through the fur of those that would permit it. She shared their eagerness to be away from the iron monsters invading their world.

Around the tent the mess was at its worst. Most of the boxes the group had scavenged from the dockside were empty, and many broken to flinders. Straw packing had been trodden into the mud and snow. Men from both Persin and Trassan's expeditions sorted through their salvaged supplies quickly, discarding whatever was not needed. Weight was the prime concern. How much they took with them determined their speed of travel through that harsh land. The expedition prioritised food and fuel. Expensive scientific instruments were discarded, any wooden parts they had stripped off for fuel. Their crates were kept. In that climate, the boxes were more valuable than the objects they held. Splintery, cheap timber burned, and would keep them warm, something a theodolite or telescope could not do. It was strange how one's priorities changed, Ilona thought. Trash became gold, in the right circumstances.

"Come on girl," said Bannord. "Stop dallying, the meeting has already begun."

He pointed at the tent, an open sided, square affair with a pyramidal roof. Though it had sides, they were currently rolled up. It was really an awning intended to protect artefacts taken from the city while they were catalogued rather than a serious shelter. It would not withstand a storm.

Men were downing their tools and heading within. There were too many to fit inside, so they crowded around it. Despite the lack of room, a clear gap existed between the rival expeditions, as obvious as that between the two packs of dogs. Bannord took advantage of this to push his way to the front, where Eustache Antoninan, the famed polar explorer hired by Trassan, stood next to Vardeuche Persin. Persin carried the satchel containing a device from the city Trassan had told Ilona to watch over. She had thought about stealing it back, but he was never without the thing.

All told, there were twenty-five people in the party, a mixture from the Kressind and the Persin expeditions; only Vardeuche Persin was very much alive, while Trassan Kressind was dead.

Persin's rivalry with Trassan's sponsor, Vand, had led him to throw in his lot with the mage Adamanka Shrane. She had subsequently betrayed him, opening a portal in the city of ice that had let a forgotten evil into the world. Persin was not apologetic about his error, for he was too arrogant to be so. This attitude did not play well with Antoninan, who was also renowned for his towering opinion of himself. Both he and Persin were Maceriyan, which, Ilona thought, explained their egos. Despite their shared nationality, they had little time for each other. They waited for the meeting to commence without speaking.

"Time to shake things up a little," said Bannord with a grin.

Bannord took his place with Antoninan and Persin. To Ilona's surprise he beckoned her forward. She made a quizzical face at him. He nodded encouragingly and beckoned her again. She joined him reluctantly.

Persin's eyes goggled in his round, bald face. He leaned in to whisper to Bannord.

"Goodman, I do not think it a good idea to involve the lady in this critical meeting. We must make plans for our survival. This is not women's business."

Bannord smiled menacingly. "Firstly," he said loudly enough for everyone to hear. "I may be poorer than you, but I am of better birth, so either refer to me as goodfellow or as lieutenant. I will have my rank respected, either social or military. I leave the choice to you."

Among Persin's seven surviving men were three who did not speak Karsarin. One of their colleagues whispered a translation in Maceriyan of the proceedings for the benefit of his comrades.

Persin scowled with outrage. He was not used to being spoken to in that manner.

"Secondly, although Trooper Kressinda-Hamafara here is technically but a lowly soldier under my command, she is also of high birth," Bannord continued. "She is the cousin of Trassan Kressind. Now he is dead, she is the representative of the Kressind family by right of blood."

"This was Goodman Vand's expedition," said Persin. "Not Kressind's."

"You would think that, being so caught up in your rivalry with Vand it drove you to murder," said Bannord. The assembled men shifted uncomfortably, for what Bannord said was true. "But I concede that you have a point. Ullfider!" Bannord called out into the crowd. The expedition's aged antiquarian shuffled to the front.

"Yes?" he said, somewhat perplexed. His spectacles fogged in the heat coming off the pressed bodies.

"You're Vand's man."

"Well, I... I suppose," said Ullfider. "I have known him since he was a boy. And yes, I... I worked with his father. I don't know about *man*... I—"

"You know what he wanted."

"I suppose you could say that," said Ullfider, casting a suspicious look at Persin. "He and I drew up the objectives for this expedition, with Goodfellow Kressind, of course," he added hurriedly.

"So then," said Bannord. "You should be up here too, to represent his interests."

"Oh I don't know—"

"Come up here now," said Bannord. "There is an army of iron giants pursuing us. We should be sparing with our time. You're joining us here, like it or not."

Ullfider shuffled to the front.

"So," said Bannord, addressing the assembly. "Myself, Antoninan, the goodlady, Persin, and Ullfider will lead this expedition, which has gone from one of exploration to survival." He glanced back at Antoninan.

The explorer responded stonily. It was he who had called the meeting, no doubt to press his position of authority over Persin's. He had not anticipated Bannord commandeering it. "I respect your rank, lieutenant, and the fact that a number of our fellows here are under your direct command. But you have no experience of survival in this part of the world. I do. It is I who should lead this expedition."

"I would say I have some experience," said Bannord. "Not as much as you, I admit, but some. I have sailed the Sorskian coast and the Sorkosan sea."

"Maybe you have experience at sea; you have none on land."

"That is true," admitted Bannord. "I agree that you should determine what we ought to do to survive. You are the expert. However, you cannot be allowed unquestioned leadership. The five of us will make up a council."

"Leadership by committee will kill is all," said Antoninan.

Persin watched their exchange with a calculating expression.

"Which is why I am not proposing leadership by committee," said Bannord. "What I am saying is that no one should lead without any form of check. Your expeditions are renowned for their high rates of fatality as much as their boldness. Would you have exerted yourself so strongly over Trassan as you do now over me?"

"We had an agreement, Kressind and I. On the ice my commands were to be preeminent."

"Preeminent, not unchallenged," said Bannord. "I and my men will follow you. I defer to your greater experience. But no major decision should be made on the expedition's fate without consultation. This is no different to the agreement you had with Trassan Kressind."

Antoninan glared at him. "Circumstances are changed. We are fighting for our survival."

"Higher stakes require more care from the gambler," said Bannord. "Ullfider, Ilona, Persin. Are you in favour of this proposal?"

Ullfider mumbled affirmatively. "I... I suppose so..."

"I think you are right," said Persin. "My own polar expert is dead, but we had a similar agreement." He looked to the others, shrugging slightly. Antoninan sneered at him.

"Ilona," said Bannord. "Do you agree?"

"I am not comfortable to be given this responsibility," she said. "But I will take it. Though I am not happy that the man who commissioned the murder of my cousin should have any role in leadership."

Bannord started to interrupt. Ilona pressed on. "But!" she said forcefully. "His men make up nearly a third of our number, so he should have some say."

Persin backed down with a small bow of his head.

"There we are then, Goodfellow Antoninan," said Bannord. "You may lead with our support, or not at all."

Antoninan was displeased. "I accept," he said, "if only because I have no choice. Be warned, I will put my opinions forward forcefully."

"As will I," said Bannord. He turned to address the others again. "Do you men object?"

Mazarine, Persin's highest ranking remaining mercenary, folded his arms. "We'll follow you as readily as him," he said, glancing at Persin. "We don't care for his orders any more. He got most of us killed. If you put us in danger we'll fight. We're in this for ourselves. Life and death."

"It's a foolish man who makes threats to them who outnumbers him," said Ranost, who Bannord had appointed as his corporal.

"This must stop now! Cast that idea from your heads immediately. We are not in this for ourselves," said Antoninan. "It is us against this land, and we must work together. You do not have the understanding of this landscape that I do. Surviving here is hard enough, and we have an army of iron monsters to contend with. There'll be no need for violence among us, if only because you will be too busy trying to stay alive."

Mazarine spat on the ground. "Agreed," he said. "For now."

"Excellent," said Bannord. "Antoninan, I believe you have a proposal."

"I do, but to begin there will be a making of a new roll. Unless anyone objects?"

Bannord shook his head.

One by one, the members of the group called out their names. Antoninan's remaining groom marked them in a small book. Seven men survived from Persin's rival expedition, and Persin himself, saved incidentally by Vols Iapetus from Shrane's betrayal.

Persin's men were Sergeant Mazarine, who was also Maceriyan. Then there were the four Olberlander mercenaries Gesentur, Krasstermann, Heisenwel and Crut, two further Maceriyans named Favreau and Jeuney, and a Musran called Devall. These latter three were the men without a command of Karsarin, a not uncommon lack in people from the Maceriyan successor states. Crut, who was something of a polyglot, translated for them.

The remainder were from Trassan's party. They were, Ilona, Bannord, Ardovani, Antoninan, Ullfider, his younger assistant Vengrise and the middle-aged Davson, the sailors Moather Fend-nereaz-Atarar, known as Mo, and Arrkan And-nereaz-Fons, known by his first name alone. They were the sole Ishmalani in the group, caught only because they had been loading artefacts for transport to the *Prince Alfra* when Persin attacked. Gestane, another Maceriyan, was the groom. Untalkative on the voyage, the death of Gestane's son, the assistant groom, had driven his last words from him. Tyn Rulsy made eleven. The remainder were Bannord's Karsan marines—Darrasind, Forfeth, Aretimus and Corporal Ranost. Fourteen all told.

The mood was sombre. All of them had lost friends. Morfaan guardian constructs had slain several, more men had died in the clash between the two parties. A great many of Persin's group had been killed when Shrane opened the gate.

"That's twenty-three. By my reckoning there should be twenty-four. Where is the other Tyn?" asked Antoninan.

"Gelven," said Bannord. "Tyn Gelven."

"He does not call his name," said Gestane.

"Where is he?" Bannord asked Rulsy.

She shrugged. "He gone, back to ship." Rulsy seemed to speak broken Karsarin, but her words were understood by all.

The men muttered to each other, making the signs of banished gods and kissing the backs of their hands in warding.

"When?" said Bannord frowning. "How?"

"When, that's after they buried the master 'neath the rocks." Rulsy stuck her lip out. "How, he go the old Tyn way, a way I don't know. He say after Master Trassan goes under that he goes back. So he goes. Walks into a crack in the world and then he's gone, from here to there." She pointed to the ground, then behind her to the sea.

"I don't understand," said Persin. He licked his lips nervously and patted his satchel. Non-Karsans were wary of Tyn. "Is he out on the ice?"

"Tyn magic," said Bannord.

Rulsy gave Persin a look of withering contempt. "You think he walked? He didn't walk. He went in a crack in the world, like I says. He back there now on the ship, with the rest. A folding of things and a quick step, that's all it takes, for those what knows how to do it, which I doesn't," she concluded peevishly.

"Little bastard," said Forfeth. "He's fucking left us here to die!"

Rulsy span round on her heel, making him flinch. "He's one of the good ones, is Tyn Gelven, you not be disrespecting him, or I'll put the eye on you," she said, staring hard at him. He dropped his gaze and shuffled behind his friend. "He's gone to help you. More danger on the road than there is on the ice."

"Can you do that?" asked Persin urgently. "Could you go back and tell them what is happening?"

"I already said no," said Rulsy. "Not my trick, don't you listen?"

"You did appear in this group without warning," said Bannord. "You weren't in the city with us, and then you were, creeping out of the furs while we were moving."

"A different thing," she said. "A short hop. I can't walk the road. He'll tell. Why you think he gone? He gone back, tell the captain you're all here. You should thank him, magic like that pushes the changes, and we Tyn don't like change no more." She flicked her iron collar with a dirty nail. "And he might die for what he did. You be uppity if you like, goodfellows," said

Rulsy. "A Tyn can only take himself, not you too. Can't say he's going to do it, 'cause you won't believe he can. Make it all difficult, that does. And then there's timing. Don't you think he'd want to hear all your lovely plans? No. He gets one chance, might not be another. So he goes. He thinks you'll head for Sea Drays Bay."

"Well, that puts a different complexion on things," said Ullfider with relief. "Do you think they'll come to rescue us?"

Rulsy poked out her bottom lip again and huddled into her parka. "If it's luck you're after, you're asking the wrong Tyn. Tyn can't do that, not for so many as you. Maybe they come, maybe they won't."

Everyone started talking at once. Accusations flew back and forth between the two groups; the Karsans complaining they would never be in such dire circumstances without the Maceriyans. The Maceriyans said they were following Persin's orders, that it was simple rivalry between rich men, and that they'd all been thoroughly duped. This line of argument found ready listeners among the Karsans, and more than a few murderous looks were deflected from the mercenaries onto their employer.

"Silence!" shouted Antoninan. "Silence!"

The men continued to shout.

Bannord tugged his gloves off with his teeth and whistled shrilly between his fingers.

"Shut up!" he bellowed. "That's an order, and I don't care if you're in my regiment or not." He stared them all down until the last words died.

"There will be no more unilateral action in future," said Antoninan to Rulsy. "Anyone who wishes to act must discuss it with me."

"Don't know why you're telling me," muttered Rulsy.

"Has he definitely gone?" asked Bannord.

"I just says so, didn't I?"

"My apologies, Goodlady Tyn," said Bannord.

"I ain't no lady," grumbled Rulsy.

"Let's get closer to the shore and make camp," said Ullfider excitedly. "They'll be coming back!"

"We cannot linger here," said Antoninan. "These Draathis?" He looked to Rulsy for confirmation, she nodded at him.

"The Draathis, the Iron Children. That's what they is called. They will track us here," she said.

"We could take the chance they won't get here soon," said Ilona. "The ship knows he's alive," she said, pointing at Persin. "They'll know we're alive. So whoever is in charge has a reason to come back. The *Prince Alfra* is fast."

Persin cleared his throat uncomfortably. "Well, let us not be too hasty. We cannot assume they'll be coming for me."

"Your own men would abandon you?" said Bannord.

"Oh, you should wager they would," said Mazarine. He clapped his hands onto his elbows and chuckled drily. "Our Captain Croutier is a merciless son of a whore. He'd leave us all to freeze if it saved his own life. I'll bet he'll not even rendezvous with Mesire Persin's other two vessels, but make home at all speed."

"I paid him fairly," said Persin angrily.

"You will have lost his respect," said Mazarine. "He doesn't know what happened to us in that chamber, but when he saw that pillar of steam and all that magic, it won't have taken him long to figure out what happened. He never did like the mage."

More shouting, until Bannord whistled again.

"Please, goodmen," said Antoninan. "I must appeal for calm. We have to decide what we are going to do."

"That is, stay or go?" said Bannord.

"We have to go," said Antoninan. He unrolled a chart that showed an incomplete map of the Sotherwinter coast and hung it from the tent's central pole. Large segments were dotted lines. Some had been recently filled in, others had been amended, crossed out and redrawn. The continent was roughly circular, and its shape was more or less known, but question marks were everywhere, mostly relating to the extent of the ice shelves piled up by successive great tides around the landmass, and the Sotherwinter interior was entirely blank. No man had ever trodden there. "We have limited supplies. Twelve days of food at full rations, perhaps. Limited fuel. Were it not for our glimmer lamps and stoves, I would not rate our chances highly. The Karsan party has seven ironlock rifles remaining to them, along with Ardovani's marvellous gun. The eight soldiers in Persin's employ are all armed, giving us sixteen weapons in total. All except Ardovani's will do little against our pursuers, but we have an adequate amount of ammunition, so we may hunt. I propose we do that. There is nothing to eat here. There are rookeries of birds and dracon-kind around the coasts," said Ardovani, "at Sea Drays Bay."

"This is a joke," said Ranost. "The bay was shut by ice."

"The punishment detail I give you will be anything but, Ranost," said Bannord. "Keep it stowed for later."

"If it weren't for our visitors, I would say we make camp there and wait for rescue. Sea Drays Bay is usually accessible from the ocean, it is mapped, and offers the chance to restock our provisions. I have left stores of equipment there. I have not overwintered on the Sotherwinter yet, but I believe it is possible at the bay. That is why I proposed it as our original landing site. There are options open to us there. Sadly, we cannot remain long. We will be caught. We must have another plan."

"They have not caught us yet," said Persin. "Who says they will?"

"I saw no conveyances, no sleds, no vehicles of any kind," said Antoninan. "If they had any of these things, they would have overtaken us already, but we can assume an advantage on their part—that of inhumanity. They may not need to rest. The heat they give out suggests to me that they will have no issue with the cold. When the weather worsens, they will catch us."

"Alright, Antoninan, stop there. You're a polar expert, not a mage," said Bannord. "Ardovani, what do you think?"

"I have never seen anything like them," said Ardovani from his place in the crowd. "The Draathis were alive. Not machines, though they looked like them. They were surrounded by magic."

"That is not possible!" said Persin. "An iron man, made by magic? Nonsense!"

"I never said they were made by magic," said Ardovani. "They are encased in it, as you are. They have the aura of life. We have souls. Souls are, in essence, magical. They can be seen by those who have the skill. These iron men have souls. Who knows how they were made? Perhaps it was magic. Remember that Iron Mages were a myth until last week," said Ardovani. "We have all seen iron and magic in action together through the mage Shrane. As far as I am concerned, anything is possible."

"A hundred years ago, the mechanism of glimmer and iron power was unknown to us," said Ilona. "I suppose if these things come from somewhere else, they could do anything."

"So they may or may not catch us," said Bannord.

"We must assume that they will pursue us," said Antoninan. "Our best chance at survival is to move quickly to the bay, with minimal rest. For the last four days we have used the edge of the ice shelf to travel. They could not follow us there, I believe the heat they make would put them in danger of falling through. They will be forced to go around this inlet." He pointed out a deep cut into the coastline near to the city of ice. "But from hereon out, the coast curves far into the Sotherwinter sea." He sketched the line of the coast on the map. "Meaning that we have the greater distance to go if we stick to the ice shelf. If they move directly across the land here, they could intercept us at any point." He tapped the map. "The rising slopes into the interior give them a perfect view out over the ice. They will cut us off."

"Then how do we avoid them?" asked Mazarine.

"If we leave the pack ice, and cut across land ourselves from this point," explained Antoninan, "we can rely on our supplies. We can travel directly east to regain the coast here. Then we must travel north to Sea Drays Bay. The mountains give out there, and the water is clear of ice most of the year, I am sure what we witnessed earlier in the year will be clear soon. Moving on this line will give us an enormous advantage. And we've already come most of the way."

"We can see them coming, but they won't be able to see us," said Forfeth. "The steam from the heat they give out. We can see it now. It must fifty leagues from here."

"Exactly," said Antoninan.

"You have seen these places, I recall from your last book," said Persin. "Did you not launch your last attempt to find the land route to the Sotherwinter from Sea Drays Bay?"

"It has been my ambition to find the Sorskian Passage for a long time. Going overland we avoid the territory of the drowned completely, save the souls of our men and avoid his tolls. It is an attractive route for those who would like to exploit the resources of the Sotherwinter. There is great wealth in these lands: metals, meat, dragon ivory, sea dray oil. More. Perhaps even glimmer deposits."

"I heard something about a rail line," said Ardovani. "You plan to build a railway?"

"Not I, but I am sponsored by men who would."

"He has to find the route first," said Ilona.

"I nearly have," said Antoninan grandly. "I have mapped both ends of the supposed Sorskian Passage, from Sea Drays Bay here in the south, and from Finewater Bight on the Sorskian coast in the north. If we can find it, and fill in the detail of this central section," Antoninan indicated a blank part of the map, "we will get home. The country in those parts of Sorksia is inhabited, sparsely, but there are people there. They will aid us. The passage must be here somewhere. It has to be."

Persin looked at the map. A peninsula poked northward toward the very southernmost kingdoms. A similar, mountainous land mass curled down from the north. The coast either side of the map area was a treacherous maze of islets and shifting ice that extended some way toward the putative link. "To make it to Sorksia, we have to find the land path, which you have failed to discover on three separate occasions, if I recollect. If you can't find a way through the mountains from the south, and you could not find a land bridge that extended all the way through Winter's Maze from the north, what chance do we have, searching in a blind panic? That is assuming this land bridge exists at all, and there is not clear ocean between the Sotherwinter and Sorksia."

"If we stray from the coast and the iron ship does come for us, then the crew will not be able to find us. We might condemn ourselves," said Ullfider.

"What if they don't come? Sea Drays Bay is visited rarely. There is an expedition to the Finewater nearly every year," said Antoninan. "I have overwintered there before. Even if we are not pursued, we will be safer at Finewater Bight when the weather turns. A few degrees can mean the difference between life and death. We can then make our way overland to the Kingdoms in spring."

"It's an idea," said Bannord.

Persin shook his head. "If we push on so far north we shall exhaust ourselves. These iron beasts will certainly catch us then, and if they don't they will outpace us. The world may be a little preoccupied with them to be sending jaunts off into the south. You are trying to match our fight for survival with your personal obsession. I say we trust to rescue from my expedition, or the *Prince Alfra*."

"It was your obsession that put us here!" said Antoninan in Maceriyan. "We can do it," he said, switching back to Karsarin. His eyes moved up a long sweep of land whose northern extremities were a cartographer's best guess of dotted lines, alternative coasts in different colours, and hazards inked in red. "I know it is there somewhere. The Sorkosans and Sorskians have told me of it many times. We have not seen it because we do not dwell there. The water churns with sharp rocks and glimmer-laced whirlpools. No one can sail within eighty leagues of it. No sending works there. It is impossible to sail the Winter's Maze, but there is a land route. I know it is there somewhere."

"You've already tried. Three times!" said Persin. "Were it not for Valatrice, your third time would have been the last. It's madness. To get there in the first place, we have to cross these mountains." He poked the map beyond Sea Drays Bay, making it flutter. "And if I recall your reports from your last, *failed* attempt, there are more mountains beyond. That's before we reach the Maze. We'll all die."

"Then what do you suggest?"

"We move as fast as we can along the lip of the ice to Sea Drays Bay, keeping watch for the *Prince Alfra* or the remainder of my expedition. If they don't come, then we find somewhere hidden to camp near to the bay."

"We can't stay in the Sotherwinter during winter. It is possible, but we are poorly equipped. The Draathis will catch us. We will die. We must move on to the north," said Antoninan.

"But my other ships are also out there. They will come looking for me, if Croutier does not."

"What were your orders to your ships, Persin?" asked Bannord.

Persin looked guilty.

"If I recall right," said Mazarine, "they were to make their way to the City of Ice and attempt to discover a way through while we held the city."

"So, they'll either fail and go home; they'll succeed, see the enemy and run—assuming we're dead—or they'll all die," said Bannord. "I don't like this second part of Antoninan's plan, but I concur with the first part. Heading to Sea Drays Bay seems our best course for now."

"The odds of finding our way overland to Sorksia are ridiculously low!" said Persin.

"We can argue about that once we get to the bay, but it may not come to that," said Bannord. "The *Prince Alfra* might be waiting for us when we arrive. If it isn't, we will discuss plans again."

"Well, I er..." said Ullfider. "I am inclined to agree with Mesire Persin."

"Are you sure? We have to move on anyway, there's nowhere for the ship to land here. If we wait for rescue, we will die," said Bannord. "When we get to Sea Drays Bay what happens next depends on which captain is in command upon the iron ship. Is it Croutier, or did Heffi see him off? That's a big roll of the dice. At least this way, we're putting ground between us and the enemy, and there is food in Antoninan's stores there."

"Um, then perhaps not?" said Ullfider questioningly. He looked to the others for guidance.

"I say we vote now. Council first, all in favour of trying the first part of Antoninan's overland route," said Ilona.

Bannord raised his hand, as did Antoninan and, with a little prompting, Ullfider. After some thought, Ilona followed suit.

"For awaiting rescue on the shore close to here," said Ilona.

Persin held his hand defiantly aloft.

"In favour of waiting for rescue, Persin. We are going to Sea Drays Bay," said Bannord.

"Lieutenant—" began Persin.

"We'll reexamine our options once there," said Bannord.

"Goodmen," said Antoninan, "we will finish consolidating our supplies, then rest. None of us have rested since the opening of the gate. Try to sleep if you can. Tomorrow, we will drive hard for the east, then the north."

CHAPTER NINE
Chimes in the Night

FAINT CHIMES WOKE Rel from a dream. In the waking world he heard only the snores of the modalmen. Their hulking forms lay sprawled around the fire, the glow of their markings dull in their sleep. He propped himself up on one elbow, sure he had heard a bell ringing. A garau snorted. The night was totally still, not a breath of wind, and bitingly cold. The rumbling of the sleeping modalmen was locally loud, but devoured by the vast quiets of the desert. It was somewhere out in all that silence that the bell had chimed. He strained his ears until he felt deafened by the rush of his own pulse. When one of his giant companions let out a thunderous roll of flatulence he gave up in disgust.

"A dream," he said uneasily, not believing his own words. Out in the Black Sands it was as likely not to be a dream, and he settled himself back down into his bed roll certain that the sounds were not a product of his mind.

He shuddered as he burrowed back into his blanket. The ground radiated heat still from the day, so though the air was freezing, he was warm enough; for a while, he ruefully told himself. Hours before dawn the sand would have leached the last of its comfort into the air, and he would wake stiff and aching, as he had for weeks.

He cursed as he always did the circumstances that had him out there at the edge of the known world, not least Goodfellow Dorion's comely wife.

He drifted off thinking of Goodlady Anellia's thighs, and what lay between. He smiled. Sometimes he thought it had been worth it.

Memory blended into the precursors of dream. Flashes of false recollection burst colourfully behind his eyes; children playing in the rainbow shadows of crystal domes. He was on the lip of sleep when the bell sounded again.

He sat up sharply.

"That time I definitely heard something," he muttered.

Darkness surrounded the camp. The fires were duller than the modalmen's patterns. A single, giant figure sat on watch atop a mound some way off. All others slept, whether hound, modalman or garau. One of Rel's hands instinctively went to the hilt of his sword lying by his blanket. The other hand went to the stock of his carbine. Quietly, he took up both weapons, and hooked his scabbard to his belt.

With his gun held ready, he ventured away from the ember glow of the fire.

The dying firelight extended only a few yards. His eyes adjusted and the wall of blackness surrounding the camp became a grainy grey. The sky gleamed with millions of stars. In the light of the God's Road the sand glittered back. The hummocks of rubble hidden by sand were indistinguishable from the lumpen bodies of his hosts.

He heard the chiming again, and the suggestion of distant voices. He followed them out into the sand-choked streets until he was a distance from the camp, too intent on finding the source of the noises to notice how far he was straying. He cast about for a vantage point, choosing a tumbled wall twelve feet in height, and clambered up a ramp of debris and sand to the top. He looked down, and found an unexpected scene.

Superimposed over the shattered walls was a phantasmal image of Losirna when it had been alive.

Whatever era the image depicted, it was the full of day. Gentle skies smiled on a multi-sided plaza of amazing complexity constructed on several levels. Huge buildings of shining crystals wove themselves together high overhead, but though enormous, they were perfectly placed so as not to block the sun. Where they did, they did so purposefully, creating cool shade over places for people to sit. The building glass acted like prisms to split the sun into rainbows, which danced in fountains and dappled the walls with shards of light that were split again, and again, so that the whole square shivered with colour.

Rel's gun stayed firmly in his hands, he was too cynical and too experienced to let the wondrous overwhelm him, but his jaw slackened nonetheless. There were thousands of people in the vision going about their business, all of them in total ignorance of their city's ruin. It was clear the people were not human, but such was the habituation of his brain to the human form it took him a few moments to realise that he looked upon a city full of Earth's past masters. The Morfaan, full of life and beauty. Rel had only ever seen ancient, stylised statues of the Morfaan. In life, they looked different to how he had pictured them.

Down a street he glimpsed a bright market. People ambled in crowds, chatting amiably with each other. The women wore glorious metal clothes and jewellery which covered them from neck to ankle. The men were as finely garbed, but more freely and in looser fabrics, with some openly displaying their smaller, secondary pairs of arms.

Scribes hurried by. Palanquins carrying high-born folk swayed past. Children splashed in the largest of the fountains.

He could hear them speaking quietly, as if heard from very far away. The bell tolled again. He searched it out, finding it atop a modest crystal spire fronted by an inexplicable machine.

He noticed then that there were machines everywhere. What he took for birds or dracon-birds he saw as flying vehicles, beating golden wings to traverse the sky. A being of living brass stalked down a sidestreet. At that, finally, his gun slipped from his grasp to dangle by its strap. In gaps and vents in the machine's surfaces the tell-tale glow of glimmer shone, but the light was far purer, and the machine far more elegant, than those employed by mankind.

The present was visible behind the vision. Paved terraces were displayed over the slumped mounds that covered them. Towers rose from stumps like ghostly markers for their own graves. The inhabitants waded through sand without hindrance. They walked in a different time. They did not see what the future held for them, and as Rel watched, the vision grew in veracity, crowding out the sad truths of the present. Ruins shivered and faded away like a mirage caught. The warding pouch Aarin had given him warmed at his side. He placed a hand on it, but paid no attention to its warning.

The vision spread. Light engulfed the foot of the wall he stood upon. Pitted stone became shining marble and Morfaan glass. Gaping, wind-blasted hollows shimmered and turned into fine windows glazed with coloured panes and alcoves furnished with golden statues.

Magic lapped over the top of the wall. His feet tingled as the light washed them, taking him from present night to long-ago day. His back was still in the cold of night, but his front was warmed by a gentle sun. As its rays touched his face, the noises of the city went from muted to immediate, and his nostrils filled with the scents of warmed stone, spices, and reptilian, alien bodies. The day was hot, but pleasantly so, not the baking heat of the desert. The climate reminded him of Irrica or one of the other northern kingdoms, so different to dreary, rainy Karsa.

The city invited him in. The warmth reached the back of his head. The Morfaan saw him and stopped. Children pointed. Adults smiled and beckoned, asking him to join them.

Rel dropped his gun. He unhitched his sword. Both struck the wall with the thump of metal on sand. The pouch at his belt vibrated frantically, collecting weight to itself that dragged at his side, pulling back toward the night, but it did not possess the power to stop him.

He took a step forward.

A huge hand grabbed him by the shoulder and yanked him back into the dark.

"I told you, I am thinking, that you ought to remain by the fire," said Shkarauthir.

The vision retreated like coloured silk pulled off objects on a table, revealing what was hidden beneath. The city day receded until only the very centre remained, tantalising him with its warmth. The bell chimed, and then it was gone. Rel blinked after-images from his eyes. He shivered in the sudden cold.

Shkarauthir peered down at him with his characteristic unreadable expression. His tribal markings shifted from red to blue in the darkness.

"Or am I recollecting incorrectly?" he said.

Rel could not decide if the giant were mocking him or asking a genuine question.

"I... The city," he said. "It was real."

"It was," agreed Shkarauthir. "You saw it as it was, a long, long time ago; a time before we true men, perhaps. You are blessed to receive such a vision, and see it as I knew it, though it nearly cost you your life."

Rel's quizzical face prompted the modalman to crouch low. He pointed his massive finger in line with Rel's eyes, so that he could follow.

"Look, by that tower. There is the thing that lured you."

At first, Rel saw nothing, then something moved, and he discerned a shape lurking in the lee of a tower's stump. It was almost invisible, a piece of blackness solid as coal. A sense of evil clung to it. Red eyes and steel teeth flashed as it turned and slunk away.

Rel let out his breath.

"What by the hells was that?" he said.

"What else? One of the lesser Y Dvar: a godling, trapped here. It uses the memory of the land to tempt fools in, small one."

"For what purpose?" Rel gathered up his gun and sword, eyes fixed on the shadows where the Y Dvar had been. "You're going to say, 'So it could eat you', aren't you?'

Shkarauthir nodded sagely. "So it could eat you. Body and soul."

"I am never going to get used to this bloody desert."

"It has got used to you, small one. You are honoured. You must be strong in will to coax the Y Dvar out. They only devour those rich in magic." Shkarauthir looked at him strangely.

"I'm not. And it doesn't feel like an honour," said Rel. "Drauthek wants to eat me, that wants to eat me, you say the other modalmen want to eat me. Is there nothing out here that does not wish to eat me?"

Shkarauthir made the grumbling hiccupping that served him for a laugh.

"Not very many. The Black Sands can be dangerous to the weak."

"Don't look at me like that. I'm not weak."

"The way I look is the way I look, as you are the size you are."

"As in, small and weak?" said Rel.

Shkarauthir laid a friendly hand on his shoulder, a gesture that nearly floored Rel. "Come. Sleep. Tomorrow your peril only grows. You will need all your strength, such as it is. We have a hard ride across deadly country. The secret ways open, for a time. We will travel quickly, but it may kill you."

"You know," said Rel, "you are lousy company."

"I am very good company," said Shkarauthir amiably. "You would be dead without me. Company that keeps you alive is company of the best kind."

Shkarauthir set off back to their camp. As always when walking with the modalmen, Rel was forced to run to keep up.

CHAPTER TEN
Prisoner of Monsters

RAFOZO AWOKE TUVACS from a troubled sleep, bringing him to full alertness with a jolt. The hooting, laughing calls of their captors boomed through the dark, along with the screams of men.

"Wake up! Wake up!" whispered Rafozo. "They're coming."

"A choosing?" asked Tuvacs.

Rafozo nodded. His eyes glinted in the dark. His skin shone with sweat.

"Don't look at them. Show no fear."

Tuvacs' heart hammered, urging him to fight or flee, but the modalmen could not be fought against by mortal men, and there was no escaping the cages.

In other circumstances the desert would have appeared beautiful. The moons had set and the stars were more numerous than children's wishes, filling the heavens so deeply across the God's Road that it was a glorious, milky white. Subtle shades of violet and blue were visible at the edges, the sort of light that the faintest illumination would destroy. Only the black circle of the approaching Twin detracted from the vista of stars. Tuvacs had never seen such skies as these anywhere else. They went unappreciated, a backdrop for his horror.

The day was a long ordeal of boredom under which squirmed constant terror. Every man in the cage dealt with their situation as best they could. Tuvacs' wits yet remained his own, though he fully expected the madness to descend upon him. Maybe tomorrow, maybe tonight. His eyes darted around the cage, all the energy his body poured into him had nowhere to go, so his mind spent it obsessively calculating who would be next. To think he had survived his wounds and his fever to die like this. Most of the men stared fixedly at the rough wooden boards of the cage floor, their manacled hands crossed over bony knees. At the time of choosing, no one could look at the empty chains dangling from the crude iron bars.

There was an older man, the Marovesi named Fulx. Ratozo said he had begun the journey a big man, well-muscled and tough, a survivor of the inter-clan warfare so beloved of the southern kingdoms. At the beginning Fulx had made light of their predicament, but his good humour was as doomed as his body. The stress had eaten away at his mind as surely as starvation had stripped his body of flesh. When Tuvacs knew him he was skeletal, his strong shoulders were hunched. His eyes were enormous above sunken cheeks. He shook with terror, chewing at his cracked lips like an animal caught in a trap.

"I can't, I can't, I can't, I can't," he said. The others glanced at him. Sometimes, if everyone in a cage was quiet, the modalmen would pass them by. The men shifted uneasily, their manacles rattling.

Dunets was the unofficial cage leader, partly by his utter ruthlessness in taking food and comfort from others, partly because he sometimes shared what he stole. He was the only one that spoke.

"Keep him quiet!" he growled. "Keep him quiet or we're all dead."

"Oh please, please!" whimpered Fulx.

"Hey, hey!" said Rafozo soothingly. "Shh, hey, Fulx. Fulx!"

The other man stared ahead, the whites of his eyes as big as saucers.

"Remember the stories you told me, about the fighting in the south, the winters, the ice dragon? Hey, remember that ice dragon you killed? You must have been really brave."

The modalmen were opening the cages, working their way down the line to Tuvacs' prison. Men in the others pleaded, screamed and sobbed as they were brutally removed from their restraints.

Tuvacs ignored them, focussing on Rafozo calming Fulx down. The young man touched the dagger-length tooth Fulx wore around his neck. Fulx glanced down at it and moaned.

Tuvacs shifted, coming as far across the cage width as his manacles would allow. "Yeah, he really liked that story," he said. "I've never heard it, can you tell it again?"

Rafozo gave Tuvacs a grateful look.

Fulx stared at them with uncomprehending eyes.

"That's right. It was a great story. How did it go?" said Rafozo.

Dunets grunted. "Strangle him. Stop your jabber. Your nursemaiding won't do shit."

"Screw you, Dunets," Rafozo said. "You found the creature with your dogs after it slaughtered your goats?" Rafozo said to Fulx.

"Yeah," said Tuvacs. "How big was it?"

The modalmen were at the cage ahead of theirs. In their corral, their draught beasts lowed at the disturbance, their markings flickering. The men in the cage shouted. One of prisoners kicked at the hands of the monster reaching in to pull out his friend. The modalman slapped him so hard Tuvacs heard the bone snap in his leg and he screamed. The modalman grasped the man he had chosen, and deftly unsnapped his chains from the cage bars. The modalman's fellows laughed at the shrieks of terror the wretch gave. When the man did not stop, his captor reached up and snapped his neck as easily as if he were a barnyard fowl.

"You must have been very brave, be brave now," whispered Tuvacs urgently to Fulx.

Their cage's turn came. Golden Rings was coming, so named for the hoops that pierced his lower lip. At the sight of him damp warmth leaked out of Fulx, wetting the cage boards. The door screeched open on dry hinges. Huge charcoal coloured hands reached in. Only one modalman at a time could fit into the opening of the cage's rear, but they were experienced livestock handlers. It used its upper arms to sort through the men, poking at them, grabbing limbs or heads and turning them this way and that in rough inspection as they shouted and tried to get out of the way. Pandemonium reigned over the caravan. The shouts and cries of terrified men shattering the peace of the night. The hands passed over Fulx, and he screamed loud enough to scare the ghost out of a man.

"No, no, no, no!" he jabbered.

The modalmen grabbed Fulx around the waist with its upper hands. An insane strength possessed the Marovesi, and he bucked and thrashed, foiling the modalman's attempts to undo his chains. Tuvacs was trapped, the modalman's heavy arms crushing him against the bars while the legs of the Marovesi battered into him. A wild kick caught Golden Rings square in the eye, eliciting a grunt of annoyance and bellows of monstrous laughter from its comrades. The modalman swatted Fulx across the face, stunning him. Rather than taking the opportunity to undo the chain, the modalmen stepped back, and pulled.

Fulx screamed at the pain. Tuvacs had never heard such agony given voice. The manacles bit deep into the flesh of his wrists at the modalman's tugging. His shoulders popped out of their sockets audibly. The modalmen twisted and wrenched, furious at being kicked in the eye, and Fulx shrieked horribly, until, with a final tug, the manacles skinned the unfortunate man's hands. Lubricated by his own blood, Fulx slipped free, and was carried out from the cage, leaving the gloves of his skin lying limp upon the cage floor.

Tuvacs blinked Fulx's blood from his eyes. He could not control his breathing. His heart hammered in his chest so hard he thought he would die. Creeping faintness blotted his vision. So fixated was he on the ripped flesh of Fulx he did not notice that the modalmen were not done with their cage, until he was grabbed, and his chains removed from the bars.

He was lifted up like a child and dragged into the night. Golden Rings had him. He held Tuvacs up appraisingly, lifting his arms and sniffing at him, grinning evilly.

Satisfied with his selection, he walked away from the cage, bearing Tuvacs from his shouting comrades. He cuffed Tuvacs about the face in idle cruelty, leaving his head spinning. The wounds in his back shifted painfully, threatening to tear. Pain and terror crowded out all other sensations. He was still weak from his fever, and unconsciousness beckoned.

Another modalman stepped into the path of his would-be devourer, halting Golden Rings. Tuvacs, who thought he could not possibly be more scared, knew the full depths of terror.

Before him was Brauctha, their captors' leader. In a tribe of giants he was the biggest of all, standing head and shoulders over the others. Upon his back was an enormous sword, long as a logger's saw. It was an impossible weapon, so huge it could be wielded by no one but the giant modalmen, and then only one so large and strong as Brauctha. He lacked his right eye. A long battle scar crossed over his brow, grey and thick as a rope at the top, running over the empty socket, then forking to mar his cheek with a pinkish lightning bolt. Whatever weapon had caused the wound had split his eyelids right through. These been stitched back together badly, and healed into a puckered mess of scar tissue.

Brauctha's head was studded with a crown of silver rivets. Gold rings and silver bars pierced his flesh around the deep grooves of his markings.

Golden Rings paused. Brauctha ruled more by fear and violence than agreement. His clan lights pulsed strong colours in challenge. The glow of Tuvacs' captor dimmed in response.

Brauctha barked at Golden Rings in their tongue. Tuvacs had a natural facility for languages, even ones so foreign as the modalmen's, and he had begun to tease out a few words from the stream of nonsense sounds. "Not" and "kill" were two of them.

Tuvacs' captor looked at his prize. Golden Rings was only slightly smaller than Brauctha. He argued back, holding Tuvacs up, prodding hard at Tuvacs' wounds and protesting.

The chief repeated his demand again. Reluctantly, Golden Rings offered Tuvacs up with his head submissively bowed.

Brauctha took Tuvacs in two gigantic hands. He was as helpless as a ham passed from butcher to goodwife. Brauctha held him with one hand clamped around his neck, the other around his thigh, which Brauctha's fingers encircled completely. He lifted Tuvacs up to his good eye, peering at him closely. The modalmen had a strange, musky odour. Given the constituency of their diets, he expected their breath to be foul with rotten meat, but contrarily it was sweet, a spiced smell almost. Out of the two of them, it was Tuvacs who stank. Brauctha's apish nose twitched, and he smiled, his wide mouth splitting so wide it seemed to Tuvacs he could swallow him whole.

"Not you," he said in gruff Maceriyan, its vowels smoothed and words punctuated by strange clicks. "You are good meat. Good spirit. You will be with me." He sniffed again. "You stink of piss. Fresh. But it is not yours. Not your stink. You are strong. Good warrior. No coward. You will live. I say before, you will live. He will not listen. Soon we reach the moot and he will see, but he want to kill you now."

Brauctha shoved Tuvacs at Golden Rings, and shouted at him. Golden Rings backed away, until he was stood with his back to the cage.

Brauctha's voice rose in volume. Golden Rings nodded, and mumbled, but as he grabbed Tuvacs' bicep in his upper right arm to take him back to his prison, his face became savage, and he reached behind himself with his lower right arm, using Tuvacs' body to shield his grasping of a long, bone handled danger worn flat across his back.

Tuvacs shouted a warning. It was not needed.

Golden Rings drew his knife halfway before he died. Brauctha's markings flared brilliant gold. With his two upper hands, he drew his sword from the scabbard on his back, swung it over his head and down onto the other modalman. The blade was more than seven feet long, and wickedly sharp. Its edge caught the light of Brauctha's fury as it descended and cleaved off both the second Modalman's right arms. Tuvacs fell. The weight of the creature's severed limb still clamped about his arm dragged him to his knees. Hot blood sprayed all over him. The injured modalman roared and fell back against the wagon. Brauctha finished him with a thrust so powerful it punched right through his back and out the other side. The blade squealed on the iron bars and gutted a man in the cage.

Brauctha yanked out his weapon, pulling out ropes of offal on the blade's deep serrations. The dead modalman fell first face onto the ground, the light of his clan markings extinguished. Brauctha spat on the corpse. Two other modalmen hurried up to take it away while another stuffed Tuvacs back into the cage and locked his manacles to the cage bars. Woozily, Tuvacs realised his injuries had split a little, spreading their hot, throbbing pain across his back.

The modalmen withdrew, heading back to their fires and the cooking pots where they butchered their screaming human victims and the slaughtered Golden Rings.

Tuvacs slumped down into the blood and piss slicking the wooden planks, too weak to move. The horrors of the night were replaced by thankfully dreamless black.

CHAPTER ELEVEN
Riding North

WITH BELLOWING CALLS Shkarauthir's modalmen greeted the dawn. Rel poked his head from under his blanket. His arm was dead from him lying upon it. Huddling into as small a bundle as possible was the key to staying warm in the desert nights, but warmth had a price, and his limbs cracked like an old man's when he stood up.

The modalmen packed their few possessions quickly, binding the bundles to the saddle horns of the garau. Rel bent stiffly to roll up his blanket. The events of the night before were like a dream, hard to believe they were real. Only his line of footprints leading away from the camp and back told the truth of it. They were quickly scuffed away by the massive boots of his hosts as they loaded their beasts.

Encouraged by sharp yips from their masters, the garau lumbered to their feet, snorting plumes of hot breath into the dawn chill. Frost clung to the most sheltered spots, but the cold would not last. As soon as the sun hit the sand, the world would go from ice house to furnace.

The modalmen would loose their hounds next. Rel wanted to be mounted before they did that. Groaning, he hobbled off to fetch Aramaz. The mauve dracon was pegged out away from the garau at Shkarauthir's insistence. Packs of wild dracons hunted garau in the modalmen's country, said Shkarauthir, and though the garau tolerated the dracon during the day, at night Aramaz's scent made the beasts skittish.

The dracon was alternately pacing about and preening his arm feathers, a sure sign of impatience. The long, sparse plumes on his head rose in greeting and he bobbed his head.

"Morning, Aramaz," said Rel. He checked the creature's reptilian hide for sores and lice before retrieving the saddle from nearby and slinging it over Aramaz's back. A dracon saddle was a complicated thing to set correctly. Rel was glad he did not have to work around a muzzle, hobble, claw sheaths and the tail-brake he had used back in Karsa. Karsan sauralier training dictated a dracon be rendered harmless when not being ridden to war. There were good reasons why the dragon-kin were not used as civilian mounts in the west. But Rel had learned from other cultures more accustomed to living with dracons, and was at last comfortable around Aramaz while his natural weapons were free. The dracon had developed a good bond with its master. Nevertheless, Rel was careful, and he left the steel scythe blades that fitted over Aramaz's claws sheathed on his saddle.

Aramaz skipped sideways as the weight of the saddle went on, but soon settled. He croaked happily as Rel ducked under his neck, giving the dracon a scratch before belting the chest piece in place. Another strap went around the base of the tail, and a girth belt around Aramaz's belly. Rel adjusted the saddle until he was happy with the fit and Aramaz ceased fidgeting. Finally, he slung his bed roll over the back of his saddle in front of the empty javelin holders, and placed his saddle bags over the dracon's shoulders between his pairs of primary and lesser, secondary arms.

"See?" said Rel, scratching Aramaz under the chin. "I didn't even notice your murder claws today. I am now almost completely sure you won't tear out my innards if I look at you funny. I must be going native."

Aramaz rattled his throat and shook out his head.

Rel placed his hand on the saddle pommel and one foot in the stirrup. He glanced back, to where the modalmen were raising a cloud of dust in their haste to break camp. They were setting the hounds loose. Not a moment too soon.

"No chance of a hot breakfast today," he complained.

Aramaz screeched.

"Yeah, I know, no food for you today either. Sorry. I suppose it is getting close to your feeding time." Rel hoped they reached the moot soon. Dracons only had to eat a few times every month, but became dangerous if starved.

Rel wheeled the dracon about. It pranced into what was left of the camp. The modalmen were meticulous in their tidying, cleaning away every evidence of their presence, burying their fires and their dung.

"Small one!" boomed Shkarauthir from atop his garau. "You are ready?"

Rel was annoyed at being referred to as little and small by others. Zhinsky had done the same, although in the case of the modalmen he admitted it was warranted. He must have looked like a child to them. "I am."

"We are near. Brauctha's clan will be close to the moot, so we may ride hard. Stay by me!"

Rel grinned. "We won't have any trouble keeping up," he said. "Will we Aramaz?"

Shkarauthir laughed. "We shall see!" he said, and let out an ululating call. The modalmen mounted their huge steeds, many vaulting onto their backs.

Waving his hand around and turning his garau about, Shkarauthir led the way out of the ruined barracks and back into the endless, gleaming Black Sands. The party broke into a lumbering gallop.

Within moments they had left the city behind them. Rel looked back. All he saw was desert, as far as the eye could see. He doubted he would be able to find Losirna again.

THEY RODE FAST, caution abandoned. Garau looked slow, but once they got going they moved quickly. There was no reason to hide their presence any more, and the modalmen allowed their mounts their head. They ate up the miles rapidly. Giant clouds of dust rose from the garau's pounding feet. Rel had never seen them move at a full gallop before. The ground shook and he grinned. Aramaz was much faster than the garau. He kept pace with them easily, falling into the strutting, quick-legged stride he could maintain for days.

"How far?" yelled Rel up at Shkarauthir.

"A hundred leagues. We will arrive in two days!" the modalman called back.

"We'll never make a hundred leagues in two days!"

"Now we need no longer hide, we travel the Road of Fire!" shouted Shkarauthir. "You see before, when we rescued you!"

Rel had seen the modalmen emerge from thin air to slay the hounds about to kill him, a move that had risked exposing them to their rivals, so Shkarauthir had explained.

"We are all connected to the Otherland, that the Road of Fire cuts in a burning line," he shouted down from his mount. "Only sometimes are its paths open to us. Last night I had a dream that the way is open again, so we ride beyond the Earth into places outside this sphere! A shortcut!"

"And what about them? The Giev En? Will we meet them on the road?"

Shkarauthir shook his head. "They have too many wagons, too much Forgetful cargo. The road is narrow. The Forgetful might not survive. They go the slow way. Maybe we arrive before them! Ha!"

"Hey!" Rel yelled over the pounding of heavy feet. "I am of the Forgetful, right? What about me? Will I die?"

"I said last night you might. You might not. It is all in the hands of the One."

"Perhaps I should stay here, on this Earth."

"Perhaps you should. Then you can die for certain."

How narrow is the road? Rel wondered. *And in what way is it dangerous to people like me?* The Otherlands could be anything, one of the heavens or one of the hells, or some other place entirely.

He was about to find out.

The garau moved in a deafening stampede. Their riders seemed inconsequential, the beasts were in control, thought Rel, not the modalmen. They snorted and lowed, grunting with the effort of running. Sweat lathered their hides, its foam collecting in the deep patterns all over their bodies.

Just when Rel thought the garau could not possibly run faster, the patterns in the hides of modalman, garau and modalhound alike glowed with fierce light, shifting from a delicate blue to a steady, unvarying red. The colour bled from their bodies, making trails in the air. The light of the sun weakened until the red outshone it. There was a shift in Rel's perception, and everything was moving as if arrested. He saw the garau's six feet striking the floor in precise patterns. Aramaz's plumage fluttered in the wind of his gallop with unnatural slowness. The modalmen looked like vivid sculptures. His own motions were likewise sluggish, though his thinking was not. He felt the first stirrings of panic, for the body is the smallest prison of all to be trapped within.

The modalmen were shouting, their voices horrible, low moans. A dazzling light burst into being over the desert ahead, its rays moving slower than arrows, so that Rel could track the progress of each beam. The light flickered languidly and became a sphere that collapsed with a boom Rel felt rather than heard. In the sphere's place was a black circle wreathed with slow fires. All this took forever, so long Rel lived his life through, or so it seemed.

Time snapped back to its proper speed unheralded, nearly causing Rel to pitch from his saddle. He had no time to react after he corrected his slide; the modalmen plunged right into the black circle, vanishing as surely as if they had passed through a wall of liquid ink.

Aramaz followed right after them in spite of Rel's shouts to halt.

REL BURST INTO a landscape he could hardly comprehend. A bright road that seemed to be made of stretched, golden flame, headed in a dead straight line into the infinite distance. A cage of streaking light separated the road from a darkness more utter than any night. But though terrifyingly deep, the dark aether was not empty, but full of sights.

Strange lands whipped by him. Whole worlds wheeled onward, spinning rapidly on their axes. Upon the surfaces of the largest he saw tiny cities and strange creatures reproduced with a model maker's skill. Other things rolled through the dark, some so bizarre he had no names for them. Some he recognised at the last moment as everyday objects magnified to a massive scale. The aether flashed away, and they were chasing clouds across a pink sky. That was replaced in its turn by ocean shallows teeming with giant armoured fish, then an endless night full of stars, and another flash and another as varied realms slipped past, fast as a river flowing down a fall.

"Behold!" proclaimed Shkarauthir; the sound of the garau's feet was quiet in that place, and Shkarauthir no longer needed to shout. "The Road of Fire. Do not stray past its edge, no matter what you see."

"What are these places?" called Rel, as amazed as he was frightened.

"These are the endless worlds, where once our masters walked. They are forbidden us. The road does not go to them, only through. Modalmen walk only on this Earth. Do not look too closely at the beings you see, lest they look back at you!"

Another flash, and they raced through a giant room lit by long, narrow suns. An enormous man in a white surcoat bent over the road, eyes large as lakes peering at them. Rel yelled at the sight, and spurred Aramaz to go faster.

"Do not be afraid!" said Shkarauthir. "None one can touch you while you are upon the road. Shut your eyes if you are scared, but you shall miss wonders! Stay on the road!"

A world of gold. A sea of diamond. A prairie of blooms over which rose an enormous, striped world. They flashed by one after the other, faster and faster, until they came and went so quickly Rel got only the briefest glimpses of them, and then they became blurs too rapid to process.

They burst through a sheet of lightning, and over a land that made no sense by earthly standards. The ethereal shades of men and women crowded leaden city streets, winding their way from bone-covered plains to turn vertically upward and run into mazes of tenements that hung like stalactites from the sky.

Another flash. A black circle flexed itself into existence across the road.

"We leave!" whooped Shkarauthir. "Onward, onward!"

The modalmen band rushed through the second circle as they had the first. Rel took a leap of faith, following them.

A forest of leafless trees rushed at him. Aramaz's feet smacked hard into black sand and he pushed off to the left, almost tipping Rel from the saddle in his bid to avoid a trunk.

The garau were not so nimble, and slammed into the trees with devastating force, shattering them into pieces. A frantic horn blew, and the modalmen drew up their charging beasts in skidding stops that ploughed furrows into the ground. They scattered, split into a ragged mob by their chaotic return to Earth, if they were indeed upon the Earth.

Aramaz dodged the trees, and jogged to a huffing halt. Rel turned him about to rejoin the others.

The trees were petrified, jutting out of the desert as if placed there by a sculptor. Many had been broken into chunks of rock by the arrival of the modalmen. A thick, chill mist hung around the trees, cutting visibility down to a hundred yards or so and giving the forest a graveyard's air.

One garau was dead, impaled upon a stony branch. Another rolled around in agony, screaming, tangled in the remains of the tree it had collided with; its back was broken and the four back legs were limp. Its rider lay not far away, dead or unconscious. Rel sat, helpless to assist the giants as they went to the aid of their comrades.

Shkarauthir joined Rel. "The Road of Fire is a perilous route. We can never know exactly where we shall regain the Earth," he said. "This is the forest of Chel, slain with the rest of these lands long ago. It is a deadly barrier to those emerging from the Otherlands close to the citadel."

"Were we supposed to come here?"

The modalmen were regrouping, bringing their mounts into formation. The fallen modalman was getting groggily to his feet. The second without a garau helped him.

The injured garau let out a shriek as it was speared through the heart. The cessation of its cries brought only momentary relief. The suffocating quiet of the mist was worse, in its way.

"The One decreed we arrive here, and so here is where we have arrived. The death of two mounts is a price worth paying for fast travel," said Shkarauthir.

He pulled hard on his reins, bringing his garau around. "We must go now. These lands are dangerous, even to us, and we have fifty miles yet to go." Shouting in his own tongue, he gathered his clan to him. The unmounted modalmen doubled up with their friends, and they rode away.

They left the dead animals behind.

THE FOREST EXTENDED over miles of hills, thousands of stone trees standing where they had died in the distant past. The modalmen often talked in their grumbling, singing way on the longer marches, but through the forest they were alert, quiet, with their weapons ready. The hounds fanned out and loped ahead at whistled commands, heads low, padding feet silent on the mist-dampened sand. It was as moist in the petrified forest as it would be in a living wood, but nothing grew there. Grey trunks, black sand, white mist in between. A dead world, stark as a woodcut.

Aramaz sensed something amiss, and was silent. The crunch of sand under the feet of their mounts and their panting breath were quiet noises made intrusive by the silence. Something out there was listening to them.

After several hours of hard riding, the land steepened into a sharp hill that the sand could not cling to. Crags of red rock sliced their way out of the flesh of the Earth. The soil weathered from the bedrock was hardly less treacherous to traverse than the sand, and the party's progress became laborious. Mist obscured everything more than a few hundred yards away, but the modalmen knew where they were going.

The hill crested without warning, bringing the party onto a shelf cut into the rock. The work of the ancients, made to carry a road whose broken paving snaked off into the murky grey.

Shkarauthir held up a hand. The group halted, facing out. The hounds scrambled quietly onto the road and passed into the centre of the group. Their silence more than their presence made both Rel and his mount nervous. Aramaz shied with a squawk.

"Quiet!" said Shkarauthir. "In this place, mists hold danger."

They stayed that way for five tense minutes, until a thunderous howling shivered through the mist.

Instantly, the modalmen brought their weapons up. Rel shrugged his carbine off his shoulder. The click of the bullet sliding home into the breech had Shkarauthir shoot him a warning look. Wincing, Rel closed the slot, and drew back the hammer, muffling the snap of the firing mechanism's engagement with his coat. A garau shifted its weight and huffed. Silence again.

A second howl, much closer this time. A heavy tread followed, and the rasping of feet on stone. Further up the road a giant foot descended from the higher slopes, planting itself carefully in the centre. It was pointed, and hard like a crab's leg. Three more followed as a gargantuan creature lowered itself onto the road.

The thing was a few hundred yards away. In the mist its silhouette dissolved at the edges into uncertain outline, but Rel saw enough.

From the waist down the creature was an aquatic nightmare. A skirt of restless tentacles waved between four arthropod's legs, prodding at the ground, snatching up stones and throwing them aside. From the waist up it had a torso reminiscent of a man's, with a pair of massive arms and heavy hands. An oversized head sprouting a single horn crowned the shoulders. No other detail was visible but these and the size; the modalmen were as small to it as a rat was to Rel, a true giant.

It stood athwart the road, sniffing the air. Shkarauthir kept his eyes fixed on it, his hand held level out at his side, ready to signal an attack.

The giant hooted wordlessly again, loud as organ pipes, and close enough so that Rel could hear the whistle of air in its throat. It swung its legs over the side of the road, and plunged down the hillside. Giant hands reached up behind it to steady its descent, pulling away part of the road as it climbed down, then it was gone.

They waited a while, listening to its howling draw further away. Shkarauthir whispered something in the modalmen language, then said to Rel, "We, go, quickly!"

They spurred their mounts on down the road. Where the creature had crossed there were puddles of hissing mucous eating into the rock.

Though many of the road's slabs were displaced by age and parts of the edge had crumbled away down the slope, the road was easy going compared to the sands. They were able to move at speed. Only when they burst from the mist into hot, golden sunshine, did Rel feel safe enough to put away his gun.

Shkarauthir called another halt. The mist formed a solid grey wall behind them. The hill the road cut into was the last of the forest range. Past it, the land stepped up unnaturally quickly into the soaring heights of the High Spine, mountains so tall the peaks brushed the underside of heaven and could not be seen from the ground.

The road wound downward from their position. The forest continued past the edge of the mist, its dead trees almost white in the full light of the sun. In the distance a haze of blue smoke roofed over a valley. The road led into this place as a faint scar on the land dotted with groups of modalmen, and behind the valley, set directly into the sheer face of a mountain, was a bright sliver of reflected light.

Shkarauthir pointed. "There," he said. "The Fallen Citadel of the Brass God. We arrive to the moot of all the modalmen clans."

CHAPTER TWELVE
The Road to Oresz

GARTEN'S VIGIL OVER the beach ended the first night with no sign of the Morfaan Josan. He was left alone in unknown lands. Far north, he thought, for the climate was sweltering. The trees foresting the clifftops were of unfamiliar types, and full of biting insects he had never seen before.

He feared he was in Ocerzerkiya. War smouldered between the northern empire and the Kingdoms. Though hostilities were restricted to privateering actions on the high seas, a lone Kingdoms man abroad in their lands would not last long.

The Heart of Mists, the giant opal Josan had entrusted him with, would bring him only more trouble, so he buried it several yards back from the edge of the cliffs. The ground was soft, the cliffs being of some friable yellow stone. He used a flat rock and his hands, not wishing to blunt his sword by digging. It was hard work, and his fingers were bloodied by the time the moons were risen and he was done. He marked the position with a trio of pebbles.

There were no lights anywhere. No glow of distant cities or ships' lamps on the sea. The jungle was a cacophony of chirps and animals cries. He recognised none of the constellations, but the moons were those of his own Earth, and the Twin was coming over the horizon out to sea, eating up the stars.

Rarely had he felt so alone. He swatted at the things biting him. They plagued him so much he resolved to spend the night on the beach, though that left him exposed. He would plan his next move in the morning.

GARTEN AWOKE TO another sweltering day. The Twin was still in the sky, its orb washed out but forbidding nonetheless. The sun was only beginning to rise, but it was already hot.

He needed to eat, soon. More urgently he needed water. The only items he had were the clothes he wore and his sword. He missed Tyn Issy. He would have welcomed her advice.

In the night the sea drew back, uncovering a huge plain of corals. Their fleshy parts were scaled away by neat stony doors. Air bubbles puttered from them, bursting in such multitudes that the landscape spoke in rippling pops. He could not hear or see the ocean.

The Morfaan gate was completely exposed, it was rooted to a platform that had been titled by an upheaval of the Earth, and so the twin prongs that made the gate were angled toward the land. They resembled the jaw bones of a sea dragon set upright. Shellfish clad every part of the prongs, and they were hung with ribbons of weed, disguising the gate's nature well. Close to the platform the remains of a road were visible under piles of shingle, blocks of stone and marine animals, now all withdrawn into their shells until the water returned, but the shore end was entirely buried under the sand. He looked behind him to see where the road might come out. He spied the grey teeth of paving stones hanging out over the edge of the yellow cliffs, and he decided he would start his orientation there.

First, he would find himself some food. He picked his way through the rock pools, hunting for shellfish and guzzling them raw where he found them. He tried some of the seaweeds, but none were of varieties common in Karsa, and all were unpalatably bitter. The sun climbed. The heat increased. Swarms of fat flies descended on the exposed seabed in clouds so thick that Garten was forced from the beach.

He clambered up the cliffs again, passing the place he had buried the Heart of Mists. The jungle hung thickly over the lip of the land, and it took him longer than he expected to fight his way through it to the road. By the time he had stumbled on the stones, he had sweated his clothes right through.

The road was covered by leaf litter that turned into soil as it ran away from the cliff, concealing it again. Garten followed the course as best he could. Though at first the ground was level where the road had been, it was soon obscured by centuries of growth. He traced it by subtle signs: blocks of worked stone turned up by the trees' thrusting roots and the occasional cut in the landscape.

Walking on the road was only marginally easier than fighting through the forest around it. Though the trees were smaller on the old road's course the undergrowth was thick, and he was raked by branches and thorns.

Garten despaired of finding his way anywhere until, quite unexpectedly, the road joined a highway that was still in use.

A slash of light in the jungle canopy warned Garten of the other road's presence. He approached the edge of the forest stealthily.

The highway ran in a dead straight line through the jungle. Trees towered over it, forced to gigantic sizes through competition with their fellows. Only at the edge could Garten see how tall the trees were, in the jungle their upper stories were hidden by the profusion of growth. The road was wide enough for four dray carts, and paved with uniformly fashioned blocks of stone. They were the same dimensions and materials as the few he'd seen poking through the forest floor, but if this highway were the same age as the buried road, it had been expertly maintained. A smooth camber curved off into shallow gutters. Yellow jungle soil showed around the edges where the foliage had been cut back. He looked toward the north, and saw nothing on the whole length of the road, but when he turned south he saw men working the verges, and a caravan passing between them. They were so far away they were as small as black ants.

Garten could see nothing beyond the jungle and the road. He needed height. The trees in the forest saved their branches for their crowns, but those by the road had the light and opportunity to put out boughs to their sides. He searched out a tree he might climb before the people on the road reached him.

The tree was easier to climb than he expected. He reached the topmost branches without difficulty and looked out over the jungle.

Unbroken canopy stretched in every direction apart from toward the east where, miles away, mountains punched their way out of the green. South, the caravan was coming closer. Judging himself well hidden, he stayed in the tree.

The caravan was of twelve immense carts pulled by teams of dracon oxen. Nine of them were piled high with material, mostly lumber, but a few were stacked with crates. The remaining three, at the rear, supported tents and wooden apartments painted gaudy colours. The carts were so large and complicated they were more akin to ocean-going vessels than land vehicles, needing eight tall wheels to bear their weight.

Armed guards in blackened steel armour marched at the front of the column. More manned small towers sat at the rear of three of the carts. Four drivers were needed to operate the equipment required to steer the dracon teams. The front of the carts were raised up and cantilevered out over their draft beasts' rumps to accommodate the drivers' station. Long reins coming off metal hoops fixed into the dracon's horns were lashed to axles turned by devices like ship's wheels. At the rear set of wheels, curved levers manned by two men apiece worked mechanisms that pushed massive iron brake pads against the wheel rims.

Garten shrank back into the shadows. No one looked up.

The carts with tents passed under him. Men lazed on the decks, served by women dressed in long white gowns that hid their shapes and covered them neck to ankle. Three of the men smoked pipes, talking and laughing.

The last cart rolled past. Behind it walked four files of people, manacled at the wrists to long chains. Men, women and children. More soldiers brought up the rear of the column, half of them mounted on black-scaled riding dracons.

They were definitely Oczerks. Garten was in Ocerzerkiya. No one in the Kingdoms kept slaves.

He waited until the caravan had passed almost out of sight before he clambered down. The work team was still a few miles away in the other direction. Garten darted across the highway and plunged into the jungle, trusting to distance and solitude to hide him.

The mountains—he decided to strike out for them. He would be cooler, and away from immediate danger. Up there, he would have time to think.

He set out, uncertain if he could make it across such rough terrain.

He never had the chance to find out. He walked directly into one of the mounted soldiers from the caravan. Broken shrubs showed the path the man had taken to double back through the jungle. Garten had his sword in his hand almost as soon as he saw the sauralier, though his duelling weapon would be little use against an armoured opponent.

The soldier undid his face mask and removed his helmet. He was dark skinned and tall, with straw-coloured hair in tight curls on his head; typically Ocerzerkiyan in appearance. He said something in his native speech to Garten. Getting no response, he shrugged and whistled over his shoulder. More men emerged from the trees, three with swords drawn, and two with bows. Their dracons made no noise in the jungle.

The bowmen nocked their arrows. The rider repeated his words. Bowstrings creaked.

Garten calculated his odds. He'd be dead before he moved.

Cursing, he threw down his sword and held up his hands.

The lead rider gestured to his warriors. Two dismounted.

One of the men came forward and kicked Garten in the back of the leg, dropping him to his knees. Another clapped irons around his wrists. At the command of the leader, they hauled Garten up, and shoved him back onto the road.

More mounted warriors came out of the forest on the other side, their dracons croaking. The men shouted back and forth. Garten took another shove in the back. The caravan waited in the distance.

Garten was escorted down the road and clapped in irons at the end of the human chain. The soldiers shouted something at him and wheeled their dracons about. A horn blew, and the caravan creaked into motion, yanking Garten's arms out in front of him and dragging him along.

Garten had been captured by slavers.

CHAPTER THIRTEEN
Captain Heffi's Quandary

TYN GELVEN WOULD be the first to admit his passage from the Sotherwinter to a moving ship of iron was foolhardy. The pain he suffered bore this judgement out. The road was wild, for the Tyn had changed greatly since the road was built, so it saw Tyn Gelven as foreign, and rebelled against his presence. Worlds uncounted whirled past him as he ran faster than any ray of light. The time between the ship and the land at that speed would be measured in fractions of a thousandth of a second, were his route not so circuitous. The road did not run straight, and passage between two near points might require a journey of a million years, were it attempted at human speeds. He searched frantically for his destination, peering into myriad realms. Five times he thought he had it, and came close to opening the door, only to see the ships he viewed were not those of his time and place, but belonged to other streams of fate. All the while the road sent coruscating flames after him that licked at his feet and burned his soul. Defences installed against trespassers turned blindly against the road's masters.

As Tyn Gelven's strength was giving out, he spied the ship, and slowed to allow himself egress into the mortal world. Golden clouds of malevolence engulfed him and gnawed with burning teeth at his body. In agony, he scrabbled for an exit into the *Prince Alfra*.

When the door opened from the place between the worlds he fell out at great speed, slamming into a shelf of tinned goods in the ship's main hold. His body was slight, but imbued with such momentum it knocked the shelving down and bent the metal racks holding it. Supplies crashed loudly off the ship's iron innards.

He lay in a heap, his flesh burned. His clothes smouldered. His hair was gone. His skin was cracked and raw.

Worse than these pains was the agony of the ship. There was so much iron all around him. Gelven counted himself fortunate, his resistance to iron's touch was greater than many of his fellows, but his ability to resist was compromised by his injuries, and the pain of the metal's presence lanced through his bones. He moved weakly, trying to get his burned skin out of contact with it. Teeth bared and panting like a Lesser Tyn spent too long with the beasts of the forest, he pulled himself up onto a rumpled tarpaulin, and lay there spent.

The door opened quietly. A nervous sailor poked his head into the hold, a glimmer lamp held in one hand, a gaff in the other.

He shouted in fright as his lamp's beam lit Gelven's smoking body, before he realised what he saw, and hurried forward.

Tyn Gelven rolled over on his back.

"Get Captain Heffi," wheezed Tyn Gelven through a grimace of pain. "I bring him news from the ice."

*   *   *

THE WHEELHOUSE BROODED with the tension between two men. Captain Croutier of Persin's mercenaries leaned against the forward window, two of his men flanking him. Captain Heffi defied him.

"You will turn this boat to the west, where we will rendezvous with the other two vessels of Persin's expedition. Then we will return home," said Croutier.

Heffi stuck out his chin. "Our comrades may still be alive at the city. Your master may still be there."

Croutier shrugged. "Nothing could survive the collapse of that city. You saw the fire, and the explosion. We all saw into the rift in the sky. Whatever caused that might still be there. And if Persin is alive, what of it? Persin was a windbag. His venture was a failure. I never trusted that mage of his, and she is surely behind all this. Things are simpler this way. We meet with the rest of our expedition. We go home. We all get to live."

The way Croutier looked around the wheelhouse suggested to Heffi that as soon as there were enough of Croutier's men on board, he would kill them all and take the *Prince Alfra* as a prize to ransom back to Vand. Heffi was well travelled. He had met far too many men like Croutier in the course of his life to believe anything the captain said.

"Or I could shoot you," said Croutier pleasantly.

"The crew won't like it," said Heffi.

Croutier smiled and looked out of the window. Icebergs drifted stately by, white on the dark sea. "You're the captain. Tell them they have to."

"Allow us to turn back and we may be less damning in our reports to the authorities," said Heffi. "If you behave like a common pirate you will be chained out at low tide to suffer the fate your kind deserve."

Croutier braced his hands behind his head and cracked his neck. "Ahh," he said. He smiled a dracon's smile. "Maybe they'll hang me instead?"

Heffi stared at him defiantly.

"No? It'll be your word against mine," said Croutier. "We are both going home without our masters. I am a common man, you are an Ishmalan. Which judge would put any stock in our words? I'll not be drowned. If you're smart, we can both come out of this well."

"If we both go home," said Heffi. "I don't trust you."

"It's like that is it? Very well. I don't see you've much choice. There's been violence on both sides. That is now done, but remember, captain, I am the one with the guns pointing at your men. That puts me in charge. So, adjust your course and take us west as I said. Or I will start shooting people."

Heffi folded his hands over his belt buckle. The soft flesh of his belly moulded itself to them. He had had a good life, and was in no hurry to leave it to face the judgment of the One.

"Helmsman Tolpoleznaen! Take us to the west. The captain here will provide co-ordinates."

"As the One wishes," said Tolpoleznaen.

Heffi bent over a speaking tube, though he left his eyes locked with Croutier's. "Engines, all ahead. Engage glimmer stacks one through four. Make full speed." He adjusted the engine dial. Acknowledgement of the order ran out on several bells.

Croutier grinned insolently. "That's better captain."

Fucker, thought Heffi.

A knock came at the wheelhouse door. The face of a sailor by the name of Fenden Hul-Skaranaz appeared in the porthole.

"Enter!" called Heffi before Croutier could say otherwise.

"Captain." The sailor made the sign of the One as he entered the wheelhouse. A blast of cold air followed him. It was stifling inside, and his forehead was beaded with sweat before he'd finished his bow.

"What is it?" said Heffi. "We're in the middle of something here."

"I beg your pardon, my captain, but you must come. There has been an accident. One of the Tyn has been badly burned."

Heffi turned to his sailor. That was all he needed, his iron whisperers dying on him. "Get him to the physic, then!"

"I have, my captain, but you should come." The sailor's eyes flicked briefly to Croutier. "It is a grave matter. The injured Tyn is Tyn Gelven."

Tolpoleznaen made to speak. Heffi silenced him with a chop of his hand. "Gelven is injured?"

"Yes captain. He is in the physic's room."

"Go back to him and tell him I am coming," said Heffi. "Keep it quiet. News like that will unsettle the crew." Heffi directed the last part to Croutier. "Tolpoleznaen, you have the wheel and command. I will be back shortly."

Heffi moved toward the door. One of Croutier's thugs blocked it. Croutier gripped Heffi's shoulder.

"Does a simple accident require the presence of the captain?" said Croutier.

"This is not a simple accident," Heffi removed

Croutier's hand firmly. "The Tyn that is injured is the chief of those left aboard, and a fine engineer."

"You worry that your cook will have no direction?"

"Not so much the cook, but the iron whisperers," said Heffi.

"You Ishmalani and Karsans working with those things," said Croutier, "I'd drop them in the ocean tied in sacks. They are wicked."

"You're more than welcome to try," said Heffi. "We won't stand idly by, nor would they."

"You would die if you tried to stop me."

"We would all die without them. Without the iron whisperers' abilities to sound out the state of the metal, maintaining this ship under arctic conditions would be impossible. Besides, it would be you who would die, because they'd stop you themselves. We Ishmalani have a saying, ancient, wise, and pertinent to the situation here."

"Yes?" said Croutier. "Enlighten me with your religious drivel."

"'Don't fuck with the Tyn,'" said Heffi. "And Tyn Charvolay is a very good cook. Do you know how much a good cook costs to hire?"

Croutier snorted. "You know, I can smell a lie. I am good at that. Ask my men. Most of them bear the whip marks to prove it."

"There is no lie. Now stand aside. You want to get to your other ships, fine. Let me do my job or none of us will be going anywhere. I don't see many sailors among you."

Croutier sneered and stepped back. "By all means, go to your little monster. But you will return in five minutes, or I will..." He looked around, and pointed to Second Mariner Suqab. "I will kill him."

Heffi looked at Suqab. He nodded back grimly.

Heffi made to leave.

"Not so fast, captain. Guando here will go with you," said Croutier.

One of Croutier's men, a killer with ice-blue eyes, a broken nose and stringy, shoulder-length blonde hair opened the door for Heffi.

"After you, captain," he said.

Heffi gave Croutier a final glare and stepped out into the cold.

"Five minutes!" Croutier called after him.

The door slammed shut, locking Heffi away from the warmth and the seat of his power. After he descended the steps to the lower deck he glanced up at the windows. Croutier looked down on him through fogged glass.

Heffi vowed there and then to kill the usurper, come what may.

THEY WERE OUT in the cool of the Sotherwinter evening for only a minute. It was quite mild, and Heffi found it refreshing after the heat of the wheelhouse. Deep blues of various shades striated the skies, dotted with stars struggling to come out before the sun stole their opportunity. For all the light, it was very late, and he was tired.

"How did he get here?" Heffi asked Fenden Hul-Skaranaz. His use of the secret Ishmalani tongue provoked an immediate reaction from Guando.

"Oi! No Ishy talk. Captain's orders. Speak Maceriyan, or Karsarin if you can't, but none of that topknotters nonsense."

"Tyn magic," Fenden replied in Karsarin.

"The One's holy fundament," swore Heffi, causing

Fenden to make the sign and ask forgiveness from their god for his captain. "Has he said anything?"

"No Ishy!" spat Guando, and he slammed the butt of his ironlock into the back of Heffi's leg.

Heffi rounded on Guando.

"This is my command, you treat me with respect. It is customary for my people to converse in their own tongue when speaking of sailing."

"It is customary for me to gut whichever cunt I don't like," said Guando. Faster than Heffi could follow, he had a giant knife with a cruelly curved tip in his hand. "No fucking Ishy, or there'll be no fucking captain."

They went back inside. Heffi used the cover of the squealing door to mutter, "These bastards are no fools."

Fenden shrugged glumly.

First Mariner Volozeranetz was at the door of the physic's office, which relieved Heffi. Volozeranetz had a good head on him.

"How is he?" asked Heffi, in pointedly loud Karsarin.

"Burns all over him," the first mariner said. "It doesn't look good."

Heffi nodded. "I'll go in and see him."

Guando made to follow. Volozeranetz and Fenden stepped in his way.

"One visitor at a time. Physic's orders."

Guando looked from one to the other and made a dismissive noise. He couldn't take them both at once. They all knew it.

"Fine, I'll wait here. Remember the clock is ticking." He made a show of checking his watch.

"Four minutes," said Guando.

Heffi stepped inside.

The physic's room was small like most of the chambers on board the *Prince Alfra*, with a wheel-locked door and solid bulkheads all around. Trassan had designed the ship well, Heffi had always thought that.

There were four beds within. The physic's desk was crammed up against one wall. The physic, Mauden, sat in his chair, exhausted. All four beds were occupied with men wounded in the fight for the *Prince Alfra*. Kolskwin, blinded in the battle against the city's guardians, moaned quietly in his bunk.

Tyn Gelven was in a collapsible cot in the middle of the room that Heffi had to edge around.

Gelven was swathed in bandages already soaked with weeping fluid. Ointment was plastered over the few patches of visible skin.

"He looks bad," said Heffi.

"It is bad," said Mauden. "He's got burns all over, from the soles of his feet to his eyelids. Whatever did this to him was no normal fire. I've never seen burns like that, or in that pattern."

"Magic?"

"He's a Tyn. I'd say that's likely. There's the question of how he got here."

Heffi shot a warning glance at the door. "Careful. He's been on board all along, do you understand?"

Mauden nodded his head and lowered his voice.

"Thaumaturgical trauma is not my speciality, but it fits the picture."

"Can you wake him?"

"Hang on." Mauden searched through a tray of medical instruments, his hands shaking. Heffi doubted he'd slept since the taking of the ship. He found a syringe, and held it up. "This stuff works on people. It might work on him."

Mauden knelt by the Tyn and held up the syringe to the room's glimmer light. The lamp sat behind a protective cage of thick glass and iron bars bolted to the wall; more of Trassan's cautious engineering. Mauden squirted a little fluid out to rid the drug of air bubbles, then injected it into Tyn Gelven's shoulder.

A moment later, the Tyn's eyes fluttered open; they flicked back and forth before focussing on Heffi.

"Captain!" he said, "I have found you."

His breathing rattled in his chest.

"Hold fast there, Tyn Gelven."

"No time. I've lived a long old while, but it's over now. My choice, my choice."

"What happened to you?"

"I got burned, walking roads I haven't walked since before the beginning of your history. I knew it would happen, but I had to come. Trassan is dead, Captain Heffi. He died at the hands of Persin's servant, an Iron Mage out of the past."

"An Iron Mage?" said Heffi. He looked at Mauden. Mauden shrugged.

"An enemy from the old times." Gelven breathed laboriously. "But the others, they are still alive. Goodlady Ilona. Bannord, Antoninan, some others. And Persin. He is with them. They have escaped along the coast."

"So Persin is alive," said Heffi.

"Goodmage Iapetus saved them. Circumstance threw them together. How long their alliance will last, I cannot say. But they are together now. Tyn Rulsy too."

"I thought she was on the ship," said Heffi.

Gelven wheezed. "If you can, you must save them, but do not return to the city in the ice. The Draathis have come to retake this world. They will kill you all, and if you do not find the others, they will kill them."

"The Iron Children?" said Heffi. "The Draathis of the holy book?"

Gelven nodded painfully. "They are no story. They are real."

"Where are Bannord and the others bound?"

"I had to leave before the decision was made, but I foresee them heading for Sea Drays Bay."

"Sea Drays Bay," said Heffi, "was blocked. Antoninan's idea, no doubt."

Gelven nodded.

A hammering rang off the door. Gaundo's shouts came through the iron, muffled.

"I have to go," said Heffi. "The ship is overrun with Persin's men, though they show no loyalty to him. I was given five minutes to speak with you. If I do not return in time, they will kill Suqab."

"Five minutes." Gelven coughed. "More time than remains to me." He closed his eyes, his speech slowed. "I could have run back to Karsa. I could have gone anywhere. I came here. Trassan was among the few men I have known who treated me as more than a danger or a slave. There are good people among your comrades. We Tyn were..." he coughed again. "We were once so much more. To learn humility from a starting point of arrogance is hard, and for some of us it has been impossible. It took me centuries. I thought I would die from hatred, or loss. But I did not. I learned to be less. I long for the times before. But I am glad to have known the little kindness from your people that I did."

"You shall have more here; Mauden will tend you. Rest now."

Tyn Gelven let out a final breath that stuck in his chest. He was gone.

Heffi covered the dead Tyn's face with the sheet.

He stood. "I have be getting back. Tell no one of what you heard here, Mauden."

Mauden blinked red-rimmed eyes at Heffi. "Absolutely. Not a word."

Heffi put his hand on the wheel lock and withdrew it sharply. It was vibrating so fast it stung his hand.

"What by the One?"

All along the shelves, bottles bounced and rattled. Liquids danced in their jars. Mauden had to lunge for his tray of instruments to stop them falling from his table.

"What's happening?" said the physic.

They both turned to look at the Tyn. The cabin shook. In the corridor, men were shouting.

The sheet covering Tyn Gelven's face slipped away. From between his closed eyelids and his half-open mouth, white light burned so brilliantly the two men could not look into it. It grew in intensity. Heffi threw up his arm to protect his sight. Through the dazzling light, Heffi saw something much bigger than the Tyn rise up; a being so tall it had to curl into a ball to fit within the room. The iron of the ship screamed. Heffi's teeth burred painfully, his eyes rattled in their sockets. The being collapsed into an orb as bright as a miniature sun that darted around the room, smashing whatever it touched. The four injured men were awake and screaming.

"The Tyn's ghost!" yelled Heffi. "The iron! It can't get out! Open the porthole!"

"What?" yelled Mauden.

"Open the damned porthole!"

Mauden was slow to act, and Heffi struggled his way past the dead Tyn and the room's bouncing contents. His ears were in agony from the noise the orb called out of the iron. His fingers slipped on the brass nuts holding the porthole shut. He was dangerously close to passing out when first one then the other loosened, the bars disengaged from their locking slots. The glass cracked with the stress of the shaking. Heffi flung open the window.

No sooner was the porthole open than the orb hurtled out of the room and over the ocean, looped around and rushed east to the horizon, where it shot skyward before the curve of the world could hide it. It punched a hole in the heavens and vanished. Green aurorae flashed all over the sky.

Heffi blinked streaming eyes, and made the sign of the One, touching his topknot, forehead and lips with his knuckles.

The door groaned inward. Guando fell into the room. His eyes were bleeding, and he waved his gun around at things he could only half see.

"What the hundred hells is going on in here?" He said, blinking blood from his eyes. He pulled back the hammer of his gun.

Heffi pointed at Tyn Gelven's tiny corpse. "The Tyn is dead. His ghost passed on." He stared at Guando meaningfully. "Now do you believe me when I say they should not be fucked with?"

CHAPTER FOURTEEN
King of the Gulu Thek

FOR SEVERAL MILES around the camp, the petrified forest had been felled. The drag marks of stone timber and the tracks of the garau headed toward the Citadel of the Brass God. The modalmen growled and made bubbling complaints about this sacrilege, and Shkarauthir became grim.

All through that country were signs of recent activity. No patch of sand was free of tracks. The modalmen called their hounds back to them, wary of confrontations between different clan packs.

Night fell as they approached the valley. The orange of firelight glowed at the foot of the mountain, suggesting a great many campfires. The smell of dung smoke drifted from the valley mouth. Steep hillsides bracketed the fire glow. Behind the valley the mountains were a sheer wall of blackness, blocking out all starlight.

On their way to the valley they passed other groups of modalmen heading toward the moot. There were differences between these and Shkarauthir's tribe. Nothing particularly remarkable—variations in stature, markings and colouring. It was the same, he supposed, as the differing skin tones and statures of the men of the Kingdoms, and the differences of the modalmen were not so pronounced.

Shkarauthir's tribe hooted and spread their four arms wide and brandished their weapons when they passed certain clans. Other times they simply ignored one another. Not once did they exchange friendly greetings.

A wide path of sand disturbed by thousands of garau led toward the valley. The ancient road was an insignificant strip of uneven paving down the centre of this trampled swathe.

They rounded a corner of the land, and the valley was before them. Shkarauthir called a halt. He and his chief advisors conferred hurriedly with each other, pointing at an incomplete palisade of petrified tree trunks guarding the camp valley. Through the gaps between firelight shone, giving the valley the appearance of a hellish gullet fronted by black teeth.

From the reaction of the modalmen and the piles of shattered stone branches heaped outside, Rel guessed this wall to be new. He stared at a torchlit group of modalmen and harnessed garau hauling freshly dressed stone trunks toward the unfinished far end. They stared back with unfriendly eyes. One bellowed and his clan marks flared, drawing Shkarauthir's attention to Rel.

"Do not stare," rumbled Shkarauthir.

"That wall is new, isn't it?" said Rel. "Why is that important?"

"This felling of the trees is sacrilege," said Shkarauthir, "and the valley of the moot should be open for all. The wall does not bode well. If it has been permitted, then war is coming, and the decision to fight is as good as made. Now Brauctha's actions can be explained."

"Why? What's he doing with my people?"

Shkarauthir did not answer.

"We not happy, small one," said Drauthek.

"Stay in the middle of our group," Shkarauthir ordered. "You are under my protection. Most of the true men will not harm you because of this, even those of the men-eaters, but there will be those who disagree."

"Right," said Rel. "Let me guess, they'll eat me on sight."

"Only if you are not worthy," said Shkarauthir.

"If I am worthy?"

"The men-eaters do not respect the right of a thing to be the thing it is meant to be. They will change the world to suit them better, as has happened here to the stone forest and the wall. They do not understand that once all the trees are gone, no more will grow. It is the same with your people."

"They not care!" grumbled Drauthek.

"If this has been permitted, then the moot might go against us," said Shkarauthir. He paused. "You may go, if you wish. I cannot say if I can keep you safe, if the decision is made. The camp may be more dangerous for you than the forest."

"And this decision is...?" prompted Rel irritably. He was tired and saddle sore. Not even the prospect of riding into a camp full of man-eating giants put him off his desire for sleep.

"The decision for change," said Shkarauthir.

"I am not leaving. Not now. Not if there is a chance of releasing those people from captivity."

"Very well. We go in. Be wary. Do not leave our camp. Do not stare. Do not answer any challenge. Do not stray. Do not wander."

Rel shifted in his saddle. "I don't like being helpless."

"Among my people, you are."

The group moved off. The road narrowed back to its original paved width to pass through the palisade. There were no gates across the gap. A line of modalmen mounted on garau blocking the entrance would be as effective as any gate.

They entered without challenge. As soon as they were through, the scale of the camp was apparent. The living lights of thousands of modalmen and huge herds of garau shimmered in the dark. They filled the valley side to side. Each clan camp was arranged in a number of interlocking camp circles with fires at their centres. These could have accommodated kin bands, thought Rel, though they could as easily have been regimental groupings. The latter possibility disturbed him; if every one of these creatures were a warrior, the Hundred Kingdoms were in great danger.

From what he understood, there was going to be some kind of vote or meeting. If those responsible for the raid on the rail gang won, what then? Would Shkarauthir and others like him be honour bound to march alongside the rest? Would there be a fight among them? Would they attack the Kingdoms? The rescue of the few dozen men and women taken from the rail camp seemed inconsequential. He had to get word back to the Glass Fort of the size of the modalman horde.

The chances of him getting away to do so were nil. All he could do was see how things played out. His hand strayed to the butt of his gun. His sword would be useless here, but if his aim were true, his gun might at least kill one or two of them.

The valley widened out behind the palisade into a bowl that narrowed again toward the mountain. An empty lakebed occupied the centre. A dry river led out from it before petering out near where Rel rode. The cursed Black Sands went right to the foot of the mountains here. He could see no sign of greenery. There were no prairies like those of Farside to the west.

Torch flare provided scant illumination. A fug of dung smoke and garau scent thickened the air to the extent that Rel's eyes were watering soon after they arrived, and he smelled worse things underneath it: blood and shit and offal.

The Gulu Thek's area was close to the centre of the gathering, on the hard pan of the dead lake. There were many hundred of Shkarauthir's kin present already, and they whooped and sang as he rode toward the centre of the group. Rel's spirits were buoyed to see so many campfires. The Gulu Thek were, so far as he could see, one of the largest groups in the valley.

More Gulu Thek modalmen raised their voices as they saw Shkarauthir passing by their fires. The effect rippled out, until all of them were on their feet and hollering booming cheers. A spontaneous dance began, the modalmen swaying from foot to foot and clapping out complicated rhythms with their four hands. They were all warriors. There were no women folk there.

"So this is an army," said Rel grimly.

That Shkarauthir's men were so numerous was heartening. Rel's group headed directly for the central ring and an unlit bonfire of wood that must have been dragged hundreds of miles. Around the fire modalmen wearing cloaks with peaked hoods sat cross legged, swaying in time to the singing. As Shkarauthir approached they got slowly to their feet and added a thrumming chant to the song. Beneath the hoods, Rel saw aged faces, deeply wrinkled and turned a whitish grey. Their clan markings were the same shape as the rest of Shkarauthir's people, but they glowed a muted, unchanging silver.

A modalman thrust a burning brand into the bonfire, and it burst into flame, announcing Shkarauthir's arrival.

"I had guessed that you were a chief or something," said Rel. "But you could have told me you were a king."

Shkarauthir waved at his tribesmen. "I am many things, small one, like all men. In the desert I am a warrior, on the road I am a guide. With my close clan band I am chief. Only here, when I am surrounded by so many of my people, am I a king. These are my kin, the people of the Light Sands, the Gulu Thek." The king dismounted, and the singing and dancing grew louder. "And while you are here, you are one of us."

CHAPTER FIFTEEN
A Powerful Foe

EDUWIN GROSTIMAN WAS thinking about a second glass of honey wine when his secretary Hensiall rapped on the door and poked his head around the jamb without waiting for a response. In Grostiman's experience, this was never a good sign.

"Goodfellow Grostiman, I must announce a visitor."

Grostiman laid down his pen with exaggerated care. A blob of ink fell from the nib onto his notes, making him tut. "Yes? Who is it? I am occupied today, as you can see." He passed his hand over the paper to show said occupation, though the notes were unimportant, and Grostiman had little to do at that precise moment other than consider more wine.

His secretary swallowed audibly. "My lord, it is Katriona Kressinda-Morthrocksa."

That would explain Hensiall's reticence, thought Grostiman.

Grostiman lifted up his spectacles and rubbed his face. "That damned Kressind woman. She was bound to show up sooner or later. You have told her I am in, I suppose?"

"I tried to veil the truth as you require, my lord, but she has the parliamentary list for today. Your name is quite clearly on it. She showed it to me. Twice."

"Yes, well, it would be. I put it there myself when I came in this morning," he said testily. All parliamentarians were required to sign in and out of Sunderdown Palace, to prevent fraudulent claiming of expenses. Grostiman had championed that motion six years ago. He regretted it now, and not only because he needed to find funds to repair his summerhouse roof. He sighed and blinked extravagantly. His eyes were small but mobile, well suited to staring, blinking, and other expressive motions. He always held it made up for their wateriness, and his lack of chin. "Send her in then. I must speak with her at some juncture. Right now is going to be as painful as any other time. I may as well get it over and done with sooner rather than later. The early scourge hurts just as much, but is over all the quicker, as they say."

His secretary bobbed his head sympathetically. "Yes, goodfellow."

Grostiman sat back in his chair. The springs creaked. The bloody thing needed replacing. His parliamentary office at Sunderdown was so small, its furnishings so mean, leagues away in terms of quality from his bureau at the Ministry of Justice. He resented having to spend time there.

A moment later, he heard voices, mostly the shrill, imperious tone of the Kressind she-dracon. He decided to pour that second glass of honey wine right then.

Katriona stormed into his office with the force of a battering ram. Although she was dressed in pretty lady's clothes, she might as well have been as armed and armoured as one of King Brannon's dracon knights. He could not stop his lip curling at such an unfeminine display.

"Goodfellow Grostiman," she said. She smiled superciliously as she curtsied. That made his blood boil.

She thinks she's already won, he thought. A vein of worry chilled his outrage. *What if she knows something I don't?*

Steady, he warned himself.

"Goodlady Kressinda-Morthrocksa," he said with a warm smile. He stood smartly and indicated a chair with his hand.

Ah, the social dance, he thought. *A smile is a shield to hide one's sword behind with the understanding it shall not be revealed. Without such smiles we'd be bashing each other's faces in with rocks. Civilisation depends on smiles.*

"And what can I do for you today?" he asked brightly, while simultaneously plotting how to destroy her.

Katriona had a larger bag with her than last time she had barged into his offices. The dainty clutch bag had gone, replaced by a leather satchel of the type employed by couriers of documents. A man's bag. She gently riffled through it, and withdrew, of all things, a broadsheet. She placed it before him, pressing a finger onto an article she had circled.

He glanced at it. He knew it well. He had written most of it himself. The broadsheet's proprietor drank at the same club as he.

"Yes. The Lemio Clothing and Shoddy Factory," he said, as if it were an item of mild interest. "I say, would you care for some wine? I have this fine honied vintage here, all the way from the volcanic terraces of Irrica's mount Hethaly."

"Why not?" she said politely, wrong-footing him. He had expected her to refuse. He had offered to make her uncomfortable. Real goodladies did not drink in the day.

Watch her, he warned himself. He poured and offered the wine with a smile even broader than the first.

"It is a delightful drink," he said, "and suitable for one of so delicate a temperament as yourself."

"I shall be the judge of what is suitable and what is not suitable for me, I cannot claim to speak for all goodladies any more than you can, Goodfellow Grostiman." She sipped at the wine, pursing her lips as she did. She had fine lips. She was, if viewed in the abstract, a beauty. Something stirred in Grostiman, a toxic mix of lust and hate.

"Quite. Now," he said, lacing his hands together and leaning forward attentively. "What can I do for you today, Goodlady Kressinda-Morthrocksa?"

She took another sip. "You know damned well what I am doing here, Eduwin." She pointed at the article. "I am here because of this. Do you think you are clever, closing your own factory down because of the breaches of the law that I discovered there?"

"My dear goodlady," said Grostiman. "It was not my factory. It was a distant relative's."

"Distant?" she said incredulously.

"Well, not so distant, a second cousin's. I had a modest stake in it. How was I to know, or indeed my poor dear cousin, that the management he had employed in all good faith," he waved his hand to emphasise the point, "were taking advantage of those poor orphans. Alas, in these competitive times, one tends to look at the results before examining the means. He has been fined for his naïvety, and will spend three weeks in the Drum, poor fellow. He has learned his lesson, and what salutary education it is for all of us! I thank you very much for bringing the abuses at the Lemio Clothing and Shoddy Company to light. I promise you that I shall be more diligent in future."

She narrowed her eyes. In her delicate lace gloves, slender fingers tensed. Grostiman imagined them bending iron, then crushing the life out of him, both images he found perversely erotic. He forced himself to look into her piercing eyes.

"I went through the court report from the trial," she said. "It is suspiciously brief. If I were a mistrustful woman, I would say that you used your position as Minister for Justice to hurry this through the courts and resolve it before anyone noticed, claiming to be horrified while being aware of it all along, and throwing your own kin under the charabanc to save your greasy hide," she said.

"Greasy?"

"Greasy. You are rich, Grostiman, yet you are not directly linked to any of the factories you actually own. You probably think that keeping yourself at one remove keeps you safe, and your reputation as an upholder of justice clean. I will not forget what I saw in your mill. You will never see the inside of a gaol. You are too slippery for that. But I can make you sweat. I can and I will force you to shut down your mills by exposing any illegal or immoral practises within, even if I have to do it one by one."

Grostiman sighed. "If we assume these outrageous claims are correct, goodlady, what good would it do you?"

"It will hurt you. Your profits will be hit. I imagine you are probably at this moment reorganising the workings of your mills to remove the stain of impropriety. Well, goodfellow, I view that as a victory, for the abuses will stop. Your lack of conscience will cost you money, a great deal of money."

Grostiman looked around his pokey office. "You see this room? I am required to work three days of every week here in order to keep my position as a landsman of parliament. If I am not a landsman, I cannot be a minister. There are checks on all our powers, goodlady, yours as well as mine, but there are also checks on the checks. When the Sunderdown was built after the War of Suffrage, the offices within were designed to be the same size for members of all Three Houses, ministers and landsmen alike, to show equality in government no matter a man's birth or station. By having us working in similar sized cells, like busy little bees, we are supposed to be humbled, put aside our ambition, and work for the common good." He smiled. "It is all the most pungent goat shit of course. The nobility rule the land as they should. You are a case in point, my dear, the daughter of a magnate banging a drum for the poor that they cannot sound themselves. The poor are poor because they deserve to be." He smiled sympathetically. "And the poor are poor because you are rich. It is only right that the strong and the clever rise to the top, and rule things for the benefit of all. Take my own family. We are not the highest nor the mightiest, but we were one of the canny few members of the aristocracy willing to seize the opportunities presented by the new industries. We are an old clan, one of the Companion Families, descended from King Brannon's knights, but fortunes wax and wane. The Grostimans were poor enough when industrialisation began not to turn our noses up at work. We were cheated and sidelined over the centuries. Now we are rich while those who spurned us see their power retreat. Your own family was nothing until a hundred years ago, but you also rose. You did this, because you deserve it, your own natural advantages put you were you are. Stop chasing after the rights of idiots and layabouts. If they were meant to be rich, they would be."

"Nonsense!" said Katriona. "You know that is not true. Opportunity has little to do with drive, and everything to do with birth. Families like ours grow fat on the milk of others, and crush those that work for them. It does not have to be that way. Support my bill, Grostiman, and you will be at the forefront of a new generation of industrialists who share wealth with all, for the betterment of mankind."

"I will be hanged for a fool, when production moves away from the high wages your laws will create to cheaper lands, and our workers starve and riot."

"They are starving already."

"Well, they are not rioting yet," said Grostiman. "Although, I recall they were rioting at your mill?" He raised his eyebrows. She made a moue of irritation.

"You are making the problem worse," he said gently. "And you will never get your proposal through the Three Houses."

"The First House has already passed the bill to the Second House, and I can win the second."

"The First House has no power! They don't approve, it's been pushed up so they don't have to deal with it. Really, my dear, you are poorly informed." He laughed. "You might win the Second, if you can persuade your own father not to vote against your motion. Even if you do, you cannot possibly win a vote in the third. Prince Alfra himself is opposed to your plan; he is the head of that house. His say is final. We are ruled by kings and the sons of kings as nature intended."

"He will only vote that way because you have filled his ears with nonsense."

Grostiman shook his head, "Alfra is not senile like his father. He is not a dullard. He has a shrewd mind, and will not be led. He can see the truth on his own. Goodlady, there is so much foolishness here. The Tyn have bewitched you. I appeal to your good sense, abandon this extremism, and we can find a better way. Conditions for the workers are not perfect, I agree. We can change this, but we cannot do it your way."

"I have no desire for your kind of tokenism," she said crossly. "Only for meaningful change. As for the Tyn, they persuaded me to help them, by showing me what dire circumstances they lived in. They only wanted their river back. Now I have given it to them, and the blindfold was lifted from my eyes. I am making a stand against a broader injustice. The Tyn have little to do with it."

"So, spurred on by this successful restitution of property, which amounts to no more than giving the Tyn a pond to paddle in, you seek to give something to people that they never had in the first place?" said Grostiman. "My family is rich again, and more powerful than it has been for two hundred years. I am the Minister of Justice, do not let this blasted cupboard deceive you. I'll be damned if I will allow a woman to strip away my family's hard-won wealth."

"As you will," said Katriona. She stood, leaving her wine on the desk. "I am going to mount a legal challenge against the findings of the inquiry into your mill. I am going to find the children you removed from there, and I am going to collect their testimonies."

"I will fight you every step of the way. You will hear from my lawyers, Artibus, Dofer and Seward. I will charge you with trespass, on my second cousin's behalf."

"And you will be hearing from mine," said Katriona. "They are Artibus, Dofer and Seward." She pronounced each name very precisely. "I am sorry," she said insincerely. "My poor girlish head. I meant to tell you as soon as I arrived that you need to find yourself new advocates. Your last agents received a better offer."

"I will buy them back."

"You can try. I am richer than you, for all your posturing, and unlike you, those three goodmen can tell which way the wind is blowing. Good day, Goodfellow Grostiman. I have an appointment to keep. I shall show myself out."

Katriona left. Grostiman drummed his fingers on his desk and pursed his lips in thought. He finished his wine, then he finished hers.

CHAPTER SIXTEEN
A Display of Piety

GILT DOORS SWUNG open upon a hall lined with mirrors. Musicians in two facing lines lifted silver trumpets and blew a clarion for Adamanka Shrane.

A courtier approached Shrane and her companions, taking the small steps of a man in heels far too high for him. He removed and replaced his staff of office on the floor in extravagant display, and stopped with a flourished bow. The wig on his head was so tall, and the paint on his face so thick, it obscured his humanity, turning him into an expressionless doll. A useful trait in hiding his distaste at Guis' stink. He gestured to further doors already swinging open, and stated with courtly disinterest, "The Comte Raganse will see you now. Welcome to the court of the Second Comte of Perus and Maceriya." He bowed the number of times prescribed for greeting a mage. Harafan and Guis did not merit this courtesy. The courtier shuffled backwards, still bowed, his court shoes clopping on the floor of rare wood.

"I have never been played in by a fanfare before," whispered Guis behind his hand.

The thing possessing Guis had done its best to cover up the stench of its stolen body. It insisted it had bathed, but the reek of spiritual corruption could not be washed easily away, and he emanated a sharp, unpleasant odour. The smell of old sweat and shit had gone, at least, and perfume went a long way to hiding the rest. The thing had sourced new clothes in the highest style, and wore full court make-up, but even to the dullest mind something would have appeared amiss about Guis. The makeup cracked on his skin, and his teeth were yellow as egg yolks. Adamanka Shrane looked askance at this servant of the gods, if indeed it were. The lesser Y Dvar were tricky things, whatever form they used. She would have to destroy it, though for the time being it served a purpose.

"Shh," said Shrane. "Guard your charge. Do not speak." She referred to the terrified Harafan behind Guis. He wore his best clothes, but in the surroundings of the Second Comte of Perus' staggering wealth he looked like a vagrant.

Shrane curtseyed to the courtier as convention demanded, her fixed smile not betraying the arthritic twinge in her hips. The courtier did not notice, nor would he have cared. His role was done. He remained bowed in motionless discomfort, as courtly law dictated.

"Shall we get on with this?" said Guis. He stared at the musicians until one blinked, then smiled with satisfaction. "He moved!" he said.

"Silence, Y Dvar," Shrane commanded. She set out down the avenue of musicians, toward the second doors.

Various kinds of expensive timber shipped from the northern tropics made up the floor, inlaid as a subtly pleasing pattern of muted browns, blacks and creamy whites, and polished to a mirror finish.

Rich men love to display their wealth, and the power it implics. The timber's cost was matched by sea dragon ivory sculptures, and gold and silver. Precious stones studded extravagant plaster mouldings that covered every inch of the walls not occupied by mirrors. The ceilings dripped crystal chandeliers lit up by the very latest in glimmer technology. Money, money, money— that was all these short-sighted fools had their eyes on, thought Shrane. She sincerely doubted the piety Raganse so professed for the banished gods. Religion was only another road to power for men like him.

As they neared the open doors, the purple velvet curtains on the far side were whisked back, revealing an even more opulent chamber, as long as a high street. A collection of over-dressed soldiers and beautiful women in tightly-laced dresses were dotted about, all motionless. They were not guards or companions, but possessions to be admired by their collector.

Raganse was a small man, but he had a very large throne, and he occupied it with all the imperiousness of a draconling guarding its nest. Either side of him stood two children, solemn faced under their thick white face paint. They had nowhere to sit.

Shrane walked with decorous slowness. She placed her iron stave's foot down with a soft, deliberate tap to accompany every step. A mage's badge of office and tool both, she wanted Raganse to fixate upon it, lest he forget what she was.

Guis spoiled the effect a little. He walked like an ape, his feet slapping and squeaking on the wood. He wore a manic expression of delight at the noise he was making. His clumsiness was as purposeful as her own studied grace. The thing inside the Karsan was childlike, disruptive. And dangerous, she reminded herself. She could not rebuke him. No one could speak before Raganse spoke.

The commoner, Harafan, followed meekly behind, shaking with terror at his intrusion. Men such as him were not permitted in places like this, not ever. Harafan had walked the halls of the Godhome, the first to do so since Res Iapetus drove out the gods, and yet he was still afraid.

Not one of the men or women decorating the hall moved anything but their eyes as the trio passed. Their stillness came from self-discipline, and the effect was more eerie for it. Shrane despised them, that they could submit themselves so totally to a mere man. What would they gain? Pay? Social capital? Better to serve the gods—any gods—at least their power was real, built on more than coin. She smiled inwardly. When Raganse got his desire, and the gods walked again upon the earth, he would see his mistake, before he died.

That was some time away, and it was a long walk to Raganse's throne.

When they reached the Comte of Outer Perus they halted and bowed. The doors, shrunk by perspective to matchbox lids at the far end of the hall, swung shut. Raganse twitched an eyebrow. The living statues broke and ran from their positions like a flock of birds scared from a tree, exiting through doors hidden in the room's plaster mouldings. On this cue, a door behind the throne opened, and Bishop Rousinteau was ushered through. He smiled ingratiatingly at Shrane, and nodded encouragingly at the trio as if he were about to present young prodigies to a visiting prince.

Shrane thought the man an arse. He had traded in his mendicant's robes for a costume dating back to before the god driving, heavy with gold and silver thread. *So the poison of greed has him as well*, thought Shrane. She comforted herself with the knowledge that she was the only devout person in the hall, and that her religion was the true one. Rousinteau's time would come, but for now she needed him. It was imperative neither he nor Raganse realise this.

Raganse's throne had a back five yards high covered in padded pink satin. A cover projected from the top, dangling an embarrassment of golden tassels. From the cushioned depths the comte stared at them. His clothes were as embellished as his room, a riot of differing patterns in grey and ivory, frogging, medals he had not won in battle, and a set of massive epaulettes. Between a collar stiff with brocade and a towering white wig a small, pudgy face wore the diffident, distracted expression affected by all powerful Maceriyans. The whites of Raganse's eyes were reddened by the kohl his station demanded he wore, but they were sharp, and calculating. He gestured to the children either side of him. They shuffled closer to his side. The older was a boy of about eleven, in whom defiance was losing the battle with fear. The younger was a girl of six or so. Tear marks tracked her make-up, and she had the dazed expression of someone recently drugged. He took a hand of each in soft, powered fingers, and held them while he spoke.

"You are Rousinteau's mage, Adamanka Shrane," he said. His voice was nasal but powerful in a way such voices usually are not. It echoed around his grand chamber, commanding response, at odds with his dwarfish body. Those that dared said he had Tyn blood.

Shrane curtseyed as deeply as her aching joints allowed. "I am, your greatness."

"But your name is not upon the official registry of mages in the Hundred."

"It is not, your greatness."

"Then why not?"

"I am of an ancient and powerful order which passed some time ago into rumour, your greatness. I am an Iron Mage."

Raganse's nostrils flared. He was very well briefed. His intelligence agencies were rightly feared. He would already have been told everything there was to know about Shrane and the Iron Mages, which was very little.

"Then how have I not heard of you before?"

"We are a secretive order," she said. "We lost faith in the world many centuries ago, and have kept ourselves to ourselves."

"Then there are others?"

Shrane hesitated. "There were. I am the last of my kind."

"My information says your kind had a religion of its own, the worship of iron gods, not those of the Godhome, who were of flesh and blood, and who I would restore. If that is the case, and you follow rival deities, why are you here? "

"My gods and yours were allies once," she lied. "By aiding them, I do the bidding of my own masters."

Raganse considered her words a while before speaking again. Guis tittered.

"Since the sorrowful death of my comrades and cousins," Raganse said, "the comtes of High and

Low Perus, I find myself burdened with new and terrible responsibilities. No longer can I look to poor Juliense for protection from our nation's enemies. No longer can I depend up Arvons for his wisdom and the administration of this city. My role was diplomacy. In service of our kings, my ancestors worked to maintain the interests of Maceriya in Ruthnia and in latter days, within the union of the Hundred Kingdoms. My dear cousin's children," he bowed his head first one way, and then the next to indicate them, "will remain as minors for several years. Six years until Jacq here can inherit his title, and Eloisa's brother is barely a year old. I must take upon myself the tasks of my departed comtes along with my own. Understand, Adamanka Shrane, the safety of Maceriya and its king are now my sole responsibility, and I do not take it lightly." He leaned forward in his throne. "And I must say that I do not believe you."

"That is unfortunate," said Shrane. "For by my efforts the gods might be reborn in Ruthnia. The Godhome will be raised from the ground, and you shall be hailed as the restorer of order to the continent. Old Maceriya will rise again. Look to the west, where Karsa gathers all wealth and trade to itself, and then to the east, where after centuries of rivalry, Khushasia and Mohaci come to an accord. Maceriya's supremacy within the Kingdoms is threatened. You will put yourself forward as candidate for High Legate. You will not succeed. Some other will take that office, though you are the best suited to it."

"My fellow Comte Juliense had his eyes on that prize, not I." Raganse harrumphed. "You mistakenly appeal to my ego. And why not? Believe me when I say that my devotion to the gods is absolute. I am an opportunist, but I believe sincerely that the balance of the world is disrupted. The dead will not go easily. There is a disturbance in the working of all magic. This has only occurred these last two centuries since Res Iapetus drove out the gods from the Godhome. It is my holy mission to restore this balance, not only to see Maceriya prosper again."

Rousinteau's smile became fixed. Shrane guessed he had expected to present her, his prize servant, to the de facto ruler of Maceriya and be rewarded for it. If she had not come forward herself.

Rousinteau had not anticipated the meeting turning out this way. Shrane had. A man who murdered his co-rulers and hid the deed so successfully the people sorrowed for his burdens would not be charmed by the sight of a mage's staff. Her contempt of the bishop intensified.

The bishop cleared his throat and scuttled forward. "Comte..." he began, and got no further.

Raganse silenced him with a pointed tut. "I know your mind, bishop. I need to hear the mage speak, not you. You speak enough."

"Then I will speak," said Shrane. The hard, cold nature of her voice got Raganse's attention. "Iapetus did not entirely succeed. There are remnants of the gods within the Godhome. Through my efforts, they have been awoken."

"The lights evident there thirteen days ago," said Raganse. He released the hands of the children and sat back in his throne. Jewelled fingers gripped the armrests. "The display has caused many problems in the city. The god are returning, they say. The guilty will be punished. The Twin draws near and the end of the world approaches. And at the same time we have the Countess of Mogawn presenting her theories of imminent disaster, albeit sadly interrupted." Raganse referred to the bomb his agents had almost certainly planted in the Grand House of the Assembly. "And yet my magister and the mages I have consulted can sense nothing amiss."

"I shall give you proof," said Shrane. She nodded back to Harafan.

"It is true!" said the commoner. He fell to his knees. Shrane and Guis took a step back to allow Raganse to see him.

"And who is this... person?" said Raganse.

"I am Harafan, your greatness," said the man. He kept his head bowed. "I am a wretch, nothing more."

"Then why are you in my presence?" said Raganse softly. There was peril for Harafan under his words; the high born of Perus did not take kindly to common folk addressing them.

"He is here because he has been on the Godhome," said Guis. He grabbed Harafan by the elbow and hauled him to his feet. Harafan sobbed. "Tell him what you saw there."

"Is it true?" said Raganse. He gave a bored sigh. "Is it true what the mage says?"

"It is, goodlord. The mage here approached me last year, she told me she had a plan to get into the Godhome. I and my friend Madelyne made a pact to cheat the Infernal Duke, to learn the way aboard the fallen city. We did. She did," he corrected himself. "She braved torment to learn the secret. Together we passed through the 5th Precinct, the part of the Royal Park haunted by the Wild Tyn. Once we were at the

Godhome's fallen rim, we recited the cantrip she had learned. Barely with our lives did we gain access, and barely with them did we escape."

"This is all very fascinating," said Raganse. "But I fail to see its relevance."

"Forgive me, your greatness, it was our trespass that brought the lights. We saw there Andrade, whose spirit lingers, and witnessed the full power of the Duke." Harafan dared to look at Raganse. Shrane was pleased he did. He looked convincingly haunted. "The gods' power is growing again. I have seen it."

"And where is this companion of yours? She sounds to have far more intimate experience of the gods than you." Raganse gave a thin, unpleasant smile.

"I do not know. I fled, taking the few riches I had gathered with me."

"So, a greedy coward who abandons his friends."

"You should listen to him, Raganse," said Guis. "Or things will not turn out to your liking."

Raganse raised an eyebrow. "And who are you? How dare you address me so. How dare you threaten me."

At the sound of these words, though spoke at no great volume, the hidden doors opened, and a troop of soldiers entered, these wearing somewhat more businesslike attire than the human statues of before.

"Who I am is not as important as what I am," said Guis. "I shall address you how I wish, for I am a servant of the gods. I am the herald of the Dark Lady." Guis' voice changed, becoming a demonic growl. He appeared to grow. Darkness flowed behind him, taking on the semblance of wings. The shadows on his face shifted, so that although the flesh did not move, his features were transformed into something utterly inhuman. "They will return if you help this mage here. I petition you on behalf of Omnus, lord of the gods. Listen to Adamanka Shrane, and you will be richly rewarded. Your assassination of your fellow rulers, your naked attempt to become High Legate, these will be forgiven, for you will be an Emperor over all." Guis' body shrank back to its previous size. "Which will be nice for you, won't it?" he said impishly.

The soldiers around the hall had their guns ready, but they were fearful, and unsure, waiting on Raganse's order.

Raganse sat back. "The Dark Lady. I do not serve her. I will not serve evil."

"You have sampled her cup already, Raganse," said Guis. "Divisions between good and evil are suspended within the ranks of the gods. For the time being. Balance is needed in any case, and one is nothing without the other."

"A trick," Raganse's painted lips snarled.

Shrane smiled. "Your palace is riddled through and through with magical protection, even my powers would struggle within its walls, but they are no use in the slightest against the raw power of the gods themselves. If you need proof, Comte Raganse, it is standing in front of you."

Rousinteau had dropped to his knees and was wailing out prayers.

Raganse looked from mage to godling and back. "What is it you require of me?"

"The gods were banished from this world by Res Iapetus. They cannot easily return. They require our help. There is beneath this city, in the caverna of the District of Ravens, an artefact of the Morfaan. This gate provides access between worlds. It is functional. If I open it, the gods will be able to return. To do this, I require you to promise my work will not be interfered with. I require that the caverna be cleared, and that you provide me with enough men and resources to unearth the gate. Currently it is only accessible via narrow passageways. It must be opened to the sky if it is to work correctly."

"And in return," interjected Guis, "you shall rule all Ruthnia in a manner not seen since the days of the Maceriyan Resplendency."

"How? I cannot expect the gods to click their fingers and make it so. Their power is limited, despite what the bishop here protests." Raganse languidly waved at Rousinteau.

"The Gods will provide you with an army the likes of which has not been seen since the days of the Morfaan," said Shrane. "With it, all Ruthnia will be yours. You will be not High Legate, but Emperor of the Hundred Kingdoms. Your statue will be raised in every land, next to the temples of the gods returned."

"If I refuse?"

"The gods are returning whether you help or hinder them," said Guis. "I am already here. The others will follow in time. They merely wish to speed their reentry. If you delay them, you will cause them pain which they will revisit upon you a thousandfold. They cannot deliver the Hundred Kingdoms to you on their own, but they can destroy your soul. Would you not rather be Emperor of Ruthnia?" He smiled, displaying his disturbing teeth.

They waited while Raganse considered what he had heard.

Raganse nodded. "Captain!" He called.

The leader of his troop ran to the throne and knelt.

"You have heard all that transpired?"

"Yes, good lord."

"Then see their wishes are carried out." He looked over the captain's head at the soldiers. "Are your men loyal?"

The captain's eyes shifted. "Yes, your greatness," he said a fraction too slowly.

Guis winked. "Leave them to me," he said.

"Wait!" shouted Raganse.

Shrane threw up a protective shield around herself and the throne, grimacing in pain at the piece of her soul expended to overcome the magical wards of the throne room.

Guis had no such problem. He turned on his heels and clicked them together. The soldiers aimed their weapons. Dark power flowed from beyond the wards of the Earth to Guis' spread arms. The soldiers fired. Bullets shrieked through the air, only to disappear in flashes of black light.

"My turn now," said Guis.

The slaughter began.

CHAPTER SEVENTEEN
The Moot of the Modalmen

THERE WAS FEASTING, and copious measures of a stinking, cheese-like drink Rel unwisely accepted that sent him into a drunken stupor. After that the night was over fast, and he woke with a throbbing head in the blue prèdawn to the trumpeting calls of the modalmen; a couple of dozen greeting the dawn in the desert had been loud, a valley full nearly killed him with fright. He went from fast asleep to heart-stopping alertness in an instant, his sword out of his scabbard. The moment of confusion passed. Shkarauthir was kneeling next to him, along with Ger and Drauthek. He was safe.

Shaking, Rel lowered himself into a crouch while the modalmen finished their ritual. Everywhere he looked modalmen prostrated themselves in the direction of the rising sun. There was not a single gap in the crowd that he could see through. He was walled in.

Unable to go far, Rel groped for his canteen, unscrewed the top, rinsed his mouth out and spat. It did little to clear the taste of the drink from his teeth and tongue, but he dared not fetch his toilet kit from his saddlebags to brush his teeth while the greeting of the sun was underway. Not that he could precisely recall where he had left his gear. The details of the last night were fuzzy to say the least. So he sat and sipped water and saw what he could see of his surroundings while his hangover improved.

The camp was obscured by charcoal-coloured backs, but no number of modalmen could hide the mountains. The peaks made the size difference between man and modalmen miniscule, both were nothing compared to the mountains' majesty. Foothills gave way to sudden cliffs that rose so high it hurt Rel's neck to look up to their tops. He could not see the mountain summits. The High Spine was a wall across the world, dividing the continent of Ruthnia from the little known north. No man of the Hundred had ever climbed it. Having seen it, Rel doubted anyone ever would. There were no known passes, and the lands bordering the Spine were rife with dangers physical and magical. Only a handful of explorers that had set out to map the nearside of the mountains had returned.

In the west the High Spine broke into the uneven, desert tablelands of the Red Expanse, eventually sheering off into the sea. Their eastern extent was unknown. Both the mountains and the Black Sands ended in a series of cartographer's fancies on every map Rel had ever seen. No representation could have captured their size, accurate or not. The cliff backing the valley was monolithic, more akin to a giant block of masonry than a natural formation. There were five faults in its smooth surface whose protruding ledges were probably wide enough to accommodate a locomotive. All but one began far from the ground. A goat would fail to reach the others. And this was the face of one mountain in a blocky chain of thousands similar.

The only other feature in the perpendicular plane of stone was the Citadel of the Brass God.

A deep arch had been cut directly into the rock. The edges were perfectly pointed, a master mason's work. The citadel occupied this niche in the mountain like a giant votive candle. A tall, narrow spire of unfeasibly delicate proportions presided over a town tightly crammed about its base. Delicate bridges and aerial walks connected buildings to the tower, but though they arced high in the air, they reached no further than one quarter of the way up the full height. A switchback way was carved into the rock, leading from the valley floor to the citadel, similar in construction to the road mounting the cliff up to the Glass Fort in the Appins.

There was no sense of scale. The citadel was enormous, but how big Rel could not decide. The way and the aerial walks could have been paths big enough for a single man, or they might have been roads sized for an army of modalmen. By his estimation, at the very least the spire was five hundred feet tall. Recent experience suggested to him that this was a conservative guess. Everything about the Black Sands was gigantically sized.

The moaning chants of the modalmen reached a crescendo, echoing from the walls of the valley and the mountain in musical thunder. As the sun burst over the horizon they changed pitch and rhythm, and continued as the first rays crept around the edges of the citadel's recess and struck upon the tower.

Lustrous black-green glass caught the first rays of the sun and bottled it within itself, kindling secret fires that displayed the amazing artistry of the Morfaan.

However, as soon as the citadel showed its magnificence, it revealed also its ruination. When hidden half in shadow, the citadel had seemed whole. With the citadel's wounds bleeding light, what Rel had taken for deliberate artifice were shown as ragged breaks in the walls. The little town of buildings were roofless shells, a peculiar collection that looked like they had never been inhabitable, with windows that served no useful purpose, and doors opening halfway up sheer walls. The citadel's spire appeared to have been broken off some way below the top.

For a minute the Citadel of the Brass God glimmered with the sun, then whatever resonance the first rays conjured from the glass died away, and it became a black, broken sculpture again.

The modalmen stopped singing. The whisper of clothes and feet on sand took over as they stood. From somewhere far off, Rel thought he heard human cries. The modalmen shut their eyes and raised their four arms to bathe in the sun.

Black-skinned giants surrounded Rel on every side. He was lost in a forest of legs. He wanted to see what was going on in the camp, and where his people were, but he could not.

Shkarauthir sighed with deep satisfaction and looked down at Rel. The modalmen began their day calmed by their observance, and their bass chatter filled the valley.

"The One is honoured. Our tasks begin. After we breakfast we go to the moot," said Shkarauthir.

"All of you are going?" asked Rel.

"All of us. This is an important day."

* * *

THE PRECURSOR TO the moot involved a long morning of dancing and singing. The king of the Gulu Thek was dressed by the elders in ritual finery of a gold cloth shirt, a cape of dracon feathers, and a tall felt hat. Rel was well used to the modalmen's outlandishness by then, but this new garb struck him as ridiculous.

All over the camp songs were sung, as the leaders of each clan were made ready for the moot. Rel could still see little of his surroundings, he would have had to stand upon the heads of the modalmen for that. He decided against requesting the favour.

The sun was high over the valley by the time the modalmen danced their way toward the moot. Rel walked alongside Drauthek, for Shkarauthir was at the head of the Gulu Thek procession.

"We see Brass God today!" said Drauthek joyously. "He is mighty. He know what to do. He punish others for raiding small people, you see."

Rel saw nothing but stamping, trunk-like legs. He was soon coughing upon the dust their feet kicked up. He was helpless. He tried to ask Drauthek questions, but the giant was caught up in the celebrations, and Rel's entire efforts became restricted to avoiding being trampled. The crowd became dense as modalmen from other campgrounds streamed in to join the throng. Their songs were all different. Some were harsh, others melodic, one a complicated syncopation of booming calls. They meshed somehow in an outpouring of united racial joy. Rel was shoved and battered, and he feared for his life, until Drauthek finally noticed his plight and scooped him up in his lower arms. Rel fought against the modalman's urge to cradle him like a child, and eventually, through a combination of shouts, prods and kicks, Rel got him to crook his elbow across his stomach, allowing Rel to clamber up and sit upon Drauthek's shoulder. The modalman accepted his new role as mount, but would not stop dancing, so Rel clung on as best as he could with his legs.

Arms waved like prairie grass from one side of the valley to the other. Rel got a fleeting impression of the size of the camp, but the modalmen demanded his attention. Though pressed into one chanting mass, their tribal groupings were apparent as blocks within the greater whole, like unmixed paints on an artist's palette. The colours and shapes of their glowing markings were all different, as was their dress.

There was a tribe whose skin was covered in ochre handprints, too small to be their own, perhaps made by human slaves. Another pierced the thick hide of their upper shoulders with the stripped quills of dracons. The tribe next to them was distinctive by the thick band of red paint that circled their heads; those beside them wore cloaks of bark.

A greater division existed than paint and beads. Half the modalmen wore human skulls polished and threaded like beads onto thongs, or other ghoulish remains. The other half did not. Sitting on Drauthek's shoulder, he thanked fate for his fortuitous meeting with the Gulu Thek, and not a tribe of man-eaters.

The tribes had almost completely merged when Drauthek growled and his dancing faltered. He patted Rel's leg with a massive hand and pointed.

"Brauctha," he said. "Chief of our rivals. His clan and ours, bitter enemies." Drauthek shook his head, causing Rel to grab hold of his ear to avoid falling.

The brute Drauthek indicated was head and shoulders taller than the warriors around him. Silver studs, driven, so far as Rel could tell, directly into his skull, shone around his head. Sharpened human bones were threaded through the skin between the grooves of his patterning, and he wore a necklace of human jawbones, the teeth of which had been replaced by glinting rubies.

"He is king of Giev En," continued Drauthek, struggling to find the right words. "There many tribes, but two kinds of true men, man-eaters, and not man-eaters. Man-eaters eat little people, sometimes eat true men. Not man-eater think this big sin. Giev En man-eaters, Gulu Thek not."

"Is it the men-eaters who fight against the men of the Kingdoms?"

"All true men fight little people, if Brass God says. Otherwise not, and not for long time now. We not fight for years. Sometimes true men fight true men. But all are true men, if eat men or not eat men."

"So now what? Will Shkarauthir fight Brauctha?"

"Not at moot."

"Will you fight us?"

Drauthek shrugged, a titanic motion that caused Rel to nearly fall. "We see. If Brass God say fight, we fight, if he say no fight, we not fight. Must be showing of hands first."

"A vote?"

"Yes, yes. A vote. A choosing by many?"

"That is a vote," said Rel. "You will vote to set my people free?"

"Not first. Not most important. First we vote for war, or no war."

"Against who?"

"The iron traitors," said Drauthek with real feeling. "They come soon. All true men unite to fight them. They are bad enemy, from long time ago."

The procession headed directly toward the Citadel of the Brass God. For all their circuitous dancing, the modalmen covered the distance rapidly. The citadel was taller than Rel had estimated. Now he was closer he could see that the way was a wide road. But the citadel, no matter how big it was, was nothing compared to the mountain standing in his way like the wall at the end of the world.

Directly ahead of the procession, between the citadel and the camp, a large screen had been set up across the road. Stout poles of wood held huge sheets of leather taut. These were single pieces, cut from the back of gods knew what. Vents were let into the sheets, to stop the wind from pushing them over. It was towards the screen that the modalmen made their stamping, singing way.

"There. There is the moot ground! Soon we see Brass God," said Drauthek, and began his singing and dancing again.

THE MODALMEN DANCED once all the way around the screened area, which proved to be a rough ellipse. The moot ground was raised a little from the valley floor, being on the beginning of the climb to the citadel, and that allowed Rel to gather more of an impression of the camp's extent.

The dried lake dominated the valley, forming a natural boundary between two distinct forms of camp. The camps on the far side were slightly more numerous and of a more disordered character than those on the nearside. Black flags predominated on the far side instead of the reds and blues of the nearer. He saw a large number of wagons under the black flags, each bearing cages like those used to transport war-dracons through civilised lands. There were people within. He rose up on Drauthek's shoulder to get a better look, but the distance prevented him seeing how many men they contained.

Drauthek turned away from the view as they moved back around the screened moot ground. With the procession having completed one circuit, robed modalmen unlaced the panel blocking the road and the chanting horde danced inside.

Rel had expected to see a flat area, or a mound, perhaps. What he saw instead was an ancient amphitheatre dug into the ground directly across the road. A few paces within the screen, the road to the citadel dropped down a hundred shallow steps to the arena floor, crossed the widest part, then climbed the same way up the other side. The rest of the arena was lined with stone benches cracked with the passing of many years. Like the screen around it, the amphitheatre was oval in shape, but formed with precision. Despite its great age and eroded appearance, the geometric perfection of the theatre remained. At either end were stone doors sealing tunnels carved into the bedrock.

The modalmen descended the steps and spread out. They moved in intersecting lines, only heading back up into the seats after several choreographed passes across the floor. The benches had been built for smaller creatures than the modalmen, and they were an inconvenience to them rather than an asset, something to be scrambled over and stood awkwardly upon. Nevertheless, once they were at their places they continued to jig and sing on the spot.

Shkarauthir's tribe occupied a vast slice of the theatre. Drauthek took Rel all the way back up to the top where six feet of stone walled the last bench in. Traces of carvings and peg holes in the cracked masonry for fittings spoke of a richer past. Drauthek made straight for this wall, whereupon he grasped Rel like a doll and placed him on the stony lip of the ground around the amphitheatre. Standing upon this small platform within the screen, Rel was able to see over the heads of the assembled horde right into the centre.

The amphitheatre floor was three hundred yards long and at least one hundred wide. A hundred thousand humans could have sat within the carved crater surrounding it. Rel estimated there to be at least twenty thousand modalmen there, so many that they overspilled the seats and filled the stepped road.

It took some time for the modalmen to dance their solemn yet awkward way into their places. Rel searched for Shkarauthir but did not see him, nor any of the other leaders of the clans. By the time the last and smallest of the clans had twirled their way to their place it was noon. The modalmen's bodies were foamed like exerted garau, and the heat of their exertions conspired with the sun to drive the temperature high. Rel was glad to be up alone on the lip. The modalmen fell into a swaying, exhausted trance.

Rel had brought his canteen, though he had no food. He sipped his water and settled in for a long, hungry day, diverting his mind from his grumbling stomach by examining the modalmen carefully, and further instructing himself in their differences.

He dozed awhile, waking when the eastern stone door rumbled aside. In walked the clan chiefs. The stupefied modalmen let out a resounding cheer at their arrival. Rel counted twenty-four of them. Beneath their ceremonial finery their skins glistened with oils.

The clan chiefs went to stand on the stage before their peoples. Then out came three times as many elders, each cowled and grey skinned. When the last was in place, an expectant hush fell. The snap and thrum of the skins behind Rel tensing and relaxing in the desert wind played an eerie drumroll.

Horns blew, and the second gate opened to an even greater tumult from the modalmen. They roared and sang and stamped their feet as a palanquin bearing a brazen figure emerged into the white light of the noon.

A dozen heavily-built modalmen carried the Brass God in to shouting songs so loud Rel's ears rang. He struggled to see through the banks of waving hands, so stood up.

A modalman richly clad in a cape of golden beads walked to the centre of the arena and shouted something, and the crowd yelled even louder.

The Brass God was borne to the centre of the arena to deafening roars. Rel got his first good look at the deity.

He had thought to see a wonder from ancient times. Instead upon a throne carved from floatstone was sat an effigy of a Morfaan made in brass and steel. Effigy was all it was. The execution was fair in the modalmen's brutish way, but it was in an abstract style that made no attempt at being lifelike. The body shell was fashioned of brass, beaten into plates and attached to a steel armature. Glass eyes stared fixedly forward. Crudely-sculpted hands grasped stone arm-rests. A suggestion of crossed smaller arms were scored into the metal making up its chest.

Rel had hoped for a being he could speak with, someone like Eliturion, the god who lived in Karsa, but the future of the Hundred Kingdoms rested upon a statue. His heart sank.

"Shit," said Rel.

The elder in the gold cloak held up his arms. The crowd fell silent. The gold-cloaked elder spoke then, and at length. Rel comprehended not a single word, so he applied himself to the situation as he understood it.

The outcome of the moot depended solely on the modalmen. If Shkarauthir talked the others round, he supposed that there would be no war. He could not assume it would work. Assumption was a poor foundation for success.

He wondered how the Hundred were reacting to the news of the Modalmen attack. Before Shkarauthir had appeared, Rel and his men had scouted out the Giev En's camp. When they were attacked, his warlock Deamaathani used magic to travel back to the Glass Fort. The Khusiak Zorolotsev would have made it back too, a few days later. Rel was glad he didn't have to deliver that particular report. Hundreds of modalmen in the desert, with a dragon! Messengers got blamed for bad tidings. Mining would have to be suspended. At the least, disruption to operations in Farside and the sands was going to cost a lot of rich men a lot of money, for the new industries were dependent on the Black Sands' output of glimmer. At best, the horde of modalmen jeopardised the entire territory. At the worst an army of monsters would pour over the Appins.

Now it was worse still. Hundreds had become thousands, and the man-eater tribes had far more captives than just those from the rail camps. Rel clenched his teeth. His father advocated disengagement from other's problems, no matter how dire, intervening only to exploit them for profit. He definitely would not approve of Rel risking his life for the men in the cages. Rel had no idea how he was going to get them out. He could risk his life for nothing. His father would tell him to bide his time, then slip away.

Rel was not Gelbion Kressind.

The elder finished, and beckoned forward one of the chiefs, who started a speech of his own.

Another modalman was called, then another. All spoke passionately to the silent crowd. They were allowed to say their piece without interruption. Then the next took centre stage, then the next. There was no debate.

Rel grasped the pouch he wore on his belt and twisted it. He wondered if the magic inside was still good. It had saved him from the procession of the dead in Farside. It had done precious little against the Y Dvar in Losirna. He wished Aarin had explained how to use it properly.

Shkarauthir's turn came to give his speech. Rel grew increasingly frustrated that he could not understand the language.

He weighed the pouch in his hand. Inside were small objects as hard as iron. When he first wore it he had fingered the objects gently, curious, but not wanting to break them. Later, he had applied more pressure, and they had not so much as flexed. The pouch was beautifully made, so light he hardly knew it was there most of the time. The stitching was too fine for human hands. Tyn work, he thought. Tyn work and Tyn magic.

"Don't open it." Rel reminded himself of Aarin's words.

He let the pouch hang from its fastenings and watched the king of the Gulu Thek speak. The crowd murmured. Cheers broke out. So positive was the crowd's mood that Rel half-convinced himself that Shkarauthir had swayed them by the time he had finished.

Brauctha was called next. The cheering that greeted him demolished Rel's hope. The man-eater modalman bounded into the arena without the stiff dignity of the others. He waved and he roared. Elders scattered around the crowd shook their heads and made other signs of disapproval, but when Brauctha took centre stage the crowds hooted louder than ever. He began an aggressive tirade, jabbing his finger repeatedly in the direction of the citadel.

"This is not going to go well," Rel said to himself. "I have a goal, I need a plan."

Time wore on. The speeches concluded, the debates began. The silence of before was soon a cherished memory as the modalmen roared and shouted at each other, or broke into discordant song. Brauctha took to his feet often. Shkarauthir opposed him. The cheers for the man eater were louder.

Rel looked into the cloudless sky. The sun was descending. He had not eaten all day and was famished. His eyes strayed to the bindings of the screen behind him. The panels moved on their laces, jerking at the posts with every breath of hot wind.

All of the modalmen were in the moot ground. If he were going to look around, now would be the time to do it.

He hesitated. They might kill him if they saw him leave. He might not get another chance. He at least needed to see the prisoners, if only to give them comfort that they were not forgotten.

"They're going to kill me anyway, if Brauctha gets his way," said Rel. "It's now or never."

He crept over to the nearest post, keeping out of sight behind lumps of masonry. If any of the modalmen saw his sneaking, they did not care.

Taking a deep breath, Rel loosened the laces holding the skin to the pole, and squeezed his way out.

Nobody paid him the slightest attention as the slipped away into the camp.

CHAPTER EIGHTEEN
Abroad in the Camp

REL HEADED AWAY from the moot ring. The depth of the amphitheatre contained the noise of debate, and the leather screens offered further soundproofing, so outside the talk of the modalmen was quieter than he expected it to be. They would not hear him. He moved stealthily nevertheless.

The valley stretched wide. Devoid of giants it seemed so much bigger. The pregnant silence of desert mountains fell on Rel as he moved down the slope to the valley floor. The possessions of the modalmen seemed huge without their owners. Rel had an insight into how a mouse must feel, stealing across the floor of a human household when its persecutors were abed.

Looking about himself warily, Rel jogged toward the wagons on the far side of the lake. He guessed it to be about a mile. He tried not to imagine how quickly a modalman might cover the same distance

"Stop thinking about it," he hissed to himself. "Your biggest threat is the hounds, Relly-o." He winced at the jingle of his gear as he ran. The hounds were everywhere. They lay unmoving in the heat, sleeping with a predator's confidence. He nervously glanced at every pack, checking for chains and running faster when did not see them.

Further thoughts on the matter of the hounds had him take a rapid detour to the Gulu Thek's camp to fetch his gun and his sword.

As he crossed the lake bed he got a better view down the valley. The palisade had been finished in the night. The far end had been closed off with fresh stone timber rooted in the ground and chained together. Past the gate the dead forest lands dropped away in rolling hills, which descended step by step like a god's stair, until they merged with the lower desert. Rel and his guardians had been gaining altitude for some time; although the foothills were modest in extent compared to the mountains, the desert shelved off gradually for such a distance that the bottom of the slope was lost to view. It was a clear day, and Rel guessed he could probably see for two hundred miles or more, but the human eye lacked the strength to make use of the mountain's height, and long before the horizon the black desert blended into one, unbroken declivity of uncertain angle, dark grey in the bright light of the sun.

He crossed the lake, passing by camp after camp. He kept to the ritual paths only partly to avoid the hounds; he wished no disrespect to the modalmen if he could avoid it. Whatever chance he had to preserve his life he would take. There was no sense breaking laws he did not have to.

There were a number of features on the valley slopes. Crumbling scarps ruptured the ground in three tight clusters. Old drystone walls sectioned the hill north of the lake bed into a baffling series of squares. To get to the cages he must pass a large oval structure of undressed rock piled as high as a modalman. As he did, a peculiar noise arrested him, a snorting, wheezy sound like a monstrous snore. He had seen an enclosure like that before. He could not resist taking a look.

Rel had never been close to a dragon.

REL CLAMBERED UP stone blocks and looked over into the pit that lay on the other side of the wall. A few feet below the wall top, the sharpened bones of giant beasts curved over a pit dug fifty feet deep into the valley floor.

The modalmen did not extend the same courtesies they had for their garau to the dragon. It was chained to a massive bronze ring set into the rock, its head bowed down with a spiked collar.

The dragon rested a head the size of a cab upon forelimbs, that, though they were larger than train carriages, it had daintily crossed under its snout. It was as fast asleep as a dray in its kennel. Nostrils Rel could have comfortably put his head into flexed with the bellows action of its lungs. The mountainous flanks rose and fell, scales rasping quietly on the ground as it breathed. When he had spied on the Giev En camp months ago, the dragon had looked big. At such close quarters it was immense.

Like all true dracon-kind the dragon had six limbs. The middle limbs were wings, as they were in draconbirds. But a draconbird was only the size of crow. Even draconlings, the six-winged cousins to draconbirds, rarely exceeded the size of a riding dracon. The dragon was as long as a floatstone merchantmen.

There were stories about dragons living in the Kingdoms, but if they had once dwelt in Ruthnia's civilised lands, they had not done so for a long time. There were scholars that doubted dragons existed at all, dismissing the stories. Sea dragons were undoubtedly huge, but the great dragons of land and air? They could not exist, they said. There were no bones in the Kingdoms. No sightings. No proof. Only myths.

But here was a dragon; it could not be any other thing.

The upper half of its body was sparsely feathered. On the wings were long, layered flight pens, as on a true bird, though the idea of something so big lifting itself from the ground stretched credulity. However, chains holding the wings shut suggested that it could.

The plumage was red in the main. On every part except the wings the feathers were thin. Hard, scalloped black scales predominated. The belly was snake-smooth and pale rose, the scales there fine enough to allow deep wrinkles. The head sported a crest of skin whose sides were fringed with black down. The tail ended in a spiked club, but in between the knobs of bone projected blade-like feathers. The lower portions were as red as all the rest, but the tops were a brilliant, iridescent blue, their tips framing a green spot ringed in black. These feathers were damaged by captivity, all but a couple broken and dirty.

All four feet had three toes with vicious talons as long as swords, with a fourth, backward-curving spur. Such teeth as protruded from its closed mouth were longer still. The beast was a living weapon. In the stories they breathed fire. Another ridiculous notion, no other type of dracon kin could do so, but if all the other details from the stories were true, why should it not breathe fire?

The smell of it was entrancing, a smoky perfume that smothered the reek of the camp, and it was hot, radiating a warmth that felt like a second sun on Rel's skin.

The dragon was as beautiful as it was deadly. Human bones were scattered all around its enclosure. Most were shattered to slivers, but enough remained whole that their provenance was easily determined. A few skulls lay about like discarded fruit stones.

Rel's position on top of the wall afforded him a fine view over the camp. At last he could get a good count of the modalmen's cage wagons. He was close enough to spy the prone figures of human beings like himself in every one of them.

There were hundreds of people there.

REL SCRAMBLED BACK down the enclosure and jogged across the camp ground of Brauctha's people. The camps of the men-eaters were altogether more grisly in aspect than the Gulu Thek's. Human skulls featured prominently in their decoration, spiked in vertical rows on poles hung with wind chimes of finger bones that rattled in the breeze. The smell of spoiling meat was everywhere, and fat, sated flies buzzed about. Rel was used to unpleasant sights, but his stomach rebelled at the stench.

Black cauldrons, thankfully too high to see inside, were dotted around the line of wagons. He passed a heap of bloody human rib cages and spines. Tornadoes of flies scared up as he ran by.

He approached the cages. The smell coming off the prisoners was as bad as the stink of rotting flesh. They were in poor shape, all of them. A couple watched him with deadened eyes, saying nothing. Most were dozing in the heat, huddled up in their rags upon the wagon's filthy floors.

"Hello! Hello!" Rel whispered fiercely, poking his head up to see into the cages. "Are there any here from the Gates of the World? Are there any here who speak Maceriyan?"

The people contained inside were of many nations, but mostly drawn from the Black Sands side of the Appins. A lot of them had the flat, brown faces and narrowed eyes of the northern mountain tribes. There were a few Khushiaks and Croshashians scattered among them, but no pale, blue or dark skin one could find in other parts of the Kingdoms. As he ran further along the line of cages they roused themselves wearily, rolling onto their bellies or hauling themselves up the bars. A few spoke to him in foreign tongues, and he shrugged apologetically. The men, he noticed all the prisoners were male, were near death.

The next cage was half empty. The men inside were little more than living skeletons clad in rags. In the next they were all dead, yellow bones covered in tight, dried brown skin clad in rags.

The wagons after that had more Kingdoms men.

"Do any of you speak Maceriyan?"

A Khusiak glowered dolefully at him over filthy moustaches. His beard had grown thickly beneath them. A few ceramic beads remained threaded onto the braiding. "No Maceriyan. Go there!" he said gruffly, pointing along the line.

Rel nodded his thanks and came to more wagons holding people whose nations he recognised. More Khusiaks, Correndians, Mohaca and others. He stopped at the first and peered within. He breathed through his mouth to moderate the stench.

"Hello! Does anyone speak Maceriyan here, high or low? Are you the party from the rail head?"

Their reaction was only slightly less lethargic, but they understood, and several nodded. Their necks were so thin their heads appeared oversized, like children's lollipops on paper sticks. Others spoke haltingly, as if they had forgotten how.

"We all do," a soldier crawled his way forward on his elbows on knees, seemingly too malnourished to get up. The backs of his hands were covered in sores. "Captain Kressind, isn't it?"

Rel nodded. "You are Sontiny of Corrend? I recognise you from the Fort."

"You've a good memory for faces. I must have seen you all of twice." The soldier said. "I hope you are the vanguard of a rescue force, and not a fucking mirage."

"I'm here to help."

Sontiny pushed his face through the bars of his cage and peered blearily past Rel. "Where are the rest? How many are you?"

"I am working on getting you out of here."

"Fuck me," said Sontiny with a groan. "It's just you isn't it?"

Rel couldn't answer, because others in the next cage began to clamour.

"Wait," he said.

"I'm not fucking going anywhere," said Sontiny.

Rel moved to the next cage. At the fore was a young man Rel recognised.

"You, you were a translator for that merchant, Boskovin."

"He is dead," said the youth. "Poor merchant though he was, I am sorry."

"I am too," said Rel. "I am sorry for every death." He looked behind him. "I can't stay long. They'll notice I'm gone and then I'll be in there with you."

"Did you bring cannon?" asked someone at the back. "They are going to need cannon. Big guns for these big bastards."

A fellow with a ragged beard and an inflamed wound on his cheek peered at Rel. "I don't see anyone else. It is just him!"

Rel looked back over the camp to the moot ground. The sounds of modalmen shouting drifted over the valley.

"Listen, I have to go, but I will be back, I have come a long way in pursuit of you; if I can, I will get you out."

"What do you mean, you will get us out if you can?" Sontiny called over from the next cage. "You can't, can you?"

"Please! You have to help us!" someone shouted in anguish. "They are eating us."

Rel glanced back at the pile of raw bones and the flies swirling over them.

"Tell me everything you can," he said. "Quickly."

But the prisoners were too exercised by the hope of rescue, and they all shouted at him at once.

"He's alone!" said Sontiny. "He's no use to us."

"Well, are you?" demanded the bearded man.

Rel's expression told it all.

"See!" spat Sontiny.

"Is it true?" someone else called.

"It is, I am sorry. It is just me. Listen, listen!" he said harshly. "Quiet down, tell me what you can. Have they said anything about what they intend to do with you? Do they have any weaknesses? Do you know anything, anything at all I might use to save you from these creatures?'

The prisoners were shouting now, making Rel nervous. The translator got the message.

"The one called Brauctha is their leader," said the young man. "He's the worst of them."

"What's your name?"

"Tuvacs," he said, as if his name were an unimportant detail. "I don't think they brought us here to eat us. It's like they have been testing us, winnowing out the strong from the weaker, though chance has played its part and killed enough of us."

Lots of men started shouting. Nearby, a hound rolled over and yawned. Another stretched and shook its head, setting its muscular body into waves of motion. A third lifted its head and looked directly at Rel.

"Please!" said Rel. "Be quiet. The more I can learn now, the better it will go for you." They quietened a little. Rel turned back to Tuvacs. "What makes you say they are testing you?"

Another young man pushed forward

"They killed the children first, then the women. They have kept only the men."

"Who are you?" Asked Rel.

"I am Rafozak. They ate them," he said with horrible matter-of-factness. "And they have argued over which of us to devour, and which to keep. Troublemakers have more frequently been spared." He spared a glance for a fellow sat in the shade, who glowered at Rel.

Rel frowned. "Then they have something else planned for you."

"What?" Asked the bearded man.

"I do not yet know."

"How come you are free?" asked Tuvacs.

"I came here with some of the modalmen, they are not all of the same mind regarding us. They rescued me, in fact."

The glowering man laughed and shook his head. The noise was rising again.

"It is true. They saved my life. They call the clans on this side of the valley the man-eaters."

"Maybe they'll save us too!" someone said. Someone else was crying. Another shouted madly.

A commotion was setting up all along the line of wagons. Rel backed away. More hounds of Brauctha's clan were waking, and staring at the line of cages. Their clan marks pulsed.

"Look, please, be quiet. I am going to have to go. If they find me out here alone they will kill me."

"What are they going to do with us?" asked the bearded man. "Are they going eat us all?"

"I said I don't know," said Rel, "but I don't think so."

"Why?" said Sontiny

"I don't know!" Rel said. He looked back to the moot. "I'm going now. I will find a way to get you out of here. They are voting now to determine whether or not they move on the Kingdoms. I do not have time!"

"Why are they attacking us?"

"They don't care about the Kingdoms," said Rel. "Most of them don't even think we're human. They call themselves the true men. There's something else, something worse coming." Rel backed away. The hounds were up, and growling, straining at their chains. "I'll be back as soon as I can. Stay strong. For yourselves, and for the Kingdoms."

He turned and ran, leaving the men in the cages to shout after him.

CHAPTER NINETEEN
A Pleasant Surprise

THERE WERE EXACTLY three female physics in all of Karsa, two of whom were based in Karsa City. Katriona insisted, of course, *of course,* on patronising one of them, even though her reputation was nothing compared to that of a man, and her office was in barely salubrious terraces at the Upper Lockside. Finna, she was called. Demion Morthrock loved his wife, and he indulged her in many things most men would rather divorce over, but even he had his limits. Gender was no way to select a physic.

Demion waited, cane in one hand, handkerchief in the other. He dabbed at his forehead and stuffed his handkerchief into his pocket, only to anxiously pull it out again. Dab, stuff, pull; dab, stuff, pull. Over and over, until the cloth was soaking. The waiting room was poorly ventilated and hot as the fiery hell, but his profuse sweating came from worry as much as the summer heat. He stared at the physic's plain wooden office door as if it was the gate to said hell, with all its torments hidden behind.

This will not do, Demion! He scolded himself, and forced himself to look elsewhere. Finna's waiting room was clean but uncomfortable, with scratched wooden benches that could have done with a good polish and a set of decent cushions. His recently enlarged behind kept sliding forward in a most undignified way. The wall's green paint bulged with unsightly blisters where the rain had got into the mortar. The windows were tiny and open, letting in little but the screeching of seabirds and the stench of the Lower Lockside further down the cliff. The floor was wood, old, varnish worn off and the planks dimpled by the high heels of working girls.

As his side, Tyn Lydar hummed tunelessly, the swinging of her legs sending irritating judders through the wood of the bench.

He met the eyes of the two other patients. They were commoners, both of them female, and one of them was definitely a prostitute. They regarded him with hard expressions, glancing at Tyn Lydar as much as they dared with a mixture of revulsion and curiosity.

It was bad enough being a man in this place without the Tyn along. Physic Finna probably performed all sorts of unsavoury jobs for women of a certain type. Why on Earth would Katriona want to come here to this abortionist's abattoir...?

He shook his head disapprovingly. The prostitute looked pointedly away.

How he wished they had gone to the Morthrock family physic. How he wished Katriona had not brought the Tyn along.

He looked at his companion sidelong. "You are close to my wife." He tried not to sound disapproving. Katriona had made it obvious how important the Tyn was to her.

Tyn Lydar stopped humming and swinging her legs suddenly and menacingly, like the cessation of birdsong in a wood that tells a dracon is near. She turned her wrinkled face up to his, and he shuddered.

"As close as one such as I can be to one such as her, aye, that it so, Goodfellow Morthrock," she said.

"Only I suppose you must be, or she would not have invited you here." He paused. The hard wooden bench pressed into his buttocks uncomfortably. Perhaps he really should lose some weight. "She will be alright, won't she? Why did she wait? A week, and after a meeting with that louse Grostiman! She must take care of herself!" He crumpled his handkerchief and gripped his cane. "You must know. I mean to say," he added hurriedly, "the Tyn have the sight and whatnot, but I do not wish to impose or—"

"Or pay a price for such knowledge as I may give?" said Tyn Lydar. Broad white teeth appeared in her wrinkled face, the flesh of a nut peaking through its shell. It was a disturbing smile. Demion was reminded of dracons again.

"Well," said Demion uncomfortably. "Quite." He stuffed his handkerchief away for the umpteenth time and wrung his cane for wont of something better to do with his hands. If he held them up, they would shake, he just knew it.

"Be not afraid, young Morthrock," said Tyn Lydar sympathetically. "I'll put no geas on you, nor exact a price for simple conversation. Yes, she will be fine, and no I will not say what is with her, that is hers to say, not mine."

"You know?"

Tyn Lydar cocked her head at him. Her brown eyes twinkled with mischief. "We got the sight, said so yourself, but what she has any can see, only you don't."

Demion coughed. When he had run the factory he let his Tynmen deal with the creatures. If he were honest with himself he was frightened of the Tyn. They were uncanny, magical, dangerous if handled badly. As a child he had wept at the sight of them and huddled behind his mother's skirts. Lydar was old as the hills and had been the Morthrocksey band's leader since the mill was built, and probably forever before that. She remembered what he was like as a boy.

"Goodtyn, that's what Kat calls you, yes?" said Demion.

"Ooh, now it is marks of respect. Perhaps this world has a little kindness left for my kind."

"I... I... I am merely trying to be polite," Demion coloured.

"No need to be on my behalf, so high and mighty a goodfellow as yourself," said Tyn Lydar. She stared at the slightly more respectable looking woman across the way. The woman looked back with a frightened, questioning expression. Lydar shook her head gently. The woman fell back against the bench's backrest in relief.

"Sorry," said Demion. "I... Sorry."

"Sorry is not needed. Your manners are welcome," said Tyn Lydar. "Your father treated us kindly, and he respected our ways, but politeness was a courtesy he did not afford us."

"He did not afford politeness to many people."

Tyn Lydar chuckled. "This is true. He was a great man in some ways, less than great in others. Like all men."

"I wish I were more like him," said Demion, downcast. He paused and took a deep, embarrassed breath. The floor suddenly seemed very interesting, and he tapped at it with the ferrule of his cane. "I know what they say about me. That I am useless, and tubby. That I have let the she-dracon into my yard. My wife runs my father's factory. She just took it over, and I let her, by all the hells, I encouraged her. Gossip is so hurtful. I am not insensitive. People assume if my wife can order around my staff, she can order me around, and that I must languish under the iron rod of the Kressinds."

"They do say that," said Tyn Lydar. "They say it a lot."

"But the truth of it is," he said, banging his cane on the parquet decisively, "I don't care. I was beyond glad to have the mill taken off my hands. I was rather expecting that I would have to pull myself together and step forward, run the company to impress her, you know. I never wanted to. I couldn't even manage that for my father. But I would have done, if it made her happy. You know what she's like. She does not like weak men, and I am a weak man. My father always forced me to take an interest, and I couldn't. All that dirt, and squalor. The smells!"

"Happy to leave us in it," said Lydar.

"Yes," said Demion guiltily. "She opened my eyes to that."

"You love her a long time. I saw. I saw you as a boy when her father brought her to your house, to the mill."

"The sight again, eh? It must be dashed useful," said Demion weakly. His humour was insipid, under the current circumstances.

"Heh. I used my eyes!"

"I longed for Katriona. I wanted her for so long. When she married Arvane... He was so dashing, and brave. He was... he was not me. I thought I might die from sorrow."

"Instead he died, and now she is in your bed."

"I felt perfectly wretched when he fell! Can you imagine me in a battle?" spluttered Demion. "He was a real man. I never expected her to love me after him, but I had to ask for her hand. I would happily have given her everything simply to have her by my side, even if she hated me. And I did. But then the most marvellous thing happened." Demion blinked fast. His voice was hoarse. *Oh gods*, he thought. *Don't let me cry in front of the Tyn.* "She started to love me too."

"Love you she does, for what you are in there," Tyn Lydar poked him hard in his chest with her bony finger. "Not what you think you should be. You humans, always try to be what you are not rather than living what you are. I speak from knowledge when I say this brings only sorrow. Be true to self, do not seek change. Change cannot be undone."

Demion nodded. "I agree. So let other men mock me for my wife's yellow-band ways. You see," continued Demion, "I cannot lose her. If she is ill, with the blood cough, or the sweats... I... If she *died*." He fumbled out his monogrammed handkerchief again and blew his nose loudly.

Tyn Lydar grasped his hand in her small brown fingers. There were hard as wood, and rough with years of work. She smiled, then burst into a low purring laugh. "Foolish boy, you are blind."

Demion frowned in confusion.

"What do you mean? She fainted. It could be anything!"

Tyn Lydar's laugh became uproarious and she patted his hand. He found it the most comforting thing in the world.

The door to the physic's office swung open. Finna was a no-nonsense looking woman in her mid-fifties. Her hair was iron grey, most of it hidden under a scarf. Sleeve protectors covered her blouse's arms. An apron covered her skirt. Her hands were pink from a fresh scrub. The scents of soap, vinegar and warm copper gusted out of her office.

Katriona came out, pale-faced, her lips clamped so tight they were a thin, bloodless white.

She stood before Demion, arms out stiffly. She took a deep breath.

"What is it?" Demion asked fearfully.

She looked down at him, the most peculiar expression on her face. She was having trouble speaking.

"Dear husband, I am pregnant," she said all in a rush, then burst into tears.

He stood up and dropped his cane with a clatter. He took her wrists in his hands.

"My dear, that is... that is the most marvellous news!"

She looked up at him, her nose red, and tears streaming down her face.

"You are not cross?"

Demion was perplexed by this new side of his wife. "Why on either Earth or Twin would I be cross with you? I am so very, very happy!"

She cried more, and fell into his arms.

"But my dear Kat, are you not happy? Why do you weep?"

She thumped him hard on the back and clasped him hard to her.

"Of course I'm happy, you silly oaf."

He patted her back softly as she wept, completely confused. Tyn Lydar winked at him from the bench.

For what must have been the millionth time in his life, Demion Morthrock found himself dumbfounded by women.

CHAPTER TWENTY
Home to Mogawn

IRON WHEELS CLACKED hypnotically on iron rails, *tickety-tick, tickety-tick*, fast as a bird's heart. The train sped out of Karsa City. The last of the brown suburbs dwindled, replaced by hedged fields clinging to steep valley sides colourful with summer flowers.

Countess Lucinia Vertisa was going home.

Grey skies rolled over grey hills. At the height of summer, Karsa could still look like a land in mourning. The few bright days of orange-gold sun was the intrusion of happy memories into nameless grief. It was going to rain. Again. Rain follows summer tides as surely as war follows peace, went the old saying. The old sayings looked to be holding true.

Lucinia's wealth afforded her a private compartment. Her injured leg rested on a padded footstool beside a small table set for morning tea. Cakes and cups besieged a small glimmer lamp, whose crystal pendants tinkled with the crossing of every rail joint. She stared at the window, not at the landscape on the other side, where her reflection stared glumly back. Her stupid, mannish face had been made even less attractive by a patterning of shiny burn scars all down the left side. The disfigurement was temporary, but although she would never let anyone know, the marks appalled her. Though she pretended artfully not to care, Lucinia Vertisa wanted very much to be pretty.

She clucked at her vanity. She was a countess, she had her own castle. She had the finest mind in Karsa. Her name was a touchstone for those wishing to advance the cause of women. She was finally respected among the circles of academe, and yet it was not enough. She wondered if everyone were as dissatisfied as she was, as grasping for the next thing; if a turnip farmer with a good crop wished for just one more turnip, or the Emperor of Ocerzerkiya wished for more gold to count.

A pretty nose. Delicate features. Full lips. That is what she wished for in the place of her hateful father's face. She would trade everything for that. She knew the yearning would not be stopped were it to be so. There would always be something else. Knowing so didn't help.

Mansanio had told her to love what she had, one night when she drunkenly wept on his shoulder. He had gone. More than that, she had thrown him out. Was he a scoundrel for making a pass at her, or was she a monster for rejecting his affections?

She shot the face in the window a fierce scowl. After leaving Perus she had delayed returning to Mogawn for a few weeks, staying in the city to quicken her recovery. During her convalescence she had avoided reading the papers. It was time to put that right.

She unfolded the *Karsan Herald* she'd bought at the station. The sky cast out a harsh illumination that made reading unpleasant, so she angled the broadsheet to better catch the steady blue light of the lamp, and commenced familiarising herself with the world again.

The broadsheet's narrow columns were crammed with advertisements of dubious veracity for everything from tooth whitening powder made of white lead, which she knew to be toxic, to cheap love philtres of "genuine" Tyn make, which almost certainly had never been within a mile of the Tyn.

Only the first few lines of each news story were included on the front page beneath tight headlines, presenting her with a frustrating hunt through the inner pages for the rest. The actual news that she was interested in was hidden in a morass of false claims and gossipy tidbits. Still, she supposed if anything really important had happened in Maceriya since her departure, it might have been a little more prominent. "Civil War in Old Empire," that sort of thing.

She found what she was looking for, hidden under an advertisement for a new kind of metal stamping machinery.

Maceriya Declares Candidate, read the headline.

> *Further information regarding the selection of the Maceriyan candidate for the post of High Legate, recently vacated owing to the decease of prior office holder Vichereu. Comte Raganse, Comte of Outer Perus, was almost universally selected by the Maceriyan Diet of Nobility in an assembly held two days since, on Twinday, 27th of Gannever month. The King...*

Here the line was clumsily cut, with no indication of where the story continued. She was forced to search through the innards of the paper for its conclusion.

...Lovix of Maceriya, gave his full and unconditional backing to the selection of the Comte, who currently presides over the Maceriyan Government alone, the children of his peers Juliense, Comte of High Perus, and Arvons, Comte of Low Perus, slain in the atrocity at the House of the Assembly, being in their minority. That the Comte rule alone is unprecedented in recent history, the last instance being one hundred and four years ago. As for the promotion of one of the Comtes to the candidacy for the office of High Legate, this is a novel occurrence in the history of the Alliance of the Hundred Kingdoms. Suggestions from members of the Three Houses of Karsa that this is a naked attempt to seize power by a single man intent on making himself dictator have been roundly denounced by the Maceriyan regal ministries. At present, the lack of an ambassador from Karsa, who was also killed along with Duke Abing of the Naval and Interior Ministries in the attack on the Assembly leaves our government unable to respond, or to further press the Maceriyans on their intentions. Outcry from the eastern Kingdoms has been particularly loud. The lesser lands of the Central Ruthnian Plateau wait to see what the declaration of the Isles will be. In the opinion of this correspondent, one misstep could precipitate a dissolution of the current state of

*amity that exists between our countries, and a
return to the uncertain years of hostility that so
bedevilled the Kingdoms in centuries past.*

There were references to other stories at the bottom
of the column, regarding the arrival of new embassy
staff on 13th Gannever, and the ensuing two-week
delay in the choosing of a new ambassador. The surge
in religious observance following the rumoured return
of the gods was mercilessly lampooned in the paper.

Lucinia had had enough, and folded the paper away.

"No more politics and foreign adventures," she said.
She wished to return to her castle in the sea, lick her
wounds, and proceed with her research.

Had she read further, she would have learned of the
disappearance of the Morfaan emissaries and Garten
Kressind following the duel between the Morfaan
Josanad and Kyreen Asteria, but she did not, and so
remained ignorant of these developments for some
days to come.

THE TRAIN DEPOSITED the countess at Mogawn-On-Land's
lonely station. She and the local tailor disembarked, no
one else. Mogawn-On-Land was her property, as were
most things within five miles of its ruined temple. The
tailor was keen to help the station's sole porter arrange
her bags in the tiny waiting room. She attempted to
engage him in conversation, but a combination of his
natural shyness and her station being so exalted over
his derailed her efforts. He declined her offer of a few
pennies as thanks, and was off as quickly as decorum
allowed. She leaned on her stick and watched him walk

down the tree-lined lane toward the village centre. Raindrops streaked the window.

"He's in a hurry, goodlady," said the porter, who was a sight more talkative than the tailor.

"He means respect," she said. "But his behaviour saddens me. My family have ruled this place for a long time. I had hoped that he would feel comfortable speaking with me."

The porter dropped his permanent smile. He swept his cap off his head and held it in both hands humbly. "If you would forgive my saying so, goodlady, the villagers here grumble that you don't speak much with them. They say that you are more interested in your numbers and mechanisms and all that, and have no interest in their lives or what they do. Since Goodman Mansanio left your employ, we see precious few people from the castle on the land, and it rubs them raw it does. Especially when they say that the old lord came down here regular, and was a respected expert in the sowing of corn and husbandry of animals and that."

Lucinia pulled a face. The mention of her father always darkened her mood. No one but her knew how cruel he was. The villagers judged her unfavourably against him, she knew. That's why she kept away. From celebrity to hag in the space of six hundred miles. Life was unfair.

"They are right," she said. "If it makes any difference to them, next time you are in the village tavern, you can tell them from me that I am sorry."

"Begging your pardon, countess, but you should tell them yourself."

She looked at him properly for the first time. He was young and attractive, well-muscled if slightly stooped from the demands of his work.

No, Lucinia, she told herself. She needed to improve her reputation. Bedding commoners in her own village wouldn't do anything for that.

"I'll bet they say worse about me than that."

The porter looked ashamed, and stared at the floor.

"You're not from here, are you?"

"No, goodlady. I hail from Avimouth on the south coast. See all the way to Girarsa on a clear day."

She nodded. Her father had given permission for the railway company to build their station in the village, and cut tracks across their land. She received a nominal rent for it and certain benefits, such as free tickets to the city, but the assets of the railway, and its staff, were among the few things in Mogawn-On-Land that did not belong to her.

"That would explain your honesty," she said, more coldly than she intended.

"I am sorry, goodlady," said the young man.

'No, no." She rested a hand on his arm. "I did not mean that to come out the way it did. You provide a timely reminder of my responsibilities. I shall act upon your words, and visit the village more often. I thank you."

The porter gave an unsure smile, and bobbed his head. Carriage wheels rattled on cobbles. Four fine drays came into view and pulled up outside the station's entrance.

"There. My ride home," she said. "If you would help my coachman with my bags?"

The porter nodded. His jovial nature returned a little at the provision of a generous tip.

"And tell him he is late," Lucinia finished.

CHAPTER TWENTY-ONE
Death's Calling

A TOUCH ON Aarin's back disturbed his scribing. He looked up from the manuscript into the cowl of a Guider. His face was swathed in black bandages. Aarin recognised him easily enough, there was no mistaking the apologetic air of Brother Harma.

"It is time," Harma said. "I am sorry."

Without replying, Aarin scraped the golden ink from his pen nib back into the pot, screwed on the lid, laid the pen quietly on the wooden ledge at the base of the desk and got down from his high stool. He was forced to rely solely on his right hand for these tasks. Harma winced at the bandage on Aarin's left hand, for he had been there when the damage had been done.

Harma was Aarin's most sympathetic gaoler. When Prior Seutreneause had Aarin hurt, Harma blanched. When Uguin, the prior's steward, taunted Aarin, Harma cast down his eyes. He did not excuse himself, or protest, but he was not happy with what the Guiders were doing to one of their own. Aarin veered between being grateful and despising Harma for being weak. Harma had not stepped in to stop Seutreneause's thugs breaking the rest of his fingers, for all the guilt he showed.

Harma stood back to allow Aarin out through the scriptorium. The other Guiders worked on without looking up, bandaged faces close to their work. Pens scratched over vellum, magnifying glasses glinted in the light of tallow sticks. They worked in shifts, never stopping. *The New Book of the Dead* took shape under their pens. More than a record of every person who had died in the Karsan isles since the driving of the gods, it was a desperate attempt to save the souls of the ghostless dead.

If he ever got out of the monastery, Aarin would not miss the tallow's smell. The monks rendered the fat from the corpses of sea dragons washed up on the Final Isle's shores. It reeked of fish and death.

At the end of the scriptorium was the entrance to the underworld. A carving of the Dead God's crucifixion filled most of the wooden door closing the way. From his cross Tallimastus stared at Aarin dolefully. An idealised depiction, Aarin thought. The real god was far less noble.

Harma unlocked the door and the two of them descended winding stairs into the Room of Names. They passed through an archway too grand for the staircase into a huge stone vault. On walls and ceiling carved from the living rock, monks worked night and day to engrave the names of those who had died since the god driving. This was also part of their efforts to save the souls of the people of Karsa. Their aim was noble. Whether it worked or not was another matter.

The dead aided the living in their labours. Pasquanty, Aarin's murdered deacon, was among them. Aarin searched out the animate corpse of his companion, and was glad to see they had finally stitched up Pasquanty's torn throat. Though his dead man's eyes had curdled to a dull white, and the treatments to preserve his skin had rendered it taut and yellowish, the corpse was still recognisable as the mortal shell of his former companion. If only Pasquanty's soul were in a better place, Aarin would have felt little guilt.

Harma and Aarin walked under the wheeled scaffold the dead and the living worked from. It had moved only a fraction of an inch down the hall during Aarin's time as prisoner there. The vault was large, and could take many names, but the space was finite.

Past the scaffolding smooth walls awaited, while at the far end of the vault was a hinged iron grille big enough for a single person to pass through. The rough character of the gateway was at odds with the precise engineering of the vault, and a sickening, unvarying wind blew through the grille, warm as breath.

Harma unlocked the gate. A short tunnel led onto a stairway cut into rotten rock. It looked like fat rather than stone. The more often Aarin saw it, the more he believed that was exactly what it was, and the stair was carved into the carcass of some celestial being.

He had walked this route three times before. Harma took a lantern from a store at the top. He lit it, and they descended into a place that existed outside of the world and of time. A steep, greasy stair, full of snags to trap unwary feet, led down an open-sided tunnel. Harma's lamp shone on glistening rock to their left. To their right there was nothing but blackness and the stinking wind.

At the bottom of the stairs was a platform of slabs supported on rusting iron girders projecting into the void. Three piers extended out into the dark beyond the platform's edge. Aarin's eyes were drawn to the leftmost, and he saw the spray of blood and heard the hopeless gurgle of Pasquanty as if it were happening again.

Prior Seutreneause awaited him, his wounding hands buried in his sleeves. Four other monks stood around a fifth whose outer habit had been removed, though his face was still bandaged. The young monk's hands were free. He offered his life freely to the Dead God.

"Guider Aarin," said Seutreneause, "are you ready?"

Monks grabbed him and bound his hands behind his back. Aarin grimaced at the pain in his fingers.

"Careful!" he hissed. "Thanks to your prior, they are broken, remember?"

Seutreneause made an equivocal face and shrugged.

"Then you should tell truth about your conversations with the Dead God, Guider."

"I am," said Aarin. He remained defiant as the Guiders slipped a noose over his head and seated it about his neck.

"I'm afraid I don't believe you. Your family has a certain reputation for bloody mindedness."

"What would I have to hide?" spat Aarin. A monk pushed him toward the rightmost pier. The young monk walked, head lowered, to the end of the left pier, where he stared at the black fanatically.

"Tallimastus raves at me. He is more interested in keeping me as part of his collection of souls, which you will soon be joining!" Aarin shouted at the young monk. The monk glanced at him before returning to his contemplation of the void. "How many times must I tell you, Seutreneause? The god is mad. He will not tell me anything. There is no point to this."

"Nevertheless, you shall continue to go until you bring me the information I desire," said the prior. "Find out how to solve the problem of the dead. Think beyond yourself, you selfish creature. There is more than your life at stake here. The afterlives of all the peoples of Ruthnia hang in the balance. If the Lands of the Dead are closed to us, what then? You took an oath. Fulfil it. Brother Marcel here is willing to die for the truth." He indicated the younger monk who was now lost in prayer, eyes closed and lips whispering.

"As am I," said Aarin. "But my answer remains the same. The god has told me nothing."

"Then that is too bad for you." Seutreneause lifted his hand and waved two more monks forward. One stood behind Brother Marcel. A third went to the central pier, a piece of vellum in one hand, a torch in the other. Upon the vellum was the detailed life story of a man recently dead, richly illuminated with precious gold ink. The monk behind Aarin placed his hand in the small of Aarin's back.

"A dead soul for the Dead God," said the central monk. He held the vellum into the fire, until it blackened and curled, then tossed it off the pier. As darkness swallowed the flame a desperate shriek blasted from the deeps.

"The first gate is open," a monstrous voice moaned on the wind.

"A living soul for the Dead God," said the monk behind Marcel. Marcel prayed harder as the older monk produced a dagger and slit his throat. Marcel toppled off the pier into the void. When Aarin returned, there would be a new animate working in the vault. How they retrieved the bodies he did not know.

"The second gate is open," said the voice.

"Now your turn, Aarin," said Seutreneause unpleasantly.

"A soul neither dead nor alive for the Dead God," said the monk behind Aarin.

Aarin took a breath that was cut short by a shove in his back. His feet slipped off the end of the pier, and he was lowered over the edge by his noose. He kicked helplessly. Although he knew he would not die, his body disagreed, and fought furiously for the air denied it.

Once more, his vision filled with spots. His back banged against rusting iron. From somewhere above, Seutreneause shouted at his underlings. Once more, Aarin choked out his last.

Dying was becoming tiresome.

FOR THE FOURTH time, Aarin sped away from his own body. The wall of fatty rock vanished into infinite black. For an age he sped through nothingness, until a bright point winked into being far ahead, and grew rapidly into a sphere of silver. The prison of Tallimastus, the Dead God.

Aarin's soul alighted gently upon the sphere. It was a tiny ball of a world, with horizons only a few hundred yards away. Quickly, he came to the Dead God's throne, and the impoverished court of ghosts he surrounded himself with. Green ghost light lit the scene in sickly shades. The newly-sacrificed Marcel stood closest to Tallimastus, his eyes full of hate.

"I told you so," said Aarin to the ghost.

Brother Marcel shouted back, his neck straining, lips gaping, but the dead cannot speak, and his words went unheard.

"Ah, Guider Aarin," said Tallimastus.

When viewed with Aarin's good eye, Tallimastus was a figure of two halves. His left side was that of a heavily-muscled man, vital looking. The other was wizened flesh, a mummified figure with an empty eye socket and shrunken skin. It was the dead half that spoke to him. Aarin squeezed shut his good eye, and looked upon Tallimastus with his blind eye, whose sight had been stolen when he was young. Through that, Tallimastus was an old man with milky white eyes dressed in a threadbare robe. The marks of crucifixion were the only commonality between the two. Neither aspect was a true vision, but Aarin found the living god easier to relate to, and so he kept his good eye closed.

"Have you come to ask me unanswerable questions? Have you come to be chased from my cell again?" said Tallimastus. "It amused me the first time, I grow bored of it now."

"Enjoy it while you can," said Aarin. His soul's voice was his original, not the husky whisper repeated stranglings had forced on his living body. "I will not survive many more trips into your domain. I will soon lose the use of this hand if this continues. He will not let the fingers heal, but breaks them every time when I convey the message that you will not talk to me."

"Why would you do that?" said Tallimastus, genuinely perplexed. "I did not intend for you to escape, but you did. I told you everything I could the first time we met. The route to the Lands of the Dead is weakening because magic is consumed faster than it is replenished. Your kind suck this world dry of magic with your machines. Weaker souls dissipate to nothing, those strong enough to resist will become difficult for a time. Eventually, there will be insufficient energy left to the World Spirit to allow the stronger souls to manifest as well. You doom yourselves to oblivion. There, I told you again." He laced his fingers over his stomach. "Tell them that."

Aarin lowered himself to the ground and crossed his legs. He was insubstantial as the Dead God's glaring ghosts, and drifted upward. His spirit tether floated behind him, a red line snaking off from his chest back to his corporeal body.

"Go on," said Tallimastus sarcastically, "make yourself comfortable."

"For a god, you are unwise to the nature of humanity," said Aarin. "If I tell them that, they will probably kill me. Or they will demand a solution, and send me back anyway. Either way, my prospects are poor. I do not know how many more times I can undergo this closeness to death."

"Your soul is thinning," said the Dead God. "Ah well," he sighed. "I will be sorry to see you go. Your success in reaching me has proved a diversion. My anger at your escapes help enliven this endless night."

"You are bored."

"What prisoner is not?" said the god. "You are imprisoned. I doubt your evenings are full of pleasant diversions."

"Do you want to be free?"

"What do you think, mortal?"

"Then help me get away from the Final Isle. I can aid you."

"I think not!" Tallimastus snorted. "Perhaps you could help me, but I doubt you will. If I did help you escape, I would not have the pleasure of watching you suffer. It is all that gives me joy. This cell is so dreary, and I say that having ruled the Lands of the Dead. Terrible place."

"The Twin draws near," said Aarin. "I have seen fires on its face. The Earth shakes at its approach. Tell me, if something ill befalls the Earth, or even just this monastery, will you not be trapped here forever?"

Tallimastus looked away, his mouth twisted.

"I thought as much," said Aarin. "Here I am. Here you are. I have a proposal for you, my lord god."

"Then Tallimastus is listening," said the god grudgingly.

"I swore an oath to guide the dead to their next life. I will keep it. Res Iapetus' driving of the gods has had unforeseen results for the living and the dead. You need to be free."

"I agree with you, Guider, if I were free then the problem might be solved. But then I would say that. How would releasing you help me?"

"Aid me. I have formulated a plan for escape, but I cannot do it alone. I will hold the way open as best I can. You will have time to oppose our captors."

"I believe you are selling me the same fish twice," said the god. "The door will swing shut, and how would that help me, I repeat? Only Res Iapetus knows the secrets of this place, and he is as much a prisoner as I am. I made sure of that."

"It is to Res Iapetus I will go," said Aarin. "Once free of this isle, I will seek out the King of the Drowned. I believe that I can reach him."

"You want to set the Goddriver free?" Tallimastus laughed. "It cannot be done."

"I can reach him though."

Tallimastus shrugged. "Perhaps. He is lost between life and death. Perhaps you have enough skill to circumventnt my enchantment, and speak with him."

"Then if he knows of the way to set you free, and I can speak with him, then I will find it."

"Yes, yes, very good," said the god tersely, as if he could not wait for the conversation to be done with. "That still does not guarantee my release."

"Whatever he intended to do, it had unforeseen consequences. He will see that. He will release you."

"How can you say that?" said Tallimastus angrily. "You never knew him. He was an arrogant little prick; he thought he knew everything. He did not!" He slapped his hand on the arm of his throne. "He will never release me. Never. He loathed us all. There is no getting around such hatred." He shook his head. "If you did release me, then fate would demand the return of the other gods, and I would be forced into union with my living aspect. He is mad. I have no desire to experience that again."

"That will definitely happen?"

"Let's say it is narratively appropriate that I be insane," said the god. "Eliturion dealt with all that nonsense, but fate does so love a good story. That is how I am seen, so that is the way I will be." He tugged at his beard. "Confound it! In a sense, my imprisonment makes me free. Insanity or gaol. It is no choice."

"We can deal with that when it comes to it."

Tallimastus laughed. "You know nothing you speak of. I am fucked, to use your expression."

"Then you prefer to remain here for eternity or death, whichever is to come soonest?"

Tallimastus grumbled in his throat. "I cannot say I do."

"Then let me put it another way. Do you have a better idea?" Aarin opened his good eye.

The divided form of Tallimastus looked down at him. His living expression was blank, only the dead side of his face moved, and the expression it wore was terrifying. "I do not have a better idea," he said eventually.

Aarin waited while the god of the dead regarded him.

"Keeping the door ajar will not be enough. I must ride with you. Hold out your arm," said Tallimastus. Dried sinews creaked as the god extended his forefinger. A sharp yellow nail glinted on the end.

Aarin obeyed.

"Hold still. For I must cut your soul." The dry flesh of the god's face creaked into a horrible smile. "I will not lie. This will hurt. A lot."

CHAPTER TWENTY-TWO

Escape from the Final Isle

AARIN RETURNED TO his body in the same manner as before: a swift tug upon his soul's tether, and he raced back to his mortal shell. This time, however, he was bloated with power, so heavy with souls he felt like an anchor snarled with weed being dragged through cold water. The distance from the sphere to the living world was further than ever. His arm pulsed with the insult done it by Tallimastus' talon. The thread of his life grew thinner and more frayed as he progressed, straining under the burdens placed upon it. A god rode with him, a burden the mortal spirit was never meant to bear.

When the platform upon the wall of fatty rock appeared above him, Aarin was close to dissipation. He felt thin, the atoms of his being smeared over too much space. He thought he might vanish into nothing before he arrived, but on he went, until he hovered over the figures crowding the flagstones. They appeared so insignificant. Seutreneause stood over Aarin's body; five monks waited near the bottom of the stairs ready

with medical supplies to revive him; four Guiders with
drawn daggers crouched at his side, ready to plunge
their weapons into his heart should he attempt to
escape. It was a laughable precaution. Aarin had been
barely able to move on his previous returns. He knew
then that they feared him, and he was glad.

This time it would be different, and daggers would
be no help to them.

Aarin flew at his body, and something ancient and
powerful followed. Tallimastus clung to his back,
while within his being boiled a crowd of angry ghosts.
Sensing their revenge was at hand, they poured out of
the glowing rent in his arm and swarmed around him
in loops, their mouths open in silent shrieks, before
plunging back into his spiritual form where they raced
the immortal circuits of his soul.

For a moment Aarin hung over his corporeal shell,
watching the seething mass of revenants plunge down
to infest his body. Above his head the gates of death
swung wide, opening the terrible rift into which the
Guiders saw. Gates was a poetic term for this gash in
reality. Green lights shimmered, and through them the
strange sights of the Lands of the Dead were visible.
Aarin had never seen beyond the gates. Tallimastus'
presence cleared the mists that clouded the marches of
life, and Aarin witnessed wonders.

"Do not look into the light," said Tallimastus. His
voice resounded around Aarin's mind, as if he were
part of his own psyche. "Turn your face from it,
and you will not die. This I swear. You are under my
protection. I am death."

Aarin tore his eyes from the Lands of the Dead. It
would be easier to deny the god and the prior their

wishes, and ascend to the perils of the afterlife alone. The ghosts sensed his indecision, and howled the louder, until his own desire for vengeance and a need to fulfil his oaths pushed him back toward his body.

He landed hard, his limbs twitching at the impact of his spiritual form. For something with so little physical mass, a soul possessed great heft. More ghosts followed him, smacking into his body one after the other. If any of the Guiders on the platform had been of the same degree of ability as Aarin they might have seen his passengers taking that fateful step from death into undeath, but the ghosts possessed his body unobserved, the only sign of their return to the material world the repeated twitching of his limbs.

Aarin's jaw clamped. The pain from his neck was worse than ever before. His flesh was compressed and bruised, his windpipe pushed to a fractional width. His spine ached from the jerk of the drop; they'd nearly broken his neck this time. Before he had come round, weak, but mobile. Now he flopped upon the cold flags like a landed fish.

"He has a palsy! We may lose him," said one of the monks.

"Then do your work!" Seutreneause said. "The secrets of the dead are his. Do not let him drag them into the afterlife with him. Do you hear that, Guider Aarin? I will not let you die, not until you have revealed what the Dead God said!"

His heart surged into action. His eyes flickered open, and he drew in an agonising gasp. The rush of breath down his throat pained him terribly, but after the first gulp of air he could not stop, and panted for the foul atmosphere of the pit, filling his lungs with it.

"He returns!" said the monk's physic. "He lives!"

Seutreneause looked down at him triumphantly, as if it were he who had risked his life and soul to speak with the Dead God, and he who had returned with all the secrets of life and death to command. Aarin hated him more than ever.

"Excellent, excellent," said the prior eagerly. "To his aid. Give him water, give him mead! Soothe his throat so he might speak."

Aarin tried to wave away the men that hurried over, but they would not relent, and set about unwrapping funnel and flask. Under the guard of the four armed monks, two others gripped his head, and inserted the long neck of their silver funnel into his throat so that it scraped against his swollen gullet. Another uncorked the flask and poured it down the funnel, until Aarin spluttered and choked and the funnel was withdrawn.

"No more!" he gasped. "No more! I have news from the Dead God!"

"Now, Guider," said Seutreneause, "what did he say? Speak truthfully, or I shall be forced to break the fingers on your right hand also."

Aarin nodded. The motion sawed at his neck across the line of the noose. Tallimastus' spirit was a weight upon his soul that threatened to drag him out of his body for good, but his loathing of the prior gave him the strength to hold himself in place, and look upon his right arm.

"Draw back the sleeve. You shall see the message Tallimastus our lord has deigned to give you."

"Success?" said Seutreneause eagerly. He was canny enough not to bend down and look himself, although he could barely hold himself back. Instead he ordered forward his monks. They grabbed Aarin's wrist and pinned it to the flags, as if he had the strength to assault them and escape. They drew back his sleeve.

"There is nothing here, prior," one said. They exposed Aarin's arm. The flesh was unmarked.

Seutreneause's face set with grim fury. "Guider Aarin, you shame our order. Why must you be so recalcitrant?"

Aarin laughed feebly, bringing on a cough that rasped at his bruised throat. "It is you who shame our order, prior," said Aarin. "Why would the Dead God favour someone like you with the secrets you crave?"

"Break his fingers," said Seutreneause. "All of them. We will miss your aid in the scribing of the book, but you leave me no choice!"

The monks worried at Aarin's fist, trying to uncurl his right hand, while another brought up a hammer and a chisel.

"You use the tools that should safeguard the dead to harm the living," said Aarin, "and you call yourself worthy." A wriggling sensation worked its way down his arm. The spirits of the dead moved in his body, chilling his blood. The Guider holding his arm gasped at the sudden change in his body temperature and released him.

"What are you doing?" demanded Seutreneause.

"His arm is like ice!" the man said.

Aarin sat, and held his arm out to Seutreneause. The pain of the cold was agonising, but he smiled through his grimace. "Look again, prior."

Seutreneause's eyes widened as the flesh of Aarin's arm parted. The smooth cut Tallimastus' nail had inflicted upon his spirit was mirrored by his body. Scarlet blood welled up and poured from his arm, soaking his black robes. The wound was deep, exposing the muscles and tendons. All power has a cost.

The magic the god had put within him burst forth from the wound in a tidal wave of light. The spirits of the sacrificed dead came screaming out of the Dead God's prison, into the world of the living.

First to emerge was Mother Moude, shrieking her fury. She arrived as a vapour that shimmered and took on human form as it streaked upward into the void, looped, and came arrowing back toward the group of men, screaming overhead and making them duck. More streaks and spears of light followed as Mother Moude's shade coalesced. As she flew she screamed with rage, her voice regained in the mortal world. Her ghost looped up and round and again then plunged downward to spear through one of the monks. He threw up his arms to shield himself, but she was something crude matter could not stop. He was frozen in this aspect of terror, his robes furred with sudden frost as his soul was torn from his body and shredded into glowing wisps on the air by the shrieking witch.

"The dead are using his body as a gate! Kill him!" shouted Seutreneause. "Quickly!"

The four armed monks lunged for Aarin. They were dead before their weapons could touch him, their howling spirits dragged backward from them by the ghosts pouring out of Aarin's wound.

Aarin lay back on the stone as dozens of vengeful spirits passed from him. The monks rallied themselves, forming back to back, using their Guider's skills against the ghosts. A couple of them had some skill, and sent the dead screaming away out of this realm and into the next. The Lands of the Dead's ragged entrance pulsed hungrily over the crowd as their essences raced through it.

With a chilling shriek the last of the ghosts hurled itself from Aarin's body. The warmth returned to his arm. His blood flowed freely from him in frightening amounts. He staggered, lightheaded and clamped his arm to the wound.

"You cut too deeply, god," he said.

"I cut as deeply as I needed," said Tallimastus. A glow surrounded Aarin, and Tallimastus manifested around him, encasing the Guider in a glowing, phantasmal form. "The gates of death are closed to you. I will hold them shut as long as I can. I swear you will not die."

"Tallimastus is here!" a monk shouted, stumbling backward from the divine apparition.

"They can see you," said Aarin.

"I stand upon the threshold of my prison," he replied. "But though my gaol, this place is part of the Lands of the Dead. We can look deeply into that country here. I cannot leave, but my powers are strong."

Tallimastus took on his war aspect, the chooser of the slain who selects the mightiest warriors to watch over the ways of the dead and safeguard the souls that travel there. In that guise he was a warrior with raven hair and scaled armour, bearing a tower shield and a broadsword, only his blinded eyes, covered over with a cloth soaked with new blood, suggested his identity.

"It is my turn to take vengeance," he said. He stepped forward. Aarin moved helplessly with him, his bleeding arm lifting as the god raised his weapon

"The sword of the dead! The sword of the dead!" A monk shrieked, and fled before Aarin. The weapon in

Tallimastus' hand grew monstrously huge, and cut the monk down from behind, slicing his back open and scattering his entrails in loops over the stairs. His soul came out of his body, and that too was cut, broken apart into pieces as it raced frantically for the afterlife.

"You expunge them!" said Aarin.

"It is no more than they deserve," said Tallimastus, advancing upon the monks. "They never attempted to release me. They took the money of Res Iapetus. They thought they could contain death." A Guider bravely stood his ground, flinging out a dozen of the iron darts that the Guiders used to pin dangerous spirits. They flew truly, right at the blind god's face, but Tallimastus raised his shield and they rang off it, and fell away into the black pit.

"Nice try," said the god of the dead. His sword descended, cleaving the monk into two. An explosion of blood washed over the flagstones. The monk's soul burned up in a flash of green. "You were my priests. You betrayed me knowingly, you colluded with the Goddriver. Man's hubris knows no bounds. You forgot I am a god! My vengeance is your reward. Is it not terrible to behold?"

Of the dozen monks who had sent Aarin off into Tallimastus' gaol, five remained alive. A pair of them retreated up the stairs, keeping the ghosts off them with their Guider's arts. Coronas of energy flared around them, warding away the vengeful dead. Where the energies touched the scabrous rock, it decayed into a mealy sand that sloughed from the wall and splatted, thick as porridge, on the steps. Two of the ghosts were pinned by iron darts to the rock. One took the opportunity afforded by the open gates of the dead and fled for the next world, but the majority were hellbent on revenge. Mother Moude soared and dived, harrying the surviving Guiders. Pasquanty's angry shade followed her, as clumsy in death as he was in life, the diabolical expression he wore more than made up for his fumbled attempts to break the Guiders' spells, striking fear in all who saw it.

The ghosts of three monks who had given their lives in attempts to contact the Dead God before Aarin gathered as a throng over the abyss and advanced upon the prior, staring at Seutreneause with empty, unblinking eyes.

"What we found, was not what we expected," they said. "What we found, was not what we expected," they repeated, over and over.

"Stop!" said Seutreneause. "You sacrificed yourselves for the greater good. You were honoured!"

"No honour is to be found in being the tool of another's ambition." The middle monk came forward, and pointed accusingly at the prior. "You lied to us. All things are clear to the dead. We were trapped, denied life after life. You knew this would happen to us, and you did not tell. Now you shall face the judgment of the Dead God."

Tallimastus swelled to gigantic proportions. Aarin floated at the centre of his chest.

"Ah Seutreneause," boomed the god. "You do not defend yourself with the discipline of necromancy, my gift to the true sons of the Dead God's quarter." Aarin mouthed the words along with him. "You do not do this, because you cannot. You are a weak Guider, prior. A quill-sharpening social climber. You used those granted power by me."

"I wanted to end the crisis of the dead!" raged Seutreneause. "I wanted to save the souls of mankind! I have held true to my oath!"

"Then you should not have taken Iapetus's money," said Tallimastus. "You should not have furthered the existence of this place."

"What could I do? For two centuries you were trapped. How could I go against that?"

Tallimastus reared back and grew bigger. His sword was the length of a ship's mast, his shield the size of a sail. Aarin was a mote of matter encysted in green light. "A true priest of mine would have made every effort to free me, and damned the consequences. Instead you sought profit, status and power for yourself. I offer guidance and protection in the life beyond. You have squandered eternity for mortal gain. You sought to end the crisis, it is true, but I know your heart, and the secret dreams you have locked within are of Seutreneause the saviour, the deliverer from damnation, lauded and loved across the world. A true servant of mankind craves none of these things. A true servant has *humility.*"

The wall trembled. Moist boulders rained down from above and crashed through the platform.

Seutreneause cowered backwards, hands held beseechingly in front of his heart. "Please, please! I was wrong. I only wanted to discover why the dead would not go easily. I only wanted to help."

"You lie. Perhaps you wished for those things, but they were modesty's cloak for your ambition. Maybe you believed it yourself, but I can see more clearly into your soul than you can. Always, those with little talent abuse those purer than they for gain. Always, greedy men convince themselves they work for the betterment of others." Tallimastus' foot descended, pinning the prior's robe under his sandal.

"Then why didn't you answer? Why did you not release the monks I sent to you? I could have helped!" shouted Seutreneause. "You forsook us!"

"You forsook me," said Tallimastus. "You left me to rot in Res Iapetus' prison, half a being, trapped nowhere. Do you know how bored I was?" Tallimastus leaned down, putting his shimmering, phantasmal face close to the prior's. "I pass judgement upon you, Descan Seutreneause. I find you unworthy of your office, and I hereby relieve you of your soul."

"No—!"

Seutreneause's scream was cut off by Tallimastus' sword. It sliced through the prior's body, smashing the flagstones beneath. The remainder of the platform collapsed, carrying off the last monk stood upon it screaming into the pit. The cliff shook. Boulders bounced down from an unseen height, spraying viscous fluid as they span off into the dark.

Seutreneause's ghost rose up from the pit. His cries had an edge of desperation as he flew desperately toward the gate of the dead and the shifting, auroral world beyond.

Tallimastus waved his sword into smoke, reached out and snatched the shade from the air.

"No you don't," said the Dead God. Seutreneause wailed. "It is over for you." The god crushed the prior's ghost into shreds of greenish mist, and inhaled them.

Tallimastus sighed with pleasure. Aarin, caught within his being, felt the prior's passing. An utter extinction of life and soul. It was the most terrible thing he had ever felt.

The Dead God shrank in on himself, and bore Aarin toward the ragged foot of the stairs. One of the two Guiders who had fought on the steps was frozen in place. The foot of his comrade lay bloody on the bottommost step. Close by, a ghost thrashed and screamed on the rock, pinned by two darts.

Tallimastus deposited Aarin between these grizzly remains, and drew back into the void. With no body to anchor him, the god's form began to fade. The cliff shuddered. Part of the wall over the stairs slipped down in avalanche, taking half the width of the staircase with it.

"This place collapses," said Tallimastus. "My prison will no longer be accessible to the living." The god looked upward, through the tear in space that let onto the Lands of the Dead. Aarin glimpsed strange landscapes, and crowds of lost souls, but they came and went quickly, and for the most part he saw nothing but waves of magical energy rippling on the skin of reality.

"I see into my immortal kingdom," Tallimastus said sadly. "Another rules in my place. She disguises herself, but I know her. The Dark Lady! Be wary of her, Aarin, she cares nothing for this world any more. She was unharmed by Iapetus. She retains all her power."

Tallimastus' warrior aspect rippled away. Once more he was a tired old man.

"I feel him, my living half. We are as one for a moment. I am whole. We were not always as we are, Aarin. We were not always gods. Forgive us for what we have become. There is great power in you and in all of your family. Fate has a role for you, and with that I cannot interfere. But I can help."

Aarin felt a sudden weight. On his left arm was Tallimastus' shield, clasped in his right was his sword.

They had become solid steel with a golden sheen. A greenish light shone in them still, marking them out as more than mortal gear.

"Take my weapons." The god was now an outline, his blind eyes pearls peeking from the dark. "They will serve as my badge and will grant you passage where you must go. Seek out the Drowned King, speak with Res Iapetus, cleave true to your oath and salve the hurts of the dead. I will hold you back from death for as long as I can. Be careful, for I do not know how long I will be able to."

The howling of the damned sounded out Tallimastus' disappearance. They whirled around each other in a rising wind, and sped upwards toward the exit from the cavern. Aarin yanked out the iron darts from the moist stone, and the pinned shade shot after the others.

He looked up the shaking stairs. Wet tears appeared in the marbled rock. He had very little time. He shoved past the dead Guider. The stairs, always treacherous and slick, jumped under his feet, threatening to pitch him into the void and its stinking wind. There would be no return this time if he fell.

He ran pellmell, barely slowing for the wide swathe where rockfall had reduced the steps to stubs.

Pillars of stone thumped down like steam hammers, shaken from their moorings by the convulsions of the underworld. Aarin cursed his monk's habit for slowing him, but he could not stop to tear it free. A fall of rock blocked his way, ramming down right before his nose. Instinctively, he lashed out with the Dead God's sword, sweeping the green blade across the rock. To his amazement the weapon cut through without hindrance, as if the stone were not there, and the blockage tumbled off the steps and vanished out of sight.

A dire howl came now on the wind. Aarin had no desire to face whatever thing possessed the voice, and was gladdened when the lamps at the head of the stair came into view. He pelted toward them, through the short tunnel and the open yett, and into a scene from a nightmare.

In the Room of Names, the dead slaughtered the living. The ghosts of the court of the Dead King ran amok, plunging their phantasmal hands into the chests of the monks and stilling their hearts. The animates stumbled in confusion. A monk ran screaming past Aarin. He raised his shield and sword, but the monk was blind with terror. A phantom flew through him, freezing him to the spot. The slaughter was done in seconds. With Mother Moude at their head, the dead flew away through archway, and up the stairs into the scriptorium, leaving the bodies of monks frozen in a tableau of fear.

Pasquanty's spirit remained behind, looking sadly at his body shambling idiotically about.

"I am sorry, Pasquanty. Come with me, and I shall send you on once we are outside."

Pasquanty's soul drifted miserably over to Aarin's side.

Aarin spoke words of command over the animates. They ceased their confused shambling and turned as one to face him. He selected six of them, Pasquanty's corpse included.

"Come with me," he said. The vault shook. The roar of collapsing stone issued from the tunnel. A crack appeared across the roof. Where it ran through the names of the dead, Aarin heard faint screaming.

"It is over. This venture is done," he said to Pasquanty's shade. The ghost nodded. "Which makes my task, our task, all the more pressing."

Holding the weapons of the Dead God ready, Aarin ascended the stairs into the scriptorium.

They emerged from the dark into the grey light of day. The monks in the scriptorium were all dead, frozen in various aspects of terror, hands flung up, mouths screaming, all of them coated in ice, their black robes and bandages covered in frost.

"This will not last," said Aarin. "The power of the dead cannot hold so long in the Lands of the Living." There were nought but the dead to hear him, and he spoke mainly to reassure himself. Screams rang from all over the monastery, and the shrieks of the dead. The voices of the living fell rapidly silent. He passed frozen corpses at every turn.

The front gate was unlocked. Dead monks lay spread around the green hill before it. Frozen as they ran, they had overbalanced and lay upended on the ground. An almost comical sight. Aarin advanced carefully down the steep path toward the flat, wave-cut pavement that surrounded the island's single hill. The stone was covered only by the very highest tides, and at that moment its numerous rockpools reflected the grey sky. A light drizzle fell. Aarin shivered; it was cold and windy, but he would not have to endure it for long.

Where the last of the grass met the round pools of the bare rock, Aarin stopped. His little band of animates shuffled to a halt. Pasquanty drifted to his side.

The power Tallimastus had unleashed was leaching away, and Pasquanty's shade was evaporating into nothingness.

Over the silent monastery the gates of the dead were open, shedding deathly green light across the Final Isle.

In liminal spaces the rituals of the dead had the most efficacy, and the border of the ocean and the land offered Aarin the best chance of helping the ghosts. Aarin thrust the sword of the dead into the green grass, causing it to wither in a circle three feet across. He leaned the shield against it. He held up his arms. The gash on his right forearm gaped bloodlessly. He should have been crippled, but the arm functioned perfectly, and no pain troubled him.

"Spirits of the dead! Spirits of the dead! I call upon you," he said, beginning the rite of passing employed for ghosts who had lost their bodies but not yet passed on. "There is nothing to fear. Life is done, but a new life beckons, if only you hearken to my voice, and heed my words."

He looked around the sky, seeking the ghosts who had followed him back into this world.

"Come to me," he said. "I shall show you the way."

A soft moan announced the arrival of the first—one of the monks Seutreneause had sacrificed. A second materialised next to him, then a third, then the four luckless others who had strayed into the prior's grasp. It was the first time Aarin had had a good look at them. They were fishermen of the southern isles, lured to their doom or rescued from shipwrecks, only to find their salvation was nothing of the sort.

"Heed me, spirits of the dead!" Aarin had never guided so many spirits at once on his own. He prayed to his rediscovered god that he could do it, and save them from extinction. "Heed me!"

More materialised, the ghosts of the monks slain in the monastery, hovering side by side with those who had killed them, peace imposed by death. He was heartened by that, only a few of them had been expunged.

Green light spilled onto the shore. Aarin looked up. The gate shone brightly. The clarity Tallimastus' presence had bestowed upon him was gone, and he saw only the shifting veils he had witnessed so many times before. Few Guiders in that age had Aarin's skill or talent, and most saw less than that.

He lifted his face to the ghosts.

"The way is open! Depart! Go from this place unto your rests. Your time here is done."

There was no reluctance on the part of the ghosts. They rose in ones and twos. Their gazes dwelled a little on the mortal lands, but by the time they reached the undulating edge of the gates they had their eyes firmly fixed on their destination.

Pasquanty lingered a moment longer. Aarin smiled at him. "I am sorry I was not a better master, Pasquanty. May you find peace wherever you go, and if we should meet in some other realm, I pray I will be a kinder friend."

Pasquanty gave a mute smile, and floated upwards. He watched Aarin most of the way, but finally he too turned his face from that world to the next so that it was bathed in light, and was gone.

One spirit remained.

Mother Moude floated in front of Aarin, her face full of hatred.

"You may go Mother," he said. "You are free."

The ghost shifted from form to form as she stared at him, going from voluptuous maiden to middle-age to rotting corpse in a sickening cycle.

Mother Moude was a wild talent, a mageborn executed for witchcraft in an age less tolerant of women with power. She should never have been killed. Her soul should never have been imprisoned in its iron box. Her sacrifice by Seutreneause to the Dead God was but the last in a long line of indignities.

In death, she retained her ability, and unlike most ghosts she could speak with the living.

"No," she said.

Aarin had had custody of her before, and though he could have, he had not released her because he feared her. He had been right to do so. She sped at him, screaming. He snatched up the shield of Tallimastus, and she slammed into it. The uncanny metal deflected her, and she rebounded off over the ocean as a screaming green light. A flash of silent lightning ushered her over the horizon.

The gates of the dead faded out of the sky.

Aarin cried out as pain flooded back into his arm, bringing forth a trickle of blood. Guiders had some healer's skills. He probed it gingerly to check his veins and arteries were not cut. The wound was grave. Without Tallimastus' aid, it would kill him. He struggled one-handed to tear off a strip of his habit and bind it closed.

"The Dead God's power fades," he said to himself. He looked up across the boundless sea. He did not have much time.

"Come," he said to the animates, and set out across the platform of rock to the cliffs at its edge.

A series of jetties projected from the cliffs at varying heights, cunningly built up from natural protrusions of the rock to allow the monks to access the sea whatever the tide. Their longboat bobbed on the water some way out, anchored clear of the stone. A coracle was tethered to the topmost pier so that it would float safely free at the highest tides. Aarin commanded one of the dead to fetch it. It obeyed mechanically, its soulless body motivated by Aarin's will alone. It went to the coracle, picked it up and placed it upside down upon its back. Aarin was still bleeding slightly, and by the time the dead man had carried the coracle down three flights of wave-worn steps to the sea, he was shivering with shock more than cold.

The animate stared at him with dead eyes.

"Go to the longboat. Draw in its anchor. Return with the boat's line," Aarin commanded.

The dead man wordlessly set about his task. The water washed over the top of the jetty currently level with the sea, and he waded through it. At the end, he flipped the coracle off his back and into the water, then clambered in.

It took an age for the dead man to paddle out to the bigger boat and start the return journey.

"The rest of you, draw it in," Aarin said through chattering teeth. He wasn't sure he could keep himself awake. If Tallimastus' influence was gone and he died, Aarin hoped he could find his own way to the next world. The thought of dissipating to nothing as Seutreneause had panicked him, and made it hard to concentrate on what he was doing.

The longboat bumped against the jetty. Aarin splashed through freezing water and half fell into it, the shield and sword of the dead banging on the boat's ribs.

"Get in," he told the dead men.

The animates clambered aboard, and took up the oars. There were eight of them. Aarin threw the extra two oars overboard. Six rowers would have to be enough.

"Take the boat about, and row into the ocean."

They did as he asked. The rain was falling more heavily. Aarin wished he had taken the time to gather more clothes and tend to his wound better. He reminded himself none of that would matter in a few moments.

The Final Isle retreated quickly. From out on the water, nothing seemed any different to the first time he had seen it. The monastery stood on the side of the hill near the rounded summit, its solitary tower spearing the grey sky. Grey rock fringed the green. Grey sea surged around the rock, rushing into a million small cavities with a growling shush.

"Stop. Here," ordered Aarin.

The undead ceased to row. The skiff slid to a halt on the sea. Aarin stood up, and walked to the prow. He looked down into the water. It was a singular grey, covered over with shifting circles of spume dappled with the expanding ripples of raindrops. It was entirely opaque to human sight. The boat lifted and sank in the swell. Aarin stared.

Without a word, he lifted his foot over the gunwale, and stepped into the water. The weight of Tallimastus' shield and sword dragged him down with frightening speed. His wound stung at first, but the cold of the ocean killed the pain. The weight of the water crushed the air from his lungs, forcing an involuntary moan out of his throat in a cloud of silvery bubbles.

He could fight the urge to inhale only for so long, but that was the plan.

What better way was there to summon the Drowned King?

Aarin's body screamed at him for breath. Daylight was a pewter gleam far above, the elongated lozenge of the longboat's hull no bigger than a seed. He could not have swum back if he had wanted to.

He could not deny his body. He breathed in, and his lungs filled with a choking wash of freezing water.

His lungs burned. His mind dimmed. Tallimastus' shield and sword pulled him faster and faster, taking him down to the fathomless deeps.

Aarin was dimly aware of cold, slimy hands grasping his ankles before he drowned.

CHAPTER TWENTY-THREE
To Sea Drays Bay

TWELVE DAYS AFTER leaving Trassan's grave, the ice ran out.

Antoninan, Ullfider, Persin, Bannord, Ardovani and Ilona stood upon a ridge. To the south the eternal white of the Sotherwinter ice cap blazed, the long tongues of glaciers nosing down from it toward the sea. To the north, the crags and stacks of the ice shelf gleamed in sunlight that was melting it into ever more fantastic shapes. Azure pools of water collected on its surface. Waterfalls rushed into the sea. Constant groans and rumbles passed through the earth, interrupted by the thunderous, glassy shattering of collapse, and the roaring of the sea as the ice was received.

The noises disquieted the dogs. The nights kept their bitter chill, but the days were getting hotter. Merciless sun blistered the skins of the party. Half the time they were far too hot, but were forced to keep themselves covered against sunburn. The insides of their noises bled for want of moisture in the air. For all the snow melting on the coast there was precious little to drink inland. The earth soaked up what water freed itself. The air sucked it away. There were no springs to be found anywhere nearby; that part of the Sotherwinter as dry as it was cold, a frigid desert. Many of the men resorted to ramming their canteens full of snow, and putting them against their bodies, although Antoninan grew furious with those he caught doing this, warning of frost burn. He scolded others for eating the ice, saying it would waste their bodies' strength. He told them all to wait for evening when they could set up their stoves to melt the snow safely. Thirst drove them to disobey.

Behind them the pillar of steam rose high into the blue of the sky. A solitary column of vapour, there were no clouds for it to join or storms to disperse it. When the winds teased it apart it always returned. An innocuous streak it seemed, but it loured over the Sotherwinter as menacingly as a thunderhead, and drove the survivors on as if it were a lash.

Their progress slowed. For a day the sleds bumped over frequent patches of rock. The dogs became ill-tempered. The men were forced to lend their strength to the effort. Antoninan ran up and down the line screaming at them to mind the runners. Then finally the shadowed slope heavily mottled with rock, and over the ridge the sunward side nearly bare. Beyond the hill the land was free of ice.

Antoninan snapped his telescope shut and said something filthy in his native tongue.

"We have to cross it," he said.

The land before them was a plain of broken rock dotted with pancakes of snow. Tussocks of grass rattled in the dry winds. Tiny flowers skulked at the bases of exposed root balls. Expansive snowfields glittered in the sun beyond, but the distance to them was considerable.

"Can we not go south, use the permanent ice there, and come back around?" said Bannord.

"A further diversion than using the pack ice in the first place," said Antoninan.

"Though safer," said Bannord. The song of the ice thrummed over the landscape oppressively. A mighty booming followed his words, warning them away.

"Sea Drays Bay is only fifteen miles distant," said Antoninan. "I can see the hills that shield it from here." He pointed to a range of black curves, gentle as a woman's body.

"You are sure?" said Ullfider. He was grey and haggard. In Karsa his life was one of ease, and he was old. After the voyage he had expected to spend his time in the comfort of the *Prince Alfra*, appraising the wonders of the past. The sled ride was hardest on him, even though Antoninan had excused him from all work.

"We could unload, take the stress off the sleds," said Bannord. "Go slow, the drays could take the sleds over. It'll slow us right down, but it has to be done. We need the speed of the sleds on the far side, or we'll be caught."

"The runners will break on the rock," said Persin. "We cannot lose the sleds."

"Travois then," said Bannord. "The dogs drag the loads, we carry the sleds. It's five or six miles to the snowfields. It'll be hard work, but we can do it."

"What will we make these travois with?" said Antoninan. "If we carry the loads and cross back, we will lose at least a day." He looked back at the steam column marking the Draathis advance.

"They will catch us," said Ardovani.

"I am aware of that, Tullian," said Antoninan testily.

"We're going to have to carry them," said Ilona. "But not all the way."

The others looked at her.

Ullfider made a dismissive gesture. Antoninan shot him a look of rebuke.

"Let the goodlady speak," said Antoninan. "Go on."

"We can go quicker if we take an indirect route."

"Nonsense!" snorted Ullfider.

Ilona ignored him. "We trace a line between the largest snow pans. The distance between them isn't so large. If we pick a good route, we can save time. We carry the sleds to the snow patches, use them to ferry the equipment across. We're going to have to carry all of the gear some of the time..."

"But not all of the gear all of the time," said Bannord, finishing for her approvingly.

"It will take too long," said Ullfider. His scoffing turned into a phlegmy cough.

"Not if we work out the best way," said Ilona, pointing. "That one there. Then to that one there. Where they are close together, further on, we can shovel snow into roads, make paths between, and save more time."

"If we send men ahead to cut more blocks from the snow pans, we can speed the process even more," said Bannord. "That's not a half-bad idea."

"My family are engineers," said Ilona. "Antoninan, what do you think?"

He nodded slowly.

"It is a good idea, goodlady," said Persin approvingly. "A very good idea."

"We shall do it," said Antoninan. He curled his lip. "Ordinarily, I have problems with too much snow, not too little. A pox on variety. But never let it be said that Eustache Antoninan avoids a challenge. Never!"

THEY WORKED HARD throughout the day. Antoninan sent ahead two parties of five men to cut blocks from the snow pans, while the rest of them set about unloading the sleds and preparing the cargo for carrying across the naked stone. When the first sled was unloaded it was taken, along with its dogs, down to the first snow pan. The ground proved to be hard going, broken up by boulders and jagged lumps of peat that crumbled underfoot without warning. Carrying the sleds was a job of six men, and still they stumbled. Soon they were cursing and sweating profusely. The air was cold, but the sun beat down on them.

"Remove your parkas!" Antoninan ordered. "If they become wet, they will freeze if the temperature drops, and you will die!"

They had little time to rest. Thirst plagued them all.

To the good, the snow in the scattered pans cut well, and if a few blocks crumbled in the hands of the men, they were in the minority. The ease of slicing and moving the snow encouraged the party to extend the roads further out across the stone field than intended. Taking the sleds across the rock was hard, and by the end of morning, the sleds and the cargo had been moved only the mile and a half to the first snow pan. However, minutes after the runners kissed the snow and the dogs had been harnessed again, the sleds had covered five hundred yards of snow pan and ice road. The elation of seeing the sleds move easily across the ice there was out of all proportion with the distance gained. The party at the second pan had made fine progress in laying a track of snow out over the rock, and so more ground was covered. They proceeded quickly thereafter, relying on the ice roads more than carrying the gear.

By the time the sun headed for its brief rest, the party had covered half of the distance over the bare ground. A band of solid white enticed them in the distance. The column of steam following them had drawn nearer, but they were all exhausted and had to stop, none more so than the dogs who had to endure the sun's heat radiating from the stone.

The party had taken to bivouacking during the nights, not wishing to spend travelling time erecting their tents. Dark was so short and the weather fair, so there seemed little point anyway. They crawled into their sleeping bags still dressed in their clothes and lit no fires to avoid giving away their position. That evening was no different.

Ilona camped at a distance from the men, with Tyn Rulsy as a chaperone; a concession to society's morals more than a real precaution. The party's situation was such that even the lustiest appetites were frozen. All they wished to do was sleep.

Ilona awoke to the sound of stifled sobs. Rulsy was not in her sleeping bag, and she cast about for her. Both moons were in the sky, though the sun was already announcing his intention to rise. It was no task to spot the Tyn sat upon a rock facing toward the coming day.

The Twin's vastness bit out a black circle from the blue of false dawn, but even it could not deny the sun. The ground rumbled, an earthquake this time. A moment later came a roar of tumbling ice from the distant shore.

Ilona approached Rulsy carefully, clearing her throat when near.

"There is no need to announce yourself, goodmaid," said the Tyn. "I can hear a mouse's sigh a hundred miles away, if I wants. Certainly I hears you."

"You are crying."

"I am crying."

"I did not know Tyn cried," Ilona said, and sat next to Rulsy. The stone had lost the heat it had hoarded during the long day. The sky sucked all warmth from the world, but paid for it in stars.

"You don't know nothing about us," said Rulsy.

"I suppose we don't," said Ilona.

"Tyn Gelven is dead," said Rulsy. "If you're wondering why I am all sad." She thrust her wizened face into her drawn up knees and let out a hitching sob.

Ilona lifted her hand and gingerly put her arm around the creature's shoulders. Tyn Rulsy was very small and fine boned, so when she nestled into Ilona's side, it felt like she held a bird. Like a bird, the Tyn was incredibly warm. Ilona's skin tingled at the contact.

"He was so old, so much older than me," said Tyn Rulsy. "He knew so much, and now he's gone."

"How can you know?" Ilona asked.

"A soul as old and strong as his makes a ripple when it goes. He went for you. He went and died because he thought you were worth it. I hope you are happy."

Ilona had no reply. Rulsy was silent. The ice groaned in the north, but at night it seemed quieter, quiet enough that the sound of the small things eking out a living between snow, grass and rock was audible.

"It's not fair," said Rulsy. "When I was young, really, really young, it was all different. Now look at the world, look at me. I know how you see me, what that magister with the sad lovely eyes says about me. I am hideous." She shrank smaller. "Once, I was so beautiful. The world was so beautiful."

"Tullian doesn't mean anything by it."

"Then why say it?" snapped Rulsy. "You people, you is so careless with your words and your thoughts and all the things you do. You don't see it changes things. You are always changing things. You changed me."

"I don't understand."

"Course you don't," muttered Rulsy. "None of you do. All be over soon anyway, all this. The Draathis have won, worse luck."

"The iron monsters. Draathis," she repeated it slowly, testing the foreign syllables on her tongue.

Rulsy snorted. "Draathis ain't no more monsters than you are. Things what don't know their place. Slaves got above their station, but they are mean. They won't ever stop. They'll walk and walk through snow and rock and water to get at you, and they will. Then when they have you, they'll kill and kill until every last one of you people is dead, and every last one of mine. Then that'll be that, and this world will be theirs."

A hiss came from Rulsy's neck. Ilona brushed her hand against the iron collar the Tyn wore.

"Rulsy! Your collar is burning hot."

"Won't be the first time I've said too much," Rulsy said. "Close to breaking my geas, I am. Tempted to do it and all."

"What would happen, if you... you know, you did break your geas?"

Rulsy looked up at Ilona, her black button eyes shone with the reflected light of the night sky. "Then this thing you see beside you, it will become all I am, and all I ever was, and the thing I was, the thing I *really* am, will be no more, and will never have been." She looked dead ahead. "Geas aren't there for fun, or for perverseness. It's magic, like the collar. Keeps us in our shapes, stops us changing any more. Don't know why we bother. It's all over. It's—"

She whimpered. Smoke rose from her neck.

"Stop talking!" said Ilona shaking her by the shoulders. "Please, I don't want you to be hurt. You've been so good to me."

"Don't really matter what you want any more, goodmaid, don't matter at all. We're all dead."

Rulsy pulled away and slid off the stone to the floor. "Best get back to bed, goodmaid." Her tone changed, as if she had not shed a tear. "We's got a day lumping sleds coming, and we best be quick about it." She glanced back at the nearing column of steam, already lit up by the coming dawn.

Rulsy would say no more, but allowed Ilona to take her hand as they walked back to their camp.

Ilona took a little solace in that.

THREE KNOCKS CLANGED against the iron door of the *Prince Alfra*'s aft hold. Volozeranetz nodded tersely. A sailor spun the wheel on the door and opened it with great care.

"Password," said the sailor.

"For the love of the One," said Heffi, pushing his way in. "If you don't know who I am or whose side I'm on by now, we're all in trouble."

Four Ishmalani, including First Mariner Volozeranetz, Boatswain Drentz and Helmsman Tolpoleznaen waited in the hold along with Trassan's clerk Godelwind; Toberan and Dellion, the sole marines in fighting condition; Ollens, Trassan's chief engineer, and the Tyn cook, Charvolay. They were all grave and afraid.

"Everyone's here," said Heffi unnecessarily, but he had to say something, and made a show of counting heads. "Good." He leaned back against the door. "This is outrageous, skulking around in my own ship like a stowaway. As you may have guessed, I have called you here to propose we do something about it, and very soon."

Heffi paused and listened carefully. Iron sang with shifts in temperature. The glimmer engine rumbled loudly. Wheels chopped through the ocean, the screw shaft whined in its housing. While through the water and the iron came the dreadful grinding and howling of the ice. There was no danger they would be overheard, even if they shouted.

"I'll keep this brief, before Croutier's thugs notice we're gone." He paused. "I have some bad news. Goodfellow Kressind is dead."

"How do you know?"

"Tyn Gelven," said Heffi. "Before he passed."

"I thought he'd sink the ship," said Godelwind nervously.

"The passing of Gelven could have," said Charvolay. "He was a great Tyn, ancient. There was a power in him, even in these diminished times. His loss is a sorry one for our people."

"Well, if anything good came out of it, it's this; Croutier is now extremely wary of the surviving Tyn. He's been a damn sight less cocky since." Heffi sighed. "The rest of it is not so good. Vols Iapetus is also dead. But many of the rest are alive, and on their way to Sea Drays Bay. If we do not turn back, we condemn them to death, and probably ourselves."

"What do you mean?" said Godelwind.

"Don't be a fool, landsman," growled Tolpoleznaen.

"In two days, maybe three, we'll rendezvous with the rest of Persin's expedition," said Heffi. "I know for a fact that Persin himself is not on board either of his remaining vessels."

"Where is he then? Is he dead too?" said Godelwind.

"He is with the others. They have made common cause. If Persin were instead here or on board his other vessels, I'd rate our chances of survival good, but I would not trust these mercenary bastards with a sack of grain meant for their starving mothers. Croutier is well aware that Persin may be alive, but he does not care. His plan is to kill us, take the ship, and make up some lying story about how we all died in the south so they can sell it back to Vand."

"How can you be sure?" said Godelwind. "Surely he's a reasonable man? We can deal with him."

"Heffi knows for sure because that's what he'd do in Croutier's place," said Tolpoleznaen.

"They can't get away with that," said Godelwind.

"Watch him," growled Tolpoleznaen. "The south breeds strange stories that are too easily believed. Verenetz's story was believed for years, and what falsehood that proved to be, from the lips of a follower of the One no less. If Croutier says we all perished in the city and they found the ship abandoned, who is going to say otherwise? The bodies might never be found. Can't use scrying magic on the ship, far too much iron."

"Right," said Heffi. He tugged at the gold rings on his fingers. "And even if he is found out and condemned to drowning, we shall all still be dead. We live for the moment because Croutier's group has no sailors among them, or not many at any rate. Not enough to sail this ship, and no engineers who can fathom out the systems. We're useful. As soon as we are not, off to the One we Ishmalani shall go, helped on our way by a sellsword's bullet, and the rest of the expedition will be spending their afterlife with the Drowned King."

"I've heard of this Croutier," said the Drentz. "He's a blackguard. Done some awful things up in the north. The Oczerks have a large bounty on his head."

Tolpoleznaen grinned. "The One shows us the way to profit. We should keep him alive, and deliver him up to them to boil until he's dead, like they do with his kind of whoreson. We'd be richer, and happier for a fitting vengeance."

"I'd say yes, my friend," said Heffi, squeezing Tolpoleznaen's shoulder. "But the more complications we have, the less likely we are to succeed. I suggest the simplest plan of all."

He looked them all in the eye, one after the other.

"We kill them all."

"I agree," said Toberan. "Say the word."

"It's just you, Toberan," said Godelwind. "Dellion's still sick. Kolskwin's blind."

"I'm better," said Dellion. He was whey faced and thin from whatever ailed him. He wasn't believed.

"And aren't most of you Ishmalani pacifists?" said Godelwind.

"If you hadn't been skulking in Goodfellow Kressind's cabin when they attacked, you would have seen the Ishmalani fight as hard as any islesman," said Toberan.

"I saw only dead men, and a ship in our enemy's hands. You can't kill them all yourself. And you don't have your gun. None of us have any weapons. Croutier's got them."

Heffi stroked his beard. "As much I enjoy lecturing non-believers on their misconceptions about our creed, I don't have time. We are permitted to fight to defend ourselves. Firearms are forbidden us, this is true, but any rule, even one of the Rule of Twenty, may be suspended by the grace of the One should our lives be in danger. We are going to have to fight. Even you, Godelwind. And you Tyn Charvolay."

Charvolay shrugged. "Not the first time I kill, not the last."

"What about the Iron Whisperers?"

Charvolay waggled his head in thought. "Might do, might not. Working close with iron changes them. They have many geas on them to protect them against iron's poison. Spilling blood is often one."

"Bah, it's only two Tyn," said Tolpoleznaen.

"Discount us, would you?" said Charvolay. "Do not. Gelven is dead because of him. There will be a reckoning for that."

Heffi nodded. "Tyn on our side, especially roused, would be good. Can anyone get to Kororsind?"

"Croutier's got him under lock and key," said Drentz. "I'm not surprised. An alchemist on the loose can do a lot of damage on a ship like this."

"That's why we need him," said Heffi. "If not a mage, a magister; if not a magister, give me an alchemist." He spoke a saying gathering popularity in Karsa at that time.

"Can we count on everyone else?" asked Toberan. "Is there any danger someone on the crew will turn on us for reward?" He looked pointedly at Godelwind.

"Unlikely, but not impossible," said Heffi. "I would move cautiously if we had more time. We do not have time. Our friends on the ice do not either. I can see profit for us nevertheless. If we rescue Persin, there will be money in it. The One would approve."

"Now you are singing to my tune," said Tolpoleznaen.

"It will convince the others," said Heffi. "We move to the signal of the fog whistle, given three times, not later than three days hence. Go to your crew mates. Get them organised. Croutier has only twenty-two men; there are nearly a hundred of us. With the favour of the One, and a little sea luck, we'll take back the ship without much loss of life."

The men nodded, and made pledges to do that.

"Now go, before we are missed! Except you Tyn Charvolay. I have an idea that I want you to put to the Iron Whisperers, and I think you're best placed to speak with Kororsind."

The others left one at a time, staging their departures at random intervals to avoid rousing suspicion. When they had gone, Charvolay gave a wicked smile of pointed teeth that shone as brightly as his silver jewellery.

"I'm all ears," he said.

CHAPTER TWENTY-FOUR
The Sisters' Barrens

THE SOUTHERN QUARTER was the largest of the four lands of Farthia, and the poorest. The triple volcano of the Three Sisters ruled. Their regular eruptions rendered a wide swathe of the land uninhabitable eastwards well into Ostria, and extending southwards almost as far as the canyon of the River Olb. The plains were riven with cracks that opened up without warning. Long black lava flows, wrinkled as a dracon's skin and black as burned rubber, extended tongues from every flank of the mountains. Seasonal flooding carved the soft ash covering the landscape into treacherous gullies yards deep.

The Sisters' most violent eruptions were visible in distant Perus, and troubled the weather for seasons afterwards. Such outpourings came seldomly, but the mountains were never quiet. Always fires glowed around the summits. The Earth's destructive industry lit the night skies for leagues, and when the Twin drew near they were at their most violent.

Arkadian Vand watched the landscape slide by. He had travelled the South Farthian road many times, but though the look of the land was familiar its landmarks rarely remained constant for long. The influence of the volcanoes extended far beyond their soaring cones. Their tantrums shook the ground, remaking it with a frustrated artist's energy.

No major outpouring from the mountains had troubled the Sisters' Barrens for two years, and the land, though deadly, was fertile with volcanic ash. For the moment large stretches were patched with vibrant green. Broken-down farmhouses occasionally interrupted the view. Sometimes, Vand saw people farming there. Only the desperate or foolhardy attempted to settle in the Sisters' Barrens. A crop might as easily be swallowed by an ash fall or dragged down overnight into a crevasse as provide abundance. Earthquakes tumbled all but the stoutest buildings. When the mountains spoke, great curls of ash fell from the sky. Molten rock bubbled from sudden fissures, turning grassland to roaring infernos. There were no woodlands. Trees had little chance to grow there. Those that did lived short lives, their charcoaled corpses standing as warnings to other seeds.

Vand had a small, fast carriage to take him to the dig. It conveyed him rapidly but it was cramped, and his knees jostled those of Zeruvias, the fat, rich Guider of Musra who accompanied him. Zeruvias was an ugly man. Beneath a bald pate, his was face marred by a dozen small bumps, and his mouth dragged down by the excessive weight of his jowls. This involuntary expression of lugubrious annoyance suited him. Zeruvias was a haughty man, his pride bolstered by the importance of his position until it had become an inviolable shield.

"They are fools to settle here," said Zeruvias, glowering at a small farmstead. "No man should tempt the wrath of the Sisters."

"Even here things are changing, goodman." Vand pointed out onto the horizon. Large, six-legged dracon-cattle cropped the grass with horned lips, their massive heads backed with frills crowned with broad racks of spines. "Kuzaks from the east. They are canny enough with their beasts to move on when trouble threatens. The Goodfellow Culon of Ostria brought them here, he rents the land from the Farthians. A delicate yet lucrative arrangement. Progress comes in many forms."

Zeruvias' face crinkled with distaste at the talk of money. "An old way that serves them poorly in their homeland. The Kuzaks are backward."

Vand struck his cane upon the carriage floor. "I could not agree more, but an old way wisely applied in a new place is a hallmark of magisterial thinking, my dear Guider Zeruvias."

Light filtered grey through ash clouds made Zeruvias look ill. "You say you bring me here because I am gifted. I am a Guider of the Dead God's True Quarter. I am a mageborn fourth son, and pledged to the service of the dead. It has been said that I am among the most gifted Guiders since the time of Res Iapetus." He said this bitterly, not with pride. "It is a curse. In the course of my duties I have gazed too often through the veil of death. For better or worse, my experiences lead me to think that all the works of men in life are folly."

"What have you seen?" asked Vand curiously.

"I do not see much, none of us do. But I cannot say what I have, you know the law. I would not tell you if I could." He looked back out of the window. "It is best not to know," he added after a moment's thought.

The carriage jounced over a dip in the causeway. Either side of the road a shallow ravine spread out long jagged fingers.

"The repairs are becoming rougher," complained Zeruvias.

"When we are done, you shall be rich enough to buy all this desolation and make them anew. All I require is a little help."

"Guiders own no property," said Zeruvias.

Vand raised his eyebrows at the Guider's large gold rings, his spreading girth, the rich clothing. "Indeed."

"Do not judge me by my appearance. I need distractions more than most," said Zeruvias. "A good life is poor recompense for the horrors of death. Why are you dragging me all the way out here, Vand? Is not Jolyon a good enough Guider for your camp? I recommended my best."

"Jolyon is more than adequate for guiding those who die at the camp," said Vand.

"If there is any issue with his ministry, you must understand any Guider sent here will be kept busy to the point of exhaustion," said Zeruvias. "These are dangerous fields you plough, Vand. Many men die here. Although given your record I doubt that is a matter of concern to you. You spend blood freely."

Vand's mood chilled at this admonishment, though he ensured his smile remained warm. "As I have told you, it is nothing to do with Jolyon. This is a matter of grave import that only a Guider of your ability can deal with. Jolyon is not up to the task, you are.

Indulge me. Stop fishing, dear Guider. You will soon see what I have to show. Do not spoil my surprise."

"I do not see this need for subterfuge."

"I have rivals. I must be careful. Vardeuche Persin has stolen too much from me. I have learnt caution."

The two men fell silent. Zeruvias stared out of the window, sunk into annoyance.

The coach rumbled off the main Farthian way onto the track leading to the site. The dig was just inside the border with Ostria, and well off the main road. Vand had been obliged to build his own access. The road was rough and the ride became uncomfortable. The day wore on, the Three Sisters grew ever larger. They stopped once to let an empty supply wagon coming back from the dig head past them, before heading on and only halting again for the night. They ate a meal in a field of dead grass as dark fell. Throughout the evening Vand had more to say to his coachman than Zeruvias, chatting with him as he unhitched the drays and pegged them out to sleep. Vand and the Guider slept in the coach. Rattling grasses lulled them, though the rhythms brought strange dreams.

Deep in the night a cracking boom startled Vand awake. Zeruvias slept on. The engineer looked out at the Sisters' fires glowing balefully on the horizon. The red light pulsed yellow. A flicker of green volcano lightning sheeted the sky, its thunder quiet. The noise ceased, and Vand was quickly asleep again.

CHAPTER TWENTY-FIVE
Vand and the Machine

VAND WOKE AT the light tap of his coachman on the door. He relieved himself in the cool dawn, his piss steaming onto the ground. Zeruvias slept through their departure. He woke an hour later, as Vand breakfasted on a dry loaf and a round of goat's cheese.

"Sleep of the dead," said Vand.

"The sleep of the dead is considerably less peaceful," said Zeruvias. He smacked his lips and pulled a face. Vand caught a whiff of night breath. He offered the Guider a bottle of scented water. Zeruvias took it gratefully, swilled the water around his mouth and spat it from the window. Vand knocked on the ceiling for the coach to stop that the Guider might toilet. Afterwards, while the coach stood waiting, Zeruvias shared the last of Vand's breakfast, then they cleaned their teeth with powdered floatstone and vinegar. One more stop and many miles saw the volcanoes grow taller and taller, the land blacker. The rare signs of human life vanished altogether. Vegetation retreated to isolated patches, much of it dead. Wrinkled sheets of old lava covered most of the ground. Earth tremors rumbled under the carriage's wheels several times.

The Sisters soared. The lowest was four thousand feet high, the tallest six. The two tallest were so close they touched, a broad saddle valley separating their cones. The third stood four miles apart from the other two. The track veered toward the Lonely Sister, then as she grew to block off the sky, turned again, curving to the southeast around the base of her cone.

"We have passed within the borders of Ostria, though the inhabited marches are many miles that way." Vand pointed between the three volcanoes. "And one hundred and forty miles to the south is the great river Olb. All the land here is waste, and dangerous. And yet there is treasure here worth risking everything for, buried in the shattered floatstone spat out by the Sisters."

Vand timed his speech carefully. As he finished, the coach came to a low rise. On the other side a wide, stepped pit a mile square opened up in the ash. A town of tents was arrayed neatly to the south, divided into quarters with an engineer's fastidiousness. In the centre of each quarter was a large blockhouse cut from the volcanic rock, refuges from eruptions. A ramp led down into the pit from the town of tents. The road skirted the edge of the pit on its way to the ramp. At the top of the ramp a number of guards occupied wooden sentry huts either side of the downward track. Recognising their employer, they waved the coach through.

A scene of great industry greeted them. The pit was cut down into soft rock and compressed ash via a series of steeply edged tiers. The bottommost was five hundred yards on each side. Further pits were sunk into the floor. The bottoms of these were gridded by lines strung from stout wooden markers, strips of fabric tied to them at four foot intervals. Huge tents covered the most important excavations. An engine house belched glimmer-tainted steam from a brick chimney. Long canvas hoses ran from it, splitting at valves that leaked fine mists of pressurised water. The hoses were directed by teams of men at the pits and the walls, jets of water blasting ash away. Other pipes pumped the waste slurry out, carrying it up the levels, finally spraying it over the lips of the pit into a holding dam next to the town. Everywhere men were at work, digging, sifting and spraying. Light dray carts pulled loads of spoil up out of the pit. Everyone there was filthy, grey from head to foot with ash, their nation and race unguessable.

"Here the Morfaan once had a city," said Vand. The coach bumped across the site. Men shouted halloos at the coach. Dogs barked. The noise was oppressive. "It was buried long since by the fury of the Sisters. Much of it is crushed, burned, destroyed beyond recognition. But not all. After the incident at Thrusea I invested most of my remaining funds here. I had a feeling that I may discover something. A good engineer never dismisses his intuition, Guider. It is good that I did not, for I have found a great deal. Within a month we had uncovered the map that revealed the location of the city in the Sotherwinter which Trassan Kressind, on a ship of my design, is currently exploring. When he returns I will be greatly enriched. I would have been content with that, but then I found something else." The coach came to a halt before the canvas wall of one of the largest tents. It was vast, its roof held up by a dozen masts.

"That object is within this marquee. I wish to ask your advice on it. That is why I have brought you here."

The coachman opened the doors and the men got out. Two workmen, filthy as the rest, held open a flap in the canvas and bowed as Vand strode through into a room partitioned by walls made of more canvas. Inside were rows of what appeared to be crude plaster statues, fine in proportion but seemingly unfinished, each tagged with a numbered orange card.

Zeruvias faltered as he stepped through the door.

"The wall between the worlds is thin here," he gasped. A servant in clean livery came to him and offered him a glass of wine from a silver tray. Zeruvias took it gratefully and gulped it down. Vand took one of water.

"These are the dead," said Zeruvias.

"Yes," Vand tapped one of the figures on the shoulder. "Morfaan, entombed by a fall of ash. We found many odd cavities on the site. My hypothesis was that the cavities were left by the bodies of the dead, so we poured plaster into them. Naturally, I was correct."

The statues were dirty grey, many in attitudes of fear or agony, arms thrown across faces, hands gripping heads. Several had strange stubs halfway down their torsos. Zeruvias stopped by one and looked closely.

"Are you sure these are Morfaan? These ones have four arms." Zeruvias pointed at small limbs. There were several with the additional limbs. On figures that seemed female they were tiny, on the males they were large enough to be useful.

"All of the figures had them. They are delicate, and broke off on several."

"I have never seen an image of a Morfaan with them," said Zeruvias.

"I have come to believe their art was stylised, and that they omitted their lesser limbs for some aesthetic reason. Puts you in mind of a riding dracon, doesn't it?" said Vand. "I hear in the duel in Perus where the male was recently wounded, that he revealed a pair of lesser arms, and that he wielded daggers in them. It did him no good against Kyreen Asteria."

Zeruvias stopped by a mass of plaster. Close inspection revealed it to be a mother sheltering two small children with her body. A hint of the terrified expression on one child had been preserved. Zeruvias recoiled. "A gruesome find."

"I expected you to be fascinated. Are you not?" Vand bent down to peer into the face of the dead mother. "It is a glimpse back into ages unknown. Can you feel their spirits?"

Tentatively Zeruvias rested a hand on one of the statues, its arm was flung up to shield its long face. The detail was poorly rendered by the natural mould, but the gaping scream of its mouth was clear. He shuddered and withdrew his hand. "Some ghosts linger, weak with time but I would be careful."

"Can you remove them?"

"They are not human, Goodman Vand," said Zeruvias. "The task is beyond the Guiders. I know not where the dead of the Morfaan go."

"No matter. They have been no trouble," said Vand.

"I apologise I cannot be of more help, if that is what you called me here to see." Zeruvias wiped his forehead. "Please, I wish to leave."

"This is not what I brought you to see, Guider," said Vand. He gestured with his cane to a canvas door. "This way!" he said. Vand's men undid toggles, and held the flaps open to reveal a much bigger space.

A sheer-sided pit opened on the far side, shovel marks fresh in ash walls twenty feet deep. Planks of wood braced against the walls held the pit open, and scaffolding provided a catwalk over the cavity. Vand led Zeruvias out onto the walk. Below, men diligently scraped at the ash with trowels and brushes. Broken walls criss-crossed the pit, their decoration and mouldings preserved as shattered jigsaw puzzles. Upon the glassy walls that stood tall enough, reliefs of Morfaan were visible.

"It is... magnificent!" said Zeruvias.

"All historically very important," agreed Vand. "But this also is not what I have to show you." He could not keep the excitement from his voice. They crossed a tall wall and reached the centre of the dig. Vand pointed down. "This is."

A pair of dark glass eyes gazed up at them from a huge, stylised, silver alien face half buried in the ash. The head it adorned was as large as a coach. The nose was fine and long, with a septum that extended almost as far as the upper lip, the eyes far larger than those of a man, the lips very full, the forehead high and narrow. Beauty was inherent to the features, albeit not of a human kind. Age had not touched the effigy. The incredible alloys of the Morfaan did not tarnish, and the metal gleamed as if freshly polished.

"We took it for a statue, at first," said Vand. "The legs remain buried, but my men will soon have the whole body uncovered."

Vand was gratified to see Zeruvias gape at the figure. From the crown of its head to the point where its thighs disappeared into the wall of the pit it was thirty yards long. It lay on its back, one arm trapped beneath its back, the other flung out. In an articulated fist it clutched a lump of iron bigger than a Torosan godling. This lesser figure was so corroded its humanoid form was not immediately obvious. Another iron figure clung to the side, arms and legs gripping the fluted armour cladding the figure. That, though scabrous and flaking, retained visible arms and legs.

Zeruvias looked up, his jowly face slack. "What is it?"

Vand smiled with pleasure. "It is a machine, goodguider. A machine. See!" he came to Zeruvias' side and pointed with his cane past the figure. The wall of the pit behind was of white masonry. "There. The city wall, I think, twenty feet tall, and I believe reduced from its full height. Twelve feet thick at the base. This machine fell upon it." Vand pointed out hints of a bed of rubble that the device sprawled upon. "There are no joins to it, like at the Glass Fort at the gates of the world, and this material is strong! I cannot break it, but this machine did."

Vand descended a ladder. The scaffold shook. "Come!" he called from the ladder's foot. "It is quite safe."

Zeruvias followed. Three men waited at the bottom, stern-faced academics as dirty as the workmen. Only slightly cleaner was Guider Jolyon, pale and tired looking in his grey robes. His greasy tonsure was clogged with ash and his nostrils sported sooty stains beneath.

"Jolyon?" said Zeruvias.

"Lord Guider," said Jolyon.

"And this?" said Zeruvias, indicating the rusted iron creatures clinging to the Morfaan machine. "They are macabre."

"We have found several dozen," said Vand. "The work is not Morfaan. I suspect they are also some sort of machine. I have not yet discerned how they were articulated. I thought at first that the joints had rusted closed owing to water seeping into the ground. But they have none. We sawed one of those we found in the streets open. It was completely hollow inside. If it were a machine, I can see no method by which it could be made to work, but it also does not strike me as a statue. Tell me, Zeruvias, how does it look to you?"

"As if they were fighting," said Zeruvias.

"Precisely," said Vand, stabbing his cane into the ash. "There are signs of battle all over this city. We have excavated only a portion, but the traces of fire and collapse are all around to see."

"Could that not be caused by the eruption?"

"I thought so, but now I do not," said Vand. "The signs are quite different, you see. The buildings that were intact have collapsed roofs due to the weight of the ash upon them, but are otherwise undamaged. Other buildings are holed, as if by cannon fire, and the outer wall is damaged. The destruction came before, not after."

"It is not a coincidence, a battle and a volcanic event at the same time?" said Zeruvias. "These could be idols. This could be some elaborate Morfaan art."

"I do not think so. Think instead on the implications of that coincidence between eruption and war," said Vand. "Why would anyone build so close to the volcanoes?"

"I have no clue, goodman."

"Think!" said Vand.

"Are you saying that the volcanoes were not here?" said Zeruvias.

"Volcanic eruption as a method of waging war!" Vand exclaimed excitedly.

Zeruvias looked askance at the machine. "Nonsense. Not even the Morfaan had that kind of power."

Vand shrugged. "Perhaps too fanciful. But as you said, the Morfaan were not human. I expect to have answers soon enough. There is a library here," said Vand. He fished out his watch chain. The fob was fashioned from a ball of bright silver, half an inch in diameter. "You are familiar with the term 'Morfaan silver'?"

"Of course," said Zeruvias. "You have a piece there."

"I do," said Vand. He played with the silver as he talked. "It is completely pure. For centuries men have searched it out. Unearthed troves of it have fuelled wars and built temples." Vand stamped his cane again upon the ground, the ferrule grinding on the gritty ash. "Our ancestors never guessed the true value of it. I confess that I was drawn to the reports of this place in the hope of digging up plenty for myself. But curiosity led me to examine what I found with more care. You see the patterns of course?"

"Of course," said Zeruvias.

"I discovered that on each orb is inscribed a series of microscopic lines, beside and within the visible lines, invisible to the naked eye. Only modern optical equipment, and I used the very finest lenses, allow us to see them. I began to consider what these lines might mean. I had them further examined. I discovered that the lines are not of uniform depth, but made up of thousands of tiny indentations. Now, I wondered, why would anyone, Morfaan or man, go to such effort for something that cannot be seen?" As often when feeling pleased with himself, Vand lectured. To his associates' regret, it was his favoured form of discourse. "It was then that I realised that they may be a sort of book."

"Were you correct?"

"I was!" said Vand, delighted at his own genius. "No book of any kind has ever been found in a Morfaan site. Paper does not last, of course, but think on the multiplicity of tomes that exist in the Kingdoms. Where are the holy books of the Morfaan? The paper and skin of their pages will be gone, but their metal casings, the fittings, jewels, scroll tubes, the shelves, even, to house them would remain. Where is all the paraphernalia associated with knowledge? Surely, they must have had some way of recording their wisdom. Signs of that should survive when the books themselves do not. Instead we find Morfaan silver, nestling in its casings snugly as a goodlady's jewellery. That led my thinking on. Maybe they had some other manner of storing their thoughts than the written word. Their culture was an ancient one, blessed with an insight beyond ours. How did they pass it on?" Vand held up his fob. His eyes gleamed fanatically. "The silver! Silver is the metal of magic, sympathetic to the workings of will. Mages have used it for millennia, the magisters make much use of it in their enchantments and their mechanisms. Even I, in the *Prince Alfra* and in many other areas employ it in my devices. The Morfaan wielded magic well. These spheres have purpose." He snatched up the fob to hold it between finger and thumb. "And therefore I divined that there must be some device to enable these baubles to be read, if I were correct." He clenched his fist around the fob.

"And is there?" asked Zeruvias.

Vand nodded to one of the waiting men. From under a cloth he produced a mangled metal construct. A box, featureless but for the dents and scratches on the surface. A pair of mangled, horn-like protrusions graced the back. Though the device was damaged, the bright metal was the same as all Morfaan steel artefacts, undimmed by its immense age. Vand took the device, held it up, and pressed the sphere into a cavity at the base. It slotted home with a soft click.

"I am often correct," said Vand. "Alas, my magisters are as bereft of ideas as I am as to how this item functioned. It is ruined beyond repair in any case. My hope is that Trassan Kressind will find an undamaged example and bring it home from the south. But I rarely limit myself to a single line of inquiry. Failure waits at the end of so many ventures." He did not reveal that he feared Trassan's expedition already lost. Vand held his secrets more closely than a gambler holds his cards.

Vand turned and held out his hand to the head of the fallen Morfaan figure.

"This machine, however, does work. My magisters investigated it thoroughly. There is a power source in there, dormant, but stable. And they detected signs of an... animus, shall we say? They duly withdrew, for spiritual matters are not within their area of expertise. That is when I asked Jolyon to investigate."

"You did?" Zeruvias asked Jolyon.

"I did, Lord Guider," began Jolyon. "But... Please, do not touch it."

Jolyon's manner concerned Zeruvias. "What did you have him do, Vand?" he demanded.

"Only what I am going to ask you to do. I wish you to contact the spirit my magisters and your own Jolyon here say reside in the machine."

"Impossible."

Vand gave him a wolfish smile, and stepped back. "I think not. Jolyon had some success. All he lacks is your talent, goodguider."

Zeruvias puffed up at the praise. "Well, it is true I have some ability that others lack."

"Don't do it, Lord Guider," said Jolyon.

"Leave us," Vand ordered. His men climbed the ladder without word. The sounds of labour ceased, and all over the pit men were called from their work. Jolyon hesitated.

"You too, Jolyon," said Vand.

Jolyon looked to Zeruvias.

"Do as he asks, Guider," said Zeruvias. "If Vand will speak with me privately, then I will allow it. I will get to the bottom of this, you have my word, and I shall demand recompense for any abuses made of your position or your person."

"As you wish." Jolyon bowed. "But don't touch it." With a worried backward glance, he climbed out of the pit.

"Jolyon is coming back with me," said Zeruvias when they were alone. "I will not allow you to misuse the servants of the dead. Look at the state of him, the poor man's exhausted."

"That is your prerogative," said Vand nonchalantly.

Zeruvias lifted his chin high. "We will see how many men wish to stay in this perilous place when there is no one to guide their soul safely from the world."

Loud bangs penetrated the canvas of the tent. The clatter of picks and shovels on rocks outside sounded faintly, but they could not hear any word spoken save their own. The men stared at each other, weighing the other's intentions.

"I will pay you ten thousand thalers," said Vand. "If you do as I ask."

Zeruvias contrived to look shocked. "Outrageous! A Guider is not to be bought! In this irreligious age, ours is the last sacred task." He held up his hand. "I cannot. I cannot!"

"Twenty thousand," said Vand. He stepped close in to the Guider. Zeruvias looked to the floor, but Vand followed him, bending down to look into his face, trapping him with his eyes. "Do you think I asked you by accident, Zeruvias? There are others are gifted as you. Not many, to be sure, but there are several of equal and greater talent. There are not, however, many Guiders who like to live the high life you enjoy. I have many of my own talents. One of those is to know who might be useful to me. You piqued my interest. Why does this man bury himself in pleasures of the flesh when the secrets of the afterlife are known to him? You came here because you suspected you might gain from it."

Zeruvias made a choked sound and stepped back.

"What if I did?" he hissed.

"You are frightened by what you have seen. Wine, money, women. They are your solace."

"Please, please!" said Zeruvias forcefully. "Do not. It is too much. The things I have seen there, on the other side. I deserve my distractions."

"There are no heavens, no opportunity of peace after death?" said Vand. He attempted to remain unmoved, but Zeruvias' revelation made him uneasy.

"Yes, yes there are those places. It is the souls who do not see the way, the ones we do not find, those we fail to guide... It is their fate that weighs on me. I will not add the hells of another race to those of our own. I am burdened enough."

"Terrible things?"

"More terrible than you know!" gasped Zeruvias.

"Tell me. A burden shared, is a burden halved."

"I cannot." He suddenly looked Vand in the face. "There are those in my order who fear something is amiss. It is all going wrong. It—" He looked behind him, eyes wild, suddenly aware of what he was saying. "No. No. I will not tell you." He cowered. Vand saw the weakling behind the facade. It was all he could do to hide his disgust.

"Then do not. Instead allow me to help you take comfort in this life. I have the money here, in my offices. You may take it away with you today. Or if you prefer, I will give you a promissory note and you may withdraw it from my bank in the Kingdoms. My notaries are forewarned and will give you no difficulty. How many warm bodies and pints of wine could you buy with that money, Zeruvias? How many good meals, eh?" He poked the Guider in the belly sharply.

"No, no please, I can't."

"Twenty-five thousand. And a stipend of one thousand per year, every year, for the rest of your life, should you discover what I need to know."

Zeruvias glanced up. He licked his lips. His hands were trembling, his posture was cowed, but he did not refuse again.

Vand was encouraged. "A short service. Talk to the ghost in the machine. Reveal its secrets to me, and you are free to go, and go rich." Sure his fish was hooked, Vand leaned on his cane. "What do you say?"

Zeruvias swallowed hard. "Twenty-five thousand? A thousand a year?"

"In cold, hard cash. Guaranteed."

The Guider remained half-crouched, trapped by indecision.

Vand waited for the moment for the subtle shift in Zeruvias' posture that would tell him he'd won. It duly came. The Guider stood tall. He regained some of his composure, and smoothed out his robe. "It would be a shame not to know the secrets of the ancients."

"Think how much we might learn! If we learn all the Morfaan knew, we might even aid the dead better. You are but doing your duty."

"Yes, I am. It is incumbent on me to do this. It is the right thing."

Gently, Vand took the Guider by the arm and led him to machine's long, alien face. "Here, I think."

Zeruvias nodded. He lifted his arms and placed his hands upon a cool metal cheek.

"There is a presence in here, very old, very angry." He closed his eyes.

"Can you talk with it?"

Zeruvias' face shifted in concentration. "I cannot find a form in it, its language is not ours. It is trying to talk, but it cannot make me understand. I sense frustration."

A rising hum came from the device. Zeruvias, deep into his guiding, did not hear. Vand stepped back, looking up and down the length of the giant figure. Nothing externally had changed, the noise came from within.

"Yes, yes, I can hear it now. It changes language. Wait, no, no! No, stop!" Zeruvias pulled back, but his hands were stuck fast to the metal. His eyes still closed, he writhed and keened, an inhuman noise that had the hairs on Vand's neck standing on end. An internal voice urged him to go to the Guider's aid, but it was small and easily quelled.

"What does it say?" urged Vand.

"It... it will not talk to me. It is trying to talk through me! It is in me!" Zeruvias screamed. The machine droned higher, thrumming the air; the pulsing reached a sympathetic frequency with the jelly of his eyes. Vand screwed them tight against the pain and took three faltering steps backwards.

Zeruvias went rigid. His hands still pressed to the metal, he turned his head as far as it would go. Muscles bulged in his neck, his face went red. The Guider let out a helpless gasp, and his spine dislocated with a series of three meaty pops. The head rotated around until he faced Vand, his eyes wide, the pupils dilated so far the iris was crushed to a hair's breadth.

The vibration stopped. A great, booming beat, like a pulse greatly amplified, shook the pit. Vand opened his eyes.

"I am awakened," said Zeruvias. His jaw was slack, the voice not his own. The words were High Maceriyan, but only just, a form of the language older than history.

"Yes, yes!" said Vand. "Speak with me!"

The machine spoke again. This time Vand struggled to understand the archaic dialect against the pounding of the machine's heart.

"You need a something... what?" he shouted.

The machine spoke for a third time. It ran through a dozen words, enunciating them clearly and individually. Vand understood none of them. "Pilot," it finally said. "Bring me a pilot."

"A pilot?" said Vand, he did not understand. "How will a boat's pilot help?"

"Will and Form, in balance," continued the voice. "Find this in one young. Bind them to me. Bring me to life."

Zeruvias made a strangled noise and fell to the ground, dead. The pounding diminished to a whine, and faded.

Vand's ears rang in the quiet. "Come back!" he shouted. "Explain!"

He ran over to the figure's head and rapped hard upon the metal with his cane. He expected the ring of a hollow cavity, instead he heard a clocking as solid as that from an iron bar.

Men were coming back into the tent, peering down at the scene.

"Get the physic!" shouted Vand. "And get off the walk! There are too many of you. You'll collapse it!" He knelt by the dead Guider. Smoke wisped from Zeruvias' ears. An expression of unalloyed horror was his last gift to the world.

Jolyon pushed through the men backing away from the edge and came down the ladder. He shoved Vand aside and cradled Zeruvias' flopping head in his hands. He shut his eyes and whispered out a hurried Guider's cant. He stopped, and stared down at his dead superior, then looked at Vand.

"What have you done?" he said.

"Nothing. He touched the machine, then this—"

"His spirit has fled. I was too late to guide him. I have no way of knowing if he made the transition correctly. This place, it is thronged with the dead! It is perilous to pass here, and I cannot see what became of him!" Jolyon stood shakily. "You must leave this machine alone!"

"Absolutely not," said Vand.

"It is cursed." Jolyon looked at the alien face. "It has you in its thrall! Clear this site, take your men from here, you are tampering with forces beyond the knowledge of any man. Begone, or pay the consequences."

Vand held his cane across his chest with both hands. "Steady, Guider."

Jolyon advanced on him, his fists clenching.

A hiss had them turn. A clunk of drawn bolts followed. The cheeks of the machine popped out an inch, opening either side of the nose. Foul air rushed out, causing Vand and Jolyon to gag. A mechanism purred inside. Vand's men shouted in alarm.

The face of the machine parted. The cheeks opened further outward. The right stopped a quarter way, something grinding within the head halted its progress, but the left swung smoothly down, revealing a dark interior.

Vand put a handkerchief to his nose and approached cautiously, ignoring the warnings of his men. He ducked his head inside, then jerked back as a seat of ivory and woven sinews spilled from within. A tangle of bones wrapped in a golden costume fell from the cradle, hitting the floor by Vand's feet.

"A body," whispered Vand. He looked at the skull and frowned. "Human bones."

Jolyon was driven forward by his concern for the dead. He knelt and laid careful hands on the jumbled skeleton, unfolding the clothes so that it lay flat. Respectfully, he lifted the skull and placed it at the head of the body. The sutures in the skull were not fully bonded. "It is a child," he said.

"Will and Form," said Vand to himself. He looked again inside. The interior was completely dark, but the seat hung out into the light filtering through the tent's fabric. A mesh of silver could be a skullcap, wands of ivory could be control levers. He understood none of it. It enthralled him.

"A pilot," Vand whispered.

Jolyon looked up from the dead child accusingly. Vand looked back. Destiny had them rocking on a fulcrum so finely balanced Vand felt the world shift as seesawed between differing paths. Vand determined then and there that he would find a pilot for the machine, and he knew with utmost certainty that Jolyon would stop at nothing to prevent that from happening.

He looked to his foreman on the walkway above.

"Clear this away, carefully! I want it examined," he ordered. "Then back to work!"

The Guider stared at him.

"Leave," Jolyon said.

"Absolutely not," replied Vand.

Something would have to be done about Jolyon.

CHAPTER TWENTY-SIX
The Sea Dragons

ON THE FINAL DAY of Gannever, the sleds crossed the last of the hills and began their descent toward the shore. Eustache Antoninan stood tall and shouted behind him to the rest of the party.

"Sea Drays Bay!" he cried. "Sea Drays Bay!"

The dogs howled joyously and the men permitted themselves to smile. Under sunny skies, the sleds coasted down long, smooth banks of snow towards the ocean.

The beach was a mix of pebbled stretches and dark sand. Low dunes, sparsely covered with hardy grass, divided littoral from land. Through piles of layered ice stacked up by successive great tides the sea was visible, cold and blue under a cloudless sky. Torrents of water bubbled from the grounded ice banks, rattling the cobbles of the shore loudly on their way to the waves. The world contained by the bay was tinted black and white and shades of pure blue, a beautiful vista that stretched along a perfect crescent for ten miles. Two imposing headlands marched from the hills into the

sea, holding off from the shore the great wall of ice
that circled the Sotherwinter. The ice that had barred
the landing of the *Prince Alfra* only a few weeks before
was breaking apart, forming a drifting maze of bergs
that thunderously ground into each other, stranding
their fellows upon the reefs of black rock strung out
between the headlands. The beginning of a major tide
was in play, and as the water pushed itself through the
ice wall foam sprayed high. But though tempestuous at
the entrance, the rising waters quickly smoothed inside
the bay, and only wavelets broke on the beach.

The dogs ran to keep ahead of the sleds, and the
party shot down toward its goal exhilaratingly fast.
Ilona laughed with joy. Even Tyn Rulsy, pressed into
her side against the cold, smiled.

There was no need to apply the sled brakes. The
slope was gentle and levelled off long before the dogs
were overtaken by their loads; soon they were pulling
again, the snow rasping under the sled runners.

"To the east, Valatrice!" Antoninan called. He
pointed toward a group of square shapes clustered
around the base of a massive boulder, alone on a stretch
of rocky ground between the beach and the dunes.

Wordlessly, Valatrice obeyed. He adjusted his
course, and the rest followed him. The boulder grew
improbably huge. There was nothing else like it in
the bay, it was as if a giant had carved off part of a
hill preparatory to making an immense sculpture, but
been called away before he could commence his work.
Ilona watched as the shapes at its feet grew and took
on details of their own. Stiff tarpaulins covered piles
of supplies. Ice-caked ropes held them in place. Several
of the coverings had torn free in winter storms, and

quivered in the sea breeze, revealing stores of timber and wooden crates, lashed together with yet more rope.

By the time the sleds came to a halt by the stores, the dogs were panting happily. Long pink tongues hung like wet flags from their jaws. A whistle from Antoninan's groom, and they collapsed into the snow, revelling in cold that would chill a man to death.

Antoninan jumped down from the halted sled. He selected four men; always, Ilona had noticed, he chose from a mixture of Trassan's and Persin's group. At his direction they made for the crates. The rest of the party clambered to the ground and worked out stiff limbs and clapped together cold hands. They talked cheerfully, the two groups united in their relief at reaching the bay.

Ilona shouldered her rifle, took Tyn Rulsy's hand in her own and followed the polar explorer.

In the shade of the boxes it was cold. Antoninan was busy inspecting his supplies, calling out orders in his native Low Maceriyan. Axes cut ropes that shattered more than broke. Crates were dragged out.

"He is an impressive leader, isn't he?"

Persin's voice at her elbow took Ilona by surprise. He walked softly for such a large man. The supplies were located well past the highest tide marks, where ocean rounded pebbles gave way to rougher, ice shattered rock, and yet he made no sound when he approached.

"To tell you the truth, I wish I had such a facility with others. There is something inspiring about him. He is a national hero at home in Maceriya, and rightfully so." Without thinking, Persin reached out and ruffled Tyn Rulsy's hood. She growled at him.

"Charming," said Persin uneasily.

Bannord strode past. "Come on soldier," he said to Ilona. "No hanging about. There's work to do."

"Excuse me," she said.

"Of course," said Persin with a small bow.

Ilona caught up with Bannord, Rulsy trotted behind.

"Thank you for that," she said. "I find him unctuous. I would despise him even had he not killed my cousin."

"The man's a prick," said Bannord brightly. "A nasty, envious, foreign prick. Still, we're all in this together. Best be nice. We can kill him later. Hey! Antoninan! How goes it?"

Antoninan turned gleefully to Bannord. Ilona had never seen him so happy.

"Lieutenant!" he said. "My cache here has weathered the past two winters well. We should be able to discard some of our less useful assets and collect better tents, food and other necessities. There is much in these stores one needs to survive in these environs, although not so much as I stocked the holds of the *Prince Alfra* with, regrettably."

"The tide is high," said Bannord, nodding at the gentle waves washing the shore. They were not due a great tide, whose limit was delineated by yet more blocks of shattered ice a hundred yards further toward the sea. "This a is a major tide coming in now, but should it come so far in?"

"My guess is the normal run of tides is being thrown off by the nearing Twin," said Antoninan.

"Maybe," said Bannord.

A group of men were pulling out long boxes, taking out the tents from within and checking them. A cheer went up as Ranost pulled out a clinking crate, pried off the lid, and pulled out a bottle of Maceriyan apple brandy.

"You have brandy. Is there any food?" said Bannord.

"There is not," said Antoninan. "It would keep well in these temperatures, but it is my custom to feast with the men before we return and use up our remaining supplies. The sea drays are inquisitive and hungry. They break open the stores if there is the faintest whiff of sustenance. I have seen them bite through sealed tins to get at the contents. If I had left so much as a ship's biscuit here, all you see would have been scattered about the beach."

"So a hunting party then," said Bannord. "We're going to have to move quickly. The men are quite well rested after that last run of snow." He looked at the sky. "We should set out immediately to find meat. The better prepared we are to run if we have to, the happier we will be."

"You insist on making camp here," said Antoninan off-handedly.

"I do. We will wait here as long as we can. I will not brave this passage that might not exist if we can sail out of here in comfort."

"The *Prince Alfra* is lost to us. The Draathis still pursue us." Antoninan pointed to the west. The party had drawn well ahead of the enemy. The steam marking the enemy's progress had diminished to a thread, finally disappearing over the horizon a few days before.

Bannord signed and kicked at the loose stone.

"Antoninan, we have talked about this. The expedition council has voted to wait, so we will wait. We need to gather food anyway. If we don't, we'll surely starve seeking out this route of yours."

Antoninan made a show of not paying much attention to Bannord, exerting his authority by directing the men in their unloading.

"Antoninan!" said Bannord, riled.

"Yes, yes." He finally deigned to look to Bannord. "There is a large colony of sea drays at the end of the bay. Naturally, their presence is one of the things that makes this site so attractive. A sheltered anchorage, often free of ice, herds of animals to hunt. All these factors determined my selection of it for my base of operations many times." He nodded, pleased with himself. He had discovered the bay. He did not need to remind the others of it again. "It is a shame the ice prevented our landing here."

"Then I shall get together a group of men and go now. How many sea drays should we take?"

"Five should be enough to feed us for a week. You will only need one sled that way. In my years here, we have ridden back upon the meat. Stay close to the edge of the colony. Pick off those that are isolated. The sea drays will not stray far from the edge of their territory. If you venture too deeply within, they will turn on you. We have no zoologist with us, but those I employed before tell me this herding is common in animals who rely on safety in numbers; it can be exploited, if you make sure it does not work against you."

"Safety from what?" asked Bannord with a half laugh. "Iron monsters?"

"Answers to questions like that are why people like me come to places like this, my friend. At the moment, I cannot say. It is a glorious mystery, like all this marvellous continent. You can be sure that where there is such a high number of prey, there will be predators"

"So we might not be the only ones with meat on our minds," said Bannord.

"I have seen nothing but drays in the bay. Here though, nothing is certain. Be on your guard."

Bannord and Ilona left Antoninan to reorder their supplies. Bannord tapped her on the shoulder, and leaned in close.

"He was a miserable bastard on the boat," said Bannord quietly. "Now look at him."

Ilona glanced back.

"You know what I think?" continued Bannord. "I think he's enjoying this far too much."

"Darrasind, Forfeth, Aretimus, you're with me. Corporal Ranost, keep this rabble occupied while I'm out. Make sure the children play nice and," he added conspiratorially, "don't let Antoninan's ego crush anyone." He clapped his hands together hard. "I need volunteers, a hunting party. Who is for it?"

"I have hunted many beasts in the forests of the Olberlands," said Crut.

"You're a very talented man, Crut," said Bannord. Crut executed a clipped, Olberlander's bow. "You're coming."

They were all speaking Maceriyan, for the benefit of those in Persin's party who knew no Karsarin. Bannord's grasp of the language was cheerfully incorrect, but good enough.

"I will come, mesire," said Favreau.

"I'll come too," said Jeuney.

"Well done. Now I need drays."

"I go," said Labarr, the larger of Persin's two Sorkosan pack leaders. He growled his words so much less beautifully than Valatrice spoke.

Valatrice rose up and stretched languidly, displaying the full length of his enormous body for all to see.

"Then I too will come," he said.

"No need, two leaders," grumbled Labarr.

"I desire to hunt."

The hackles on Labarr's back rose.

"We can both go," said Valatrice. "You and I. We shall have a contest, and see who hunts the best."

"Right, fine," said Bannord. "We need two sleds anyway, one for us and the other for our kills."

"Antoninan said we should take one sled," said Ilona.

"Antoninan can go fuck himself," said Bannord. "He's not going to be happy anyway, with his prize pup coming with us, I'll wager. So what's a few more dogs?"

Labarr curled his lip and slunk off to his own pack. Unlike the leaders, the other drays had been pegged out. Morsia, the third leader dog, lay in the snow, her white coat camouflaging her perfectly. She was smaller than the males, but wiser. Her tongue lolled in amusement at the others' behaviour.

Antoninan was unhappy about Valatrice's inclusion, and displeased with Bannord taking two sleds, but would not argue with his dog or with Bannord in front of the expedition.

Persin sat apart while the hunting party prepared, the satchel on his knees. Neither Bannord nor Antoninan wished for his help, and he poked at stones with a plank of wood taken from a crate until, with a final jab, he stood, and made his way over.

"Balls," said Bannord under his breath. "He wants to come with us too."

Persin called one of his mercenaries to him, and after a brief argument, relieved him of his gun, swapping it with the satchel.

"I can shoot," said Persin.

"It looks like you can eat too," said Bannord, with a look at Persin's gut.

Persin's face hardened. "This expedition would be far more pleasant if we were polite with each other, mesire."

"I'll settle for surviving. If you're coming, fine. Don't expect me to be your very best friend."

They harnessed the dogs. Ilona helped Antoninan's groom, Gestane, put on their tackle.

"The sea drays are like dogs," said Ilona to Valatrice. "Does it not trouble you?"

"Not at all," he replied. "I have eaten them many times before. They are not drays, but of the dracon-kind. Their coats look like fur, but they are made of feathers. They resemble we dogs superficially, but it is coincidence. I have no compunction at killing them at all. And, my little stowaway, you should know, I would have no issue in eating my colleagues here, were they dead. And no issue in eating you either, if the situation called for it. No offence meant."

"None taken," said Ilona, though she looked at the dog with fresh eyes.

Valatrice's long mouth grinned.

"But only if you were dead."

"WELL WOULD YOU look at that," said Bannord

The hunting party headed away from the sea a little and approached the sea dray rookery from the landward side in order to scout the ground. The hills were higher toward the headland, and they looked down from a hundred feet or so onto their quarry.

Thousands of sea drays roosted at the northern end of the bay, nesting on conical piles of rocks the height of Ilona's waist. They were large animals, half the size of a dray dog, with glossy black coats and pointed, whiskery faces. Valatrice's assertion that they were a type of dracon was clear enough. They had six flippers. The two forward pairs were muscular, and allowed them to walk in a clumsy fashion. The rear pair pointed backwards, and they carried these off the ground, almost like a tail.

Sea drays came and went from the ocean half a mile from the rookery. They looked to be taking advantage of the major tide to bring as much fish as they could up to their brooding partners, dropping mouthfuls of it in piles to be consumed later. Nearly every nest had a dray atop it. They never left their perches, but when they moved a flash of pale blue betrayed the presence of eggs. Dracon-skuas screeched above, hovering for a few seconds then darting away, on the lookout for exposed eggs. Those that came too close to the nesting creatures were chasing off by bared teeth and angry barking.

"Look there, lieutenant," said Crut. "We should go back down and attack from the ocean. These are sea creatures, they will run for the water. If we come at them from the sea, they will be panicked and be easier prey." He pointed to a towering lump of ice in the process of being sculpted out of existence by the sun. It chilled its surroundings, allowing a patch of snow some hundred yards across to persist around it. "There is snow there. We can run the sleds over the sand dunes right to it. It is perfect. The wind is blowing toward it, they will not smell us, and we can load our kills easily once we are done. We can make this easy for ourselves."

"Everyone agree?" Bannord asked. No one objected, and so they came from the hills and down onto the sand. The dogs strained at the increased friction, but they were back on snow soon enough, coming at the sea drays from the southwest.

They untethered the dogs. Men and drays fanned out. Ilona was close by Ardovani and Darrasind, who, following his drunken pass at her on the ship, still found it hard to look her in the eye.

She took position behind an abandoned nest, right at the edge of the rookery. The pebbles were roughly stacked and cemented together with droppings, so it stank. Feathers lined the bottom. Inside were broken eggshells, their white insides smeared with blood dried black. It was built far out from the rest, perhaps a young dray's first, unsuccessful attempt at parenthood. The drays at the periphery of the rookery seemed smaller than the ones nearer the middle.

Valatrice and Labarr led their packs past the ice block to the water. The hunters were completely silent. Darrasind leaned against a tumbled nest. Apart from his back and hooded head, Ilona saw none of the others. She could have been all alone.

The honking barks of the sea drays was a physical wall ahead of her. Their stink cloyed her throat. Small black flies buzzed around, feasting on the guano cement. This was the sea drays' world, not hers.

For several tense minutes they lay in wait.

Howling broke the calm, and uproar reigned.

Ilona stood up. Men appeared from their hiding places. The sea drays barking became deafening. Pebbles clattered as they slipped off their nests. A black ripple emanated from the hunting ground as the sea drays fled in slithering stampede. The sea was white with the entry of so many bodies into the water, but the dogs came barking and snapping up from the ocean, turning many about. Several large males attacked the dogs. Valatrice led the fight back. Canine bodies tumbled over slick, black, sea drays. The ferocity of their battle was awe inspiring. Such energy unleashed. Their warring knocked down nests. Blood, feathers and fur flew everywhere. The sea drays ran from the dogs. The dogs pulled down stragglers, and tore out their throats. Many came toward the men's position. Now was the time to act.

"Fire!" bellowed Bannord.

It seemed an age had passed, but only seconds had. The sea drays stampeded. Nests tumbled. Dracon-skuas cried and dove, spearing abandoned eggs with long beaks.

Gunfire intruded into the contest of tooth and claw. Ilona drew a bead on a sea dray surging toward her. It was magnificent. Muscles rippled under protective fat.

A single shot made it still. The men were all firing. Only Ardovani restrained himself, his weapon too powerful for hunting. He came, he said, to offer protection. Ilona thought he did not want her to spend time alone with Bannord.

"Cease firing!" shouted Bannord.

The sea drays were calming. Those further away followed nature's cold calculations and remained atop their nests, seeing no danger to themselves. The ones driven off into the sea bobbed about in the low swell, baying mournfully as the dracon-skuas pecked into their young.

Several score of nests were vacant. The eggs would freeze. Already Bannord was calling Valatrice back from his kill, getting the dogs ready to haul the dead sea drays away from the colony to where they might be safely butchered. Nine were dead. Hundreds of eggs would fail so they could eat. Ilona was saddened. All her life she had read of these places, but now she despoiled them.

A frantic honking came from the sea, and the sea drays were suddenly returning to land, swimming so fast they jumped out of the waves and landed awkwardly upon the rock. At first Ilona had the absurd idea the sea drays were seeking revenge, but then she saw they fled a greater threat.

The broad blue head of a sea dragon emerged from the ocean, not five hundred feet from her position. It leapt up, and dove under the surface. A second appeared some hundred yards further away. She saw their arrowed bodies as pale ribbons under the sea, and they burst out of the water with even more power than the sea drays, screeching loudly, scattering their prey before. Now the entire colony was in uproar. More animals abandoned their nests, even those far away that remained on theirs craned their necks and swayed nervously to keep watch on their hunters.

But the dragons were nearest to the men.

THE FIRST DRAGON came out of the sea close to Forfeth. At ten yards long it was more than five times the size of the sea drays. Light blue scales covered the upper half of its lithe body, white banding covered its belly. A long head supported a snout lined with recurved teeth and backward-pointing spines. Frills depended from its jaw, four horns crowned its head. It too had three pairs of flippers, rhombus-shaped things that ploughed long, curved furrows into the mix of ice and stone at the shore.

Forfeth watched it in terror. He could not escape. Sea drays bounded past him, forcing him to dodge. He dropped his gun. In pursuit of the fleeing animals, the dragon didn't see Forfeth and caught him a glancing blow so hard he flew with a scream through the air. He landed badly. Then it saw him. The dragon waddled to stand over this strange creature. It arched its back and cocked its head, watching Forfeth drag his broken leg behind him. Spray blasted from the nostrils atop its skull. It ignored the men crowding it, shouting at it and waving their arms, and gave Forfeth an experimental lick. Liking what it tasted, it stabbed its long snout at Forfeth, snatched him up in its teeth, and shook him until his bones snapped. It threw him up in the air, caught him, and extended its neck, ready to gulp him down like a gull swallows a fish.

Guns banged. The sea dragon screeched, dropping Forfeth and curling around to turn upon its attackers. A long serpentine tail bearing forked flukes lashed out, catching Favreau in the chest and propelling him so high he slammed into the beached iceberg and thumped lifelessly to the ground.

The second dragon responded to the screams of the first, and carved a broad trail of ruin through the sea dray's rookery, directly toward the hunting party, flinging pebbles everywhere with powerful thrusts of its muscular flippers. Eggs smashed. Dracon-skuas sped past it, to snatch up the feast leaking into the beach.

Ilona's bullet tore a long red furrow in the dragon's shoulder. Blood slicked its pale blue scales black.

Like the first it showed no pain, all Ilona achieved was to gain its attention. Its head snaked around; it gaped and hissed and sped at her, flippers propelling it through the rookery at frightening speed.

Her fingers were numb. She fumbled her next bullet from an ammo pouch on her bandolier. It fell into the sand.

The dragon was yards away. A gun went off. A small crater appeared in the beast's side, veiled by a puff of blood.

A body collided with her, slamming her out of the dragon's path. Next she knew, she was face down, spitting wet sand.

Guns were going off everywhere. The dragon screamed. She rolled over to see it thrashing in a hail of bullets. Persin advanced on it, calmly shooting and reloading, aiming for the head. Still it would not die, until Ardovani's gun shone its beam of death, cutting at an angle through its neck. Abruptly it fell silent, its head flopped to one side. The stench of burned flesh and feathers washed over her. A jet of blood fountained high, thick as water from a hose, and the dragon fell dead.

She got up, fished her gun out of a bed of snow. Her fingers burned with the cold. The metal was chill as the ice.

Men were running to the fallen. As far as she could see, Forfeth was dead, as was Favreau. Two of the dogs were down, a third whimpered, trying to rise but failing. The first dragon was shrieking, snapping at the men shooting at it. It snatched up a dead sea dray and bounded toward the water, disappearing back into the waves smoothly as a knife into flesh.

Bannord was shouting something, but she couldn't tell what. There was nothing wrong with her hearing, but she seemed to have lost command of human speech. The thunder of blood in her ears took precedence over all. Her breath rushed in and out, as if her body were shouting, *I'm alive, I'm alive, I'm alive*.

Someone lay pinned under the dead dragon. She ran toward them.

Darrasind was trapped beneath the beast's head, impaled on the spines curving back from its jaw. His face was drained of colour. A slow red stain crept through the snow. It was beautiful, like a talented murderer's depiction of a sunset.

"Hold on! Hold on!" she said. She dropped to her knees. Diluted blood, already chilled, soaked through her trousers.

"I'm dying." He coughed. Dark blood welled through his lips. "I'm dying."

"You saved my life."

He reached up and touched her arm gently. "I am sorry about before. On the ship. You are so pretty I never saw anyone so pretty as you. Got drunk... Only way... I could ask for a kiss... Man died because of it..." His words hitched, his breath gurgled in his chest. Pink blood frothed around the spine penetrating his side. "Do you think... do you think... could you give me that kiss now? It's funny... but I... but I... never... kissed... anyone... before..."

She smiled through her tears, and nodded. She swept her hair from her face, and bent over his head, and planted a kiss on his bloodied mouth.

He smiled. His eyes closed.

"Ilona, come away, come away!" Ardovani hauled her back from Darrasind's corpse. "Lost gods, you're covered in blood. Are you hurt? Are you hurt?" He shook her. She pushed him off.

"I'm fine. It's all Darrasind's," she managed.

The barking of the sea drays lessened. They were returning to their nests at a frantic pace, hoping to warm their eggs before life radiated away.

Feet crunched on pebbles. Her eyes were locked on Darrasind's dead face. His dark hair stirred in the sea wind.

"We were lucky the dragons were immature," she heard Bannord saying to Ardovani. "If either had been as big as the one we saw on the voyage, we'd all be dead. Get the meat. Collect the eggs. Leave the dragons. Too big."

"What about the ivory?" someone asked.

"Leave it!" shouted Bannord. "And don't start skinning them here, Aretimus! For fuck's sake. Gut the sea drays, get them on the sleds! That bastard might come back."

A single shot ended the injured dog's whining. Valatrice and the others began to howl.

Ilona wiped Darrasind's blood from her face. Her knees were cold. The sea drays were loud. The dogs sang in grief. Surf pounded the shore. Dracon-skuas cawed. So many vital stimuli entered her mind, but she was aware only of death.

"Are you alright?" Ardovani said. He pulled her to her feet and peered anxiously into her eyes.

"I'm a soldier now. People die. I've seen plenty of death on this voyage. I'll be fine."

"You're sure?"

She nodded. She recovered her gun, and helped secure the meat to the sleds as best she could, though she remained numbed until they were pulling away from the rookery.

Ilona could taste Darrasind's death on her lips all the way back to the camp.

CHAPTER TWENTY-SEVEN
Two Instances of Skullduggery

A FEW DAYS after returning from the Three Sisters, Arkadian Vand sent for his chief of spies.

He was eating an apple when Filden entered his office. An innocent enough act he thought, for a man bent on murder. Zeruvias' passing had required a lot of work to cover up satisfactorily. His men were easy to lie to; the ones that weren't fooled could be bribed, the ones that couldn't be bribed could be intimidated.

Still, he was left with two issues to be resolved. The matter of the child for the machine was the first; the second being Jolyon. Neither solution was pleasant, hence his thoughts of apples and innocence. There was nothing inherently blameless about the fruit, but in the past he had considered that someone bent on black deeds should not be able to do anything but fixate upon them. Surely an evil man would not eat, or drink. He would do nothing but plot his wickedness.

And yet there he was, eating his apple.

Vand wondered, *Am I wicked?*

Filden was old, in his later fifties Vand would have said. He didn't actually know, because Filden was protective of his personal information. Vand could have found out, but Filden was the man he employed to find things out for him, so there was little chance any enquiry, no matter how discreet, would go unnoticed.

Seven years had gone by since Filden had come to work for Vand. He'd been highly recommended by one of Vand's less pleasant contacts. Filden had done something in the army. Filden wouldn't say what, but Vand knew it was unpleasant. If Vand had been a little less self confident, he would have been afraid of the man. Most sensible people were.

Filden arrived wearing the green and white suit that wasn't a uniform but looked like one. Green and white was the Vand Company colour. Vand liked to refer to Filden as his personal army. It was a joke Filden never laughed at, but the clothes and the deep scar running from under his left ear down his neck onto his chest meant he looked the part.

Filden could handle both matters, Vand was quite sure.

"Ah, Filden," said Vand, as if he had not been expecting the ex-soldier. He concealed his disquiet at the events at the dig under officiousness. "I need you to drum up some of your old contacts. I've a couple of very sensitive assignments that need taking care of."

"Of course, goodfellow."

Filden clicked his heels and bowed sharply, the way a sauralier might. Vand liked to play a game with himself where he would attempt to guess where Filden had served. It made the old solider seem a little less intimidating. He might do one thing like a marine, another like an infantryman, a third like an artilleryman.

Vand needed him to be an assassin.

"Cavalry today is it?" said Vand.

"Might I inquire as to the nature of the assignments?"

Vand did not answer straightaway, but took a bite of his apple. He gave Filden an appraising look as he chewed and swallowed. He debated which was the least unpalatable task.

"You're not going to get squeamish are you?"

Filden glanced at his employee. "It depends on what you are asking me to do, goodman."

"I need you to find a child." Vand sat forward quickly. Now decided, his usual firmness reasserted itself. "A very specific child." He took another loud bite of his apple, and spoke through the pulp. "It's not what you might think. I'm not one of those."

"If you were, goodman, it would not be my concern."

"Well I'm not. Watch your tongue," Vand said more sharply than he intended.

"I make no judgement while I am on your payroll. Who is this child?"

"That's it, I don't know," said Vand. He took a final bite of his apple, leaving only the core. "It's a particular type of child rather than a particular child."

"Without further information, I cannot do anything personally for you. You are considering magical assistance?"

"I should say so. You know that shady magister, whatshisname. Can he help? I won't ask Hissenwar."

"Dequince?" said Filden. "He's not so shady he'll hunt for children. He won't touch anything like this, and he'd talk."

"And still no mages?"

"No mages, goodman."

Vand sighed angrily. "Damn it. Well, someone needs to do it." He twirled the apple stalk between thumb and forefinger, setting it spinning. "Let me be straight with you Filden, if I assume I have your confidence?"

"The utmost, goodman, as always."

"The machine I uncovered. We opened it. It requires a pilot of some sort."

"Like a boat?"

"No, not like a boat. More like a driver for a drayless glimmer wagon, but it's not so simple as that."

Filden, who was used to both sensitive assignments and those that made little sense, waited for Vand to gather his thoughts. There was little the machine or the Guider had given him to go upon.

"There is a bloodline, I suppose, of what sort I am as yet unsure. Not only do I require a child, but I need somebody who can help me find which kind. Tell me, do you know anyone who might make a start on this?"

"How far are you willing to go?" asked Filden quietly.

"Oh?" said Vand, his interest piqued. "It's not like you to be circumspect, Filden."

"There are things I do not care to meddle with, goodman, but there is one who might help. A Tyn, someone who I employ when... occasion demands. He is a tool of necessity, to be employed wisely, if at all."

"A Tyn?"

"A Free Tyn, collarless. A finder, to be exact. That's what he calls his profession, though finding is not all he does."

Vand smiled craftily. "Are you frightened of him?"

Filden gave him a reptilian look. "I used the first time on the advice of a Fethrian warlock. There was a matter of missing pay in the barracks. He found it alright, but the situation turned ugly owing to certain irregularities. I swore I wouldn't use him again. This *fellow*, shall we call him, told me otherwise. Sure enough, I had need of him not long after."

"You are at least wary of him then."

Filden looked uncomfortable. "I have killed men. I have done worse than that. I do not care for the law when it gets in the way of great effort. I obey you because I respect you, and I agree with what you are trying to accomplish. But this Tyn. .. Yes, I am wary of him."

"Why suggest him at all then, Filden?"

Filden abandoned his habitual stance at attention and looked his employer directly in his face.

"I would not suggest him if I could think of anyone else who would find what you need. He'll know what you require better than you do, and he'll get it done quickly."

"Speed is to be desired. What's his name?"

"Goodman, as with all of these things involving the Tyn, what appears straightforward is not. What it calls itself... it's not his name. I suppose it's a title. Or a black joke."

"Get to the point. Tell me the thing's name."

Filden shook his head. "I will not utter it, because I do not need him. I will write it down for you, then you must say it. As soon as you do he will become aware of you. Let me stress, goodman, to have him aware of you is no good thing. He must be controlled, he cannot control you, or he will be your undoing. He can find things no one else can, he knows things no one else does, and he will sell them, if it pleases him to do so. His geas are many. Unlike some Tyn, he will deliberately try to trick you into breaking them, and even if you avoid that, his prices are very high, and often unconventional."

"Marvellous," said Vand. He leaned back onto his desk and put his feet carelessly onto a pile of plans. "Is there anyone else?"

"You want this done quickly?"

"Yes."

"Then no, there is no one else. I will tell you his name only if you are certain you want this now. I am sure we can hit upon other options, given time."

"I have none, you have none, but..." Vand leaned back in his chair and toyed with his apple core, his face thoughtful. "I want to bring this engine to life. It would be a triumph. More so when I learn its secrets and reproduce them. And I will get there before that bastard Persin can return from the south blowing his trumpet. If he returns."

"So you do want me to tell you the name?"

"Yes, yes damn it man, spit it out!"

Finden gestured for paper and pen. Vand's feet slammed onto the floor. He shoved a sheet at Filden and indicated he use the ink pot and pen set on his desk. Filden scribbled the name fast, as if he couldn't get it down quickly enough. He tore off a strip of the paper and held it out in front of his master. "If you desire to use him, then say it aloud. You will never find him by other means."

Vand reached out. Filden hesitated a moment before handing the paper over. Vand snatched it from his man and immediately read it out. "The Sniffer? The Sniffer? What the hells kind of name is that?"

A strange fancy settled on them that there was suddenly something else in the room. Both men looked up, breath held.

Nothing happened. The day went on as normal. Dogs barked in the street, the wagons they pulled rattled over the cobbles.

Vand laughed loudly, the way men do when an expected fright does not materialise.

"By the driven gods, Filden! I thought the bloody thing would pop out of the privy, tootling on his pipe!"

"It is not wise to joke about him," said Filden, but he felt foolish, Vand could tell.

"I'm glad we got that out of the way, because there is something else you need to do, and this is arguably harder, if not so distasteful. I thought I'd build up to it, because it is a difficult request to make, but you've rather taken the buoyancy out of the floatstone."

"And what is that, sir?"

Vand paused. He had considering how to put his request. He knew Filden would do it, or else he wouldn't ask. Ordering the death of a man was never easy.

"I'll just say it baldly," said Vand. "Filden, I need you to kill the Guider, Jolyon."

"Very good, goodman."

Vand nodded solemnly.

"This is a grim business Filden, but I see no other way. We must think of the future."

"As you say, goodman," said Filden. He executed a short bow and departed.

Vand stared into the middle distance, thinking on the exigencies of success. "It can't be helped," he told himself. Shaking himself from his reflection he consumed the apple core, stalk, bitter pips and all. He was a man who took everything from life he could, good and bad.

WHY VAND WANTED Jolyon dead didn't matter to Filden. Vand did not advance an explanation, and Filden did not ask for one. A life of following orders, mostly unsavoury in nature, had blunted what little curiosity he once had. Filden genuinely did respect Vand. However, unlike Vand, who needed approval and praise, and pursued his engineering and archeological plundering for the acclaim as much as the wealth, for Filden money was a greater motivator than any form of respect, whether given or received.

Filden liked money. He did not look it, but he was a rich man already, with hundreds of thousands of thalers secreted in the banks of four different kingdoms. He had planned to earn a small fortune and retire young. The problem with small fortunes is that, once acquired, it is rarely fortune enough. Filden wanted more. His ambitions for a townhouse in Perus became dreams of a castle in Marceny; one young lover became several, and so the desire for tens of thousands became the need for hundreds of thousands. By the time he was thirty-six, he had exceeded his original goal. He did not stop. From his forties onward he continued to accumulate money. Every fortune gained was the catalyst for greater avarice, until the gathering of wealth became the end rather than the means, and his dreams receded into memory.

His humanity had been scooped out of him piece by piece by the demands made by his former masters.

His own greed concluded the process. He wasn't a man born with a surfeit of kindness anyway. Perhaps he could be no other way, and his path in life was inevitable, but Filden wasn't introspective enough to think about all of that. Questions that would have kept a more moral man awake all night went unasked.

Filden slept very well.

And so, for reasons that he almost grasped but never would, he found himself pursuing murder yet again, many years after he thought he would be done with it.

Guider Jolyon had been smart enough to leave the dig in Farthia, but not smart enough to go very far away. Nor was he as holy as his office suggested. Filden followed him from a low-class tavern in the Locksides, down the stepped streets that led eventually toward the sucking mud of the foreshore. In the warren of warehouses and boarding houses crowding the cliffs there were many brothels. The order of business for most sailors coming into Karsa city was drink, sex, and sleep, in that order. Other men in need of discretion took advantage of the facilities that sprang up to service those needs.

A series of unseasonably high tides had spurred a flurry of trading, and the port was crowded. Filden followed Jolyon at a distance, but without undue care. He behaved as if he had business in the thronging quays of Karsa's port. Skipping from shadow to shadow was the easiest way for a man to be noticed. He'd exchanged his gold and green suit of clothes for a merchant's garb, and he walked with purpose. The outfit was deliberately plain. He wore no obvious indicators to show what he might trade in to lessen the chances someone might stop him to attempt a deal. Not that anyone would, one stern look from the ex-soldier had most men hurrying on their way. No one noticed him. As a precaution, he trusted to the glamours of a Tyn-made amulet to blur the memories of those who did. Such was his skill that he rarely needed to call upon the magic.

Jolyon was similarly disguised. Filden admired his careful skirting of the Guider's Law. His robes were covered with a waxed cloak; the distinctive haircut of his order hidden under a hat. It was forbidden for a Guider to hide their calling. Dying unghosted was the greatest fear of most Ruthnians, and the Guider's oath was strenuously enforced. They were required to act immediately in the case of sudden death, and so Jolyon had been careful to wear clothes suited to the weather that just happened to conceal what he was while he headed to his appointment.

Jolyon's hypocrisy made the assassination easier for Filden.

There was a rickety building jammed between a chandlers and a wine warehouse down the street, narrow as the truth and tall as a lie. It had no signage describing its trade, but it obvious it rented out flesh by the hour.

The Guider was almost as skilled at hiding himself as Filden. He walked toward the brothel without looking like he was heading for it, turning at an abrupt right angle and stepping neatly inside. Had Filden been less focussed, he could well have missed that. He smiled at the Guider's cunning.

Filden waited a few minutes nearby. He bought a loaf of bread and ate it leaning against a wall in the watery sun. He was hungry anyway.

A shower of rain pelted him briefly. The warm streets steamed after it ended. When enough time had passed for the Guider to have chosen a consort for the afternoon, Filden crossed the street and went through the brothel's open door.

A bead curtain hid a small waiting room that smelled of sweat and frustrated sailors. A fat woman sat on a stool behind a scuffed counter which had once been painted gold. There was one other man in there, an Ishamalani bosun, by his dress. Filden gave him a level stare. The man looked away.

"Good day, goodfellow," said the fat woman. Her face was as badly painted as her furniture. Cracked powder failed to hide old sores.

"I am no nobleman," he said.

"You're whatever you pay us to treat you as in here, my love. What is your passion? We've got everything here. Holes for every taste." She smirked lasciviously.

"I don't like whores," Filden said. He leaned over the counter, the woman flinched as his face came close to hers. "The Guider, where is he?" he whispered, too quietly for the sailor to hear.

"There ain't none of the Dead God's quarter in here."

Filden drew back. He pulled out a silver thaler piece from the pocket sewn inside his coat, and pushed it deliberately across the counter. It scraped on the wood.

"This one is for your silence," he said, pulling back his coat enough so that she saw the brace of pistols at his right hip. He took out a second coin and pushed it after the first. "This one is for you. Now where is he?"

She licked her lips. Fear and greed tipped the scales. "Upstairs, third door on the left."

The sailor was making a show of not listening, which meant he had heard. The amulet should cloud his mind sufficiently to make identification impossible. Filden fixed the man's face in his mind in case he needed to deal with him later. The looks Filden gave the house madame and sailor carried enough threat to silence both. Filden doubted the man would talk, the Ishmalani were close-mouthed, doubly so when breaching their religious rule. She was more of a risk. Chances were she'd call the watch anyway, seeking to profit as much as possible from a murder she couldn't stop.

He had to be quick. He drew his first pistol as he walked up the stairs. The building was badly built and the treads creaked underfoot. Sunlight shafted through gaps in the walls. The sounds of desultory lovemaking came from a couple of the rooms, otherwise the stuffy landing at the top was quiet, the hubbub of the docks muted. Water from the a leak plinking into a chamber pot at the side of the landing was the loudest sound of all.

He pressed his ear to the door. Talk came through the boards, a man and a woman's voices. He grasped the handle lightly and pushed it open. The small room behind had a window of cracked panes, letting onto the street outside and lighting the room with a deceptively romantic glow.

The Guider was speaking.

"He died. He put his hand on that machine and he died. I've always tried to do the right thing. I am pledged to my cause, truly, and that was not right. Zeruvias was no provincial ghost talker, and he's dead! If Vand finds me—"

The whore saw Filden first. Her squeak had the Guider turn and leap from the bed. He stood naked in front of the assassin, holding out his hands and hunched a little in a pleading, submissive posture Filden had seen dozens of times. Jolyon was contemptible in his nakedness.

"Wait!" said Jolyon.

A magister's mark carved in the butt of Filden's gun flared as he shot the Guider in the head. Magic swallowed the sound of discharge. The silenced round sprayed the Guider's brains out over the window and the room turned red.

Filden swivelled on the spot, drawing his second ironlock pistol on the girl. She was young, late teens. Her lips were cracked and her arms covered in fingertip bruises and puncture marks. She whimpered and pulled the sheet up to cover herself. Filden wrenched it away on a whim, to better see her.

"He told you what he saw in the Barrens."

"He told me nothing goodman!"

Her eyes were wide but somewhat dead. The emotion she showed was a facsimile of fear, as put on as her charade of love. He doubted she could feel much of anything. Moonflower addiction was common enough among whores like her.

"He told me nothing at all," she lied. "He's a regular client, comes here all the time, talks me half to death about the dead. He thinks I'm his girlfriend. It's sad."

"No," said Filden. He held up a single finger in admonishment. "No. I heard him speaking."

"He didn't—"

"That is unfortunate for you."

The girl sank into the pillow behind her. She seemed resigned more than scared. Filden raised his gun. He was probably doing her a favour.

The girl's life was cut short by another silenced shot.

Filden shut the door gently behind him and headed for the rear of the establishment. There was a back entrance, but he favoured a rotting window on the landing that opened onto the sloping roof of the neighbouring warehouse. He wrenched it open, wriggled through, and was away over the tiles.

There were whistles and running feet coming from the street as he lowered himself into an alley a hundred yards from the brothel. He rejoined the main road, where he blended into the crowd without much fear of arrest. There were hundreds of murders every year in the Locksides, and Filden, despite being responsible for more than his fair share, had never been caught.

CHAPTER TWENTY-EIGHT
The Temple of the Brass God

DAYS PASSED WITHOUT incident in the camp of the modalmen. They greeted every sunrise with song, then danced away to the moot. Rel accompanied them a few more times, but his inability to understand their language discouraged him. When he realised no one objected to his remaining in camp he stopped going, glad for a respite from the giants.

While the modalmen were at their debates, Rel explored the barren valley. There were signs of building foundations on the banks toward the mountain, and the eroded remains of an ancient jetty protruding into the dry lake. One day he followed the lake as far as he could. At the far end the bed was broken into a series of shallow steps that lifted toward the mountain. Beyond this anomaly was the dry course of the river that had fed the lake. He followed it, and the mystery of the lake grew more perplexing. The river ended abruptly at a wall of rock where the cliffs of the mountain rose from the ground.

Puzzled as to how this could have happened, Rel returned to the Gulu Thek camp and checked on Aramaz before going back to Shkarauthir's hearth. There he sat staring into the fire until the king returned. Long clouds streamed over the mountain peaks, obscuring more than half the sky. Without the sun, the high desert was chilly, and Rel shivered under his blanket. Maybe the mountains had been made after the lake. He could recall no legend that told of such things, and as used to works of magic as he was, Rel found the creation of a mountain range in that manner incredible.

He agonised about breaking out his countrymen from the cages, but he could see no way. His own position was perilous. Shkarauthir allowed him his explorations, but had forbidden him from wandering into the man-eaters' camps. Fearing his actions would lead to a direct confrontation between Shkarauthir and Brauctha, and dismayed at his inability to help, Rel avoided returning to the cages, and occupied his mind with questions of geography.

In the evenings the modalmen left the moot subdued. They did not dance or sing, and few of them spoke. The first day Rel had seen this he assumed some awful thing to have occurred. When it happened a second time, he realised it was simply another manifestation of their peculiar ways.

The giants came back exhausted from the moot, and quietly made their meals. Sometimes Drauthek would speak with him, and they would exchange stories as best they could. Rel worked to improve Drauthek's Maceriyan, and from the modalman Rel learned a little more of their language.

Four nights after their arrival, Drauthek was trying to teach Rel how to describe past events in their tongue, his efforts causing Drauthek no end of hilarity, when a heavy hand touched the shoulder of the modalman, and he got up and left without a word. A serious-faced Shkarauthir took Drauthek's place at Rel's side.

"The moot goes badly," Shkarauthir said. The firelight blended with the light moving in his whorled skin. Shkarauthir's deep, animal smell enveloped Rel. Not unpleasant, but strong as a bull-dracon's odour during musth.

Shkarauthir picked up a piece of dung and tossed it onto the fire.

"Those who despise your kind see no value in your people as warriors. Even those who are favourably disposed toward you do not think an army of yours could best a horde like this. For the last hundred years, at the command of our god, we have largely maintained a peace. That is changing. The iron ones come to make war. The man-eaters say you will side with them as many did the last time, or get in our way. They say strike now, and be strong for the coming fight against our enemy. I say you lesser men are good warriors, with many new machines. That you will kill many of us before we kill all of you, and we shall be weakened. That way, the iron Draathis win."

"Doesn't he realise how many people there are in the Kingdoms? This is a large horde, but we have cannon and many, many guns. Any war between us would cost the Kingdoms dearly, but you would be destroyed."

"This is so," agreed Shkarauthir. "I have said all of this. Those of my opinion cannot convince Brauctha's followers that you will join us gladly, and there are smaller clans between ours and the man-eaters who fear your betrayal even if you open your arms in friendship. They see no choice but to fight."

"I wish there was something I could do," said Rel. He looked into the fire.

"There is something," said Shkarauthir. "It is why I have come to speak with you." He looked at the mountainside. "Up there, in the cliff, is a cave. Within is a temple from the long ago times. Should a worthy man go to it, the Brass God will speak with them."

"The statue is not the god?"

"It is a statue," said Shkarauthir. He looked at Rel seriously. "You think we are savages, creatures without understanding?" He was offended. "To us, you Forgetful are the savages." He shrugged. "This is the way men are, always full of suspicion of each other. We are not how you think we are. We know many things you do not. The Brass God dwells in the mountain. His effigy allows him to see all we do in the moot. He will not come down until the decision is made, and the time is right. To this moot, I think he might not come at all."

"Because of Brauctha."

Shkarauthir nodded. "Because of Brauctha. Much of his talking at the moot has been blasphemous. He says the Brass God has lost his way. The god will not come to advise unbelievers, and this makes it easier for Brauctha to deny his power." Shkarauthir's clan patterns gleamed. He looked thoughtfully down at Rel. "You are fated, small one. There is magic in you. I can smell it. In the Y Dvar armies in the old days, mages of your kind fought by our side. You are like them. You have power of your own."

Rel hunkered deeper into his blanket. "I have no power. I am a soldier. I'm a good shot. That's about it."

"Then your talents must be hidden," said Shkarauthir. "My kind have no ability to manipulate the force of Will. We have no mages, but we have an affinity for magic. We can feel it, it flows in us, in our marks," he patted his arm. "It allows us to run the Road of Fire. I see it in you, as clearly as my own clan patterns. Tell me truthfully, are there ones strong with magic in your family?"

Rel stared into the flames. There was Aarin, there was Guis. There was their mother, or so he suspected. Her addiction to moonflower was telling, and his brothers' abilities had to come from somewhere. He didn't like to talk about their mage taint. Most of the time he ignored it. Aarin was in command of his senses, but madness had seeped from their mother's veins into Guis. He nodded, his gaze fixed on the dancing flames.

"I thought so," said Shkarauthir. "You are here for a reason, small one. The Brass God only reveals himself to those that are worthy, but fate has put you here. You are worthy. He will speak with you, I am sure."

"You want me to go and speak with your god?"

"I do. And I want you to do whatever he tells you to," said Shkarauthir. "And I want you to get him to come down off his mountain, before Brauctha makes good on his threats and brings disaster on all our clans." He stood. "Now. More lessons from Drauthek. If you could speak our tongue, things would go easier."

"THIS WAY, LITTLE Rel," said Drauthek. He pointed at the rough trail winding up the fault. What appeared as a clean line from the valley floor was an unstable crack cluttered with stone blocks and floored with gritty sand that rolled under their feet. The trail was forced to swerve around these obstacles accordingly. If it had been clear the fault would have been broad enough to carry a highway. In practise, the various hazards left only enough room for a goat track. Smooth rock dropped off to their left thousands of feet to the valley floor. The height made Rel's head spin. The cliff above was set back from the path, but in many places it leaned out, half covering it over. The weight of a mountain was supported by nothing, ready to drop and squash them.

"You are sure it is safe?" asked Rel. He was discovering a new fear of heights, and of being crushed.

"Path safe." Drauthek spat over the edge of the drop. "Cave not safe."

"Great," said Rel.

Drauthek grinned at him. "You want talk with Brass God, you talk with him this way. There no other way. You go in cave, go temple. There he talk."

"It was only a comment," grumbled Rel.

"Huh?"

"An idea, a thought, a picture in my head given voice. A joke to control my fear! A comment."

"No fear. Keep good picture in head. My picture is little Rel speak with god, god come down and put an end to Brauctha's shouting. Good picture, so when Shkarauthir tell Drauthek, 'Go help little Kingdoms Rel,' Drauthek go help."

The climb was steep, and Rel's skin was slick with sweat. Once the sun was up the desert warmed, though if Rel stopped moving he started to shiver. Hot sun, cold air, like spring in the isles, only more extreme. It was a recipe for catching a chill. He scrambled over a cube of rock. A socket in the cliff above showed from where it had fallen.

"You know, I thought the god was in the moot place."

When Drauthek laughed he snorted like a dog. "That not god, that just statue. God is in the mountains, god is in heart, in head. You find him here, in old place."

"That's what Shkarauthir said. I understand why you people think I am ignorant."

Drauthek stuck out his lip. "You know nothing. Is true."

Rel looked ahead. The trail went on as far as he could see, leading steeply upward. "How long until we get there?" he said.

Drauthek managed to shrug with all four of his shoulders. Modalman anatomy was bizarre, the uppermost parts of a man's torso doubled and stacked. It shouldn't have functioned. Somehow it did. Each of Drauthek's arms was as thick through as Rel's chest. Heavy gold armlets circled his biceps. He had taken his sword with him, a weapon so big the modalman needed two hands to wield it. It was taller than Rel, and as wide as Drauthek's forearms. There was nothing in the mountain close by that necessitated such a large weapon; he had admitted he carried it to protect Rel from the other modalmen. Some of the looks Rel had received on their way through the camp had been hungry.

"Sun go there," Drauthek pointed to a place on the southern horizon that the sun would reach in about an hour. "Rel run fast, we reach cave. Brass God come," he shrugged again. "Who know? Maybe today, maybe never."

"Thank you so much," said Rel.

"Drauthek tells truth."

The path went up in a gratuitously difficult manner. In several places it narrowed and they had to edge around protruding masses in the rock so far that Drauthek's toes pointed over thin air. In others the cliff curved over the path and dropped so low that Drauthek had to bend double to proceed, and Rel had to duck. The modalman faced death coolly. Rel did his best to copy him. He had been sent far from home, battled monsters out of nightmares and been lost in the desert, but the height was too much. He forced himself to ignore the flipping in his gut, keep his eyes ahead, and try not to think about how high they were climbing.

After a time, his fear became a sort of bland background to effort. Scrambling over the dangerous path took all his concentration. He was not expecting Drauthek to stop when he did, on a ledge broader than most. The cliff roofed over the path fully there, so that the ledge was not far from being a cave itself. Otherwise, it was unremarkable.

"Cave here," said Drauthek. He pointed far to the back of the ledge. A narrow crack in the rock opened into the mountain, almost too narrow for a modalman to squeeze through, and thin enough to be taken for a shadow. Rel approached. A steady, cold wind blew from inside. When his eyes adjusted to the gloom he saw that crude figures with four arms were painted in faded pigment all around it, many of them applied atop older, barely visible images. A stack of brushwood tied in bundles was set against the wall a little further along next to a patch on the floor greasy with old fires. A water urn with a cracked lid was situated next to that.

Drauthek went and sat down by the firewood. He pulled a handful of dried meat from a pouch at his waist and fed a strip into his mouth.

"That's it? I just go in?" said Rel.

"Why be waiting, small man?" said Drauthek.

"No time like the present." The crack was the darkest thing Rel had ever seen.

"Huh?"

"Something we say in the west," said Rel. He took a step toward the gap, then stopped.

"What do I do?"

"Walk, until you find god," said Drauthek. He unhooked a wooden ladle from his belt, took the top from the urn, and lifted water to his mouth.

"He won't object that I am not a modalman?"

Drauthek washed his meat down and smacked his lips. "He is not modalman. He does not care. Any can speak with him, if he worthy." He pushed another piece of meat into his mouth, folding it carefully several times, and set to work on it. He looked out at the void of air before him, as if he were an old man on a bench in the street, spending his last days watching the world go by.

Rel shook his head. "Fine. I will see you soon."

"Maybe not," said Drauthek.

"Bloody literal bastards," muttered Rel to himself, and went into the dark.

FROM INSIDE THE cave daylight appeared, as glaring as the crack had been black. The sun penetrated only as far as a niche surrounded by geometric designs a few yards inside. Darkness beckoned. Inside the niche, Rel found a bundle of torches made of tightly bound twigs soaked in pitch. He took out his flint, iron and fire cotton, and had one of the torches burning in a few moments. He roped three more together and slung them across his back. Though the torches were heavy, being sized for modalmen, the thought of being lost in the dark of the mountain encouraged him to make the effort. Carrying the lit torch in his left hand, he went forward with his carbine in his right. The gun was too awkward to shoot one-handed effectively. At least the close environs of the cave precluded having to aim.

A jagged tunnel led upward. He scrambled up a couple of high, natural steps to where a second passage branched off from the first. He held his torch aloft, unsure of which route to take. The flame roared in the cold wind coming from the new tunnel. He turned into it, and the wind blew stronger, chilling his face. Reasoning that the wind had to come from somewhere, he took the second tunnel.

A few feet further on the last of the day vanished, leaving Rel reliant on the unsteady flames of the torch.

Time lost meaning in the dark. He supposed he had been climbing for nearly an hour when the first torch guttered out. He swore, and threw it aside. Red embers on the torch stub went out quickly, leaving him in total blackness. The second torch took longer to light than the first. He wished for a glimmer lamp, or a simple oil lamp, something that would give a steady light. Sparks spraying from his iron into his fire cotton lit up the cave with disorienting flashes. He wondered if he would have enough torches to find his way out again.

In the dark, his imagination ran wild. What exactly was this meeting with a god going to be like? Was he a brass-armoured primitive, savage as his worshippers? Was he a corporeal being like Eliturion? Rel gave out a snort of black laughter. He would have much preferred to be listening to that old bore in the Nelly Bold than stuck in the bowels of the mountain.

Finally, his wad of fire cotton caught. It nearly blew out in the tunnel wind. Swearing again, he sheltered it with his hand and coaxed the tiny flame into a small blaze, and lit the torch from it. Once the torch was alight, he patted out the cotton and stuffed it back into his tinder kit. He was acutely aware that his resources were limited. He supposed he could find his way back in the dark if he had to, so long as the path didn't diverge more than once, but he would prefer not to have to face the challenge.

If there's a damn labyrinth in here, I'm a dead man, he thought.

He pressed on. The path went always upward, getting steeper and rougher. Sharp rocks poked through clay that became increasingly moist, and he slipped several times. The wind began to moan, quietly to begin with, becoming shrill and insistent as the rocks got sharper and the tunnel narrower.

As the second torch was burning low, Rel came to a part of the tunnel that levelled out and snaked around a number of tight switchbacks. He had to stoop to get by. A modalman would have had to wriggle through. The ground was smoothed over by the passage of many bellies.

"I must be going the right way," he said to himself, running his hand over the compacted clay. The wind moaned louder in response.

The further he went into this new section, the harder the wind blew. His torch went out as the tunnel was broadening again. He continued a few paces, until the wind slackened and sang from distant surfaces. There was a sense of wide space in front of him. He stopped dead, wary of unseen drops.

He knelt to pat at the ground. Finding damp clay under his hands and not a chasm, he breathed a sigh of relief and took out his third torch. He had one left after that.

Sparks flashed not on cave walls but upon masonry, and rows of giant, fractured pillars. He slowed his efforts, striking sparks to take in his surroundings. Nearby, the monumental, blank-eyed head of a Morfaan statue looked at him from the clay.

"The temple," he said.

The torch stubbornly refused to light. There was the sound of movement in the dark. He paused, ears straining. The sound came again, moving closer, and he redoubled his efforts. A soft, eerie whining echoed round the room, and the hiss of metal moving on metal. Points of glimmer light shone in the dark. The sparks of his flint reflected from a cluster of glass eyes mounted in a triangular metal face

The light grew, illuminating the cave in a low blue glow. Rel had only the most fleeting impression of his surroundings, not much more detailed than that provided by the sparks. It could have contained every wonder of the past, but his attention was held entirely by the machine heading toward him. He abandoned his torch, got up, and aimed his gun.

The machine appeared bent double at first, before Rel saw that it was not humanoid, but insectile, with a domed carapace and many limbs. Pistons hissed, powering a score of multiply jointed arms. A dozen legs gave the machine a smooth, unnerving gait. Superficially it resembled a giant beetle. It was far in advance of anything a human engineer could build.

He pulled back the hammer on his gun. "I am here to see the Brass God!" he proclaimed. "Are you he?" Growing up in a city with its own resident deity had bred a certain lack of reverence into Rel. He thought he should have been more respectful, but he had no idea how.

The machine's blade-tipped feet pressed into the clay. Humming workings propelled it toward Rel. It was thirty yards away, moving down an aisle between toppled columns.

"Gods," Rel said. "You might be the coal hauler for all I know." He backed away. The beetle moved up and over a pile of rubble as smoothly as a millipede.

"Stay back!" he said, as it came closer. He adjusted his aim, centring it on the head. "Stop! I don't want to shoot!"

If this was some sort of test, he was failing it miserably.

"This is my last warning!"

The beetle came closer. The broad head tilted to one side. In its jaws was a glass capsule full of liquid lit by internal glimmer light. Mechanical mouthparts scissored against each other unpleasantly.

"Oh for the love of the lost gods," Rel said, and fired.

The blue-white discharge of the ironlock momentarily blinded him. The bullet drew a line of sparks off the creature's armoured back. The beetle continued to move on him, no faster and no slower than before.

"Shit!" he said. Rel snapped the gun open, and reloaded quickly, bringing the barrel up and firing in one movement. Rel was well practised, and his bullet shattered a glass eye. The light behind it went out, but the mechanical creature had plenty to spare and continued its advance without slowing.

Rel backed away as he fired, getting off two more shots before he decided to run.

"I can't hurt you, can I? Stupid idea," he said, diving for the tunnel. He slipped and fell, landing hard on the clay. He waited for the hot pain of metal entering his flesh.

None came. He turned on his back.

The mechanism was too large to fit inside the tunnel. It stood at the entrance regarding him with its dead, artificial eyes.

When the creature made no further move against him, he got slowly to his feet, and held up his hands.

"I'm not sure what I'm supposed to do here," he said. "I need to see the god. I'm sorry if this isn't the right way to go about it. I'm new to religion."

A hiss of air delivered a sharp sting to his arm.

"Damn it," he said, looking down at the long dart protruding from his bicep. His vision doubled.

A long, banded metal whip shot from below the mechanism's mouth, wrapped itself around Rel's legs, and yanked him off his feet.

He was unconscious before he hit the ground.

REL CAME TO crumpled against a wall, his mouth the flavour of an old sock and a headache to rival the worst hangover he had ever had. His surroundings had him forget both discomforts.

He was in a hall of stone with the texture and colourful qualities of fine marble and the seamless nature of Morfaan glass. Ribbed vaulting supported a high ceiling integrated so organically with the greater structure that he had the vertiginous sense of being trapped inside a monster's ribcage. The hall's vertical cross-section and its floorplan were both oval, and so perfectly symmetrical it looked wrong. The rear wall was blank and the front a vast window, though they were otherwise identically shaped. The clear glass grew from the stone glass, if that was indeed what either substance was, and looked out over the mountain foothills, the valley, and the desert beyond. The view was so sharp and clear, lacking the fuzzing of distance, that he suspected it had been magically sharpened. Several large sculptures were arrayed along the centre of the room, abstract shapes that turned soundlessly a few inches off the floor. Light came not only from the window, which let in the strong sun, but emanated also from the material of the hall itself.

Hands slipping on the smooth glass, he pulled himself up. A curious note sounded nearby, like that of a trumpet, followed by the clicking of metal feet. The mechanism from the cave emerged from behind one of the sculptures.

In the light the machine was not as intimidating as it had been in the dark, but it was frightening nonetheless. It tilted its multifaceted brass face toward him, and let out the same noise, which though wordless had the intonation of a question.

Rel's hands went for his sword. The scabbard was empty. His gun too was nowhere in sight. He held up his hands and backed away toward the giant window.

"I mean no harm!" he said.

Multiple legs rippling in sequence, the device took a step forward.

"And I'm sorry I shot you."

The creature blurted out a rasping noise. Rel backed off another step. The mechanism did the same, and stopped at arm's length from him.

Rel frowned. He took another step back. The beetle took another step forward. It made no move to come any closer than that. Haltingly, he reached out his hand and touched the thing's brass casing. His fingers encountered warm metal that vibrated with the working of internal mechanisms.

A voice spoke from the machine, though it had no lips or visible means of forming words. "You are awake," it said in archaic Maceriyan.

"Yes." Rel peered at the device's face. The broken eye was an ugly scar on its alien beauty. He had never seen anything like it. It was so finely made it was hard to see it as a machine, and not as a bizarre, metallic artwork.

"I have come in search of the Brass God," Rel said loudly and clearly, feeling foolish for it. "The god of the modalmen. Are you he?"

"It is not the Brass God," said the voice from the machine.

Halting footsteps came from behind Rel. He looked about for the source and found an opening in the side of the hall that had not been there before. From this tunnel another machine came. This was humanoid. Its face was a skull fashioned in metal, and it had two smaller arms partway between its arms and hips mounted on ball and socket joints. Rel recognised it as the same kind of device he had seen in his vision at Losirna, although this one was damaged, and therefore lacked the smooth, effortless motion of those machines.

"I take it *you* are the Brass God," said Rel. "Your worship. My lord, um..." He flailed about for the right turn of phrase. He settled for a short, sauralier's bow.

The mechanism limped closer. The left leg had been patched with inferior metals, and the knee no longer flexed, so that the device had to swing out its leg to move forward, and for most of the step its heavy foot dragged across the floor. The lesser of the left arms was bent out of shape and immobile. A hole in the skull exposed busy cogs lit by soft glimmer light. The dragging foot scratched the marble, but it rippled and healed itself as soon as it was damaged. For a moment Rel was reminded of his father, and his crippling by apoplexy.

The being's mechanical eyes whirred at Rel.

"I am the Brass God."

CHAPTER TWENTY-NINE
The Brass God

THE BRASS GOD looked down at Rel. His delicate mechanical irises whirred, metal petals behind the glowing glass.

"This is my companion, Onder," the Brass God said gesturing at the beetle machine. Onder waggled its head from side to side and made a pleasant sound. "You hurt him."

The Brass God's face was a death's head fashioned from brass and silver. It therefore had little in the way of expression. Small motors whined in its neck as it bent its head down. It was not as tall as a modalman, but at over seven feet tall, it was far bigger than Rel.

"He meant you no harm." The Brass God's voice echoed, like a person speaking into a metal tube. "You came to seek me, he is the means of conveyance. There was no need to discharge your weapon at him."

"I am sorry," said Rel. "I wasn't willing to take the chance. I did not know it... he... Onder was friendly."

"He is not friendly," said the Brass God. "He is not aggressive. He is not really even a he. He is what I command him to be. At the moment, I desire him to be friendly. Are you going to give me reason to change my mind, and therefore his?"

Onder presented a limb ending in a wicked pair of steel shears that rasped open and shut with unmistakeable meaning.

"There's no need to threaten me. I am not here to fight," said Rel.

The Brass God looked from mechanism to man. His joints made delicate, metallic noises as he moved.

"You are either brave, or stupid. Humans are quite often both, but I shall give you the benefit of the doubt." The Brass God's body shifted to maintain its balance with a dozen small corrections, as a human's does. Its behaviour uncannily mimicked life, unlike Onder, who only moved with a machine's purpose. A pulsing light flickered in the god's chest in place of a heart. Glowing blue tubes threaded their ways through hollow spaces visible in gaps in the outer casing. "I brought you here to talk. Time is growing short, and we have much to discuss."

"I have come to talk," Rel said.

"That pleases me. I have waited for one like you for a long time. Perhaps fate works in our favour, Rel Kressind, as the modalman Shkarauthir believes."

"You know who I am?"

"I know a lot more than who you are. I cannot leave this citadel, but the devices of my kind allow me to gather information from across the world. I will explain, as best I can. Much of what I have to say will be beyond your understanding. Firstly, I know you, but you do not know me."

He held out his working lesser hand. Rel looked at it stupidly.

"Do you no longer shake hands in Ruthnia?" said the god.

"Sorry, I've only met one god before. He is a little different."

"I am not a god, nor is the personage you refer to. There is only one god, the One, the creator who made this world and the realm of stars in which it spins, and the void around it. He is more than I or Eliturion can ever be. We are... We are different to one another, but neither of us are gods."

Rel took the hand in his own. The fingers were layered constructions of plate metal, and uncomfortable to hold.

"So, you probably wonder, if I am not a god, what am I? I will tell you. My name is Qurunad. I am, or was, of the Morfaan. I am deathless, but I have never been divine."

"I thought there were only two gods left in the world. They are not machines."

"I was not always a machine," said Qurunad. He had a schoolmaster's superior air. "Before my spirit was forced to inhabit this mechanism, I was one of the last of my people, a survivor of the long war that again engulfs this Earth."

"The war. You are speaking of the iron men?"

Qurunad nodded. "The Draathis are our enemies of old. The modalmen were bred to fight them, and heed our ancient decrees still, though we are no longer masters of this place. The lights on the World of Form are their signal to gather, and so they come."

"Shkarauthir said something about that. That's a start."

"As I said, there is much to discuss," said Qurunad. He turned laboriously around and headed back the way he had come. Seeing no other option, Rel followed.

The Brass God led him out of the hall into a second. Onder trotted behind them like a dog. The wall sighed closed behind them, sealing itself so thoroughly no trace of an opening was left.

The next hall was similar to the first, only much bigger and dirtier. The first hall's immaculate state seemed intended to impress. This second room appeared a little more honest in the way it matched the ruinous exterior of the Fallen Citadel. Scores of machines stood around its periphery in various states of disrepair. A half dozen things like Onder lined one wall, none of them complete. Bits of broken machine lay on the floor next to them. None of the machines in the room seemed to be in working order. The most complete of them sat on marble tables growing from the floor, displayed like museum pieces. All of them except Onder's brothers were of unguessable purpose. The light in the wall was mostly out, being confined to sickly-looking blotches. An even bigger window than in the first room looked over the valley. The camp of the modalmen was a collection of black dots on the pale mud of the lake bed; they went to and fro between their tents, smaller than fleas.

"We are in the Citadel," said Rel.

"That is what the soldiers call it."

"You know, you speak Maceriyan excellently. This is happening to me a lot. I did not expect either modalmen or their god to have any knowledge of our speech."

"I speak Maceriyan, because it is a debased version of my language." Qurunad looked down at Rel. His mechanical face may have been limited in expression, but his hauteur was clear enough. "When we brought your people to this Earth, you came from hundreds of worlds and had a thousand tongues. We taught many of you our language so that you might speak with one another and with us. We imprinted the leader caste of the modalmen with this knowledge also, though we gave them their own language so they might converse among themselves."

"You brought people here?" said Rel. He stopped and held up his hands. "Wait, wait. You brought us *here*?"

"You heard me correctly." The limp of the damaged god was pronounced, but Qurunad's voice was unaffected by pain, and was oddly flat for the lack of discomfort. "I can speak Karsarin if you prefer," he said, in perfect Karsarin, "or any one of mankind's crude languages. This Maceriyan is a bastardised child of Morfaan. I do not care for it, but it serves." The Brass God set off again. He went through an aperture into a round corridor where lights flickered. "Your antiquarians are beginning to uncover the past, though some of your culture's recent attempts to understand the world are so wrong they amuse me. Perhaps you might enlighten your scholars to the truth, should we all survive the next year, for I shall tell you much that is not known in a few moments. No more questions. Patience, please. I wish to sit. Walking tires this body. There is a pleasant place this way where we can talk."

They entered a corridor whose outward face was also of clear glass. Rel saw they were in one of the walkways he had seen from the ground, near the top of the Citadel. The little town around the base of the tower was a long way below. It appeared even more ruinous than it had to his earlier observations. Tangles of rustless metal lay in the hollow spaces of derelict buildings. Shattered piles of glass twinkled under coats of sand.

The walkway split in two. One tube led off around a sharp bend. The Brass God took the other turn toward what appeared to be a dead end. The wall sparkled with glimmer light and parted as they approached, opening into an indoor park where trees and grass grew under a glass sky. Rel recognised less than half the plants. Murals of human soldiers in archaic armour and riding strange, mammalian beasts filled the wall. They were depicted in the throes of combat, battling a race of bizarre creatures who appeared like nothing more than ambulatory mushrooms whose stalks were split by fang-rimmed mouths.

The Brass God lowered itself awkwardly into a throne of greened bronze and pointed out a bench of marble much lower than his own seat. Rel swept off a covering of dead leaves, and sat.

Onder scuttled away to a corridor on the other side of the little park, leaving them alone.

"I have sent Onder for water. Your body will need it to clear the after effects of the drug I administered."

Rel rubbed his head. "That is kind. My head does hurt."

"It will pass quickly. The drug is designed to be short-lived. I apologise for the need. I cannot have the access to this place discovered."

"You are afraid of Brauctha."

The Brass God stared, letting Rel know he disapproved of his rudeness, before continuing. The pulsing clicks of his artificial body sounded like crickets under the trees. "I would offer you food and wine, but I no longer have need of mortal sustenance, and so there is none in the Citadel. Nothing grows in these lands anymore. This garden is all that is left of the variety they supported. A pitiful collection."

Onder returned with a small machine clasped in a number of its limbs, a jug in another, water in a flawless glass in a third, and a small casket in a fourth. Rel accepted the water and drank it gratefully. It was bitterly cold, but delicious. "Thank you," he said. His headache receded as quickly as the god had promised. Onder refilled the glass from the jug. Rel gulped it down, for the water intensified his thirst rather than satisfying it. When he had drained the second glass, his headache retreated to lurk at the rear of his skull.

"What you are drinking is snow melt from the high peaks filtered through the stone," said Qurunad. "You will find no purer water anywhere in the Kingdoms. Certainly not in these fallen times." The god pronounced everything the same way, slightly brusquely, as if delivering an important lesson to uncomprehending students. "Now, to business. I will not delay. Please listen carefully. What you are about to hear is very important. You will most likely not believe it, but you must if your people and mine are to have any chance at survival, and this world is not to be transformed into a burning wasteland to match the World of Form."

Qurunad clasped his primary hands. His functional secondary arm waved as he spoke, gesturing emphatically to illustrate his points. Again Rel noted that he did not behave like a machine but like a living being. He shifted in his seat, and made all the other trivial movements a man might as he sat by the fire, telling a tale.

"The beginning," said the Brass God. "Whatever your mythology or your science tells you is wrong. The One made these worlds, and then he made his children. First were the twin worlds. Other spheres followed. After that, he made life, and from life, thinking beings. From five thinking beings, he made a race that could create. Our masters were the Children of The Five, a great and powerful race," Qurunad said. "Are you familiar with these terms?"

"From a folktale, told to me by Shkarauthir the modalman. He said much the same"

Qurunad nodded approvingly. "That will suffice. Good. It will save us time"

"The One is the god of the Ishamalani," said Rel. "I worked that out for myself."

Once more the Brass God gave Rel his disapproving stare. "You are quite facetious for a human being meeting a god."

"It's a problem I have. It gets worse the more scared I am."

"Contain yourself. These are matters of the utmost seriousness. The religion of the modalmen and that of your Ishmalani is similar," said the Brass God. "They contradict each other, both are incorrect in many details and some fundamentals. But, broadly speaking, their creeds are true, and the god they worship is the same.

"As the One made his children, so his Children of the Five made their own. The ones we must concern ourselves with were of two strains, conceived for different purposes. We Morfaan were raised up by the Children of the Five from the beasts of this earth to be their pupils." He paused. His artificial irises purred smaller in his lidless eyes. "The Children of the Five made many terrible mistakes in their stewardship of this world. Maybe our creation was one of them. The creation of the Draathis certainly was.

"While we Morfaan were made to be their companions and servants, the Draathis," he went on, "were created by the Children of the Five as slaves. They are machines of a sort, though they are made with such artifice and imbued with such a measure of will they are closer to truly living beings than this device I inhabit. We Morfaan were made of flesh, and were granted more of Will and less of Form. The Draathis were born of iron, so are more of Form and less of Will. Iron is the epitome of Form. It is inimical to what you understand as magic, but the reaction between magic and iron, as your own engineers are discovering, can produce powerful results. The indomitable Draathis soul was one unintentional consequence. Have you witnessed them yet?"

"I had never heard of them until I met Shkarauthir, and then only after a long time with the modalmen."

"To see the Draathis is to know fear. They are iron giants, big as the modalmen, with blood of molten metal and cunning minds. You will know soon enough, when you face them."

Qurunad reached out his hand. Onder offered up the machine. It was a small, flat metal box, with what looked a little like the horns of a lyre projecting upward from the back. The front was featureless, except for a small, hemispherical depression. Qurunad placed the machine on the arm of his chair. He then took the casket from Onder and opened it to show Rel the contents. Inside were stacked trays, each holding a dozen spheres the size of children's marbles. Each ball was of pure silver, and etched all over with delicate lines.

"Do you know what these are?"

Rel looked up at the god. "Morfaan silver."

"These are the books of my people. For generations, your kind has looted the ruins of our cities for these spheres, seeing nothing in them but the value of the metal they are made of. You were blind to their true worth, for upon each is a library of information. How many millions of these precious books have been melted down in ignorance by your kind," he said sorrowfully. "The knowledge of ages made into crude coin."

"I'm fairly certain no one knew what they were. Your emissaries could have told us."

"I agree," said the Brass God. "The others would not allow it. I argued that we should provide the reading machines to you, and reveal the truth of the silver in order to speed your development. I was outvoted. One of many catastrophic errors made by our ruling council. They decreed that the people of the Kingdoms be left to find their own way, with minimal guidance from our kind. If we did not leave you to raise yourselves up, it was argued, you would become powerful too rapidly. Inevitably you would learn the truth of your existence here, hunt the last of us down, and take the world for yourselves." Qurunad picked up one of the spheres. Rel could see no difference between it and the rest. Qurunad slotted the ball into the depression on the machine, where it clicked home.

"I will show you. Look between the projection prongs. Let the machine find harmony with your mind. No harm will come to you, do not be afraid. The more readily you accept this, the more I may show you."

The ball started to spin, building up speed until it rotated in a blur, becoming a solid, unmarked silver. A greyness formed between the horns, thickening into a flat mist.

"I take it this will not be like reading?" said Rel.

"The analogy between this technology and a book is imperfect," said Qurunad, taking Rel's words at face value, not hearing the impudence in them. "It is the only one you might comprehend. Obey me, and look into the grey!"

The greyness formed a skin that undulated like a sheet in the wind. A dancing circle of lights spun in the centre. Without any prior indication, Rel's perceptions shifted, and he felt that he was no longer within his own body, but separate from it by a marginal but crucial degree, so that his vision drifted rightward and his sense of touch moved out of synchronisation with his limbs. Nauseated, he attempted to look away, but his head would not turn.

"Keep your eyes on the grey!" commanded the Brass God. "Look within!"

The world turned on its side, and Rel found himself elsewhere.

CHAPTER THIRTY
The Day of Betrayal

THEY WERE IN the air, many hundreds of feet above the ground, but the sky was as solid as stone under them. Rel was not flying, instead he stood in the sky without falling from it. He could see for hundreds of miles in all directions, to misty horizons greened by patches of forest and the broad savannah lands between. Far away, Rel saw the spires of a white city. Though the vista was far-reaching, the chief element of the scene displayed to him were two mighty hosts arrayed against each other. A battle about to begin, frozen in time at the outbreak of hostilities.

"This is what I have brought you to see," said the Brass God. Qurunad's metal body was gone. In its stead was the form of a living Morfaan. He was slightly taller than Rel and roughly human in overall appearance, with a hint of the reptile to his banded throat and flattened nose. Long robes covered him from his neck to his feet, concealing his lesser arms, although there were embroidered slits in the cloth to allow him to employ them should the need arise. His upper arms were heavily muscled, and bare from the elbow. Around his wrists were wide bracelets so finely fitted and the metal that comprised them so thin that they flexed with the play of his muscles. Pouches and strange devices of silver and crystal hung from a thick belt of dracon hide about his slender waist. His voice had lost its metallic echo, but remained haughty, and the look from Qurunad's eyes of flesh was no warmer than those from his eyes of glass.

"Have you taken me through time?" asked Rel. "Is this the effect of Morfaan magic?"

"This is a true record of times long gone," said Qurunad. "Preserved in the silver so that it might be seen again. This is a distillation of time, captured the same way a mindless phantom is sometimes trapped upon the fabric of the world, when the conditions are right. This device is far improved over the natural phenomenon."

Qurunad inclined his head. They swooped down and across the landscape, as if they were in a painting, and flying at will through the scene.

The armies facing each other were not, as Rel might have expected, one of Draathis and one of Morfaan, but a mix of both species arranged in similar, checkerboard formations three regiments deep. In the first line were thousands of Draathis, and Rel got his first look at the beings who wished to ravage his world. They were blocky, dark figures with only two arms. Their heads were square, and though they appeared to be wearing armour, it was quite clear when Rel flew close by them that this was merely detail sculpted onto their iron skin. Their flesh was roughly cast, and purpled with oxidisation. Frozen in time they appeared as statues.

Their bodies looked to be incapable of movement for want of articulation. The fires in their eyes and mouths though were alive, lighting the ground before them orange, and rippling the air with arrested heat. They were caught in postures of aggression, fists clenched and raised, mouths open in silent howls. For all their belligerence, they had no weapons.

The second line was of Morfaan dressed in ornate armour of differing metallic shades—blues on one side, reds on the other. Unlike the iron giants, the reptilian creatures had all the semblance of living beings captured in a moment, which when ended would see them move again. Their regiments were varied in armament, some with polearms tipped with curved sword blades engraved all over with flowing script, others with swords and tall shields. A lesser number carried giant crossbows etched with blazing rune marks. These missile men were interspersed between the units carrying close quarter weaponry, so that they could support one another in battle. The warrior's lesser arms were half-hidden by the designs of their armour, the vambraces and gauntlets covering them fashioned so that when the arms were folded in, as most were, they looked like part of the warriors' breastplates.

The third lines consisted of more Morfaan. Among the hindmost regiments were massive cannons of strange design. Some of these were in the process of firing. Clouds of blue fire billowed from their mouths, out of which speared lightning bolts stopped upon the instant of striking.

On the wings of each army were hosts of dracon riders. Hundreds of flags flew from the standards in each group. They were glorious armies, beautiful and exotic, with such colours that they shimmered as rainbows across the land. Pretty and poison as oil on water.

The similarity between them was peculiar. The diversity of troop type and tactics seen in the Hundred's armies was lacking. Both armies were armed and armoured the same way, with only minor variation, and there were similar numbers on each side. Their deployment differed only in the detail. The red army favoured wider frontages and shallower formations in its infantry, the blue had more cavalry. They looked more like a parade ground show or armies for a war game fought upon a table than real forces.

At the centre rear of each army the generals oversaw their troops, and these were of a third type of being. Qurunad and Rel flew past these two—there were no more—without lingering as they did over other parts of the field.

"The Children of the Five," Qurunad said. "We must pass them quickly. Their power and might is preserved in this record, so it is possible for them to notice us."

"They transcend time?"

"It is more and less complicated than that," said Qurunad dismissively. "You would not understand."

The Morfaan's masters were tall, slender creatures, lofty as trees. They were beautiful by any human standard, with fine faces and slender limbs. Like the Morfaan, they too had four arms, but theirs were all of equal size, and freely displayed. They blazed with inner radiance, a pure, white luminance like starlight, so bright their armour's colours were washed out by it.

The red general had long blonde hair braided into complicated tresses tumbling down its back. The swell of breasts and a wideness across the hips indicated it was female. The blue was a male, with brown hair blowing free in the frozen wind. Both had piercing blue eyes with white pupils. The sclera, the white part of the eye, was in them black. They were girded for war, outfitted in gloriously made armour, three swords of light belted to their sides, and shields as tall as men upon their lower left arms.

Qurunad looked over the Children of the Five dispassionately. "Our masters were beautiful, but they were flawed. They were the sons and daughters of god, given dominion over these worlds, and they squandered their legacy. What could have been glorious was instead ruined. They waited so long for the One to return that they lost their way. There were many schisms between my masters down the aeons. Two occurred a long time before my people and the Draathis were made by them. The last saw the remaining few pure lords and ladies fall from their intended path entirely, and become obsessed with petty display. Hundreds of thousands of my kind died for their amusement in wars fought for no reason other than to entertain. You see them here at the final play of their power." He gestured grandly. "This is the day of the Great Betrayal."

A sucking boom set time into motion. Rel was rocked by a sudden explosion of noise. Cannons firing, Draathis howling metallic war cries, the sounding of horns and the singing of battle songs. Dracons more numerous than a forest's worth of birds screeched and roared. The armies lurched towards each other, bent on the other's destruction.

From the cannons blue orbs of energy flickered over the heads of the front lines, landing with thunderous force and carving bloody lanes into the regiments on each side. Warriors caught directly in the blasts were obliterated. Skeletons showed as black silhouettes within the Morfaan, their flesh white, and they burst apart in showers of ash. Draathis hit by the cannon exploded, flinging out sprays of molten iron in secondary waves of death.

Somehow, though they were again now high above the field, Rel fleetingly saw scenes close to. He watched as a handsome Morfaan captain levelled his pennant, and his squadron of dracons galloped out. He saw the female Child of the Five's black and white eyes darting across the battle, reading the movement of her foe. He saw the male hold out his two right arms, swords flickering with energy in each, bringing forth a flurry of semaphore from the signallers around him that prompted swift changes in the formations of his soldiery.

The Draathis of both armies moved toward one another under heavy fire, the ranks of Morfaan hard behind in close support. The iron monsters built up speed slowly, but once they were running they were unstoppable, outpacing the second and third lines, opening up space between them and their comrades. Their formations became a little ragged for their charging, but the iron giants of both sides met nearly simultaneously right across the front of the battle, with a clanging of metal on metal like the ringing of ten thousand muffled bells.

The Draathis brawled with fists, smiths' hammers beating on hot metal flesh. Their blows were phenomenally powerful, knocking their targets over, or sending them staggering many feet back with dents in their skin. Rel imagined the effect of one of those fists upon a human body. How could they even be killed? A bullet wouldn't stop one, he thought. A cannonball might.

The Morfaan of both armies spread out in measured synchronicity. Their formations held perfectly. They covered the lines of their metal comrades, tackling breakthroughs of Draathis from the opposing side, though many died doing so, as a dozen Morfaan were required to fell one Draathis. The Draathis wrought bloody havoc where they could. Rel watched as one, clutching the head of a slain rival, barged through the line of enemy Draathis into the red Morfaan. Using the head as a bludgeon it felled ten of them before enchanted glaives and the concentrated fire of two cannons brought it to smoking ruin. Even in death, the Draathis was deadly. Molten iron sprayed from its wounds, burning and maiming the Morfaan engaging it.

The tumult was harshened by the screams of Morfaan and dracons. Still they fought, responding without question to the orders of their glowing, inhuman masters.

By now, the cavalry wings on each side had engaged. The red cavalry drove off the blue in disarray, and reformed on both flanks, angling themselves inward to attack the rear ranks of the blue army's second line. Seeing this, the female Child of the Five went into a frenzy of activity, sending out orders via her flagmen to prepare her infantry to fend off the charge.

More Draathis were breaking through into the blue lines. Crossbows spat bolts of screaming magic at them. Where they breached the iron skin they left holes aglow with dripping metal and the Draathis fell lifeless, but as often as not the bolts ricocheted off.

"Now we come to it," said Qurunad. "The moment history was changed. The Draathis were clever. They waited until my people were fully engaged before springing their trap."

The red cavalry charged, horns blaring, in two directions, one half of them slamming into the rear ranks of the blue's second line, the other racing and feinting in front of the third. As a soldier, Rel could see they were doing so to draw the fire and attention of the back line away from the attack on the second. It was a callous manoeuvre, achieved at a horrible cost in lives. Broken dracon bodies wheeled upward, blasted skyward by the force of cannon immensely more powerful than those possessed by the Kingdoms.

A hallooing call sounded from somewhere amid the Draathis. It was loud, but barely audible among the raging battle, until it was joined by another, and another, until in chorus the calls of the Draathis gradually overcame the clamour of arms. Draathis from both sides disengaged from their opponents. They stepped back from their melee, and threw their lumpen heads upwards, mouths wide, and sang out notes as blaring as steam horns. The song spread quickly, and soon all the Draathis were singing, and had ceased fighting. Their bodies shimmered with the heat issuing from their mouths.

At first the Morfaan and their masters were unaware what was happening. The blue general noticed before the red, and became paralysed in horror. His banner men looked to him. Finally, he marshalled himself, and sent out a rapid succession of orders. By then it was too late.

Moving as one unstoppable formation, the Draathis from both sides poured uphill into the blue lines, slaughtering the Morfaan by the hundred. The smell of cooked blood fouled the battlefield as Morfaan were crushed underfoot by hot iron. Caught between the advancing Draathis and the red cavalry, the blue second line broke catastrophically. The red cavalry, still ignorant of what was happening, sounded horns for pursuit, but as they hacked down the fleeing blue Morfaan, they were caught by the Draathis of their own side and slaughtered. Dracons' heads exploded under Draathis fists. Morfaan sauraliers were ripped from their saddles and torn in two with contemptuous ease.

By this point, the generals understood the day was lost. The blue made a rapid pattern of ritual gestures and disappeared in a spear of light that soared skyward, leaving his warriors to their fate. The female screamed at his cowardice, and launched herself upward. She flew without wings, raining down lashes of fire and black storms of unmaking that annihilated everything they touched. Though combat between them continued sporadically, the Morfaan from both sides trained their guns on the conjoined Draathis horde, blasting holes in their lines. Molten iron blood set the grass afire. Smoke and steam fogged the field. More bass singing had the Draathis change formation. The centre pressed on into the scattered remnants of the blue army, while the Draathis flanks reversed course, and began a jog toward the red lines that became an unstoppable charge.

The blue guns fired for a brief few rounds before the Draathis ploughed into them. They smashed down the crewmen, and wrenched the guns from their carriages, which they then wielded as cumbersome shotguns.

The newly armed Draathis ignored the artillery pounding them from the red line, and aimed for the female general sweeping their ranks with death. Cerulean blasts arced toward her, each discharge of energy accompanied a thunderclap. She flew gracefully through them, her robes streaming behind her and energy trailing from her hands, and responded with awesome might.

Draathis cannoneers disintegrated into showers of iron dust, their stolen weapons thumping smoking to the turf. She turned about, spiralling around, unleashing power Rel had never heard of, not even in the most far-fetched tale.

She slaughtered over a thousand Draathis, but there were too many of them for her to prevail. Her grace and agility were no defence against the lightning chasing her across the sky. She managed a second pass before a column of energy tore off her lower left arm and smashed a hole through her side, and she fell shrieking to the earth.

She survived the fall. Her wound was as large and ugly as a dracon bite, and bled glowing blood that soaked into the torn up ground. She was trying to rise, pushing herself up, when the Draathis surrounded her. They lifted their heads, but no singing came. Instead they gave voice to a horrifying roar of triumph, impelled by centuries of pent up rage.

Rel turned away as they stamped her to death.

Qurunad looked down at Rel. "It is foul, is it not? Our masters were cruel and arrogant, but even they did not deserve to die like this. They thought themselves masters of everything upon this globe. This battle was a shock to them. The same day, Draathis all across the world rose up and slaughtered the Morfaan and the Children of the Five alike. It was the first battle in a war that has lasted for thousands of years. Far worse was to come. This battle took place a few hundred miles south of where my citadel now stands. If you look north, you will see there were no mountains then. The city in the distance is Losirna, which you visited on your way here." Qurunad looked over the untamed prairies to the city in the distance, and the rich fields that surrounded it. "The Black Sands was not always as it is now. Once, it was the heart of our empire. Ruthnia, where your Hundred Kingdoms squat in the ruins of our world, was but a province. The Draathis destroyed it all."

The battlefield froze and shrank from view. Rel blinked, disoriented. He was back in the Citadel's park, staring at a grey patch in space that snapped closed as Qurunad's mechanical fingers pulled free the piece of Morfaan silver from the machine. He contemplated it before placing it back into its tray, and shut the casket.

"This box contains the history of our wars," he said, resting his hand upon it. "In here is every atrocity visited upon the Children of the Five and the Morfaan by the Draathis."

"What happened to the Children of the Five?" said Rel. "I have never heard of them. In the Kingdoms, it is accepted that you Morfaan were the masters of the world."

"We ruled this world for thousands of years, once they were gone. So they were forgotten," said Qurunad. "The Children of the Five were much diminished in number and in potency by the Draathis' betrayal. In time, they withdrew to the fringes of the world, leaving us to fight their creations without help. Our war continued against the Draathis for scores of centuries. They evolved a cruel intelligence of their own, and a technology to go with it. Eventually, we were victorious, but at incalculable cost. Victory resulted in the destruction of our heartlands and the creation of the Black Sands by weapons of such power you could not possibly imagine them. We drove the Draathis through the greatest of the World Gates to the World of Form, but they returned, and returned again. Every 4000 years, every time the Twin draws closest, they make another attempt to take this world for themselves."

"What about us? What about humanity?" asked Rel.

"Under the Children of the Five we thrived, though we were servants to them. We learned many things at their urging. Some of the Children of the Five were not the idle things you saw in the battle, spending blood for leisure, but were thoughtful beings who desired above all else to find their god. We helped their search, and in doing so we discovered the way to many worlds, places that are closer to us than our own skin, but forever invisible." He stroked his broken lower arm with one his upper limbs. "Our explorers travelled the spheres, visiting thousands upon thousands of worlds in dozens of existences. We found no trace of the One or any like him. But in many, many places we encountered your kind. When the war dragged on and our people dwindled, your kind were brought here to fight for us. We do not have the art of our creators, and although we could make things such as this," he gestured at his metal body, "we cannot create life. So we brought you here, along with the animals and plants you depend upon. With your help, we beat the Draathis."

"You won thanks to us?"

Qurunad snorted metallically. "Not in the most important sense. It did not work. To all intents, we lost. Though you were numerous, and the strains we teased from you potent, you could not win us the victory we needed quickly enough. When it was finally won, you remained numerous, while we were few. We were outnumbered in our own world. Those of us that were left decided to shepherd you, and rebuild the world for both peoples. We would do better than our creators, we thought. After the Draathis returned for the first time, we built and took up residence in the Parrui, that which you call the Godhome, and began our great endeavour. The period you refer to as the Maceriyan Resplendency was the result."

He looked away from Rel at the murals for a while. When he resumed his account, he spoke quietly.

"We should have left, but grief and arrogance blinded us. Although the Maceriyan Resplendency ushered in an era of prosperity for your people, it was a crude memory of the Children of the Fives' civilisation. The world sickened. We discovered our kind had made a grave mistake bringing you here at all. Everywhere your kind were discovered, your creatures had supplanted those that were there before. Our world was no different. You corrupted the One's holy creation. Your animals drove the draconkind to extinction, your crops choked the flowers of His fields. Your piss and your shit poison everything, and now you enter an era of filthy machines. Where ours held harmony with the world, yours only take. Their manufacture scars the land. Their operation sucks the soul from the Earth."

The Brass God stood, and looked up through the clear ceiling, where the sun shone against the cliffs climbing vertically out of sight. "As if your goats, your dogs, your wheat, birds, fish, rats, mice, and the million other things you infested this sphere with were not bad enough, worse by far were your minds. We saw you as weak and plentiful, the perfect slave, but you are not weak. Our numbers dwindled ever faster. Few Morfaan took children to term. Our young became rare things, treated like princes, to their detriment. We did not know why, until we found too late that your will is greater than ours, especially when there are many of you. As you increased in number, so we died away. You have reshaped this world merely by your presence. We were fading, as the Children of the Five faded.

"When the Draathis returned, they tore down our civilisation. We sealed our World Gates, confining ourselves to this one reality in a bid to shut them out, but they returned again. They forwent the gates and crossed the airless spaces between our worlds, raining from the sky in iron ships. They found common cause with the men of the north, whom they beguiled, laid waste to the lands there, and marched upon Ruthnia. Once more the world was brought to ruin, millions of Morfaan and men died, the Resplendency was brought to an end, though compared to the struggles of olden times this Great War, as your people called it, was a skirmish. Somehow, the Draathis had mastered magic, an impossibility, we thought, but they, like us, used you as their pawns, and so our third error was revealed. Their Iron Mages succeeded in enchanting the world, rendering the light of the sun here poisonous to our bodies. We remained a while, to see some of what was lost regained, forced always to travel in the mists, before it was decided we should finally leave altogether and await the Earth's return to grace. The last thousands of my people were put into sleep. I was one of seven chosen to watch over them in a fortress built beyond any world; two, the sibling-spouses Josan and Josanad were chosen to wake from time to time and travel as emissaries to our lost home. Their role was to guide you as best they could. You will know of them. But there were five more, who gave up our flesh to advise the two. We intended to wait out our foes. The Draathis' last incursion was weaker; desperate, we thought, in its vindictiveness. We assumed they would die in exile. The world of Form was a paradise, they made it a hell. We thought nothing could live there. We were wrong again."

"But you are here, not in this other place," said Rel.

"How marvellously astute," said the Brass God drily. "The plan did not work. The Draathis are ready to take the Earth. It is we who have grown weak while they have grown stronger. When I realised this, the others would not listen to me. They had become cowards, clinging to forlorn hopes. I tried to convince them to reopen the world gates, and take the Heart of Mists to a new land, reawaken our people from its confines and start again far from this wreck of a sphere. I encouraged them to leave you to your fate. This was the second time I did this. For the second time, they would not listen. So I broke my vows, escaping here, where I had left this body for my refuge. I have dwelled within this citadel alone for a long time, watching, waiting, until the modalmen gathered for a last battle. I expect they will lose."

"If you doubted your own plan from the beginning," said Rel, "I see little reason to trust you."

"I was an engineer, never an idealist," said Qurunad. "As your civilisation developed, I saw a time when you would remaster the old technologies and magics. Without our guidance you began to draw overly much on the world spirit that is the source of all magic, and weakened the wards upon the gates. The Draathis have been waiting for the same thing. The end comes. They will come this time in migration, not invasion."

"Out there there are thousands of modalmen," said Rel. "Who are they? They are not men. Did you bring them here as you brought us?"

"In a manner of speaking," said the Brass God. "We made the modalmen as warriors. They were forged upon anvils of pure will to be the greatest threat to the Draathis. They are strong, resistant to the heat of the Draathis' blood, and imbued with a life force that sings with magic. As iron is anathema to magic, so too is magic anathema to iron. They think of themselves as the true men, as do you. You are both correct. Their culture is closer to the original. Your form is. They are you. They were once like yours."

"I see," said Rel calmly. 'You said you were expecting me?'

"My kind had machines with limited abilities to predict future events," said Qurunad. "There have been several times when a man of the Kingdoms looked to be coming here, only for his path to diverge and the present that emerged to differ from the future I saw. When my machines provided model futures in which you arrived here, I had little hope. That is why I say perhaps your presence is fate. Perhaps the One hears my prayers, finally; after all these hundreds of thousands of years, he looks to his first children again, these worlds of Will and Form.'

'Then why did you not warn us?'

'I cannot leave this place. I needed someone like you to take a message back to the Kingdoms and inform them of the coming of the modalmen, the Draathis... all of it. If you do not do this, there will be war between the modalmen and the people of your lands. If you can convince the governments of your kind to allow the modalmen through, and fight by their side, you may stand a chance in stopping the Draathis. Your technology is not as well progressed as I hoped, but there are many of you. If there is no unity of purpose..." He stared at Rel. "Well, you have seen the battle between the Draathis and my kind. You are a soldier. You know what the Draathis will do to your armies. You will need every ally."

"How will I deliver this message?" said Rel.

"I shall aid your escape. There is a phenomenon the modalmen call the Mountain's Breath. The modalmen see it as a sacred blessing. While it occurs, they will not stop you."

"But you said yourself your powers of prediction are imprecise. How can you be sure? I won't be able to simply walk out of here. A lot of them are itching for an excuse to kill me."

"The breath of the mountain is not weather. It is the product of the machines like these you see around you. They will do nothing to stop you, because they will not be able to. The Mountain's Breath was a device to teach the modalmen new things, to imbue them with more strength, to ensure their loyalty. It had many applications. None of them work now, but the trance can still be induced. It is one of the last controls I have over the modalmen."

Rel leaned his elbows onto his knees and gripped his head. "This is nonsense. Even if I make it back to the Hundred, I will not be believed. I was sent to the Glass Fort for an indiscretion with a lady. I was a laughing stock. Even if my record were clean, I am only a captain in a single army. There are scores of them in the Kingdoms. My word is worthless. *If* I survive the journey." He looked into the Brass God's chilling face. "If you created the modalmen, they are yours to command. Can you not ask them to deliver this message? Can you not go yourself? Why do you not go below and command them?"

"To answer your second question first, this body is dependent on the citadel. It draws power from the glimmer matrix of the buildings and the roots it puts into the mountain. If I left, it would die within three days. I have attempted to access your telesending network to send a direct message to your rulers, but your technology is so far behind ours I cannot make a signal that will reach your devices over the interference generated by the Black Sands. If I were a mage, then there would be other means, but I am not, and so there are not. To answer your first question, the modalmen are beyond my control. They have changed, and divided into two principal factions."

"I noticed," said Rel. "Half of them think I'm a pet, the other half want to eat me."

"They hate the Draathis because they were bred to hate them, but I cannot order them as I might once have. I am no general, in any case. If I were to go to them, this Brauctha who leads their man-eating clans might well destroy me. Their culture is of conquest. He who slays a being takes all his possessions by right. I cannot let that happen. The moot underway now will determine how they approach the Kingdoms. The balance of opinion among them is shifting toward open hostility. Many moderates see the Hundred as an obstacle to their goal of destroying the Draathis. They remember the betrayal of the northmen in the last war and see no difference between your peoples. Your actions toward the modalmen in the interim have not helped. If the Kingdoms respond to the modalmen's arrival peaceably, it will greatly strengthen the faction who regard you as lesser men rather than beasts, and reassure those with doubts. If we are fortunate, the man-eaters will not win out and you will convince your kind to allow the horde through the Gates of the World to fight with you. Once they see your weapons, they will not wish to engage in war, and it will be settled. Then our position will be tenable, and the world may survive another age."

"If, if, if," said Rel. "This plan is desperate! Fucking hells!" He slapped his knee. "You are a poor god."

"I am no god at all. These are desperate times. I am taking a terrible gamble on you, Rel Kressind. I have watched your people spread across this world that was once our own. You burrow into the corpses of our cities like maggots. Your machines burn the souls of our dead. How do you think that makes me feel?"

Rel frowned in question.

"What do you think the glimmer is?" said the Brass God. "It is the crystallised remains of the souls of the Morfaan and the Children of the Five, trapped and scattered across the world when these lands were blasted by the Draathis. The final, most terrible revenge of the Draathis on we Morfaan. And you burn it like coal. I should hate you, but I see no choice but to help you. I prefer to look to the middle past, when our peoples enjoyed an age of harmony, when neither were slaves nor masters. We can have that again."

"And it all depends on me," said Rel. He rubbed his face.

"Unfortunately, yes. Will you do it?"

"There is another issue. My people in the wagons. Why have they been brought here? Shkarauthir says they are gifts for you. I can see no use that you might have for them."

The Brass God lowered his head. "I was afraid you would ask that."

"Why?"

"It is better you do not know. Reconsider your question. Forget them. They are lost."

"Really? Because I would love to know what is worse than being eaten alive."

The Brass God hesitated. "We made the modalmen from your people."

"You said."

"The modalmen have no gender. There are no women, no infant modalmen. They are immortal, so long as they are not slain in battle, but they fight often among themselves."

"Then there should be very few of them." Rel leaned forward and pointed at Qurunad. "Unless you are adding to their numbers."

The Brass God nodded. "I change a handful of humans every century. A man deemed worthy of transformation is ripped apart down to the most fundamental level and refashioned. When they are rebuilt they remember their old selves sometimes, but the man they were is effectively dead. They will gladly turn on what they once loved. The machinery is here, in the citadel. I intend to use it again. It is cruel, but necessary. Without it, the modalmen would cease to exist. And they need to increase their numbers."

Rel shook his head in disbelief. "I cannot let that happen."

"You must. There are a few thousand human beings in the cages. Think how many will die if you do not make your way home. I will die if I do not reinforce the clans. Brauctha will take what he wants. Then no human will be safe. Do you want that?"

Rel stared at him. He hated Qurunad then. He hated fate and circumstance and all the powers that had led him to this moment. Rationally, there was no decision to be made. Rationality was the order of the day in Ruthnia. Rel had never cared for it. It made men inhuman.

For the first time since he was made an officer, Rel felt the burden of responsibility. Before there had always been someone else to make the hard decisions. This was his alone to make.

He looked at his hands. Hands that held the world.

"I suppose I have no choice," he said.

"You decide well," said Qurunad, in relief. "Watch for the Mountain's Breath. I will bring it now. The trance effect begins with a nimbus of light around the peak above the Citadel. When it blows hot, and the sand rides in sheets within the valley, then you should go."

"What if I am mistaken?"

"This will be like no wind you have ever witnessed. You cannot mistake it. A storm will follow. This will be the first of the dangers you must overcome."

"Right," said Rel.

The Brass God walked to the centre of the lawn. Gears squealed in his damaged leg. He gestured that Rel follow.

"Please, Goodfellow Kressind. Do not attempt to help your people here. It will greatly reduce your chances of success."

An oval of light opened at the Brass God's side.

"A short range gate, similar to the Road of Fire you rode upon. It will take you back to the temple," said the Brass God.

Rel nodded, and stepped toward the gate. The light was harsh, but somehow it did not hurt his eyes. He paused. "I can't just leave my people behind," he said to the god. "I've come all this way to help them."

"You must abandon them," said the Brass God. "The fate of the whole world depends upon it."

The gate swelled. The light swallowed Rel.

A SHIFT IN his gut, and Rel found himself in total darkness. By striking repeatedly at his flint he discovered he was back in the temple as the Brass God had promised. His weapons and last torch were in a pile at the entrance. The sad howl of the wind from the mountain was oppressive after the quiet of the citadel, and the dark pressed in on him, eager to devour the tiny noises he made. By the time he got the torch alight he was fighting a gnawing dread.

Firelight shone off cracked reliefs and broken statues. There were many in the kingdoms who would have spent what little light the torch provided in exploring the temple; such places were highly prized by academics and grave robbers alike. Rel only wished to leave.

He had to race the burning of his torch back. The wind blew stronger on the way down, nearly putting out the flames. Intermittent darkness when the torch guttered limited the speed of his descent. There seemed to be more side passages than he recalled. From them the wind moaned with a multiplicity of voices. By the time he emerged from the crack the wind was blasting from it. It pushed at his back, hurrying him along, and he feared he might be swept over the edge to his death. Stumbling at its shoving through the cave entrance, he threw himself to the side before he was hurled off the cliff.

Drauthek looked up at him. It was dark, and he had lit the fire. He was still chewing on strips of dried meat.

The White Moon was high, its brilliant light turning the Earth silver, while the Twin behind remained a looming black. On the Twin fires danced at random. It was so close Rel could have touched it.

"See god then?" said Drauthek.

Rel nodded his head dumbly.

"He happy. Mountain Breath start. Good sign. Not if blow you away though!"

The giant modalman got up, his blanket sliding from his back. He put the lid back on the water urn, and stamped out his fire.

"Come. We go back now. You tired, but this no place to stay for night. Too holy, and too dangerous."

CHAPTER THIRTY-ONE
The Second House

"My dear, I am sure that there will be enough support to get this bill through the Second House. After that, I would expect defeat in the Third."

Master Fendol was an earnest man of middle years, though he looked younger, being without the belly good living had bestowed on many of his peers. His small realm was the ladies' salon of the Sunderdown Palace. Custom demanded women wait within its confines while the Houses' gathering rituals were completed. Fine plasterwork and delicate brass sculptures decked the room in opulence, a sign of Karsa's growing wealth, but it oppressed her. Her attention strayed constantly to the double doors leading onto the ladies gallery. Shortly, they would be opened, and she would be able to watch the gears of Karsan government at work, grinding up her proposals into nothing.

"I intend to take it all the way to the end," said Katriona defiantly. "And if it does fail, then I shall try again until I do succeed."

"She will!" said Demion. "And I will support her every step of the way."

"Thank you, husband."

"That is admirable, goodlady," said Fendol, "but it will do little but waste your time and money."

A small group of sympathisers sat with them. Mill owners who shared Katriona's concern for the plight of the city's workers. A couple were there simply because they saw advantage for themselves in tighter regulation of the labour market. Katriona counted maybe nine of the eleven as sincere. They were all men, because female owners like herself were a rarity.

"You should count your victories. Your threats alone have led to a better application of the existing laws," said Goodfellow Martenion, of the famous weaving family. "Although I wish for more myself, you should not be too disheartened." He patted her on the hand gently.

Demion pointedly took his wife's hand to prevent further impropriety.

"Many children are begging on the streets, as factory owners expel them to avoid prosecution under the new law," said Demion.

"Existing laws, dear husband," Katriona corrected him.

"Well, whether existing or not, you have caused a stir. I myself have become involved, and have our agents scouring the city for such waifs. We will offer them a home, and employment, and schooling."

"You are involved, Demi?" asked Goodfellow Brask, who knew Demion Morthrock socially, although took a far more active interest in his factories than Demion did in his own.

"Yes, even I," said Demion. "Katriona here has changed me for the better."

"Well, if she can do that," said Brask. "She can do anything."

"I believe she can," said Demion Morthrock fiercely.

"If we cannot succeed politically," said Katriona, "we shall lead by example, until the others are shamed into action."

"Well said!" said Martenion.

"My dear goodfellow," said Olwin Barnes, the richest of them all, "that is all well and good for the likes of us to promise, but not all of us have such deep pockets. The law has to change, or it will be for nought."

"We are willing to lend you our support, but only if the proposals become law," said another. "If they do not, then those firms that adopt the new standards will be penalising themselves. Our costs will increase enormously, leaving us at the mercy of our competitors."

"That, my goodfellow, is a defeatist attitude, and though the easier path, it will lead to greater troubles further down the road," said Martenion.

Watching all this quietly was a man in far plainer garb than the others. He was rougher featured from a life of manual labour. He was, in matter of fact, poor, and everything about his appearance and demeanour screamed it. He was uncomfortable in the richness of the lounge, but bullishly ignored it.

"You have the support of the Agglomerated Labour Associations, my goodlady," said the man. "When the time comes, and the factories of every man who stands against you come a halt, my people will keep on working in yours."

"Goodman Monimus, your support is appreciated," said Brask, "but you people have no power."

"Who turns the metal, who weaves the cloth? Who repairs the machines and moves the coal and tends the drays? We can make that stop," said Monimus.

"Your movement is in its infancy."

"But growing fast. There will be a reckoning. There is only so much the people will take before they rise up."

"I am uncomfortable being associated with this revolutionary," said Brask.

"We are all revolutionaries, goodfellow," said Martenion.

A woman approached the group demurely. She smiled in the socially approved manner, and dipped a curtsey to Katriona.

"Goodlady Kressinda-Morthrocksa," she said.

"Goodlady Thrivena-Andasy," Katriona said.

"My husband sent me to say that there are those that are sympathetic to your cause, who believe what you say is right. Or so I hear. Many perhaps who would back you, but who fear that, should they act before the law demands it, they will be ruined."

"It is the right thing to do," said Katriona.

"Sometimes the right thing to do is very much the wrong thing to do," said Goodlady Thrivena-Andasy. "Good day."

The doors to the ladies' gallery swung wide. A wigged footman emerged.

"Goodladies, goodfellows, and fine citizens," he said, "the Second House is in session. You may enter the gallery to witness the debate if you wish."

The occupants of the saloon downed their drinks

and made their way to the door, some still engaged in passionate political debate. Many were of the same social class as Katriona—new money aristocrats, their families recently ennobled. Most of these people were against her and glared their disapproval. Ironically, the old money crowd who were ordinarily venomously opposed to anything the new industrialists offered to the house, were enthusiastically in favour of her reforms. In her movement they saw a way of curbing the power of the newcomers.

It was a mess. People from all factions despised her. Many who said they supported her did for selfish reasons. Others who would support her kept their opinions to themselves fearing the judgement of their peers. She could not trust anyone. *Damn the lot of them*, she thought.

To stiffen her resolve, Katriona held in her mind the children toiling their lives away in factories, the families starving as they worked themselves to death, the workers dying from the filth they lived in.

Head held high, she entered the Ladies Gallery. Her supporters formed up around her.

Women were only allowed into that one space, whereas of course the men could go where they liked, and that included the Ladies Gallery. Demion, Brask and the rest sat around her without a thought for that fact. For them, it was natural. For her, it was an affront.

Once she had won the war for the lives of the poor, she thought she might attempt to change the lot of women too.

*   *   *

THE KARSAN GOVERNMENT was a multi-layered thing, cumbersome in its multitudinous departments and cursed with several layers of interleaved, duplicated authority. Despite all that, its system was among the most liberal in the Hundred Kingdoms.

Unlike many other nations, Karsa's head of state, the king, did not have absolute power. Complicating the situation, King Demes was unfortunately mad, and his son Prince Alfra ruled for him. Had he been sane, his power would have been limited anyway; after the Lord's Rebellion three centuries before, the nation had been governed as a constitutional monarchy.

Three Houses made up the parliament, each with a hundred members. The First House had once been made up of priests. Since the days of the god driving, its members had been professional bureaucrats. It had no legislative power. The First House existed solely to decide the legality of any motion to be put before the other Houses of the parliament, and gauge the true intent of the petitioners in suggesting motions to be debated.

The Second House had much more influence. Its ranks were drawn from the merchants, lesser aristocracy and bankers of the realm, with a smattering of philosophs and other wise minds to grant it a veneer of intellectual respectability. They were all directly elected by the populace, although suffrage was restricted to the wealthy.

Many of the new, industrial nobility occupied the landsmen seats of the Second House. They further scrutinised what the First House had deemed as acceptable for possible legislation, and voted upon its implementation. Should the motion be passed, it was then sent to the Third House.

In the Third House the roar of democracy became a timid presentation of fealty. The Third House had evolved from the King's Council of earlier centuries, and performed a similar role, though its membership had been greatly expanded to match the hundred of the lower two houses. The Third House's landsmen were the hereditary lords, most descended from King Brannon's companions. The remainder were drawn from the richest industrialists. Prince Alfra himself headed its proceedings, in the stead of the king.

Katriona was well versed in all this. Her father's contrary attitudes towards his eldest daughter had encompassed bullying her to learn all about politics, then rejecting her because she unfemininely excelled at its study.

She was grateful there was little chance of Gelbion Kressind showing up to vote. He still had his seat in the House, but had withdrawn from politics after his illness several years before, and had not voted on any issue since. Even so, she resented her father's presence in her thoughts. Had he actually deigned to come...

She clenched her hand until her manicured nails bit into her palm through her lace gloves. She had far more pressing issues to consider than her father.

Plutocrats, careerists, old money, new money, slave drivers, shirkers, inheritors and parasites of every cloth waited to foul her political ambitions.

If Katriona's motion were to pass the Second House's vote, it would fail in the Third, as the members there had the most to lose from it. Though the industrialists made up a minority in the Upper House, most of the richer companion lords had money invested in the new industries. But the Second was by no means won. The poorer landed aristocracy would vote for the motion to cripple the industrialists. The industrialists would vote according to the relative weight they attached to their consciences and their wallets. She could not even decide with any certainty if her bill of laws would be voted for by those who professed support. They all had their games to play, and they hid their hands well.

According to the spirit of Karsa's national character, her challenge should have been welcome. Before the days of glimmer engines and factories, Karsa had been an agrarian nation. The Little Agreement made between the lords and the peasants after the Lords' Rebellion cemented the rights of those who tilled the land, and the responsibilities of those who owned it. She sought to extend the spirit of that agreement to the relationship between factory owner and worker. There was, as far as she could see, no difference. She knew the rest of them saw she was right, that all this new wealth depended on the blood of others.

Fortunes were at risk. Unsurprisingly, the issue was hotly contested.

The crowd took their seats in a gallery so steep that the feet of each tier's occupants were close by the heads of the people in the row below. The observers clung like seabirds to a cliff over the assembly of the Second House. The chamber was in a pit beneath, shaped like a floatstone hull in recognition of Karsa's maritime traditions.

In another land, in the Queendom of Pris, Katriona would have been down there presenting her own case while the men looked on powerlessly. In Karsa, she must rely on men. She found it tiresome. Having achieved so much, she knew she could achieve more if only her gender did not stand in her way.

In her stead, the speaker of the Second House set out Katriona's bill in reduced form. Most of the men (again, she noted, they were *all* men), had copies of her motion in their hands that they peered at and flicked through. Some had obviously read it back to front. Others had just as obviously never set eyes on it and looked at it as if they had no acquaintance with documents whatsoever. Of the hundred seats, fewer than half were occupied. The members' absence was a mark of the lack of seriousness with which the house regarded Katriona. That was another thing that would have to change. A fiery mix of impatience and outrage clenched her heart. Through injustice and thwarted will are revolutionaries made.

Speeches were given on her behalf. Those in favour came before the rest. Two were allowed per side, all strictly timed upon a large brass timepiece to the right of the speaker's chair.

The first speech came from Goodman Polko Vreesen, a manufacturer of bricks out of Stoncastrum. He was a dull fellow whose first name Katriona could never recall; she was sure she would forget it again before the end of the proceedings. He had been chosen by his male peers, not her. Frustrated enormously that she played no part, she watched men she barely knew hijack her reforms.

"Rich men are not necessarily blind to the suffering of those they make their money from," Vreesen began. "Wealth does not automatically lead to an erosion of morality. We all of us know wherefrom our wealth springs. It is not from the sweat of our own brows, but those of the workers who toil for us. In their suffering is gold, and we mine it ruthlessly." His voice droned like a hive of bees, soporific and irritating. "Our Goodlady Kressinda-Morthrocksa has achieved much where other reformers have failed, embarrassing our Ministry of Justice into ensuring existing legislation is properly enforced. I say she is right to want to go further!"

Demion leaned in to his wife.

"I cannot simply stand by," he said. "I support you fully, my dear. This is all beyond me, but I will find the children for you. You know that I am striving to do that?"

"I know, my husband," she said, her attention on the proceedings of the House.

"I love you my dear," he said. "You are strong, and talented."

She turned to him with a half-smile. "What about beautiful?"

"I would not reduce you to the characteristic of beauty," he said seriously.

She laughed softly. "I am a woman. We are contrary creatures. None of us wish to be judged by our looks, my dear husband, but most of us wish to be thought beautiful."

"But you are beautiful."

She put her hand through the loop of his elbow.

"And you are kind, and generous. And a good lover," she added mischievously.

He reddened.

"And I love you very much also, but now I ask you to please be quiet, because I am trying to listen to the speeches."

"Of course, of course my dear."

She smiled again at him. His bumbling manner she found endearing only because, beneath his bluster and his obsession with horses and cards, Demion was an upright man.

The first speech ended to applause from more than half the House. The bells of the clock chimed a moment later.

"A good sign," whispered Martenion from the row behind. His back popped as he bent low enough to speak in Katriona's ear.

Katriona nodded. Martenion had helped select Vreesen to speak first. In her opinion, his speech had been unforgivably dull, and full of platitude. Martenion did not have enough regard for her, or her own choice would have delivered the opening speech. Still, Vreesen's message was clear. Morality must play a part in profit. There was a mark in their favour.

The second speech was less inspiring, and drew a half-hearted response. She breathed hard against her corsets. If only she could speak herself!

The bells rang before the speech was finished. The first speech against was announced.

The first speech against was simply, "No, no, no, no!" delivered by a man brandishing the paper bearing her proposals as if it were a murder weapon. Worryingly, the applause for that was the loudest yet.

The second against was equally thunderous in tone, though more traditional in scope. A short, round man announced as Goodfellow Dwin gave it, a man Katriona was wearyingly familiar with.

"These proposals cannot pass!" Dwin explosively roared, his face turning shockingly red, as if a lever had been thrown and sent the pistons of his heart into sudden motion. "They go against every principle of Karsan free enterprise, the very virtues that have made this nation great! The poor should not be coddled, they should have no allowance made for them!" He whacked the proposals on the board of the speaking lectern in time with his words. "If the poor are granted these concessions, they will become lazy, and presumptuous of aid. Where will be their incentive to better themselves, and to raise themselves to a higher state of life? No! I say no!"

Laughter greeted parts of his speech. Men shouted, "Hear hear." Others jeered back at them, naming them heartless and slavers. Shouts in support and against what Dwin said echoed off the high ceiling; through all Dwin ploughed on regardless, with the manner of a man who would be heard no matter how long it took.

"He's certainly stirred them up," said Brask.

"We are fools to pander to the lazy few," Dwin continued. "For the sake of our tormented morality, we would toss our economic might upon a bonfire. If we are to do this, then I will remove my manufacturing operation to the continent. In Maceriya they have no such laws. Do not think our competitors of other lands have not seen this, or that they do not rub their hands at the prospect of this law's enactment! Without these restrictions upon their own manufactories, they shall drain the industry from these isles, and take the money from our pockets. This woman," he pointed up to the gallery, "should remain at home and raise children, a situation better suited to her compassion. See, my goodfellows, the danger that lies in allowing women to participate in men's affairs. They are a disruptive factor to an ordered world, and the result is this!" He threw his papers down. "It is anti-competitive, it is unpatriotic, it is economic suicide! I for one hope that Katriona Kressinda-Morthrocksa's tenure at the Morthrocksey Mill remain an isolated experiment, and that she enters no further into the field of politics. Enact this ruling at your peril, goodfellows! Mark my words, mark my words!"

"Dwin is among our worst opponents. Many of the older men respect him," muttered Brask.

"I know him well," said Katriona. "He has tried to cheat me twice on wholesale silver prices for my munitions factory, thinking me a weak-minded woman. I corrected his opinion there. It appears he requires further correction."

"I am sure you will provide it," said Brask, amused.

The Second House went into a brief recess. The clocks were reset. Drinks were brought to the members too occupied in conversation with their fellows to leave the chamber. They were also served to those too indolent to bother, or those too ridden with gout to move. The difficulty was, Katriona thought to herself, in telling the tribes apart. There was no mechanism for separating men from one another as there was for wheat and chaff. She wished to toss them into a machine, and see what virtues were collected, and what sins bailed like straw.

"If only there was such a machine," she murmured.

"What my dear?" Demion asked. He held out his arm to her. She consented to be led into the Ladies Saloon.

"Nothing," she said.

Fifteen minutes ran by at breathless pace. Faces came and went, their owners presenting themselves in case advantage might be got in future, or come to condemn. Several were all for enforcement of existing laws, but no more than that. Fingers were wagged. Demion brusquely escorted two gentlemen away whose admonitions were too animated. Wine was offered her, refused twice, finally accepted, but when sipped, found to be insipidly warm.

The chamber bells rang. The footman came out and declared the vote would be taken. Katriona was lightheaded, she feared she had drunk too much, though she had but a mouthful. Now was the moment of truth.

IN THE CHAMBER two large urns had been set up. They were mismatched, cracked, their bronze pitted with corrosion. Legend told that King Brannon had been presented these ancient artefacts by the Tyn as an offering of peace when he had crossed the neck. They had been used in voting in Karsa ever since.

Between the urns was a bowl full of identical white glass beads. The principal was simple. The urn on the left was for votes against, that on the right votes for.

"Goodfellows," said the speaker from his throne. "You may begin voting now on The Morthrock Motion."

There were offices within the House which granted their holders precedence; the master of the rolls, the heads of the loose party groupings, the secretary for records and a few others. They voted first, beginning with the speaker. He stepped down from his elevated perch, and solemnly cast a glass bead into the urn for against. Several others followed. Beads clanked into the urns. The vote was public. Everyone watching knew exactly who voted for what.

After the officials voted, the general mass of members were permitted to vote. The braver men made their opinions known first. Such courage could make a career or ruin it. Men of slyer character held back, to see which way the vote went before adding their choice to the winning side. So was politics done in Karsa.

The votes were barely begun, when a minor commotion began at the back of the hall. The doors to the chamber opened. A dozen members arrived to cast their vote.

Katriona was occupied with counting the tally of votes for her motion, and so at first did not see who led the latecomers, until his name, harshly whispered, made its way down the Ladies Gallery.

"Gelbion Kressind!"

Katriona's stomach turned to ice. Her father was limping determinedly down the open area at the centre of the chamber, flanked by old men like himself.

"Gods!" said Brask. "That's the cream of the new nobility, right there."

Whispered speculation was rife in the gallery as everyone debated which way Kressind would vote. Katriona knew in the pit of her stomach that he had come to destroy her ambition. He was a callous man, with no time for workers' rights.

His progress was slow. The disease that crippled his left side made walking extremely difficult for him, but he refused all help, and doggedly forced his malfunctioning body toward the voting urns.

He stopped at the basket. He shifted his stick to his withered hand, and used his right to reach for the beads. He almost overbalanced, but righted himself, and snarled at the men who rushed to his side. He scrabbled a bead from the basket, and threw it into the urn.

Katriona stood up so fast her folding chair banged back into the upright position.

Her father had voted for.

Without saying a word, Gelbion Kressind made his laborious way back to the doors.

All the men who had accompanied him cast their votes the same way. Seeing their betters vote, the lesser industrialists followed suit.

"Gelbion Kressind voted for!" The words were repeated everywhere.

Katriona ran for the door.

"My dear!" called Demion. "They will be counting the vote soon." But she was out of the Ladies Gallery, and running as fast as her restrictive clothing would allow for the atrium of the palace, where she hoped to intercept her father.

NOW SHE HAD to run, she hated the corsets and hoops, the heels and the stays that her womanhood forced on her. Katriona liked being a woman. She liked dressing as one. She had no desire to emulate the Countess of Mogawn. The idea of wearing men's clothes in high society appalled her, but at that moment she wished for a choice of something more practical. A memory of running through the woods of the Kressind country estate with her brothers came to mind. There had been no lacing of her body to constrain her breath then, no padding and crushing and forcing. She wore trousers to roam the hills with her siblings.

When her father was away, only then.

Skirts held high, she rounded a corner, nearly slipping on the polished marble as she headed for the staircases leading into the palace's vast atrium. Forced to run at an undignified trot, panting against her corset, she made it down into the entrance hall as her father was leaving.

He was in his wheelchair, having condescended to be helped out now his gesture was made, and was being pushed toward the doors. That must have hurt his pride.

"Father!" she called.

Gelbion's servant continued to push.

"Father!" she said, and ran to the front of his chair. It stopped dead.

Gelbion Kressind lifted his face to meet his daughter's eyes. One side was slack with infirmity.

"Daughter," he said.

She faltered. There was nothing but hatred in his expression.

"I... I wanted see you. To say thank you for backing my motion. I am so pleased you have found it in your heart to think of the poor."

Gelbion looked away, his jaw working. He did not look back to her as he spoke, but whispered with controlled fury.

"I care not a jot for the fate of the poor. They are poor because they are meant to be poor. If they had more intelligence, then they would be rich."

"Then why?" she said, confused.

"I voted for your pathetic humanitarian folly to prevent this family's name being dragged through the mud. You are a Kressind, I will not fuel the furnaces of gossip by publicly opposing you. Nor will I stir up trouble in my own workforce. You put me in a very difficult position, child. My workers look to you and make trouble. In my own circles, I am a laughing stock because of your antics. A woman, running a mill, whipping old Horras' boy like a servant so he'll do your bidding. Marrying him to get your hands on his wealth, like a common low rank goodmaid. You are disgusting. Your marriage was supposed to strengthen our family, not gift you some doll's playset to make believe with."

"Father!" Katriona said. "It is a good match. And the Morthrocksey Mill makes more money now than it has for years. Demion and I are happy together. I admit, I saw an opportunity when he proposed the match and you approved." She paused, the admission was hard to make. It made her seem so calculating, just like her father. "It is love that—"

"Love!" scoffed Gelbion. He gave a sidelong look at his daughter. Perhaps there was a little respect in it. "Out-manoeuvred by a woman. I blame myself. I should never have educated you. I was too indulgent. Demion is weaker than I thought possible, and between us we have made a monster every bit as bad as the Hag of Mogawn. What you are doing is against the rightwise order of things. No doubt you indulge yourself in Prissian practises. You should go there, where women like you are wanted."

Katriona's face hardened. "Do not accuse me of perversion. I am a good woman, and I am my father's daughter. You taught me well. I am as capable of fury as you. You spurn me, very well, it makes me more determined. Things are changing, father. You should recognise it, before it is too late."

"Perhaps I could have forgiven your gender. Demion is a feeble excuse for a man, and for all the unnaturalness of it, you have shown that you can run a mill well, certainly better than Morthrock or any of your wastrel brothers might," he grumbled. "I heard you have diversified into arms."

"We made some already," said Katriona. "I decided we should concentrate on them. I have turned over much of our capacity to the manufacture of ironlocks."

Her father nodded, and for a fraction of a second he appeared to be close to approval. "Wise, in a time of uncertainty." His reasonable expression vanished. "I will not bless your actions. Now I have done what I need to save this family's reputation, I will not aid you through the Third House. When this goes before the prince, it will rightly fail." Gelbion waved his good hand at his servant. "Simeon, take me home."

His servant pushed him hard, forcing Katriona out of the way.

"Father!" she called after him. "You will see, one day! You will see. I am right!"

"You will fail in the Third House," Gelbion said. "Repent your ways, daughter, if you desire our affection." Doormen held open the palace's doors, and he was wheeled out.

Katriona's cheek was wet. She dabbed at it with her hand. Her glove came away dirtied with a mix of powder and tears. She was crying without realising.

She touched her belly protectively. She hadn't told him she was pregnant. She wasn't sure she ever would.

CHAPTER THIRTY-TWO
A Fortress Remembered

THE TAIL END of Gannever came and went with barely a day of sunshine. Rain clung to Mogawn even when the mainland was bathed in light. Flat skies and seas suited Lucinia's mood. She was not miserable, exactly, but her spirits were subdued. Her leg troubled her, and when she slept at night she relived the moment of the explosion more than once in her dreams. She could not abide the sight of raw meat, for it reminded her too much of the aftermath.

She paid little attention to what went on in the outside world, leaving her broadsheets unread and letters unopened. The events of the last year had exhausted her, and she fell back into the simple rhythms of Mogawn gladly. They were a comfortable bed she had been kept out of for too long. The rising and falling of the castle to the pulse of the tides soothed her back toward health. Gradually her leg started to heal. Six weeks—thirty-six days— the physics in Karsa had told her it would take, but among the countess's eclectic store of knowledge was a deal of medicine, and she knew it would not take so long. The healing magister in Perus had been among the best that nation had, and the magical marks he had stained her leg with speeded the knitting of the bone considerably. She reckoned it would not be long. She was confident in her prognosis; she always was in matters of rationalism, whatever the branch.

By the beginning of Seventh her strength was returning The splints would have to stay on for most of the month, but the pain was less, and with a little application she could manage the stairs so could at least access her study and observatory where she tried, and mostly failed, to work.

The dreams continued. A muzzy disconnect from reality refused to lift. The business of the castle went on without her input. She needed Mogawn, but it did not appear to need her. That made her sad in a way she found perfectly ridiculous, but could nevertheless not shake.

The month finished with incessant drizzle. The motions of the sea were pushed out of their usual patterns by the nearing Twin. Seventh opened with a modest Great Tide that brought with it foul weather off the ocean. A blistering westerly blew in successive waves of belting rain so hard half the harvest on the coast would rot in the fields. Such was the trouble of cultivation in the rainy isles. A good percentage of her income depended on the farms of Mogawn-On-Land, but she could not motivate herself to find the industry of farming more interesting than she did. In part it was because her father had taken such pride in agriculture. Farming was a human problem, the grubby question of day-to-day survival. The improvement of dracon breeds and crop rotations were the province of dull yeomen scientists. She preferred the soaring, the ineffable. The divine, dare she say it.

She was reading when the soldiers came. Her study was snug from the fire burning in the grate. It took a heroic effort for the fireplace to raise the temperature of the stones of Mogawn, but once heated, they stayed warm, and the damp of the castle was driven back for a while. Lucinia had toyed with installing more modern systems of heating, but there never seemed to be any time.

Outside, the bad weather persisted. By rights it should have been warm still, with Seventh the last month of summer, but rain tapped at the window, announcing the possibility of an early autumn. She guiltily remembered her unfulfilled promise to visit the village as she stared at the water coursing down the glass, then promptly put all thoughts of the land from her mind.

She sighed. She could not concentrate on the book, and set it face down on her outstretched leg. The top and bottom of it was that she still had not been into the village as she had said she would to the railway porter, but had instead closeted herself away with her books.

"When my leg is better," she said to herself. She was uncharacteristically bad-tempered, she knew. The explosion had shaken her. Waking from nightmares of bodies blasted to pieces every day was exhausting. Terror gave way with the dawn to a more generalised sadness that doubled the effort of any task. People could carry a trauma like that through their lives, she knew. She had seen the psychological effect of battle and tragedy on others. She would be fine, she told herself. She just needed time.

That is why you are not speaking to anyone, or bathing, she said to herself.

"Traitor," she hissed.

With scowling care she lifted her injured leg off its footstool and hobbled from her couch to the shelves where she slotted the book back into its place.

Titles danced before her eyes. Most of these books she had read, of course, but familiarity meant comfort. That was why she had come home. She squinted at them, but they would not be read.

I need to get out of here, she thought. *I will go mad.*

She pulled a tome out at random. It was written in Ferroki, a language she had difficulty with. Maybe the challenge would help her concentrate.

"Why the hells am I so damned fretful?" she grumbled.

She had just eased herself back into her chair and got her leg out at the least uncomfortable angle when a knock interrupted her.

"What is it?" she bellowed.

The door opened a crack. Light from the room illuminated a stripe of her housekeeper Astred's face. "Begging your pardon, my goodlady, but there are men here."

"Men?" said Lucinia. "What men?"

"Soldiers. So they say," said Astred suspiciously. Most of Lucinia's staff distrusted strangers. Island life bred that mentality.

"How many?" said Lucinia uneasily.

"Fifty or so."

Fifty men. In its day, Mogawn had been one of the greatest fortresses in Karsa, it still was, but without warriors to man it, a fortress was nothing. She quickly counted her staff in her head. She had twelve, mostly goodmaids, men past their prime and youths too young to leave for better work. Ardwynion was ancient and mostly blind, the younger Aldwyn was lazy, and his sons were still boys. Only Ardwynion's sons—sired late in his life—were vigorous, and hadn't the eldest gone away to the military academy in Stoncastrum last winter? She couldn't remember. She hadn't seen him for a while. There was Holless of course. Her coachman was young and loyal, but he was the only man in the prime of his life resident at Mogawn.

Fifty men could kill them all.

What the hells am I thinking? she thought. *What foreign power could reach me at Mogawn?*

"It will be the government. A patrol, or an inspection or somesuch," she said, waving her hand in annoyance. "Send them away."

"Begging your pardon, goodlady, but it ain't no inspection or the like. I think they mean to stay." Astred opened the door fully. Her doughy peasant's face was creased with worry. "Holless only let the one in, well two. He says he's their leader. A captain. He's on a dracon!" she said, with a little flash of excitement.

Lucinia set her book down. "If he is riding a dracon, then he is at least a soldier and not a bandit." She shivered with sudden relief, not realising how seriously she had entertained the possibility of attack. She would never have reacted this way before. What was wrong with her? "What the hells do they want here?"

She rose slowly, pushing her weight up from the chair with her arms to save her leg.

"Shall I tell them you are coming down?" said Astred. "Ardwynion says he's going for his gun."

"Tell the soldiers the mistress of the house is coming down, and tell that old fool Ardwynion to keep his gun locked away. He'll only shoot himself in the foot, or get us all arrested. Or both."

"Yes, goodlady." Astred executed one of her catastrophically bad curtsies, and hustled off.

Lucinia considered changing her clothes. She was wearing a skirt, for once, for the ease it gave her in moving her broken leg, but it was dirty, and coupled with a labourer's jerkin it was wholly unflattering.

"Driven gods woman!" she scolded herself. "You're supposed to send them packing, not screw them. Anyway," she smiled wryly, a touch of her old manner returning to her. "Fifty is too many to bed."

She dragged a blanket on as a makeshift cloak to ward off the chill, and hobbled downstairs.

ASTRED, HOLLESS, ARDWYNION'S younger son Barniby, and Aldwyn's lad Bolth, the cook's boy, were drawn up in the door of the great keep in an ineffectual battle line. The stairs were slippery in the rain, doubled back awkwardly on themselves, and had no railing, all minor details of Mogawn's formidable defensive architecture, but the captain had ridden his dracon to their summit nonetheless, and stood dismounted holding its bridle. When the countess hobbled into the door he bowed.

Barniby, who acted as kennel boy, regarded the reptile nervously, but the officer did not require him to take it.

A fine army, Lucinia thought. She was touched by her servant's protectiveness, though irritated by their suspicion toward the soldier, for he was very plainly what he claimed to be.

The majority of the captain's uniform was hidden beneath an oilskin poncho, but his sodden legs were visible. He had the knee high shiny boots favoured by a sauralier, coupled with the tight, yellow-piped black trousers of an infantryman. Rain streamed off his oilskins in miniature waterfalls. He was soaked. It was then that she realised she knew him.

That was potentially embarrassing. They had met at the revel of Katriona Kressinda.

The countess pulled her blanket closer about her. It was unseasonably cold, the Twin was wreaking havoc on the weather as much as the tides. Looking at the wet man made her feel colder.

"What do you want?" she said imperiously.

"I am Captain Qurion, of the Twenty-Second Foot," he said. He affected to look proud. He was as handsome as she remembered, but the effect was spoiled by the water dripping from his moustaches.

"Right," said the countess. "We have met before, though I did not get your name the first time."

Qurion's face betrayed nothing. "You are the countess of Mogawn, Lucinia Vertisa, that is correct?"

So he wants to play it like that then, she thought. He was pretending not to recognise her. It increased her temper.

"Yes, that is correct," she said snappishly. "This is my castle. You are stood on my bloody threshold. I am the bloody countess. What do you want? You haven't come all this way to propose to me, I take it."

Was that the hint of a blush? She thought.

It was not. It was the dawn of realisation.

"You're not expecting us," said Qurion "You didn't know we were coming."

"No, I didn't know you were coming. Why have you come? Please be quick. I am cold. I have recently been injured. I do not wish to add influenza to my catalogue of ailments."

"My commanding officer told me you had been written to. He said that it was all arranged."

"I have received no communication. Nothing has been arranged, and had I known about it, nothing would have been. We are all fine here, thank you very much. Now please go. There is an inn in the village. The tide will cover the causeway in less than half an hour. If you go this minute, you will not drown."

"I'm not sure about that," said Qurion. He looked skyward. Large raindrops bounced off his face. Lucinia felt a little sorry for him, in spite of herself.

"Bad weather for the harvest," Qurion said. "Bad weather for anything. Can I come in to talk? I'm sopping wet. We are here for your safety."

"I think not," she said, appalled at the brittleness in her voice.

"Please," he said. Some of his pride left him. "We have been marching through this rain since dawn. There is a big tide tonight, you are right. We are stuck with each other, because I am not going anywhere. Do you think we might come into the castle, or shall I go outside your walls, and spend my remaining moments before I die of the cold writing to my superiors to tell them that the hospitality of Mogawn is not what it was in your father's day?"

The countess's nostrils flared. Her father was twelve years dead. She still hated him. She hated all reference to him.

"It is a frightful night. You must be gone before the leading wave comes."

"Goodlady Countess, the causeway is already covering over."

"Then you must swim."

Qurion clenched his jaw. "Fine, fine. Then I will explain here, where I am extremely uncomfortable. I had hoped to keep this pleasant, but seeing as you are poorly disposed to me and my men, I will have to do it this way."

Qurion tugged off his gloves, and reached inside his streaming poncho to draw out a leather message tube. Ardwynion, ridiculously, tensed before the tube was revealed. As if such an old man could wrestle a pistol from the captain's grasp.

"I'd read this inside," Qurion continued, holding out the tube. "Or the ink will run. I can tell you what it says, if you like. This is an official missive from the Interior Ministry invoking Article 19 of the Defence of the Realm act, which, as I am sure you know, names Mogawn as a Fortress of Karsa. We are here to garrison the castle. I have my orders. I cannot leave."

The countess snorted. "That clause hasn't been applied for a century."

"That is because we have not been at war for a century," said Qurion.

"Are you speaking of the events in Perus? There is no threat there. I have recently returned from the city."

Qurion looked thoroughly put out. "It is not Maceriya you should be concerned with, goodlady. Some weeks ago, the Ambassador of the Drowned King delivered a notice to Garten Kressind of the Admiralty stating that the Drowned King is considering retaliatory action against the Isles of Karsa for the trespass of the vessel, the *Prince Alfra* into his territory. The Prince naturally rejected the Drowned King's complaint. I don't think that will make the Drowned King very happy. Seeing as Mogawn was among our primary defences against the drowned in centuries past, my superiors expect that any action against the kingdom will begin here." He regarded her. There was a shine in his eye. He recognised her. He was asking her to play along. She rather liked that, she had to admit. "Looking at the vast forces arrayed before me, I can see that you have things under control. If you prefer, we can go home when the tide is amenable."

"We are at war with the Drowned King?"

Qurion shrugged. "It may come to that, goodlady."

"But this happened weeks ago?"

"While you were in Perus."

"You took your bloody time then."

"I am not party to diplomacy, goodlady. I have been told to anticipate the possibility of retaliatory action, that is all. A raid, perhaps. I doubt we will see a full blown war. Maybe nothing will happen."

"We better hope it does not!" she exclaimed. "The Interior Ministry sends me fifty men against a horde of the undead? You are partway between an infuriating inconvenience and a token gesture."

"Fifty men is what I have, and it's more than enough to defend this place. I've not seen it before, but I've studied the plan; formidable is the word I'd use. In fact, I've always wanted to see it. It takes fewer men to hold a castle than you'd think. With the cannon I've been provided, it will be accomplished."

"Mogawn is less formidable than it was."

"We shall see about that," he said. "Or perhaps we will be lucky enough not to." He shivered. "There are further stipulations in the decree commanding you and you servants off the isle until it is safe, but I suppose you won't pay any attention to them, so I won't bother informing you. We'll just take it as read you won't go."

"You're damn right. I am not leaving my home. I don't care who's coming."

"Then let us meet on the middle ground, and get me in out of this rain. I am now very cold. Where shall I billet my men?"

"Hmmm," said Lucinia. The drumming rain and inconstant gurgle of malfunctioning downpipes took the place of conversation.

"We could put them in the barracks," said Holless finally. His expression and tone suggested he didn't want to say that, and that he wanted the soldiers gone, but nobody was moving and it was getting late.

Lucinia rolled her eyes and groaned theatrically. "Why does everyone want to put all our visitors into the barracks?"

"So you agree we can stay?" said Qurion.

"The damned barracks is full of holes." She pulled a face. She'd given in. "Stick them in the great hall."

Qurion smiled. "Goodlady, we are soldiers. Soldiers belong in barracks, not halls. I take it your barracks have their own cookhouse, stables and latrines?"

"Of course they do, or they did... Captain, the barracks have not been used seriously for the better part of eighty years. They are in a dire state. Part of the roof has collapsed. The rest of it is leaky as a sieve. The stoves are rusted through, the latrines filled in and it is full of junk. I doubt your men will like it."

"Is it drier than where I am now?"

"Naturally," said Ardwynion unpleasantly.

"Then I will take it and I will like it," said Qurion. "We shall withdraw there. I shall consider it a personal honour if you allow us the favour of repairing them for you. I find an idle soldier is a troublesome soldier, and nothing motivates him more to good, honest toil than his own comfort."

"Captain..." began the countess.

"It will keep them out of trouble." He winked at her. He actually *winked*.

"Very well. The barracks. Holless, open the gates. Let the rest in. Rouse the cook. Have him prepare a stew or something."

"We're all out of meat," grumbled Ardwynion. "Market's not for two days."

"Then fish, gods-damn it man, fish! We live in the blasted ocean, don't we?"

"Fish," sneered Ardwynion, as if it were a terrible curse. Ardwynion went off on his errand, muttering to himself about the pains in his joints and the impositions of duty.

Qurion tipped his sopping hat and clambered back onto his dracon. The beast rattled miserably. Its coat of feathers was so wet they were plastered to its skin, and it was consequently sluggish in the cold. Qurion was obliged to employ his spurs to get it moving back down the steps. Once in motion it strutted across the bailey, its clawed feet splashing in puddles in the uneven cobbling.

Holless and Aldwyn swung open the gates at his approach. The lesser bailey within the gatehouse was cluttered with rubbish. The salty atmosphere had stripped the paint off the inner gates and the bottommost planks were rotted through. The outer gates, which her retainers hurried to swing open, were in even poorer repair. Only now they might be required to hold an enemy did she notice their parlous state. Her gaze wandered over the castle, to the semi-derelict great southern tower, the barracks with its slumped roof, the lesser towers weakened by the addition of windows. Iron fittings eroded by the sea air spread the majority of their mass down walls as long orange stains. Bronze and brass were bright green with verdigris. The great hall, kennels and the kitchen block were in more tolerable condition, but barely. The whole castle was rundown, little better than a seed-peck baron's provincial domicile.

She blinked and frowned, as if the arrival of actual soldiers into the castle forced her to see all of this for the first time. Her home was a mess. Mogawn, once reckoned the third greatest fortress in the western Kingdoms. What armies could not reduce, neglect had.

She was embarrassed by that.

Qurion's men entered Mogawn to the squelch of soaking boots. There was a mix of artillerymen and infantry, with a small accompanying staff of officers. Water streamed off the oilcloth-wrapped weapons slung over their shoulders. The wheels of gun carriages and tenders caught in the mud. The paired dogs that pulled them were soaked. The best any of the men, dogs or dracons could manage was stoic acceptance of the rain. In the main they were weighed down with the misery of the truly sodden.

Thick blue smoke curled out of the barrack's chimney, its exhaust added to by the burning of eighty years of birds' nests, cobwebs and dust that had accumulated inside. At least it worked, there was that.

She could think of no more positives. Cheeks aflame, she turned her back as her kennel boy nervously helped Qurion and his three subordinate officers take their mounts inside.

CHAPTER THIRTY-THREE

Lessons in Astronomy

THE COUNTESS CAME awake in the close dark of her curtained bed. She half sat, not daring to breathe, fearing an explosion that did not come.

The banging of hammers broke her fear.

The tide had come in, lifting Mogawn free of the mud flats. The gentle rocking of the floatstone isle was not to the dracons' liking, and they shrieked from the kennel block with every shift in the swell. The hammering started up again, drowning out the reptiles' complaints, and the stop-start sawing of wood joined the racket. She heard men shouting.

The soldiers.

She pushed aside the bed curtains and picked her way through the detritus cluttering the floor of the bedchamber. Only her books, her laboratory, her observatory, her wardrobe and her love life were properly organised, and the last only haphazardly so. As she kicked a boot out of the way with her good foot, she resolved there and then to do something about the state of her castle. Mogawn would be tidied, whether it liked it or not.

She limped to the window, and screwed up her eyes in anticipation of opening the curtains. A moment of painful blindness followed their withdrawing. She blinked against a bright grey sky of that headachy intensity found only in the isles. She regretted the flask of wine she'd drunk before bed. The masked sun seemed intent on flattening her brain against the back of her skull. It was a small mercy that it was no longer raining.

Down in her muddy courtyard men went to and fro, carrying long planks of raw yellow wood. Qurion stood at a table made of an old door and a pair of sawhorses, consulting plans with a man in the garb of a military engineer.

"Hmph," she said, blowing a stray lock of hair out of her face. "They brought timber. They expected to do work here." She was freezing in spite of her long woollen nightgown.

"Astred!" she called. "Astred! Get me a fire going in here!"

Lucinia emerged into the courtyard shortly after, washed and better dressed than the day before. Annoying though the intrusion of the soldiers was, it had shaken her out of her melancholy. The thought of new people to bait put a spring into her step. She had Astred dig out one of her finer outfits. It was last year's, but the mannish styling was still shocking to the average Karsan. The left leg had be cut off the trousers, but in a way her naked, splinted leg only increased the outfit's potential for offence.

"Good morning captain!" she called cheerily.

Qurion looked up from his work and raised his eyebrows at her clothes.

"Good morning, goodlady. I am relieved to report a cessation in the rain."

"Your work may proceed more quickly. Lucky you." She looked over at the barracks. The tiles had been removed and neatly stacked, exposing the rafters. The soldiers, though tired, were nevertheless enthusiastically pulling out rotten timbers in preparation for replacement.

"And here was me thinking your offer to repair my barracks was made from the goodness of your heart, captain."

She looked pointedly at the fresh timber and the engineer. The engineer grinned. Qurion gave him a sharp look, and he stepped back.

"I'm afraid it's more than the barracks, my lady," he said. "Perhaps I might come within your keep, where we may discuss this like people of good manners?"

"Why are you always trying to get yourself into my keep, captain?" she said, cocking an eyebrow.

"Your reputation for innuendo is well earned."

"I assure you that is the first saucy thing I have said in weeks. I've not been feeling myself. The arrival of fifty fine young men can wake a lady's appetite."

He laughed.

"You have a soldier's sense of humour," he said.

"That's not all I have in common with soldiers. Come on then, come into the keep. We shall discuss your plans while I have breakfast."

"Breakfast? It is nearly noon," he said, coming out from behind the trestle.

"If you tell me I have missed the best part of the day, I shall shoot you. I prefer the hours of the night. The morning is a blasted inconvenience."

"I had no intention, goodlady."

"Very kind. You may have an early lunch, I shall have my breakfast."

THE COUNTESS HAD the table in the keep's hall set for two. She took responsibility for moving the mass of papers heaped on it, but restricted her other preparations to barked commands at Astred, the maid Hovernia and Bolth as they brought in food. Dried fish, bread warm from the morning's second round of baking, small beer and pickled seaweeds plucked from the underside of the island at low tide appeared on the table with varying amounts of efficiency. Hovernia was particularly clumsy, being flustered by Qurion.

"Hovernia! Stop gawping at him!" the countess snapped. "I realise that now he is uncovered and dry he is a comely man, but please remember yourself."

Astred smacked the younger maid around the head. Hovernia went a deep crimson, practically dropped the last wooden bowl on the table and made a hasty retreat.

The countess and the captain sat opposite each other under the orrery. Its engine was disengaged, and the globes were still. She looked at him carefully. He was as good looking as she remembered.

"Do you always have that effect on women?" she asked. She picked up a mug and poured herself some beer, then filled another and handed it to Qurion.

"Not always," he said, accepting the drink.

"You do remember me don't you?"

Qurion grinned widely, an expression that transformed him from stern captain to cheeky boy. "Of course I do. It was a fine revel, and we had a fine time at it, as I recall. I apologise if you were offended yesterday that I offered no recognition, but I do not think it appropriate to allude to my nocturnal adventures directly in front of my men."

"The sanctity of the revel must be honoured," said the countess with mock solemnity.

"Quite," said Qurion.

"So have you come here solely for the warfare, or are you pursuing me?"

"I would not be so forward as to do that," said Qurion. "I was not lying when I said I have always wanted to see Mogawn, and the few words we exchanged spoke of a certain rapport. I volunteered."

"You could have written to me, I am glad of the occasional guest."

'Well, I am here now," he said.

The countess smiled and bit into a pickle with a loud crunch. "Please," she said, "eat."

Qurion helped himself to some fish.

A fire flickered inconsequentially in its grate, failing to raise the temperature. She shivered.

"Two cold summers on the run. It's a couple of degrees from being able to see your bloody breath on the air," said Lucinia.

"Perhaps we can help with that," said Qurion. "We knew that Mogawn required a certain amount of preparation to make it secure, although not exactly how much. We can clear the chimneys and effect general repairs besides improving the fortifications. It will be only a little extra work."

"The place is a mess," she said. "I have let it go to ruin while I concentrate on my science. Your arrival has made me painfully aware of it."

Qurion smiled apologetically. "We have enough lumber, and enough hands. Engineer Koby is a good man, very talented. We are to improve the defences and see to our own accommodation, but if there is anything else we can do, we shall, and I mean that without any condition."

"Koby? Is he the one that looks like he is twelve years old?"

"Yes," said Qurion. "I find that happens as one gets older. Everyone is suddenly younger than you are."

She snorted. "You can't be over thirty."

"Thirty-two," he said.

"Try nearing forty," she said. "That feels like age, even though I know many people who are older, I do not look forward to living through the years they have. This is the top of the mountain my lad, only downhill from here."

"I understand you are thirty-six."

"My, your intelligence is good, but not perfect. Thirty-seven," she said. "A month ago."

"Then a belated happy birthday."

Qurion looked up at the orrery hanging over them.

"This is your science? They talk a lot about your discoveries in the city nowadays. I must admit, I was interested in meeting you as well as seeing Mogawn."

"The reputation of my mind will never outmatch that which my body has brought me. Not that I care."

"Is that really true?" he said. "I know goodfellows and goodladies who would either die from shame or shine with pride to be so gossiped about as you are, but rarely would they not care."

"Captain, you are forward, despite that you protest you are not." She finished her pickle. "The answer is yes and no. I do and I don't care. I suppose I must care less than I might. If I really cared, I'd probably make more of an effort to keep my underwear on. But then sex is so much fun." She stared at him as she said this, awaiting one of the usual array of reactions: embarrassment, lust, a polite ignoring of what she said, nervous laughter, or all of them.

Qurion merely nodded in agreement. "I enjoyed myself the time we last met." He put down his beer and poured himself a cup of Ocerzerkiyan tea. "What you say is too true. Why is something so pleasurable so frowned upon? I myself have courted trouble in that department." He picked up his cup and sipped. He pulled a face.

"Sorry, the tea is awful. That is why I gave you the beer," she said. "I was absent for several weeks in Perus. My staff have not replenished my stores since then, though I did send word. I have a large shipment of reasonable food coming."

"They seem a..." he thought carefully. "A likeable crew."

"Likeable, but largely useless."

"I do not understand why women must deny their passions. Your science, your loves," he said. "You are commendable for following them."

She picked up another pickle and pointed it at him. "Now I know you want to take advantage of me."

"I mean it sincerely. You have more admirers than you know."

"Maybe," she said. "I was quite the darling of the Perusian fashionistas, though I doubt one of their empty heads could comprehend what I do here. They liked my clothes. Once, that would have been enough for me. Now I need more."

"There are many in Karsa that do understand your mind, and that admire you for it."

"The times are changing," she said ironically.

"I know for a fact that Katriona Kressinda-Morthrocksa praises you highly."

"Ah, the Kressinds. I assume you know them, seeing as you were at the wedding?"

He nodded. "I know some of them. I attended the same school as a couple of the sons. I got to know the sister through them."

"How well?"

"Not as well as you are implying, although I was good friends with her late husband, Arvane. I was there when he died, in fact." He said no more, though she waited.

"It is a small island. You are of the nobility?"

"Very minor," he said. "Nothing like them, certainly nothing like you. Barely gentry."

"That explains why our paths have never crossed."

"The wrong circles," he agreed. "I'm far too lowly to have met you socially."

"So the career...?"

"Like most officers, I'm afraid my captaincy was purchased. A useful way of disposing of a middle son. But I like soldiering, and I'm good at it, so don't worry if the drowned come. They have not sent you some milk-blooded aristocrat. I can actually fight." He said it fiercely. He had defended his position before. The reputation of bought commission officers was poor. He paused before he continued. "I understand Guis came to see you."

She couldn't stop her face hardening. "A cold-hearted bastard that one."

"I would never have heard him described so," said Qurion. "In our adventures, it was he who always scolded me for my free and easy morals."

"Those who maintain the higher moral ground are often there by circumstance rather than choice. He bedded me then rejected me. I liked him, a little too much." She surprised herself with her frankness, but could not arrest her mouth. "I believe he was worried what his friends might say. I am not a beauty. He was weak."

"Yes well, Guis is far from perfect, though he affects superiority. He and I parted on bad terms last I saw him, now he is missing," said Qurion.

"And you thought I might know where he is? I don't." She tore a strip of bread from the loaf unnecessarily hard, and stuffed it into her mouth. "And I don't care either."

"I am sorry," he said. His natural confidence seemed a little dented to her. "I had to ask. He and I are close. We were close," he added. "I am not so sure now."

She shrugged.

There followed an uncomfortable silence.

"Tell me about this device?"

"My orrery? You want to change the subject."

"You don't?"

"Well," she said, speaking through a full mouth and waving her knife up at the bronze and brass spheres on their iron arms. "These balls represent the worlds around our own. That one there," she jabbed her knife toward a middling-sized object, "is our Earth."

"I see. The Red and White moons are there, and that must be the Twin. I take it the machinery replicates their orbits?"

She swallowed and nodded. "I had it turned off when I left for Perus. The engine is a direct glimmer device, very expensive to run. However, now I am back, I think I will turn it back on again."

"It is a fine astronomical instrument."

"I used it to prove my theories. I don't need it on any more, but I would like to see it move again."

"Your theories about motion, the attractive force and the Twin?"

"It's about more than that," she said, stuffing more food into her mouth. After picking at her food for weeks, she was suddenly enormously hungry.

"And what is that?"

"The end of the world," she said with a wild grin. "I discerned in the planets' movements a coincidence in our histories between the fall of civilisations—the Morfaan's, the Maceriyan Resplendency and possibly more—and the drawing near of the Twin. Although it draws near then away from us, so causing, in conjunction with the moons, the Great Tides, its orbit is ultimately erratic. With each passage it comes nearer. It comes to its closest approach once every four millennia, then everything goes to shit. You have felt the increased incidence of earthquakes and so forth—the weather, the disruption of the tides?"

"There is the talk of the gods' return also," said Qurion.

"Maceriyan hysteria, but perhaps it is connected," she said. "Who knows what adverse effects the proximity of the Twin has upon the human mind?

Who knows indeed, what is coming to our world?"

"You seem pleased."

"I am pleased my theory is correct, that is all. Although the exact nature of the destruction eludes me."

"Well then," said Qurion setting his tea aside and taking up the beer again. "We had better discuss the plans for reinforcing the castle, hadn't we?" He unrolled his drawings. She obligingly moved aside her breakfast and brushed away the crumbs. "There is no harm in being prepared for the worst."

CHAPTER THIRTY-FOUR
The Sniffer

THERE WAS TEA that nobody drank. Vand looked over the cooling pot at Veridy on the other side of the table.

"Don't you have anything to say to me?" said Veridy. Her eyes and nose were again red from weeping.

"There is no news. I have Magister Hissenwar working constantly to locate the *Prince Alfra*. As soon as I have notice, I will let you know. The slightest thing, I swear."

"I am not upset for lack of news, father!" she said exasperatedly.

"Then why are you upset?"

"Because of you," she said harshly. "You behave as if nothing has happened. You go on with your plots and your plans." She pointed at a half-rolled blueprint of a new ship, bigger than the *Prince Alfra*. "We do not even know if Trassan lives or is dead, and already you are planning a new vessel!"

"I am planning lots of things." Vand looked at her in bemusement. "What do you expect me to do? I have interests that must be taken care of. If Persin returns with the contents of the city, then I will be disadvantaged."

"Interests!" she shouted, and stood suddenly. "I should be your interest! Trassan, who was a like son to you, should be your interest! Not all this..." she flung her arm out. "Cold iron! You are dead inside, you show no emotion at his loss, none whatsoever. You are inhuman! I hate you!"

She broke from the room in floods of tears, leaving Vand to sit sadly alone. He laced his fingers in his lap and sighed. She was young, and didn't understand men well enough to see that he grieved in his own way.

A stab of vindictiveness pricked at him. Perhaps if he revealed Trassan's infidelities to her, then she would forget him. He could wheel in the woman Trassan used as an occasional mistress behind Veridy's back, or the doxy he bedded at his sister Katriona's revel.

Vand stopped his train of thought dead. Maybe she was right. If he was thinking how to hurt his daughter to get her to shut up, he had lost something. Maybe ambition had got the better of him.

It was a thought quickly disregarded. The matter of the pilot for his machine was ever on his mind. The Sniffer had not appeared as Filden had promised when Vand had spoken the name. He was going to have to dig him out. He rang the silver bell on his desk. His assistant Kasagalio came in, his air of self-importance as deliberately projected as it always was.

"Where's Filden?" Vand snapped.

"He is out, Goodman Vand," said Kasagalio. "He said not to expect him here until the morning."

"Morning's too late. You'll have to do. I want you to get down to Tyntown and hunt out this Free Tyn for me." Vand tossed the scrap of paper given him by Filden across the desk. It was wrinkled, and the ink smeared from the many times Vand had crumpled it up and smoothed it out again.

Kasagalio was horrified.

"You... You want me... You want me to go to Tyntown?"

"Yes. Yes I do Kasagalio, I want you to go to Tyntown, just like I said," said Vand, with undisguised contempt. "So go to Tyntown. Don't be a coward. You don't want to test me today. His name is on paper."

"The what?"

"His bloody name, you stammering ninny." He pointed to the paper.

Kasagalio plucked it up as if it were unclean. He frowned as he read it.

"Say it," said Vand.

"I'm sorry?"

"If you don't say it, apparently you can't find him. Tyn magic. Say it."

Kasagalio blanched.

"Say it!"

"The sn-sniffer?"

"Yes, I know," said Vand, though Kasagalio reacted only with fear to his request, and not puzzlement. "Damned odd name. Go and find him."

"Sir. Please, there is a very good man who would be far better suited than I to—"

"I don't want a very good man to go and find him, I want you to go and find him," roared Vand. "That's why I gods-damned asked you to bloody go, you gods-damned fool!" Vand wasn't good at grief, but anger came easily to him. All the annoyances and pain of the last few weeks burst from him at great volume, and in a shower of spittle.

Kasagalio wavered.

"Out!" roared Vand. "Find the Sniffer, find him now!"

Kasagalio pranced out of the room. The door slammed behind him.

"I am surrounded by idiots!" Vand muttered to himself. He smoothed his hair and sat himself down.

The door burst open again, and in came Kasagalio. He was white as a sheet.

"He is here!" he shrieked girlishly. "He's in there right now!"

"Who?" snapped Vand.

"The Sniffer!"

Vand frowned. "Maybe Filden wasn't talking rot after all. Show him in then."

Kasagalio turned and looked out of the door. "He's gone!" he said, equally shrilly.

"I'm right here, your worships."

Vand and Kasagalio faced the corner of the room. Vand had a pair of chairs there, either side of an Ocerzerkiyan shaque board set up like he was about to play, though he rarely did. The chairs were in full sunlight, but one was occupied by an indistinct shape, like it was hidden in shadow.

Not a small shape, as Kasagalio would remember that night over two bottles of fortified Gallonian wine. Short, yes. But broad across the chest, somewhat powerful arms, with a large, misshapen head topped with wiry grey hair like a sort of hideous turnip. People laughed at Kasagalio when he described the Sniffer that way, but it was the only way he could think of it. Like when a farmer pulls a humorously shaped vegetable from the earth, only this wasn't funny. It should have been, it was so mismatched and comical like a lot of Tyn, but it wasn't a thing of humour. Unexpected, a shock. It shouldn't be, it was just a... a... "A vegetable?" one of his friends said and laughed. But it was horrible, he insisted.

It was when he started talking like that that Kasagalio thought he might be going insane.

The Sniffer's nose was long, emerging first into the light from the broiling dark birthing him. He had a richly rounded mouth as wide as a shark's and full of small, square teeth. A baby's teeth, thought Kasagalio, but yellow with age and hiding behind a smile that dripped with poisonous guile. Then he popped out from the shadows all at once. The way the Tyn landed on the carpet suggested he was heavy. His over-large hands pulled first a fine cane, then a large carpet bag out of the dark behind him, and he stood there complete. The darkness fizzed out of existence, leaving the whole of him available for scrutiny. He was lopsided, hunched, repellent to human sight. Disproportionately long arms reached far lower down the leg than a human's would. He wore a velvet frock coat of Quireadan red, a rich and autumnal shade. Breeches, rings, shoes with fashionable heels and three buckles; all the trappings of a goodfellow about town, cut and refashioned to his unnatural proportions, right down to the long lace collars that almost, but not quite, hid the brown scar where he had once worn an iron collar.

All was filthy, his clothes as seamed with dirt and scuffed and stained as the skin of his hands and face.

Kasagalio almost died of fright when the Tyn addressed him directly. Its eyes glinted with cruel mischief.

"I hear your master is looking for me, Dosion Kasagalio."

Kasagalio pointed sideways at Vand.

"Well, you found me." He did a mocking bow, throwing out his long arms wide to balance himself. "You've found old Sniffer."

"Tyn," said Vand, attracting the thing's attention. "Why come now, why not come earlier when I said your name before?"

The Tyn shrugged and waddled over to Vand's desk in a manner that suggested a deformity of the bones or joints. It stopped where Vand could see it and leaned on its cane. "I come when I please, and arrive where I will," it said. Faint amusement bubbled under its every word, as if it found the world ridiculous.

"Kasagalio, leave us," said Vand.

"He must stay, he was the one who summoned me." The Sniffer smiled evilly at him. Kasagalio mewled with fear.

"Release my servant. It is me you will deal with."

"Is it now?" said the Tyn. Its tone was mild enough, but menace clung to it. Vand's perceptions stretched, and a persistent ringing started in his ears. Reality seemed affronted by the being before him.

"Release him, or you will get no work from me."

The Tyn shrugged. "I know what you want, Goodman Vand." It licked its lips with a pointed, bright pink tongue. "And I know what you want, Dosion."

Kasagalio went paler, though further whitening seemed impossible.

"Leave him be," said Vand.

"Very well," said the Sniffer. "I release you for a glass warm milk from a goat milked this morning. Add in a drop of red wine while the milk rotates away from the sun. You may not stir it with any metal, only bone. Bring it here. If you do this well, you will never see me again. If you do not, well..." It let insinuation bite at Kasagalio's nerves. "I know you now, Dosion Kasagalio."

Vand's secretary stood staring at the creature in shock.

"Go on then, get out!" said Vand. His voice caught. This thing disturbed him.

Kasagalio almost fell from the room, banging the door shut behind him in his haste to be away. He was shouting down to the kitchen for the things the creature demanded before he was out of his office.

"So," said the Sniffer. "Here I am, like you wanted. I can find what you seek, but it's a rare thing you need."

"What is it I want?" Vand challenged him.

The Sniffer snickered. "Don't trust old Sniffer, eh? There are greater powers in this world than soul dust and steam, engineer. I know alright. Close by the Three Sisters, in the old cities of the young masters, you have found a machine. Human blood it needs to walk and make war, and a human heart to drive the blood, and a human mind to pump the heart. A child, that's what you need, a child of a very special sort." It leaned forward and snatched an apple from the bowl on Vand's desk with its long, thief's fingers. "This blood and the child it runs within is of an old sort bred by the young masters, much diluted now. The bearers are one in a million. But it exists still. If you wants it, I can find it."

"It will make the machine work?"

The Sniffer wagged a finger at Vand. It popped the apple whole into its mouth, and did not speak until it had finished crunching it to nothing and swallowed it down. "Answers to questions are finding as well, in their way. Separate price for those."

"Name it then," said Vand. "I won't employ you to find this child for me if it won't work."

"Them apples," said the Sniffer. "The whole bowl. I'm hungry."

Vand lifted both hands to indicate the Sniffer should take them. The Tyn waggled his fingers and surveyed them, making a show of selecting the best, before plucking one up almost too fast to see. This second apple it consumed like the first, crunching it up whole.

"Well," it said, when it had finished. It hooked its cane over the back of its chair and folded its horrible hands over its little round belly. "The machine is a thing of war, made by the young masters, the Morfaan as you call them. I don't know anything about machines. That's why the young masters were made by my brothers and sisters, but I do know the truth, and the truth is it won't work without the child. If you do it right, it will walk again, and the rewards you receive shall be just."

"I will be rich?"

"Your company will flourish. You will be more famous than ever before."

A smile broke through Vand's unease.

"Steady there, Goodman Vand!" said the Tyn, its eyes widening and a hand coming up. "You better hear the price first."

"What is it?"

"Nothing too esoteric," said the Tyn. It took a third apple, which it swallowed whole, like a dracon wolfing down a stone to work in its stomach. "I want a night with your daughter."

Vand's smile vanished.

"Get out," Vand said.

The Tyn moved his hand like a fish swimming through the sea, becoming momentarily absorbed by it. "Careful now, I could exact a higher price for that request. You want rid of me, you have to do it properly." It dropped its hand into its lap. "No harm will come to her, body or mind. One night I need, for purposes of my own, which I will not speak of, and nor shall she. She will be richer, live longer, and be wiser than if she does not stay the night at my side. This I swear. There is the matter of the child. Be aware if you do not employ me, then you shall never find what you seek, and the toy of the young masters will never move for any man."

"You're lying."

"I can't lie," said the Sniffer. "Geas, you see. There are other constraints on a Tyn than an iron collar." It tapped its neck. "The mightiest take both, I took the one over the other," it said. "I can deceive, and I do, but the deception is always due to poor interpretation on the part of the deceived. Any word out of this mouth of mine is the truth, especially where it concerns the future. It's what I don't say that you want to watch." It gave a hideous grin. "What will win out, Goodman Vand? Riches and fame throughout the Kingdoms, or paternal duty?"

Vand sat, impossible calculations running through his sharp mind. The ship had failed. Persin was breathing down his neck. Already he'd taken a big risk with the Guiders, and blood followed blood, as they said. He was getting deeper into it. For the briefest moment, he had a flash of insight into what sort of monster his ambition was making him, but ambition was all he had. After the explosion at Thrusea, and now the probable loss of the ship, his fortune was stretched thin.

The glint of Morfaan silver caught his eye. Unreadable still.

He could not afford another failure.

"Very well," he said stiffly. "One night, and one night only." He felt filthy inside as he said it, as if he'd drunk a quart of engine oil.

The Sniffer jumped down from his chair and clapped his hands. "Consider it done!" he said.

"Do you know the child?"

"I can sense her, a fine lassie she is too. I don't know where she is, not yet, but I will, I will! You shall hear from me within the month, and the child shall be yours."

It snatched up its cane and its bag, and capered directly out of the office.

A second later, a very flustered Kasagalio came running the opposite way into the room with the Tyn's drink.

"Where did it go?" He said, looking around wildly for the Sniffer. "Where did it go!?"

"You didn't see it on the stair?"

Kasagalio shook his head. He looked miserably at the milk.

"I wouldn't worry, Kasagalio, it told you to bring the milk here. It did not specify it should receive it. These things are terribly literal."

Veridy would understand, he thought. Of course she would. The needs of the family business had to come first. Not that there was any way in which he would stick to his agreement, he thought quickly. He thought of the thing's hands all over his daughter. He felt ill.

Kasagalio dared not take the milk away, and set it on the game board beside where the Tyn had appeared.

Vand stared at the cooling drink for ten minutes afterwards, wondering what on Earth he had done.

He needed Filden again.

CHAPTER THIRTY-FIVE
A Momentary Kindness

THE SAYING GOES that fate is cruel, and that is true. What is not often acknowledged is that fate is far crueler to the poor than it is to the rich.

The poor were much in evidence upon the Golden Lane, the high road out to the north of Karsa City. This was because Golden Lane had yet to be redeveloped by Per Allian as part of the rebuilding of the city, though that was on its way, and so the poor flocked there.

From the new boulevard of the Grand Parade, the architect's ruthless demolitions devoured the capital street by street to the northeast and southwest, while new roads straight as wheel spokes radiated from the plazas at the either end of the Parade. Everywhere, grimy old Karsan vernacular was toppled in favour of new, shining buildings in the Maceriyan revivalist style.

Allian's forest of cranes had reached the southern end of Golden Lane, having already reshaped Far Reach Road, the way that had continued Golden Lane into the centre. Where Golden Lane met Far Reach Road, the road had kinked around Wicker Square, a hamlet swallowed not a hundred years since when the growing capital ate up the last of the farmlands within the outer walls. Chiefly, Wicker Square was known as the location of an ancient structure, whose foundations had, until recently, been visible in the base of a basket weaver's shop. Scholars speculated it to be of Morfaan build, others said Maceriyan. No remains of either civilisation had been found so far west anywhere else.

The point was now moot. Per Allian had little respect for things that did not fit into his vision of the future. Weaver's Square had gone. The kink in the road had been ironed out. History had been erased to make way for his grand idea of what a capital city should be. Impressive maps in the Sunderdown Palace depicted an ideal Karsa City. When Golden Lane's redevelopment was completed, it would be possible to see all the way down its length from the old Northgate to where the city plunged into the basin of the Lemio river. A pair of fine towers would frame the view of the Spires, the fantastically carved ridge where the nobility dwelt, dividing Lemio from Var. A view of the rich, designed by the rich, for the rich.

The poor, as always, were displaced.

As each crumbling tenement and higgledy-piggledy mill was brought down, its occupants were flushed out like rats, away from the demolition gangs and into the parts of the city Allian did not care for or had not yet reached. The last mile of Golden Lane held out, for now. In this refuge for the past, individual tradesmen battled crippling rents and ever more proficient industry to earn a living. Families lived ten to a room. But though these people were desperate, and in some cases starving, they were not the poorest. The poorest could be found on the street.

Golden Lane thronged with beggars chased out of the new city. Many of them were children who, thanks to the crusading efforts of a certain Katriona Kressinda-Morthrocksa, found themselves unemployed.

Lavinia Tuvacs shivered under her threadbare shawl. Unlike the other children begging up and down the street, who shouted and bawled for the attention of people barely richer than they, she kept her eyes downcast. Shame made its home in her hollow heart. She had never begged in her life. She had always worked. As a young child, she had run with the gleaner gangs in Mohacs-Gravo, always poor, but never a beggar. To find better work, she and her brother Alovo had risked crossing a continent. She remembered their journey, running from the gang bosses, leaping in the night onto passing trains, and fleeing to the glorious west.

"Look Lavinia, we have crossed half of all the Hundred!" Alovo told her one sunny morning. He yanked back the sliding door of the millet truck they rode. She remembered it well, the rattle of the train as it crossed an iron bridge hanging incredibly over a gorge thousands of feet deep. The future had seemed so promising. Karsa's industries attracted people from all over Ruthnia. There would be work for them, perhaps even prosperity.

A hopeful future is the lie of the past, they said in the land of Mohaci. The old saying was right. The jobs they found were near slavery, their accommodation infested with lice and dripping with Karsa's hideous damp. Her brother had been forced to thieve. He had been caught, and taken from her. The threat of the gang bosses in Mohacs-Gravo were paltry in comparison to the facts of her current life. The present was hellish.

Her clothes were more filth than thread. She was so hungry her ribs showed through her dress. After Alovo had gone, there had been the lie of the dice factory. The contract Boskovin had secured her had been sold on to the Lemio Clothing and Shoddy Company, where there was no food, many beatings, and thundering machines stole her hearing away. Then, another of hope's false dawns; release under laws rarely enacted before. A dray wagon took them away in full sight of outraged worthies, only to dump most of them in the slums around the Northgate.

Now there was less food, and more violence. She could barely sleep for fear of rape, or worse. Several times she had been propositioned, tempted to sell herself for money. The men varied from the leering to the nervous to the sympathetic, but all of them wanted the same thing. Every time, she had refused. She feared there would come an occasion when she would not. Hunger would compel her, and then she would be lost.

She was going deaf, she knew. Everything she heard since the Lemio mill was perceived as though through a heavy woollen blanket. In the stillness of the night, the muffling in her ears showed itself as a persistent, irritating whine that cheated her of other noises.

Her face stayed impassive as she despaired. Her bonnet delineated her world, framing a view of shit-caked cobbles between shoes too small for her growing feet. Her toes poked through split seams.

Misery had her so tightly she was numb to it. She would die there, on the streets of this foreign land. Alovo had abandoned her. She did not even have the comfort of the letter he had sent her, dictated to his employer and written in the goodfellow's neat hand, explaining why he had to go. Alovo had never learned to read or write. The letter had been lost when they were released from the Lemio mill.

Both of them had run from freedom. In this land of Karsa a person could not be bought and sold, but their terms of service could be. It was a legal modesty for the outrage of slavery. In the letter Alovo had said he would return for her. She had read that part a thousand times. There were dark moments when she doubted if it were true. She had not heard from him since he had gone.

The clattering of dracon cattle bells had her start from her misery too late. She failed to catch the beggar's alarm. A boy pelted past, showing the blackened soles of his bare feet as he leaped over her knees. His bronze bells clonked right by her ear, but they sounded so far away. His shout came as if from underwater.

"The watch! The watch is coming!" He said, then he was away, cursing at the coins spilling from the hat clutched against his chest. A boy of four or less scrabbled for the change. A well-heeled man kicked him out of the way and pocketed the money.

She got to her feet. A dozen constables were working their way down the side of the busy road, kicking over begging bowls and yanking waifs to their feet, sending them staggering away with blows of heavy wooden truncheons. The constables laughed and shouted as they worked, though their words were inaudible to her. Too often, the watch was the day job of nocturnal criminals. She turned to run, slamming straight into the arms of a waiting watchman.

"This area is to be cleared! Demolition starts before winter. No beggars. Beggars first out!" He shouted into her face. He raised his arm to strike her and she shrank back, hands up in front of her face to protect herself, knowing as she did that he would hit her anyway. The blow would shatter her fingers and he would not care.

A hand grabbed the watchman's arm. The watchman turned his head very suddenly, like he were not in complete control of his own anatomy. His eyes and veins in his neck swelled almost comically, and his smile became a snarl.

"Unhand me, goodman!"

His challenger did not release him, but stepped into view and prodded him in the chest with a ringed finger. He was a young man, with long, curly hair that was shaved to the scalp on one side of his head. A neat goatee, and long, waxed moustaches graced a handsome face. The style of his clothes, which were fine, and his jewellery, which was almost immodestly abundant, announced him as hailing from Renia, a morsel of a kingdom sandwiched between Marceny and Corrend.

"Stay your hand, goodconstable," he said. His Karsan was fluent, though strongly accented. She caught most of his words through the muffles circumstance had placed on her hearing.

"I said get off!" said the constable. He threw the Renian's hand off. "Who are you to stop a member of the watch about his lawful duties?" The man had a rough, gutter voice. A dockland whelp.

"If I were the Prince, I would spend less time on buildings and more on reforming institutions that employ men like you," retorted the Renian. "Striking young girls is no lawful thing."

The constable smacked his truncheon into the palm of his hand.

"Care to say that again, and you can be beaten first, if you want, you filthy foreign dog."

The Renian swung his left foot and arm wide, displaying the sword, pistol and dagger, all hung close by one another on his belt. "Be my guest, my friend. We will see who lives." He placed his hand on the butt of his gun.

"You're threatening an agent of the peace," said the constable. He did not strike.

"And you obstruct an officer of the district," the Renian said. He pulled out a small sheet of paper. "My license. I am here to remove these children, by more peaceful means, at the behest of the North District council."

"Child catcher," the constable said. He stepped back. "Why weren't we informed you were operating here?"

"I am no child catcher," scoffed the Renian. "I am no menace to these people. I am empowered to help the poor, like you. Unlike you, I also have the inclination." He hurried on speaking as the constable began to object. "I did not know until this morning that Golden Lane was scheduled for clearance. By all means, beat them and drive them off, they will be back tomorrow. I have a request from Goodfellow Morthrock for young workers to be housed and fed at his expense."

"Philanthropists," growled the constable.

"Tell your colleagues," said the Renian calmly. "Have them corral these youths. I will assess them, and take those that best fit the Goodfellow's requirements." He looked at the huddled children. "Today, I will take thirty off the street. I will not even ask you for payment for doing your job for you."

The constable scowled, but turned away, whereupon his voice was lost to Lavinia.

"Come now." The Renian looked down at her with a warm smile. "I am not going to strike you. You are safe."

She hesitantly lowered her hands.

"Well," he said, "you're a pretty young lady." A calculating look came to his face.

The intensity of his gaze made her drop her eyes for a moment, but she quickly raised them. More and more she relied on watching people's lips to hear their words. She was experienced enough in poverty to see an escape from her current predicament. It would vanish if her impairment was apparent to the Renian.

"Have you any experience in the factories?" he said.

"Yes, goodman," she said quickly. "At the Lemio Clothing and Shoddy Company. I had many duties there. I am a good worker. I—"

He silenced her with a hand on her shoulder. It was so clean it accentuated her own filthiness; she flinched, ashamed at the state of herself. He gripped tighter to prevent her flight.

"No need to babble." He looked her up and down. "I think, I think you're exactly the kind of person the goodfellow wants for his factory. Your accent, you are Kuzaki?"

"Mohaci," she said softly.

"Well, not that it matters," he said. "I am curious. I am Goodman Donati, of Renia. Say it to me, so you don't forget."

"Goodman Donati, of Renia," she said.

"Good!" he said. "Now, you will be coming with me."

She hoped he would leave her alone, but he gripped her bicep tightly and marched her down the street to where a ring of constables surrounded the group of shivering children. How she hated the watch's uniforms. When they had arrived and arrested Goodwife Agna at the factory, they had been saviours, now they seemed like demons, sent to drag her away from one hell to a worse one.

Donati looked over the gathered children. "My, what a pitiful lot." He said this strangely, with a mix of contempt, humour, and sympathy. "At Morthrocksey we will fatten you all up, and get you clean."

He took out a silver whistle and blew on it hard, waving up the street.

A long dray wagon, very much like the one that had driven Lavinia out of the Lemio Clothing and Shoddy Company, came down the street. The constables loaded the battered children onto it. The Renian shook his head at a few of them, and they were removed from the group.

They left the weakest, the sickest and the youngest behind. The drays pulling the wagon started out so slowly that she felt she were drifting by on a cloud. Life had become unreal, a waking nightmare that tormented her with snatches of dream.

The-four-year old sat in the gutter with a bloody nose, weeping piteously.

The Renian winked at her as the wagon drove by the child, leaving him to his fate.

CHAPTER THIRTY-SIX
The Army of the Drowned

AARIN NO LONGER needed to breathe. He revived to find his heart still beating and water flowing in and out of his lungs.

Tallimastus' gifts were gone from his hands, but they were not lost. He felt them, close by, and he thought should he need them he might draw them forth from wherever they waited. Two drowned men pulled him at an unnatural pace through the ocean, holding one of his wrists each. Aarin thought for a moment that some magical means or even mechanical aid dragged them so, but when his vision cleared further he saw two giant fish ahead of them, their tails thrashing. Rope ran from copper hooks embedded in their fins into the outstretched hands of the drowned. By this means they were pulled through the deeps so rapidly the hair of his escort streamed out behind them.

It was at that point that Aarin also realised he could see under the water, with none of the distortion a person ordinarily suffers when submerged. He blinked, amazed, at the murky landscapes passing under his trailing feet.

The fish were phenomenally strong. Aarin's robe dragged at the water. The two drowned men were heavily armed, carrying wide scimitars and bucklers on their belts, but the fish swam tirelessly, their muscular tails sending the sea in to vortices that caressed Aarin's face.

The seabed was a hundred feet beneath Aarin, a pale expanse of sand dotted with rocks and patches of submarine vegetation. The surface was about the same distance above. The deepest water below was dark and inky, but above it became increasingly blue until the shining, dappled sky of the surface roofed all over.

Aarin looked at his escorts. Both were recently drowned, their skin still whole and bodies not yet puffed up with the absorption of water. He tugged at his arms, but they held him fast, and stared fixedly ahead at the murky horizon.

A darkness approached. Such was the occluding effect of distance under the water that for a long while Aarin could not see exactly what it was, until the barrier turned a dark green and broke into individual shapes. Tall fronds of kelp that stretched the full distance between seabed and the world above resolved themselves, and he found himself drawing closer to an undersea forest.

The fish dove, dragging their passengers into the weeds. The drowned moved not a muscle, they may as well have been carved of wood, and so Aarin could not decide if they directed the fish, or the fish knew the route they were to take without command.

Across the flats of the tidal plains, kelp draped itself in giant mounds at the lowest water, stinking of ocean chemistry and alive with transient clouds of flies. Aarin had always associated the plant with rot. To witness the length of these living ropes reaching for the distant light, their flat, bladed leaves moving in the gentle ocean current was to appreciate them in a totally different way. It was a verdant landscape, rich as any terrestrial woodland, whose birds were colourful fish, the flowers anemones blooming on rocky beds, the animals slow moving sea drays nosing the silt and blowing up columns of sand.

For a land dweller, the sea was deadly. So high were the tides, and so deadly the perils, natural and supernatural, that few men took their living from it on Aarin's Earth. It was mysterious, and feared. But now the roles of land as life giver and ocean as death were reversed. Under the water, it was the air that was strange and menacing, and the sea that was rich with life.

Aarin's piscine drays burst from a thicket of the kelp, and into a wide slash cut through the submarine trees. There, he encountered the army of the Drowned King.

Across a broad, sandy road through the forest of kelp, the drowned were marching to war.

The rearguard travelled in tattered, mixed columns, for death makes no distinction between gender, age, race, or degree. Every type of man and woman, and a few luckless children too marched together, undead comrades in arms. Amid this army were many nations, from the Hundred Kingdoms of Ruthnia and beyond. There were tribesmen of the Deep South, clad in thick coats of sea dray feathers and rotting, dogskin parkas.

There were dozens of peoples from the diverse empire of Ocerzerkiya, and men in odd costumes whose like Aarin had never seen and could not guess at the origin of.

The drowned wore no uniform, being garbed only in the apparel they had sported in life, whether that remained as a full suit of clothes or was absent depended on the circumstances of their drowning and the length of their submersion. But they were all armed. In fingers bloated by water the drowned carried rusted swords encrusted with barnacles, and spearheads whose worm-devoured shafts were nothing but memories. Boat hooks, tools for carving float stone, sail maker's knives, and fishermen's gaffes were mixed in with halberds, cutlasses, daggers and all the other tools intended only to bring about the death of men. Glimmer weaponry they possessed too, though their gunners were in no formal groupings of their own, but scattered among the horde. The earliest examples of ironlock technology were present as corroded lumps fronded with seaweeds, the holes where iron filings should be poured to react with a glimmer charge clogged with half-moon shells. Later guns held more of their form, the very latest were barely rusted, their wooden stocks unmarked but for the odd wormhole.

Aarin's guards took him down the long column, and it became apparent the massive rearguard was a militia, poorly equipped and ordered, for toward the front greater organisation was in evidence.

Next came the artillery, a mismatched train of guns taken from every kind of ship. The dead had worked to preserve this artillery from decay, encasing the barrels in tight, waterproof skins of leather. By contrast to the care given the guns, the carriages were rickety, being of sun-bleached driftwood and bone lashed together with the sinews of undersea beasts.

Ahead of the guns regiments of dead men marched in drilled squares. The warriors toward the front of the column were the most decayed. Many were entirely fleshless, little more than animate skeletons in whose cavities sea creatures dwelled. These soldiers marched with surer purpose. They wore armour fashioned from panels of shell, and their weapons were of glittering stone, sharp and unmarred by the ocean's corrosive waters. Officers went ahead of them on composite mounts stitched together from the corpses of many beasts. Shoals of seahorses accompanied some as gaudy pets, while anguillon elvers glided at the sides of others upon leashes fashioned from their parent's leather. Like all the spectacle of the drowned host, examination of the detail left a poor impression. Their proud officers were unlovely parodies of parade ground heroes. Their helmets were full of holes, their hats rotted. The feathers in their headgear were sprigs of seaweed wafting in the current generated by the passage of the army.

Through billows of sand kicked up by the trudging feet, Aarin was taken toward the very front. The column moved at a snail's pace, leaning into the water to push its way through, further belying its impressive first appearance. Every curtain of sand pulled back revealed another tawdry glory or bone-chilling horror. Upon the backs of adolescent anguillons rode drowned knights, their lances the spiralled tusks of oceanic monsters, their helms outsize cowries, their shields the nacreous upper shells of giant oysters.

These swept back and forth over the marching infantry in impatience at their sluggish speed.

The undersea road wound downwards, and the kelp thinned and gave out. A wide plain of broken rock formed the seabed ahead. Every army requires its staff and its general. Upon the plain at the head of the host they were to be found.

A hundred bearers carried banners. Some were made of scavenged sails and stolen flags, their colours bleached by salt water. The flags were of all nations, many fragmentary, selected seemingly for their colours' prettiness rather than any meaning they might carry. Only two thirds of the standard bearers bore such devices, the rest made do with tall pennants of kelp, their rubbery stalks stripped, the upper part left with an unruly mop of fronds. Musicians marched before the banner men, carrying beneath rotting arms great conches and other shells, and brass trumpets greened by long exposure to the deep. A bodyguard of huge warriors, mostly again skeletal, marched ahead of them.

In the midst of this fearsome bodyguard was the Drowned King.

THE RELATIONSHIP BETWEEN the drowned and their liege was poorly understood by the peoples of the land. The Guiders said the drowned and their king were one and the same, that his soul was composed of the spirits of the world's drowned and the rest had no will of their own. Other wise men disagreed, maintaining that the king held the drowned in thrall, preventing their escape to the afterlife. There were drowned souls before the coming of the King, their opponents argued. Not so many, said the others. So scholarly debate went back and forth in university cloisters of dry stone, safely away from the terrors of the deep.

For those that witnessed the King—or worse, suffered his wrath—the argument was immaterial. The King was mercurial, dangerous and oftentimes wicked. His subjects were legion. Air-breathing men feared to join them.

On the last occasion Aarin faced the Drowned King, he had been a giant composed of many corpses, a gestalt horror of storm-lost sailors and shattered boats. The day Aarin saw him striding across the rocky plain, the King was still a giant, still made up of a thousand dead men. But his body that second time incorporated trees swallowed by the sea, their roots and branches coiled like sinews in the corpse flesh of his limbs, while his head and chest were made of the coiled cadaver of a giant sea dragon, the rotting face of the beast furnishing the lord of the drowned with a new, bestial visage.

The fish dived lower, swooping over the hooked spears of the army's foremost regiments, passing through the fluttering array of flags. The drowned released their captive, depositing Aarin ahead of the army.

Aarin stood alone before the horde.

Through the eyeless sockets of the sea dragon carcass the Drowned King looked upon Aarin. He held up an arm made of drowned men, wood, the corpses of giant fish and other things besides, and brought his legions to a halt.

Silence. Sand churned up from the bottom by the army floated away in the watery breeze of the ocean currents.

Guider, spoke the king. No words issued from his mouth. No sound carried through the water, but Aarin heard him nonetheless; a cold, black, boneless presence in his mind, chilled by sunless fathoms, whispering to his soul. *Upon your brother's ship you committed a crime against my people, sending them away from our home beneath the waves, into the uncertain hells of the hereafter. Now you are drowned, and you are mine.* The Drowned King beckoned to him. *Come forward, let me free you of the memories of your dry life, so you may begin anew in the nation of the water.*

I will not, replied Aarin. He was not sure if he could respond, but thought back his words at the vile sensation intruding into his mind. *I have an errand to complete that will determine the future of all the dead, and must be resolved.*

He was heard. The Drowned King's stolen head reared high upon its serpentine neck.

You speak! The presence hissed, a maddening sensation worming deep into his spirit. It was all Aarin could do not to hammer at his skull to try and claw it out. *How is this so? Ghosts have no voices.*

This one does, replied Aarin.

Then you have a powerful soul.

Perhaps, Aarin replied. *I am not dead, nor am I alive. I am between the two, under the protection of the Dead God himself.*

The water was perturbed by the king's emotions. Swift currents tugged at Aarin's clothes. From behind the banner men, a cohort of drowned emerged, weapons levelled at the Guider.

Tell me before I kill you, what business Tallimastus has with the dead of the sea.

Business left unfinished at the time of the driving, said Aarin. *When he was captured, and he turned the tables upon the man who imprisoned him. I have come here in search of that man, so that I may release him. I come here in search of Res Iapetus.*

At the uttering of the great mage's name, a ripple of movement passed down the column's length.

That name means nothing to me, said the Drowned King.

You lie, said Aarin. *Look inside yourself. To your heart. You know who you are. Speak with me. Tell me how I may free Tallimastus. He will free you in return, and we may repair the damage to the way of the dead.*

You appeal to the wrong monarch, I care nothing for the fate of the dead of the land, and I have no heart! laughed the Drowned King. *Why would I wish the dead to depart? You would rob me of my kingdom!*

The skeletal warriors advanced, the eyes of fish dwelling in their ribcages gleaming at Aarin.

I will stop you. I will use my gifts.

You cannot. You may guide one or two of my warriors from this world before you are torn apart, that is all. You have no mage to help you this time. Dead God's boon or no, you will die. After this interruption is concluded, I will march on to my war against the dry folk. You shall be no more.

The dead legionnaires advanced, shields overlapped, long spears pointing at the Guider.

Aarin's heart sank. *Then to all the souls bound into your service, who languish here in the depths when they should fly free across eternal skies, I offer my apologies. But I must do what must be done.*

With a thought, Aarin conjured the weapons of Tallimastus into his hands. The shield gleamed brassily in the feeble undersea light. The sword burned with green fire. At their summoning, all weight of the water fell away from him, and he moved unencumbered by the ocean's press. Raising the god's weapon, he ran into the warriors surrounding him, and set to work.

The sword boiled the water. Spear heads fell slowly to the sea bed. Shields of shell exploded into fragments. The sword cut through armour and then through bone, biting finally into the atrophied spirits of the drowned. They were dragged from their bodies and torn apart. Freed for a moment from the Drowned King's bondage, they saw the fate awaiting them, and they screamed as Aarin cut them from the Earth's tale.

Green flashes lit the kingdom of the drowned as Aarin destroyed the souls of dozens of damned men. Like his brothers, Aarin had been instructed as a youth in swordplay. This combination of shield and sword was unfamiliar to him, an outdated, military form of combat. But he was empowered by the wrath of a god, and he cut through the Drowned King's soldiers with ease. Not one of them could touch him. They died the final death, the expunging of spirit. Aarin would weep for what he had done, if he were not so driven to solve the problem of the dead. Lives must be sacrificed, souls must be sundered.

He did not know if these thoughts were his, or the sword's.

Soon enough he had cut through the regiment, leaving them as bone splinters and rags of cloth drifting off into the ocean's darkness.

You cannot kill them all, said the Drowned King. *Thousands of souls are mine to command!*

You must speak with me, Res Iapetus! Aarin responded.

I do not know that name.

Bubbling horn cries sounded. The army of the drowned moved forward, the column splitting, regiments arraying themselves for battle. Their sudden advance pushed the water forward as an invisible force. Anguillon knights came shoaling from the murk behind the king, their lances levelled at Aarin. He lopped them off as they charged, cut the giant eels in half, dismembered the corpse-warriors and sent their souls into shrieking oblivion. But there were too many.

A spiral lance slammed into Aarin's side, breaking off and leaving its point embedded in his ribs. A scream escaped his mouth in a cloud of bubbles. His shield dropped, allowing a second lance to enter his body. The knight released the haft; the weight dragged Aarin to his knees. The Drowned King laughed.

His laughter turned to rage as Aarin forced himself up, slicing the second lance's shaft away with the Dead God's sword.

I am under the protection of death. I cannot die, he said, and leapt forward, his sword raised to strike.

Tallimastus' blade cleaved the snapping dragon's head from the Dead God's shoulders, and continued down the chest. Where the blade touched the sodden flesh of drowned men, it shrivelled to black mud, and the feeble candles of dead souls were snuffed out. Aarin cut one of the King's legs away, the sword of the god shearing through the five men who made up his thigh. The Drowned King tumbled down, his arms flopping uselessly. Aarin cut his other leg away below the knee.

Aarin turned his attention to the torso again, hacking his way through the King's chest. Wisps of spirit and rotting flesh clouded the water, and the screams of the damned burned his soul. He ignored the blades cutting at his back as the drowned desperately worked to protect their king. Holed, drowned, pierced by blade and lance, he did not die, and his heart still beat.

One final blow brought forth a flood of light that drove back the drowned men attacking him. Aarin fell from the Drowned King's chest. A second explosion of light blasting back the water, the shockwave knocking flat the troops of the king for half a mile around.

Aarin got to his feet, coughing water from his lungs. His back was a mess of bloodless cuts. Like the one in his arm, they bled but little. He and the Drowned King were in a hemisphere of air upon the seabed. The drowned circled outside, those that had recovered from the blast attempted to get within, but there was some barrier they could not breach, and they clawed helplessly at the edge of the water with their bony fingers and puffed corpse flesh, dead jaws snapping their frustration.

"Guider," a weak voice said.

The Drowned King had disintegrated into a pile of corpses and marine debris. The stench was overpowering.

"Guider!" The voice came from the centre.

Aarin clambered over slippery corpses. At the very middle, half-buried in reeking dead flesh, was a living man. The family resemblance with Vols Iapetus was unmistakeable, although the man lacked Vols' less fortunate features, being strongly muscled and handsome, with a full head of hair.

"You are Res Iapetus," said Aarin.

The man nodded. He was spread-eagled and naked in the filth. Only one of his arms was visible. Around the hand was a silver ball that blended with his skin. Magical lightning sparked around it.

"I am Res Iapetus, the driver of the gods," he said with self-mocking pomposity. He appeared very tired, like a man recovering from a long sickness. "I only have a minute or so before Tallimastus' magic overpowers me again. So listen carefully. I understand why you want to free the Dead God. Do not do it, no matter how many people seem to be suffering."

"They are not suffering," said Aarin. "They are dying, forever. That is your fault."

"Maybe," said Res Iapetus wearily. "Maybe not. There is much at play here. Knowing what you do, you may think me foolish for driving out the gods and precipitating this crisis, but my work was unfinished. I was hoping to save the world from what is coming. Had I completed my task, we would all be safe."

"What about your wife?"

"There was that too," admitted the mage. "Her death made me look closely at the gods, and why we are beholden to them. I did not much like what I saw."

Spirit light shone in the air. Souls coalesced. They sank toward the broken bodies of the drowned, and were absorbed.

"It is beginning," said Res. "Even Tallimastus's sword cannot destroy these souls. See, they reform."

"Impossible!" said Aarin.

"They are here by his enchantment. They are my gaolers. I will become the Drowned King again, Tallimastus' last gift! Listen, and listen well. Only one of my bloodline can stop what is going to happen."

A corpse twitched near Aarin's foot. Another rolled over, and embraced the first. A third wriggled into place against them, entwining fingers with a fourth. Others plucked at Aarin's robes as they crawled together. He tugged them free in disgust.

"My only descendant is Vols Iapetus."

More corpses wriggled together. The initial knot of them were taking on the semblance of an arm.

"I know him," said Aarin. "He is with my brother in the south."

"He was with your brother," said Res, speaking quickly. "I have watched Vols in my dreams, the only place I am free. He has the potential to be the greatest mage ever to have been, greater even than I. He can finish my work. He can save all humanity, not only the Kingdoms. He can stop them all—the Morfaan, the Draathis, and the Y Dvar."

"Tell me what he must do!" said Aarin. "I shall get word to him."

"Ah, I would, but there is a problem," said Iapetus ruefully. "He is dead." Iapetus made a pained noise as his legs were pulled taut.

Corpses rolled under Aarin's feet, binding themselves together by embracing. He stepped back, stumbling over them, until he reached the safety of the sand. The corpses inside the hemisphere ignored him, but around the perimeter of air more and more of the drowned were gathering, thronging the ocean bed, and were staring in at him with murderous eyes.

"Then what can I do?"

"You have power. You are of the Dead God's quarter. All true Guiders are mageborn, but you are powerful, I can see it. You must go into the Lands of the Dead."

"Impossible!" said Aarin. "I am no necromancer."

"A poor word for a powerful man. It is possible. You know it is. Tallimastus has rendered you immune to death. It is probable he foresaw this chain of events." A dead man rolled onto Res Iapetus' chest, making him breathe quickly. "Return Vols to this world. He can save it. Only he can save us all."

"What about Tallimastus?"

"Forget about him! Do not trust him," shouted Res Iapetus. Squirming limbs were covering him over, drawing him back into the heart of the Drowned King. "He will destroy you. Do not trust any of them."

"He is a god."

"He is not a god, none of them were," gasped Res. Only his face was visible now. He shouted quickly, desperate to get out his message. "Those we worshipped are pretenders. They were the Y Dvar, the children of the One. They abandoned their path. This is what I discovered; all of them, the wild, the collared sneaks who live among us, the gods—they are the same. I was going to drive them all away, because they have fallen."

Res gagged as corpse fluid poured into his mouth. Writhing cadavers smothered him. They slid over Aarin's feet in their rush to rejoin the composite body.

"Listen to me! Listen!" choked Res. "Do not trust the Children of the Five, do not trust any of them or the creatures they made! Do not trust the Tyn Y Dvar!" He screamed then, a sound cut off as his face disappeared under a drowned sailor's fish-white, sagging skin.

"The Tyn Y Dvar?" said Aarin. "The Tyn?"

But Res Iapetus was gone, drawn back into the heart of the Drowned King. Drunkenly, the king sat. His gestalt body grew steadier as more dead bodies flowed into it, bringing it back to unlife.

The air bubble wobbled, and shrank.

Aarin did not know what to do. Iapetus was trapped. Tallimastus may or may not have been trustworthy. If he did bring Vols back, should he release the god?

Another thought struck him. If Vols was dead, what of his brother, Trassan?

He looked up. The air bubble was shrinking further. The Drowned King was groaning. There was no escape from this place.

He was being manipulated. Triesko, Seutreneause, Tallimastus, and now the Goddriver. He wouldn't have it. He would not have it at all.

His face set with anger, he hefted the sword of the Dead God.

"Heed me, oh dead," he said, beginning the cantrip that would open the way to the afterlife. He had spoken it a thousand times, only never for himself. "Hearken to me, gather to me, release your earthly cares, so that I might send you on."

A green light wavered in front of him. He continued his chant. The souls of the drowned nearest him rose from their bodies with grateful sighs. "Go into the light, go into eternity. Begone from this world of pain and hollowness, and into a new place, where reward awaits the just, and the wicked might be redeemed."

The light strengthened. Aarin gripped the sword and shield of Tallimastus tightly. The drowned around the air bubble collapsed, their ghosts drawn toward the rift. Aarin's power was magnified. The rift was wider than it had ever been. He saw through it, clearly, to a land of green mists and twisted buildings. So strong was its power it pulled at his soul.

Aarin took a deep breath his body did not need. With a shout of defiance, he ran at the gates of the dead, and hurled himself through.

Against all the laws he had ever known, Aarin vanished from this world. A moment later, the rift collapsed. The air pocket erupted upwards in a boiling storm of bubbles.

The Drowned King clambered to his feet.

Under the wrathful gaze of their rotting monarch, the dead regrouped, and recommenced their march.

CHAPTER THIRTY-SEVEN
The House of Arms

THERE WERE A couple of days in an empty warehouse for the children. The Renian Donati promised he would return to them soon, explaining that he had preparations to make, and entrusted them to the watch of a stern, uncommunicative pair of goodwives who scowled at any noise, but otherwise left the children alone.

In the warehouse they were served hot food. For most of them it was the first meal they had had in days. There were beds to sleep in, and clean water to drink. The conditions were not much better than at the Lemio mill, but for Lavinia it was a heaven compared to the street.

Lavinia knew few of her new comrades. They had come to Golden Lane from all over the city. There was only one other girl from the Lemio factory among the thirty children in the warehouse. The workers from the Lemio mill had run everywhere after they were dumped. One boy she had seen dead in the street, naked from the waist down. Others had vanished, probably to similar fates.

A few of the children in the warehouse were spirited sorts, but none of them attempted escape. They didn't seem to have much in common, except that they were healthy, and there was a good proportion of pretty girls and handsome boys among them. She reassured herself that in people like them, prettiness was a mark of health. Not one was under the age of ten. All of them were strong.

If Donati's master required workers, then he had chosen well.

Mostly they slept and devoured what food was given. Lavinia continued to eat long past the point of satiation, anticipating no more to come. After they rose in the morning they carried their bedding around wherever they went. One of the goodwives tried to explain their blankets would not be taken from them, but the children trusted no one. Still, she was unmolested. No one tried to steal her food. No one argued. They talked very little, but sat in fearful, individual worlds.

The second morning, Donati returned full of smiles. He distributed sweet treats among the children.

"My apologies, young ones," he said. "My last day was full of form filling and rubber stamping. I am sorry you have no new clothes, but you shall have them today. Now the bureaucracy, that is all done with. I may now take you from this place to your new home. Come on! *Avanati!*"

He smiled as the children gathered up their bedding. "Leave it. There is no need young ones, all will be provided at Morthrocksey."

Only two of them dropped their blankets. The others clutched theirs defiantly. Donati chuckled.

"Very well! It matters not. Goodfellow Morthrock's largesse is great. He can afford for you to keep these, but there will be more, and better! Come! Come!"

Men dragged back wheeled doors. The children spilled out into the street, where once again dray wagons waited for them. When they clambered aboard it was with a little less wariness than before.

Donati climbed up last, and sat by Lavinia.

They rode through ranks of blank, windowless warehouses. Commercial dray trucks rumbled past them, piled high with goods hidden under tarpaulins. Iron rails were embedded in the centre of the road, and down this chugged a small glimmer engine pulling a modest train of eight wagons loaded with crushed stone.

The wagon turned up a wider street. Three train lines came in from the opposite direction, running alongside the carriageway. Ahead were several, large buildings, walled off from the rest of the district. Giant chimneys spewed glittering smoke into the sky. Men and women in worker's overalls and caps went in and out of the gates. A steam whistle blew hard enough for Lavinia to hear. Otherwise the scene was to her eerily muffled, the other sounds that undoubtedly made up an industrial din hardly perceptible.

"See ahead the Morthrocksey Mill, that which we call the House of Arms!" Donati proclaimed. "It has recently become the greatest armaments factory anywhere in the Kingdoms. All this you see here, it belongs to my master Goodfellow Demion and his wife Goodlady Katriona." He was proud of all these things that were owned by other people. "They are very wealthy, and very successful, and they wish to spread his good fortune to the likes of you, poor deprived children. You are lucky."

They approached the mill's high brick perimeter. Lavinia wondered why the wall needed iron spikes along it, if the mill were such a grand place to live.

"The South Gate," Donati explained, as happily as if he owned it himself.

The buildings behind the south gate were of new, fresh brick, still pale from their baking. Mortar stood out in crisp white lines. Everything was red brick or grey stone. Sharp angles dominated. Not one green thing grew there. The sky was low, brown with smog that spat flurries of lightning caused by glimmer pollution.

The dray wagon passed under the buildings' shadow a hundred feet before they reached the factory wall. The buildings were so huge they barred the sun from the city.

The warehouses lining either side of the way stopped. Wide roads ran right round the factory. Beyond them on the left were ranks of tidy terrace houses, on the right a vast rail yard.

The wagon's wheels bumped over rails, and it went under an ornately curled cast iron arch which had a huge glimmer lantern at its centre, burning in the middle of the day. Below it the factory's name was picked out in gold lettering wrought in the most fashionable of fonts.

A portico fit for a palace fronted the factory offices. Huge columns held aloft a brick pediment moulded with images of industry and progress. The frieze continued around the portico, and off down the factory's sides.

The entrance to the offices was equally grand, with main doors of twenty feet tall, spiked bronze, the sort of thing found on a fortress or barracks rather than a mill. Fittingly, they were guarded by a pair of uniformed men carrying shining ironlocks.

Five stories of large windows surrounded the portico. An open-sided spire speared the sky from the centre of the main roof, housing a large bell below its golden onion dome.

The children did not enter this way, but were driven around the side of the office building. This was a big square block of a thing, joined at the back to the featureless brick walls of a sort more commonly associated with the industrial buildings of the era. The second building was new, of just two stories, its roof a saw-tooth of alternating glass and slate faces angled to catch the sun. A river ran in a square, brick channel along the street there, disappearing into a culvert under the factory. Further along its length were young trees in pots, and places where the bricks had been pulled up and plants allowed to grow. It was the only vegetation Lavinia saw. At the far end of the street, was a second, even larger gateway. Close by it a number of buildings had been burned out, and were surrounded by scaffolding and screens that did not manage to hide the scorched brickwork.

They drew up beside a metal door painted black. Donati leaped down. From within came the pounding of machines.

"Come!" He spread his arms wide and faced his charges, smiling all the while. The doors opened, and the rumble of manufacture became very loud. "Come down, come see! Come and look at the future!

Welcome to the greatest factory in the world!" He said. He stopped by the open door. The factory floor spread out behind him. Beneath iron beams holding up the roof, long axles span belts that ran hundreds of machines. These were arranged in specialised rows, as per the doctrine of Thortha Bannda of Irruz. Men, women and children in identical uniforms worked on guns, each making a single part or assembling sections before putting the weapon onto trolleys to be wheeled further down the chain for the next stage to be completed. "At Morthrocksey we make many things, from pans to pipes, but guns are our speciality."

The concrete floor was freshly painted. The machines were new under their coatings of black oil. The belts that drove them were unscuffed, and all the axles shone under generous dollops of fresh, yellow grease. The glass of the roof let in the sun. All was light. It was a world away from the broken down Lemio mill.

Donati summed it up, when he said, "This, my little friends, is the epitome of modern manufacturing writ large." He had to shout over the noise. Lavinia's growing lip-reading skills gave her an advantage. Now it was her new friends' turn to strain to hear.

"This is one of the most important places in all of Ruthnia," said Donati. "You are about to embark on a lifetime of worthwhile work." He held up his hand. "Who among you boys here wants to be a soldier?"

Several of the boys put up their hands. Soldiering pay was poor, but regular, and at least the troops were fed.

"I am not surprised!" Donati shouted. "You will serve your nation, yes?" He bent down conspiratorially and rested his hands on his knees to speak at the smallest boy's level. "Let me tell you, you can serve Karsa here!

You will be more important than any soldier. A soldier without his gun is nothing. You will give him power, because you will make his gun! From here, weapons are sold to every army in the Hundred Kingdoms. This factory is so crucial to the honour of our realms that it is, in a way, an army of the Kingdoms, as much as any on the field of battle or aboard ships fighting the Ocerzerkiyans on the ocean waves. You, my friends, are its latest recruits. How do you feel about that?"

The children looked back at him with hollow eyes. Lavinia had a desperate urge to run out of the factory. Being around the machines threatened to send her into a panic. The lure of food and shelter kept her where she was.

"That enthusiastic, eh? Well, does anyone want to leave?" He put his hands on his hips and looked at them all. "Think before you do. Look around. Many of the children you see here..." He searched about. "...like him." He pointed at a boy at a lathe. He was gaunt, but not starving. He held a chisel in his hand. Curls of wood drew themselves off a block of wood at the blade's touch, and a gun stock took shape quickly under his guidance. "He was going to die, now he has a job. He has shelter and food, and education. Now," he said, clapping his hands together, "I ask again. Does anyone want to leave?"

Nobody moved.

"Bravo!" he said. "Then come this way!"

LAVINIA'S TURN IN the washhouse could not come quickly enough. She enviously watched her companions go into the three small rooms grubby and ragged and emerge scrubbed pink and clad in new factory uniforms. When the maid gently touched her shoulder to get her attention and led her inside, Lavinia found a small room covered floor to ceiling in neat white tiles, with a slit window at the top to let in the light. A motto picked out in small black tesserae within blue borders was the sole ornament.

Cleanliness is virtue, it read.

Austere in decoration though it was, to her amazement there was not only a washbasin in the room, but also an unexpected luxury—most of the space was taken up by a deep ceramic bath set partially into the floor. The dirty water within spoiled the effect, but she had been about to climb into it anyway when the factory girl shook her head.

"No, goodmiss," was all she said, before letting out the stopper.

Black grit and scummy water flowed away, the sins of another soaked off and dispensed with. An absolution by soap, she thought. The bath was rinsed for her, and fresh water drawn from the copper taps set high over the tub.

"Take as long as you need," the maid said, and retired. At the side she left a clean towel neatly folded with a cake of soap on top.

The water was hot when Lavinia got in, almost painfully so, but she lowered herself into it with a sigh of pleasure. She scrubbed and scrubbed but there was always more dirt. The cleaner she got the dirtier she felt, her hair in particular was driving her mad. It was caked with filth that came out in endless crumbs, and now, halfway between clean and filthy, it began to itch. The soap wore away to a wafer, the water grew cold. She felt like she would never be clean until, miraculously, she was.

She lay back in the grey water. Her clothes lay in a stinking pile nearby. Now she was cleansed, the reek coming off her dress, shawl and bonnet disgusted her. The thought of putting them back on made her ill. She wanted to see them burned. The thought of not getting a uniform like everyone else agitated her.

It was quiet in the room, enough that the infernal ringing in her ears was all too audible. She had the sudden urge to scratch at them, to enlarge the holes and ram her hands into them, as if scrubbing them out would rid her of her deafness like it too were dirt.

A knock came at the door, very loud. She supposed she missed the first attempt. Slipping into the water up to her shoulders, she crossed her hands over her chest, covering her youthful breasts.

"Yes?" she said.

She expected the factory girl. She flushed when Donati walked in, a fresh uniform dress over his arm, and a linen bag in his hand.

"Hello, hello, my goodlady," he said with easy charm. "Here are you new clothes." He laid the dress over a bar projecting from the wall. "Here is your new underwear, a toilet kit, socks, rags for your monthlies and a belt of rope for the same..." he grinned with affected bashfulness. "All the things a young lady needs."

The ringing in her ears outcompeted the higher registers of his voice, so she watched his lips.

"Thank you," she said.

"This and more will be provided you here at the House of Arms, goodlady," he said, bowing with a little flourish.

She stared at him. "It is a demon's bargain," she said.

Donati sighed and hitched up his sword belt. "You are no fool, my dear. It is a deal with its downsides, but that does not make it a worse deal than what you had," he said reasonably. "Here you will at least not die. Let us be honest. What Goodman Morthrock is doing for you is kindness, but what I am doing is not solely down to that."

"I did not think so," she said. She wanted to get out of the bath and into her clothes. She did not like being alone with him.

"Owing to certain agitation among the factory owners of Karsa, there is a surfeit of labour in the city at the moment. It is something of a crisis, you might say. My master's wife is the cause of this upheaval. She is kind, but no fool. She is offered money by the council of this district to take young people like you off the streets. I do this work for them. In return, I can pay you very little, because so many of you are looking for work. That makes me look good to them. We all win." He shrugged. "Life is cruel, but laws never acknowledged before are suddenly being enforced, and new ones even more stringent will probably come. Then, you might well be able to name your own price for your time and your labour. But who knows how long the new laws will take to be passed? Until that day comes, I have the use of a large, virtually free pool of labour. The essence of business is disruption, *mio chicina*, the goodfellow said so to me. He says many wise things to me, though I think his wife told them to him. I take it to heart. I get cheap labour. The Morthrocks get to salve their conscience. We all make money."

Donati knelt by the side of the bath and swished his hand through the dirty water.

"You will get your clothes wet," she said nervously.

"I do not care!" he said dramatically. "The Morthrocks treat me well. I have many suits of clothes." He looked sidelong at her dress. "Would you not like the same?"

"I am glad for the uniform," she replied.

"I am a shift boss, do you know what that means?"

"Yes."

"You will be joining my crew. There is prosperity here, for those with the right..." he smiled again. "Attitude."

"I work hard."

"There are other routes to riches than simple work. How old are you?" he said. He reached out and stroked a strand of hair away from her ear. "You are so very beautiful, a flower in the most glorious phase of womanhood."

Anything said to her had to struggle past the ringing barrier in her head, but though she did not hear every word, his meaning was clear.

"In my land, a girl is a woman when she bleeds," she said. "I started my bleeding two years ago." She trembled under his touch, a mixture of unlooked for arousal and fear. "I think I am fourteen summers, maybe fifteen."

"A good age," he said. "Here, in Karsa, a woman is not a woman until she is twenty-one years of age, no matter whether the blood flows or not. But who decides these things? Surely, if you can bear children, you are a woman? That is the way in my own land."

"What are you doing in here?" she asked.

He laughed. "Can you not guess? You are not so young."

She pushed herself away from him and looked at the wall, willing him to go.

"Which factory were you at?" He folded his hands on the side of the bath. He spoke more clearly now she was facing away. That sent a chill down her spine.

"The Lemio Clothing and Shoddy Company," she said, looking back at him.

"Grostiman's venture," he said with a nod. "He is typical of the mill owners, and my mistress's enemy. They treat their young workers so poorly it is cheaper to throw them out before they are caught flouting the law. Too many of these factory owners are doing that now. They are untouchable. Their underlings are arrested instead of they, charged for offences that seem new, for they have never been enforced. All that is changing."

She looked at him quizzically.

He smiled, though his intention in doing so was masked. "Do you not know, my pretty little one? The goodlady who runs this factory is your champion, although for how much longer remains to be seen. Many of my master's associates are convinced she will put herself out of business. Although, I say to myself, and never, ever to them," he gave her another white-toothed smile, and grasped her gently by the chin, "if that is the case my lords, why are you scrambling to divest yourself of these youthful liabilities?" He let go of her face and rocked back from the bath on his heels. "You can see from how you are being treated here that the Morthrocks are good people. But they will not bankrupt themselves. Life here will be dull. You will work hard in return for their protection. I can make it better."

"Is this true?" she asked. "Is the Goodlady Morthrocksa fighting for us?

"It is true, *mio chicina*," he said. "Right now, at Sunderdown she goes against all three houses. Can you imagine? I do not think Goodlady Katriona will get her bill through, but it will make change. Action always makes change. She is not alone, though her supporters sit on the side of the match field, in case she loses. If she does not they will all leap up and claim their own victories. They will say, 'See, I too am a champion of the poor! I always have been!" He laughed. "If she fails, conditions will still be imposed upon the mill owners. Life will become freer, better for people like you, perhaps worse for people like me. But don't you worry about that. That will not happen for a long time, so if I were you I would make the best of this situation as you find it." He gave her a look loaded with meaning, "You are pretty. If you can keep your looks, in a few years you might marry yourself out of this situation. More likely, you will marry another drudge in this place and bear litters of brats to toil alongside you. It would be better if you had someone to watch over you. A real man, with means and money, not a boy or an exhausted factory worker who will drink your wages away and beat you in his frustration with life."

She stared back, refusing to speak.

"If I need to spell it out, very well. I offer my services, in exchange for a few of yours. What do you say?"

She shook her head.

"Ah, my dear, my dear little one. We both know something that the good lords Demion and Katriona do not. I know that your hearing is affected."

Her blood ran cold. "It is not."

He smiled. "Oh it is. An unfortunate result of your work in all these factories," he said. "Many are afflicted with it. A ringing in your ears, yes? A ringing that drowns out all other sound. If you do not take precautions, it will get worse. The goodman is kind, but I have little time for persons with the smallest flaw. It affects my productivity, and that affects my purse."

She choked on a sob.

"Shhh," he said. "I will not be unkind. I am a good man, skilled in the art of love. I believe that women, like flowers, have a perfect age, did you know that? Those first, perfect years, unmarred by pest or age. Those are the golden times for women, and they are so often overlooked."

He stroked her shoulder.

She shook her head, using the motion to avoid his hand. It followed her face and continued to caress her. Conflicting sensations put her on edge. Her body stiffened against his touch, freezing her in place.

His hand fell lower, drawing circles around her collar bones, then down over the upper curve of her breast. She felt her nipples tighten, bringing a wave of disgust. "Pick a flower too late, and its beauty has gone before you know it," he said. He ran his hand up to her face again, the strokes becoming firmer. He pulled her lower lip from her teeth for a moment. He looked at them, similar to the way a breeder inspects the teeth of a dray. "Pick them as flowers, and they wither and die so quickly. Pluck it just before it blooms, and you may enjoy beauty for a long time before it sadly flees." He took her chin again and tilted her face toward him. "I prefer to pluck my flowers while they are yet buds. That way I get to enjoy their opening." He breathed into her face. His breath was sweet with spices, redolent of warmer, drier lands. "I can get you things. Food. New clothes, not just these factory smocks." He gestured dismissively at the uniform. "I can provide protection for your ears, so you need not lose your hearing completely. I can love you, if you behave correctly. This warm water I bring you all, I did it for you, you see?" His smile took on a predatory air. "I do it because you are beautiful. I can see in your eyes that you and I, we may have a match in our souls." He pointed at her then at himself. "I can help. All I require is a few small considerations on your part, easily achieved." His voice dropped to a whisper. "I will not force you to do anything you do not want to." His laugh, so beguiling and kind before took on a sinister edge. "Well, not unless you want me to force you."

His hand trailed lower, dipping into the water. She squeezed her thighs shut, but he stood without touching her again. He playfully flicked the water from his fingers, and looked down from on high like a man surveying a patch of ground he would till.

"Think about it. Your life could be very boring here, though it will be safe. The Morthrocks are profiteers like the rest, but they have a few more morals than most industrialists. Sadly, your disability may shorten your stay here. Or," he smiled again, and all things positive had gone from his handsome face and the glint of his ivory teeth, "it could be exciting, and not limited to these brick halls alone."

He glanced up at the motto and snorted before sauntering out of the door.

She had been asked to sell herself many times since Tuvacs had gone.

A week after she arrived at the Morthrocksey Mill, she finally gave in.

CHAPTER THIRTY-EIGHT
The Taking of the *Prince Alfra*

"SMOKE ON THE horizon!" The lookout's warning was conveyed from the watchnest to the wheelhouse, his voice hollowed out by the speaking tubes. "Smoke on the horizon!"

Croutier's back expanded and settled as he took in a deep breath. Heffi couldn't see his face, but he would bet his last nose ring that the mercenary was smiling.

Heffi looked sidelong at Suqab. The Second Mariner's eyes met his. Heffi nodded.

"Sound the whistle," said Heffi.

Suqab pulled the whistle cord three times. Its two-toned lowing blew out over the choppy sea, sorrowful as the widows of the drowned.

"What are you doing?" asked Croutier affably.

Heffi raised his eyebrows. "I assume you want them to be able to find us? I am merely speeding them to our location."

"Is that what you're doing?" Croutier drew his pistol and pointed it at Heffi's head. "Because someone told me that when you blew three whistles like that, you would attempt to take back the ship."

"I've no idea what you are talking about. Tol?" Heffi asked the helmsman nonchalantly. "Do you have any idea what he's talking about?"

"None at all," said the helmsman, his eyes fixed on the horizon.

A trickle of sweat ran down Heffi's temple.

"You're all dead," said Croutier.

Three of Croutier's thugs came into the wheelhouse, weapons ready. Godelwind was hauled in by Guando.

"Tell your captain what you told me," Croutier demanded of the terrified Godelwind.

"I... You didn't say I'd have to look at him," stammered Godelwind.

"I prefer men who are not ashamed of their convictions." Croutier swung his gun round to point at Godelwind without taking his eyes from Heffi. "Tell him now."

"I told him," said Godelwind defiantly, "I couldn't let you do it. These are reasonable men. We would all have died."

"Coward," said Heffi. "He's going to kill us all, you know that."

"Oh yes I am," said Croutier. "You see, the thing is Godelwind, that's your name, isn't it?"

Croutier waited for a reply. Godelwind nodded frantically.

"Thank you," said Croutier. "Where was I?" he scratched his nose with his pistol barrel. "Ah yes, the thing is, Godelwind, is that your captain was right."

Croutier pointed the gun at Godelwind's head.

"Wait!" said Godelwind.

"To arms!" yelled Heffi. He stamped his foot so hard the iron deck rang.

Croutier's gun came round for Heffi. A less ruthless man might have made a quip at that point, Heffi thought. Croutier just fired.

Heffi was saved by a sudden upwelling in the iron of the wheelhouse floor. Metal shrieked on metal. The bullet went wide, sparking from the wall an inch away from Heffi and ricocheting into the window. Croutier swayed on the buckling plating.

"What by the lost gods..." Croutier swore.

The whole of the forward section of the wheelhouse deformed and lifted, sending the room's occupants staggering. Metal screamed in parting. Rivets pinged from their holes, shattering the glass, smashing instruments. One of Croutier's men was peppered by flying iron. His skull broke, and he went down.

The Ishamalani went into action.

Drentz was on the mercenaries fast, knife in a man's throat before he could react. Tolpoleznaen felled another, the belaying pin hidden in his sash appearing in his hands as if by magic, knocking his target cold with a single blow.

Croutier was screaming wildly, with an abandon Heffi would have thought out of character for the man. But then, reflected the captain in later years, he was being crushed alive by a giant, flat hand made of metal that peeled itself away from the floor. Long fingers wrenched themselves out of the structure of the ship with ominous plinks, and curled themselves about the mercenary captain's body. The shifting metal opened the wheelhouse to the deck below, and from that newly made gap the iron whisperers emerged, gliding uncannily up a ramp of metal, eyes aglow.

The Tyn chanted a song that hurt the soul. Metal danced to its tune. Marks Heffi had never seen before glowed white hot in the Tyn's skin, and their veins showed as black patterns through their flesh. Their eyes blazed with the heat of a forge, and the smell of hot metal washed off them in searing blasts.

Heffi took an involuntary step back. The iron rippled closer to the wheel housing.

"Not the wheel!" he shouted. "If we lose the rudder now, we're all dead!"

With obvious effort, the Tyn reined in their magic and turned aside the squeezing hand. The splits in the metal plating ran up to the foot of Heffi's station, stopping inches before they tore open the structure around the wheel and destroyed the *Prince Alfra's* ability to steer.

Croutier thrashed and screamed in the grip of the enchanted metal. He pushed at its fingers in terror, slicing open his palms on the jagged edges, but he was held fast. He could not escape.

Guando got a shot off as he backed towards the door, catching Suqab in the throat and felling him. Sounds of fighting came from all over the ship. The isolated bangs of ironlocks going off were outcompeted by bloodcurdling Ishmalani shouts. Not battlecries, exactly, for battle was forbidden, but in a situation like this such rules were suspended, and their prayers screamed at volume were as terrifying as any warrior's cry. Guando went down to a shot from behind. Toberan burst in, followed by Dellion. Tyn Charvolay pushed past them, blood dripping from his chef's knife and wearing an expression of such savagery it frightened Heffi.

The Tyn's chanting reached a crescendo. Croutier's screaming followed suit. The iron fingers had him about the waist, covering him from chest to knee. As they constricted, his bones snapped one by one, then all at once. Croutier gave one last spasmodic twitch and fell limp. His upper torso hung from the fist, his pulped innards held in the bruised sack his skin had become. Fluid pattered onto the deck.

It was done. The Tyn attempted to stop their magic, but it had got away from them. One screamed and fell down, smoke pouring from his clothes. The second could not stop his chanting. He locked his teeth, but the words had him now, and forced themselves from his mouth. White heat bathed the wheelhouse in light. The Tyn's back arched. The chant was cut short. The light went out.

A few bangs and shouts came from outside the wheelhouse, then silence, and cheering.

The musical, crystalline sound of metal settling played a discordant song aboard the bridge.

Heffi dropped the arm he had raised to protect his face. Melded to the deck in seamless union was a statue of the iron whisperer. Everything, from his wiry hair to his teeth, even his clothes, had been transformed into a single piece of iron, perfect in every detail. All except his collar, which remained apart around his iron neck, rapidly cooling from orange to cherry red.

Tyn Charvolay let out a cry, and rushed to the smoking body of the other iron whisperer, and patted him.

"He's still alive! Call for the physic. Get him cooled down. Oh, disaster," said Charvolay.

Toberan nodded, and ran out with the marine.

"I have never seen such a thing," said Heffi in wonder.

"I never thought it was possible."

Charvolay wiped tears from his face with the back of his hand. "You know what powers this ship. You know the Tyn of the Morthrocksey band made it possible. The knowledge to manipulate iron and magic together is not limited to the Morthrockesy alone, curse the world that it is so!"

"But this..." Heffi gestured to the inert iron fist, dripping with the crushed remains of Croutier.

Toberan returned with help. Kororsind had been released from his alchemist's lab, and he assisted the physic, Mauden, and Baudlein, the ship's tynman, as they helped up the last iron whisperer. Heffi didn't know the Tyn's name. He didn't know its sex. The iron whisperers were a breed apart, even among their people.

Charvolay pulled a face. "It is a power from the ancient times, little used now. Few dare to attempt it." Charvolay shook his head sadly at the transmutated Tyn. "Two Tyn dead in weeks, we who can live forever. Immortality thrown aside for your benefit, Ishmalan. Do not forget this in the coming months. Our sacrifices must be remembered, or you will pay."

"In the name of the One, it shall be so," said Heffi.

"Your prayers are wasted," said the cook. "Pray to a better god. The One forgot his children long ago." Charvolay left with the rest, talking urgently to the fallen iron whisperer in words no one else could understand.

"Captain, the ship is taken. We have the survivors of Croutier's mercenaries held captive," said Toberan.

"How many dead?" said Heffi. He pulled out his telescope while he spoke. He gave the approaching vessels a rapid scan. Though floatstone, they were as revolutionary in their design as the *Prince Alfra*. Their hulls were tall and strong, finely shaped and smoothed, fit to survive the rigours of a direct crossing of the southern ocean, a feat few had attempted and fewer survived.

"There are six of ours dead, eleven wounded. Three will die. Four of Croutier's men remain. The rest we killed."

"Toss the survivors overboard," said Heffi.

Toberan was taken aback. "They'll die for sure. No one can live in that water for more than a few minutes."

"A few minutes will bring their fellows to their aid, if they desire to stop. We will not be responsible for their deaths. If they do die, I care not. No one takes a ship from the Ishmalani. No one. They would have done the same to us. The Drowned King will welcome such scoundrels into his service."

"And what about him?" said Toberan, pointing to Godelwind, who cowered in the corner.

"Lock this dracon's arsehole up somewhere I don't have to look at him," said Heffi. "I'll think on it. The penalty for mutiny is unpleasant, it may suffice."

Godelwind whimpered.

"As you wish, captain," said Toberan, and again left the wheelhouse.

Heffi clicked his telescope shut. Persin's ships really were remarkably quick for floatstone.

The crew began firing the *Prince Alfra's* few cannon, small calibre swivel guns attached to the rails. Guns that size would do nothing to Persin's monsters. But the *Prince Alfra* had a greater weapon: speed. More speed than any other ship on the sea.

"All about!" shouted Heffi. "Engage all glimmer engines. Immerse the cores! Prepare screw for engagement!"

"All about!" repeated Drentz.

"Counterspin the paddles!" Heffi ordered.

"Counterspin paddles!" shouted Drentz.

Tolpoleznaen was back at the wheel. He threw it round. As the rudder pushed the ship into a steep starboard turn, the paddlewheels spun in opposite directions, and the *Prince Alfra* slewed around, tipping to port with the violence of its motion. Grey water whipped white by the ship surged up the side in sheets of spray.

The pop-pop-pop of cannon fired at range crackled behind them. Cannonballs shrieked after them, trailing blue glimmer. Spouts burst from the ocean where they struck. A single ball clipped the stern, making the hull boom. Heffi grinned. No glimmer cannon could penetrate the *Prince Alfra's* iron hide.

"Turn complete," said Tolpoleznaen.

"All ahead full!" shouted Heffi. "Engage screw!" His orders were repeated by his men.

The floatstone ships were coming closer. Croutier's men shouted for mercy as they were tossed from the side. One of Persin's ships slowed to pick them up. The other continued at full speed, its funnels belching black coal smoke, paddlewheels chopping hungrily at the fractious sea.

Another round clanged from the ship. Columns of water fountained around the *Prince Alfra*. The ship lunged forward as the screw and paddles bit into the ocean. Cold air streamed through the broken windows of the wheelhouse.

Heffi grinned savagely. The two ships of Persin's expedition fell behind them. The cannon fire became less threatening, diminished by distance to the volume of children's popguns. Impact spouts were far to their stern. No other rounds hit home.

"This is a very fine ship," said Heffi, patting his damaged console. "A very fine ship indeed."

He rested his hand a moment on brass fittings cold in the breeze.

"Make course for Sea Drays Bay," said Heffi. "Tolpoleznaen, you have command. I must inspect the damage to our vessel, and pay my respects to those who died to save it."

CHAPTER THIRTY-NINE
The Breath of the Mountain

A MODALMAN FACED another, smaller warrior from a different clan. His nostrils flared, his clan marks pulsed out a threat. The second reacted, shoving at the first with his huge, upper arms. In seconds they were grappling on the ground, all four fists punching and gouging. The large pinned the smaller, landing multiple blows on his head. Then the smaller managed to block and lock the arm of the larger, and flipped him off his chest onto the ground, where the tussle commenced anew.

Drauthek clapped loudly with his lower hands, cupping his upper hands around his mouth. "Yes! Yes! Good throw," he said, almost knocking Rel flat as he clapped. The modalman laughed joyously and shouted some more, "hit him," and "bring him down" being words Rel now understood in modish, having seen several impromptu wrestling bouts over the preceding days. The modalmen were feeling the pressure of the wind. Aggression flared, but they were also deliriously happy.

Rel moved away from Drauthek. It would be highly ironic if he were incapacitated by an accident only hours before escape. Out of the shelter of his giant friend's body, he wrapped his scarves about his face tightly against the gathering storm.

As the Brass God predicted, lights played around the citadel's towers. Hot wind blew directly down the face of the mountain. The vortices it generated as it hit the ground were visible to the naked eye as standing waves of dust. From there the wind raced out into desert. Funnelled by the valley sides, the wind picked up speed, stirring up dust devils on the dry lake bed. These tore through the camp, tossing the modalmen's possessions hither and thither. Tents boomed and shook with the force of air hurrying from one place to another. An occasional whiplash crack accompanied the collapse of a shelter. The modalmen were invigorated, almost giddy, but their animals were less than happy. The garau huddled together, feet folded under them, bellies pressed close to the earth. Their eyes were shut and their eyelashes coated with sand. Like the garau, the hounds lay motionless with their rumps facing into the wind. The animals waited out the storm without eating or drinking. They were so still sand collected on them, making them appear like so many boulders.

Laughter greeted each falling tent and spontaneous altercation. The modalmen sang wild songs, and gave their praise not to the sun in the morning, but instead to the wind. If it dropped, they were glum, only to become joyous again as it picked up and lashed them all anew.

"It is a common wind in these parts, it comes from the high peaks, hot and vigorous," Shkarauthir explained.

He had become voluble again, buoyed up by the wind. "It brings painful heads and short tempers, but when it comes it blasts out all bad thoughts, and fills us with the energy of the One. It is his gift to us, if we are strong enough to use it."

This was the Breath of the Mountain. It made Rel twitchy. There was an energy contained in it that made his skin crawl, although there were other reasons for his nerves, and they had little to do with the wind itself. Every day as the wind picked up, he wondered if that day would be the day it reached its height, and if he should strike out. He awaited the trance the Brass God promised, but if anything the modalmen were becoming more energetic, not less, and he feared he might be squandering his chance to get out.

Besides that, the wind was an enormous irritant. It was very hot, hotter than the desert itself. Its unvarying direction and mostly constant speed was maddening.

"Like being stuck in a bread oven," he muttered to himself. Blown sand got into his food and his face and his bed. His sole comfort was that Aramaz, ostensibly better adapted for life in those conditions, seemed as miserable as he did.

It was while he was commiserating with his dracon that the change in the modalman began. Aramaz had scraped out a depression in the ground, like the nest of a desert fowl, and settled himself into it. Rel sat by the dracon's head, picking grit out of his dried meat and fruit and letting the dracon lick the residue off his fingers. The dracon's inner eyelids were permanently shut. His pupils were just visible through the thin skin, which allowed him to see a little while keeping the sand out of his eyes.

"I wish I had two pairs of eyelids," said Rel, whose own eyes were constantly full of dust. He hunkered low over his bowl to shelter it, but a rush of sand fell from his robes into his food. In disgust, he set the bowl by Aramaz's snout. The dracon noisily ate, croaking happily.

"You enjoy it," said Rel. "I don't have much stomach for grit."

He dusted his hands off and stood up. The wind blew stronger and hotter than ever. There was not a cloud in the sky, but his view was partially obscured by persistent airborne sand that formed a brown smoke extending a hundred feet into the air. It was a strange wind. If he went up the valley sides, he was out of the worst of it. It clung close to the ground. On ridges further than a half mile from the main range of soaring cliffs no veils of dust blew at all. The infrequent grasses of sheltered spaces did not move. Over the valley, the wind ran at differing speeds, creating spectacular laminar flows, rivers of dust moved as independent sheets over each other, so they appeared like living strata of rock. The effect was entrancing, when the wind wasn't blowing into his eyes.

"This wind is not natural," he said. But of course, he knew that. He kept his eye on these sheets, because the Brass God had told him to expect them. The time for his departure neared.

He leaned down and scratched Aramaz's head. The dracon's plumage rose and fell in pleasure, tickling the underside of his wrist.

The tuneless clonking of a modalman gong sounded through the wind. Others joined it, until the valley resounded. Rel had Aramaz tethered a way from any modalman hearth. The giants were hazy forms in the murk. Their laughter had stopped, and they were walking purposefully, all of them heading toward their kin bands. Already those nearest to their camps had found their place, and were gathering in circles about extinguished campfires.

Horns warbled.

"It's beginning," said Rel. He looked down at Aramaz. "I hope you're ready. I'll be back in a few minutes. Don't go anywhere."

Aramaz croaked as Rel headed off back toward the campground of the Gulu Thek.

WHEN REL REACHED Shkarauthir's hearth the Gulu Thek were in the final stages of preparation for their rituals. The clan elders anointed the warriors' foreheads with smudges of white paint, then red, then dotted the stripes with black. Already modalmen in nearby camps were standing motionless with their arms spread wide as tree boughs, eyes closed, humming in tune with the steady moan of the mountain's breath. Their light patterns pulsed slowly, falling into time with one another, more sluggishly than when they slept. Their song blended eerily with the voice of the wind.

Rel pelting into their midst upset the tranquility of the scene.

"Shkarauthir!" Rel shouted.

The king of the Gulu Thek turned soft brown eyes on Rel and raised an arm in greeting. "Little Rel! You are here in time for the dreams of the breath. It is good that you return. We shall meditate. You will be alone for a while. Do not stray. The world changes while the mountain breathes. It will not be safe." He looked to his followers. "Leave us," he said in the modalman tongue.

The elders bowed to their king, and took their bowls of pigment away. Grauthek stood next to his lord, extended his lower arms diagonally to the ground and placed his upper hands, palms flat, together above his head. He stared at Rel and shut his eyes, then began to hum. Ger stood on the other side of the king, and likewise began to meditate.

Shkarauthir took a deep breath, and led Rel a little distance away.

"Of course, you will be leaving imminently," said Shkarauthir, once his tribesmen were out of earshot. "The Brass God came to me in a dream, and told me so. We will all succumb to the trance, and you may go without risk. That sack there," he pointed to a large bag, "contains supplies that should keep you alive until you reach the end of the petrified forest. Past there, you will come to a green country like your Farside. The land is hard, but you may hunt, and there is water. Follow the mountains, after many days they will turn south, and become the Appins. Northern Farside is not far after that, from there you may make your way home. It is a long journey, but with luck, you will return to your people."

"Drauthek drew me maps in the sand. I can find my way."

"Be safe, little one," said Shkarauthir. The king of the Gulu Thek turned into the wind, and gracefully moved his arms into the same configuration as Drauthek and Ger.

"Shkarauthir!" shouted Rel over the rising wind. "My people are starving in their cages. What will you do? Will you challenge Brauctha? I need to know whether this army you have here is going to go to the Kingdoms in peace or in war. What if I get back to the Kingdoms, secure safe passage for the modalmen, only for them to attack?"

Shkarauthir's eyes slid open a fraction. Ger and Brauctha's humming had a soporific effect that made Rel tired. He fought against a desire to join the modalmen in their strange prayer. The wind's strength was increasing.

"What will be will be, little one," said Shkarauthir, with the patience of a parent for its child. "We cannot rush things. Whether we go in war or peace I do not know. I hope for peace, but the true men are split equally. Perhaps in the voice of the wind, we will find guidance. Perhaps the Brass God will come and tell us his desires in person. What you told me is encouraging, but it is not enough."

"What if he does not come?"

"Then we will wait some more." Shkarauthir's eyes closed.

"I would be happier if you killed Brauctha."

"Now you sound like the man-eaters. I will not fight him, not while the peace of the moot holds. You will stay away from his encampment, little Rel. No good can come of it if you interfere. Leave your people. Our god warned you. Heed him." The light in his markings was pulsing slowly.

"Can you smell that?" said Rel, pointing behind him. "The rotting meat? The wind can't hide it. Tell me that you will see what you can do for them."

"I will do what I can for them," said Shkarauthir. "Do not aid them yourself. The risk is great." His words were slurring. "Good fortune to you, small one. May we meet again under propitious circumstances."

"Shkarauthir!" said Rel, but the king's tribal marks pulsed lethargically around the circuits of their tracks, and fell into time with those of the others. Shkarauthir was lost to the mountain's breath.

Rel took a couple of half steps backward, circling around. The wind was picking up. Modalmen stood still as the stone trees outside the camp. They faced the same direction, all tribes and clans, closed eyes pointing at the mountain.

"Shit," he said. "Shit!" This was it. He had to leave. He grabbed the sack.

The wind blew so hard it threatened to push him down. Rel leaned sideways into it. His progress was pathetic. A gale howled through the giants. Hurrying sand rattled off Rel's nomad clothes. Lumps of grit were carried in the blast, and they stung his skin through the layered cotton. In any other circumstances, Rel would seek shelter. This was a killing storm, the sort that would drive a man off his path and leave his corpse buried in the sand.

After a long struggle he reached his mount. He roused Aramaz with great difficulty. The dracon screeched and croaked, reluctant to go into the storm. Rel stowed the supplies, and clambered onto the reptile's back. The wind and Aramaz's movements made that hard, and he was almost spilled from the saddle.

Aramaz gladly broke into a run when his face was turned from the mountain. The wind pushed at

Rel's back, hurrying them through the camp. With the wind at the dracon's tail, it was not so bad. The modalmen loomed out of the sandstorm like statues. Aramaz dodged past them, leaping over their hounds when they appeared suddenly on the ground, hidden by the drifting sand. Like their masters, the creatures of the modalmen remained utterly still, few of them even stirring as Aramaz galloped past.

They reached the road. The palisade was ahead. Visibility was down to tens of feet. The edge of the valley was near. A sole campground stood between Rel and freedom.

His heart sank.

The men in cages were waiting for him. He was their only hope.

He yanked hard on Aramaz's reins, making the dracon shriek. He turned Aramaz around, and looked back up the road.

"I'll let them out," he said. "Then I'll be on my way."

TUVACS WORKED AT the loose bar in the cage. The modalmen had gone into a trance, prompting him from surreptitious picking at the wood into outright attack.

"Quickly!" snarled Dunets. "Get the iron out! Get their keys! Release us all!"

"We're working on it," snapped Rafozo.

Only Rafozo and Tuvacs were close enough to the loose bar to get their hands on the wood. With no tools, they had to work at individual splinters with their fingernails to make a hole.

"Stop a moment," said Tuvacs.

Rafozo moved back. Tuvacs ran his chains to the bottom of the bar and yanked hard. The bar shifted nearly all the way out of its socket, then jammed itself fast.

"Almost got it!" He said. He kicked the bar back into place and yanked back and forth on it until it was rattling with every touch.

Their lookout whistled from his station at the rear of the cage. "Driven gods, someone is coming! Work faster!"

Rafozo grabbed Tuvacs arm. "Stop," he said. "We should save this for another time."

"There won't be another fucking time!" snarled Dunets. "Get out of here. Get the gods-damned keys, or I'll kill you myself."

"It's too late," said Rafozo. "If they're awake, then getting Tuvaco out of here will make no difference."

"He won't be dead," said Dunets. "That's a start."

"They'll kill him!"

"They'll kill us all anyway. Get out, Mohaci boy!"

Tuvacs continued to yank hard.

"Stop, Tuvaco!" said Rafozo. "There'll be another chance."

"There won't," said Tuvacs.

The lookout squinted into the wind. "It's not a modalman! It's a man, on a dracon!"

Men ran their chains up the bars they were bound to so that they might stand and see.

The rider drew up next to the cage, retrieved something from his belt and tossed it within.

A bunch of keys clanked on the boards. There was a plain one for the door, and a number of identical manacle keys.

"Captain Kressind!" said Tuvacs.

"That it is," Rel said. "Get yourselves out!" He shouted over the wind howling through the bars. "I took enough keys from the guards for all the wagons, but we don't have much time. Get out, flee! Head west, along the mountain's feet. There is good land in that direction."

Dunets had already snatched up the keys and was undoing his manacles as Rel was riding away.

REL RODE UP and down the line, tossing bunches of keys into cages and shouting at the men inside to rouse themselves and escape. "Head west!" he shouted. "Follow the mountains, there is a gentle land a few day's west of here."

The men were wretched, broken things. Whether the modalmen chased them or not, a handful would make it. The rest would die. But it was better that they die as men than experience the agony of being remade and having their personalities stripped away.

The wind blew now at a ferocious pace. Truncated lightning stabbed down from the clouds of sand, hitting the modalmen. Their clan markings flared brightly with these strikes of power, but they were unharmed, and did not move a muscle.

The storm reached its climax. Through the hurrying veils of sand and dust the blue sky was occasionally visible where it had not been before. Rel had to be going. There were three bunches of keys in his hand still. He dithered, he could ride off, and give the last of the keys to the men to free the others. Looking back he saw them spilling from their cages. They were so feeble. He was faster, if he delivered the keys quickly, he would be away, losing but a little more time.

"Hyah!" he spurred Aramaz on. The creature shied at being ridden into the abrasive wind, but did as he was asked. Rel rode at full tilt up the line of wagons, tossing the keys into the cages as he went. "Release yourselves, flee!" He called. "Head to the west, go home to your families!"

Aramaz leapt over a stinking tangle of bones. Moving together in perfect synchronicity, Rel and his mount leaned far to the side, running around the last wagon and turning back toward the gate. As they sped back toward freedom, the wind once again at their back, he threw the last bunch of keys into the cage of bone situated upon the wagon bed.

Rel spurred the dracon on. Aramaz arrowed forward, scattering escaping men before him. The wind was dropping. More blue streaks of sky showed through the sand. The last of the lightning cracked down from the sinking clouds, and the howling diminished.

"Run you fools!" shouted Rel. Men were sinking to their knees. Now they were out they did not know to do. Others would not leave their cages, so conditioned by fear they had become. Those still possessing some strength and wit were running away, most toward the gate in the palisade, though a few scattered for the hills, trusting to broken ground to slow their pursuers. And they would be pursued. The storm was dropping quickly. Rel rode hard through the fleeing prisoners. They called after him to stop. He swerved when a man stood in his path, arms waving. Another grabbed for his bridle. Rel yanked Aramaz's reins to the side too slowly. The dracon bit at the man's arm, severing it above the elbow, and he fell screaming.

"Get out of my way!" he shouted. "I have to deliver a message, I have to tell the Kingdoms they are coming!"

Men sobbed as he rode away from them. Abuse fell upon his ears. The sandstorm was abating. The modalmen had thankfully yet to move.

He was a fool to stay behind. In finding the keys and handing them out he had given up over an hour's advantage in travel. The garau could never catch Aramaz, but the hounds would. He should have left his countrymen to their fate.

He swore at himself for thinking that. He could still make it. The gate in the palisade was near. Nobody guarded it.

"Fly Aramaz!" he yelled. "Fly! Fly!"

The gate beckoned. The petrified forest lay beyond. On the other side was safety.

They passed the gate in a blur of colour. Aramaz's bright plumage streaked the air. Rel whooped with joy. He had never known his mount to run so fast. The bond between them was complete, they moved as one, master and beast.

As they passed the gate, a rope jerked upward from the sand, catching Aramaz's feet and catastrophically tripping him. Aramaz screamed as he fell at full pelt. His leading leg smashed into the ground, and for a moment it seemed he might right himself, but his foot hit badly, he rolled, sending Rel crashing into the ground. The dracon scrabbled with all six limbs to get up again, and had regained his feet when a broad spearhead slammed through his side, showering gore over the stunned Rel. Before his eyes, Aramaz fell face down, throat rattling in death.

Brauctha's face appeared over Rel, blocking out the sky; in his hand was the bloody spear. He bent low and pulled Rel up off the ground like a doll.

"Shkarauthir's last mistake," said the modalman evilly. "I knew you would run."

Rel was bundled into a stinking sack and dragged back into the camp over a modalman's shoulder. Through the cloth, the shouts of modalmen and the baying of their hounds mingled with the screams of men.

CHAPTER FORTY
A Spy Spied Upon

THE DOOR TO Hissenwar's workroom was open. Vand allowed the magister plenty of space for his work, and his room was full of half assembled devices, Morfaan artefacts, books and mugs of congealing tea. It was late, and all but a single wooden desk with a leather top was dark. The desk was of the sort with a high back full of small drawers. Three glimmer lamps were screwed into the uprights. The piece was expertly made, but poorly used. It was scratched, stained and battered by its careless employment as a workbench.

Hissenwar had removed his magister's jacket, and worked in his shirtsleeves, intent upon a tiny mechanism in his hands. This could conceivably have been the reason he did not see Filden approach, though it was not, because nobody ever saw Filden coming.

"Do you have it for me?" Filden asked.

Hissenwar jumped, scattering the pieces of the machine he was working on across his desk and the floor beneath.

"Omnus' balls, Filden!" he snapped as he hunted for the spilled components.

Filden cocked his eyebrow.

"Do you have to sneak up on a man like that?"

"Force of habit, Magister," Filden said.

Hissenwar grunted as he folded his ample frame double to retrieve the pieces from the floor. His fingers failed to gain traction on the components, so he licked their tips and dabbed them up. He held them up to the arrangement of magnifying lenses covering his eyes. "Ruined!" he grumbled. "Look! Covered in dust!" He held out his fingertip in accusation. A tiny golden flywheel sat on the ridges of his fingertip.

"It is just dust," said Filden.

"To you, it is just dust!" said Hissenwar. He was very angry. His cheeks were florid with it.

Hissenwar had never allowed himself to get so furious at Filden. *Every man has a trigger*, thought Filden. *And here is another I can pull.*

"To me it is not just dust. It is a mess of organic particles lousy with residual life memory, rogue glimmer, electrostatic charge and other forces and contaminants that will render this piece unusable!" He peered at it again. "Oh! I shall have to cast and enchant another. You have wasted me an hour of my spare time."

"What is it that you are making?"

"Nothing," said Hissenwar, hunching protectively over his work. "A hobby."

He looked at a perfect one-to-one scale model of a finch, clamped wings spread, upon a small stand. Entirely made of metal, it had a marvellous plumage of copper, bronze and steel. Hissenwar noticed Filden follow his glance, and cast a handkerchief over the bird.

"Will it fly?"

"Yes, no. I don't know," fumed Hissenwar. "It will take me longer to find out thanks to you."

Filden plucked a coin from his belt and tossed it onto Hissenwar's desk in one swift movement. Hissenwar noticed the flight of the coin too late to catch it, and cringed as it sailed toward his delicate engines, but it landed, perfectly flat, upon one of the few clear spaces.

"For your troubles, in addition to our agreed fee. Now, have you finished what I requested?"

Hissenwar pulled off his headgear. His owlish eyes blinked at Filden. "I have. It's not the sort of work I would normally do. Tyn magic. I had to go to the Watermarket. It took me several attempts get one of them to help me. They're only too pleased to sell me the ingredients, but entirely resistant to the idea of teaching me how to blend them." He pulled open one of the many small drawers of his desk, and fished out a small, waxed paper parcel sealed with blue wax. "You open it. I can't touch it." Filden took the parcel. Hissenwar grabbed his wrist. "Nobody but you can touch it, do you understand?"

"I have utilised magic before, you know."

"Even Tyn filth?"

"Even that." Filden broke the seal and unwrapped the item in the paper. It was a small amulet, covered in odd Tyn runes, similar to the mind-clouder he already possessed.

"I don't care for the aesthetics," said Hissenwar. "But it will work." He grinned. "I too have had dealings with the little bastards. I had the one that did the work geas himself up to the arsehole with negative consequence should it fail. That's the best guarantee of their work there is."

Filden weighed the thing in his hand. It was light, looked like steel but had the greasy feel of lead. His fingers numbed while he held it.

Hissenwar held out his own hands warningly toward Filden. "Don't!" he said. "Don't keep it in contact with your bare skin for long, and don't let anyone else touch it. As soon as it is touched by any other human being or Tyn, the enchantment will be reversed and the…" He almost said the name, but caught himself in time. "The target, will become aware of you, and will be drawn to you. You will not be able to hide from him, quite the opposite in fact."

Filden nodded, and slipped the amulet into a leather pouch.

"You'll need this too," Hissenwar said, handing over a silver die stamp. "The Free Tyn are an odd lot, but they have their friendships and alliances. I couldn't trust the fellow who made it with the target's name, and he probably would have had a fit had I told him. You need to stamp it in yourself. That's all you need to do. I made the die. It should work. Do test the amulet first, mind. And when you stamp it, remember the die is silver. It is soft. It will only stand a couple of strikings before it loses definition and becomes useless, so make sure you hit true. I have a hammer…" He pulled objects off one another as he searched his desk, finally fishing out a rounded cobbler's hammer from under a pile of paper. "There you are. Go into the next room and do it. You have to be alone, focus on the name and the target's face. Then please bring both back. As soon as the die is used, the silver must be melted down. I've warmed my crucible. I'm ready."

Filden, whose actual depth of experience with magic would have shocked the magister, nodded. "Simple," he said.

"Are you sure you want to do this? I've had a few of my contacts ask around. This Sn..." He gulped. "This *Tyn* is not well liked by anyone, and he has a reputation. They say he is very dangerous."

"So am I," said Filden.

The look of fear on Hissenwar's face was gratifying.

FILDEN KEPT TO the shadows. He preferred the night. He was at home in it. The dark embraced him like a lover.

Being abroad at that hour in those streets was risky. The watch patrolled the lower parts of town in force. They worked on the assumption that anyone about at three in the morning was either up to no good or drunk, and they tended to arrest both sorts. Filden's outfit of dark clothes, hat and mask put him firmly in the camp of ne'er do wells, but he had nothing to worry about. The watch would never see him, let alone catch him.

The White Moon shone brightly on the Lemio district, turning it into a charcoal sketch of chimneys and tottering apartments. This part of Karsa was not scheduled for rebuilding, it being safely out of the way of Per Allian and Prince Alfra's idealised vision. It would remain, therefore, a maze of modest factories, and all the small businesses required to fuel a city of Karsa's size. Most of them reeked; backstreet abattoirs, tanneries, bone renderers, wood cookers and the like, all crammed up against people's homes. Modern sanitation helped not one bit. The smell of clotted blood welled thickly from inadequate sewers.

Filden's new amulet vibrated in its pouch, rattling softly against the stiff leather and drawing him toward the Sniffer's location. He saw the Tyn intermittently. It moved far more quickly than it should, disappearing from view into the deepest shadow and reappearing scores of yards away. Its humpbacked shape scuttled over rooftops and vanished. The next moment it crept from an alleyway. Filden remained at a safe distance, wary of the Tyn's preternatural senses. He waited while it tottered precariously on a roof ridge, its large carpet bag out to balance it. The Sniffer did not fall, but dropped to all fours and ran, like a black, bloated spider, its bag in its teeth. It bounded down the slant of the roof. It paused, looking back toward him, nose quivering, then ran vertically down a wall in a way that gave Filden pause. From there it leapt through a window. A moment later a scream chased it out, and it bounded impossibly along the wall.

Filden looked about to make sure he was not seen. The street was deserted. He slipped after the Sniffer.

For a time he lost sight of the Sniffer, relying on the intensity of the amulet's vibrations to draw him on. This was nervous work. He had tracked and slain many men in his old role, even a few Tyn. They had been difficult to kill, and none had been like his current quarry. The Sniffer was the being he went to when his own prodigious skills were inadequate. He played a dangerous game following it. But he followed it because it was dangerous, and because he was afraid of it.

Filden feared nothing but the Tyn. There was a thrill in this chase utterly lacking from all his other hunts.

The amulet led him away from the flatter part of the Lemio bowl, toward the steep hillsides where the moors around the city began their curtsey to the sea. The slopes were as built over as the flat, full of precipitous streets and buildings that optimistically defied gravity. There were a couple of scars in the cityscape there, where the tremors stirred up by the approaching Twin had brought down parts of the hill and the houses on it.

Filden found himself by the Lemio itself, at a place where one of its many small tributaries joined its flow. The Lemio and Var were short rivers, but fed by the moorland's many streams, they grew rapidly. The Lemio itself was young there, stepping down old weirs and rubbish-choked cataracts toward its truncated, overbuilt flood plain. From there it flowed around the new docks toward its old meeting place with the Var at the Lockside, though the rivers were now forever divided by man's artifice. A bridge crossed the Lemio ahead, the road turning to follow the river up the hill on the other side. The road in front of him rose gradually toward the east. He turned to face each direction in turn, paying attention to the signals of his amulet. It thrummed as he faced the bridge, so he crossed it, and went upward.

THE TYN WAS in an old mill perched halfway up the hillside. "The Lemio Clothing and Shoddy Company" its sign read. Filden recalled news of the mill orphanage's closure in the broadsheets a little while ago. That led him to guess the girl the Sniffer hunted was among their number. Such information would be useful. His opinion of the Sniffer lessened; men made mistakes like that. He expected more.

The mill gates were barred, but there was no one on watch, and Filden climbed the wall around the place quickly, landing with a soft thud on the far side. A few buildings were within the yard: an engine house, a newer building, and an ancient watermill, its origins clear from the structure over the water which had once held the wheel. According to the amulet, the Sniffer was in the old mill.

Filden ran silently across the moonlit courtyard. A glance at the main sliding door, and he saw chains locking it shut. Filden dare not chance picking its padlock or cutting the links, so crept around the building until he found a door that was easily forced.

He was in the same building as the Tyn. He had to be careful. He pulled out a four-shot pistol, loaded with specialised bullets made for killing the Sniffer's kind. The core was glimmer covered in thin silver, as in a normal bullet, the projectile impelled when the sliver jacket was struck and pierced by the iron firing pin. But the front of Filden's bullets were also coated in iron, a substance deadly to the Tyn. Magister's marks enchanted them with increased accuracy, and warded them against Tyn spells. Creating such a bullet from so many layers was dangerously tricky. Imbuing them with magic more so. They were therefore very expensive.

Old machines filled the factory floor, covered with scrapper's signs. Since the orphans had gone the machinery had probably become uneconomical to use, though it was as likely that the Grostimans were being quick to wipe away all traces of evidence, Filden thought.

He held his breath, moving with all the stealth he could muster. The Sniffer was nowhere to be seen. A noise drew his eyes to the floorboards of the storey above. Holding his pistol lightly, he went to the stairwell door at the side of the factory floor, and crept upstairs.

The first floor was empty, everything gone. A few scraps of cloth and a thick dust of fabric particles made it likely this was the shoddy room. Still no Sniffer.

The second floor had been a dormitory. Beds were heaped untidily in one corner, ready for disposal. It was a grim place, full of draughts.

The Sniffer was in the centre of the room, muttering to itself. Filden retreated out of sight.

"We'll find you my pretty," the Sniffer said, and tittered to itself. "For this we have a night with a goodlady!"

Filden's eyes set over his mask. He thought Vand had been rash to promise his daughter to this thing. Even Filden had limits.

Humming a song popular a hundred years ago, the Sniffer unclasped its tatty carpet bag. Witch light shone up from the interior, bathing the room in a ghoulish glow. The Sniffer peered inside, thrust its arm in and rummaged around.

"Where are you?" it growled. Its arm went in right the way to its armpit, so far in the Sniffer had to lean its head against the bag. His tongue poked out between his teeth, he would have looked comical were he not so grotesque. The bag could not possibly be so deep.

The Sniffer put his head into the bag, then his shoulders. Then he slipped inside, all of him, though the bag was far too small to contain his body. Singing came from its depths. Filden cocked his pistol, the precision engineering rendering the action soundless.

A moment later a bundle wrapped in a rag flew up out of the bag and thumped onto the floor. The Sniffer scrambled out and crawled to fetch it. The Tyn seemed more comfortable with this manner of locomotion than walking on two feet.

Cackling softly, the Sniffer unwrapped the rags, then squatted, caressed the contents, and kissed it.

"Go on my pretty, find her, find the Mohaci girl for old Sniffer."

The Tyn stood, and rolled the thing along the floor like a skittles ball. It was uneven, and rumbled loudly in the emptied dormitory. Filden squinted at it as it rolled around in a spiral outward from the Sniffer long after it should have stopped. From an aperture on one side, a trail of gleaming dust was laid, painting patterns on the floor.

"Come on, come on Jerame, show the Sniffer what he needs to see."

The ball rolled right past Filden's hiding place. Few things horrified Filden. He had killed and tortured. He had confronted monsters of the worst kind, human and otherwise, but the ball repulsed him.

It was a mummified child's head, its eyes, nose, lips and ears closed with fine Tyn stitching. A hole in its forehead let out the stream of glowing particles.

Filden stepped back, in case the ball saw him. But it rolled by, switching direction unexpectedly, until it suddenly came to a stop, rolled over onto the crown of its head, presenting the patch of skin tucked over its severed neck, and span violently on one spot.

"Now we know where she slept!" said the Sniffer. He swaggered over to the spot, kicked the head out of the way, and searched the spot closely with spread fingers and beady eyes.

"Aha!" He said, holding something up between his forefinger and thumb. "A hair! A hair is there! Now we can know where she *is*." He put the hair into a paper bag, and tucked it into his pocket, then whistled. "Hup, cup Jerame, back into to yer wrapper, back into the bag!"

The Sniffer bent down and spread the rag. The head rolled noisily at it, and the Sniffer wrapped it quickly, as if he were trying to prevent its escape, then tossed it carelessly into the bag, which he then snapped shut. The green light went out. The Sniffer made a horrible gurgling in his throat, then its head whipped round.

The Tyn looked directly at Filden, eyes glowing like torches in the dark either side of its long nose.

Filden ducked back smoothly, trusting to long experience to avoid being seen. Quiet followed. A minute passed, then a second. Filden risked looking back.

The Sniffer had vanished.

A Mohaci girl, resident at the Lemio Clothing and Shoddy Company. It was not much to go on, but Filden never required more than that.

He smiled. Next time he saw the Sniffer, he would kill him.

CHAPTER FORTY-ONE
Last Orders at the Nelly Bold

THE HOUR WAS so late it was early. Three bells until sunrise, and the Off Parade was a ghost town lit by glimmer lamps. A handful of people hurried home through a light mist, making sure to look purposeful lest they fall afoul of the watch.

The doorbell on the Nelly Bold clattered as the last customer was bundled out into the night by Arto the doorman. The man shouted in the cheerful manner of drunks who were quicker to laughter than to violence. For a moment the street was noisy, until his warbling song drew away. A dray dog barked in its kennel. Someone shouted at it to shut up. The door slammed out the Off Parade's night sounds, ringing the bell on its spring a final time.

"That's it Ellany!" Arto called back into the main bar. "He was the last!"

"He was not the last. I am the last. The last one is still here," said Eliturion, god of wine and drama, who was hard at work overseeing the first of his divine responsibilities. He sat with a pot the size of a barrel in his hand, in his giant chair in his usual booth. The booth was the largest in the place, more of a room to itself, positioned so everyone could see him when they headed to the bar, but positioned out of the draft. The Nelly Bold's proprietors were careful to keep their greatest draw happy.

"You don't count, my dear," said Ellany gently to the god. She was the latest in the Nelly Bold's long line of landladies. She had grown up with the god. Eliturion was practically family to her. "Have you checked the privy?" she shouted to her doormen.

"Yes, goodmaid," Arto called back. He and his two assistants were going around the three interconnected rooms that made up the main bar, checking behind chairs and benches for overlooked drunks.

"No one here, no one here," they half sang. They too had been enjoying the Nelly Bold's wares while they worked. Liquid payment kept their wages affordable.

"You and the boys can help me sort out this keg then you can be off," Ellany said, pointing at a large barrel.

Arto summoned his men to his side. "You don't need one of us to stay over?" he said.

"Nah," said Ellany. "The day staff are in at six bells. Besides, I don't think I'll be shifting his lordship out of here tonight, and he's the best guard dog there is."

"It's cold out there. There's wine in here. The fire is warmer than the company, I'll grant, but both are more delightful than night's mist!" shouted the god, hoisting his massive tankard high in comic salute.

Ellany rolled her eyes at him.

The three doormen manhandled the large beer barrel into the cellars, then took a quick sup of brandy. They gave their farewells in good spirits. The doorbell rang them out.

Muffled laughter came from the street, and the pub was silent.

Ellany fetched herself a rag and began to wipe down the tables with great efficiency. If she were lucky, she'd be able to get four hours sleep before the next day began.

It was a hard life, but she was free. Her gratitude for that exhibited itself in the thoroughness with which she did everything. There were ship's captains who were less diligent than Ellany.

She shivered as she moved to a table away from the fire. "It is bloody cold," said Ellany. "Drops right off when the drinkers are out. Another chilly night, and it not yet Takcrop." She shook her head as she polished beer stains away. "Must be the Twin, so I heard. Lots of strange things going on because of that. If this keeps up, next year promises to be something."

"I would not sound so excited about that if I were you," said Eliturion. He took a long look into the depths of his tankard. "I would pray that the Twin's closest approach passes quickly and without incident, and that the worlds complete their long dance without bringing the Earth into peril."

Ellany snorted. She rubbed down another table until it shone. "Who do I pray to, Eli, you?" she scoffed.

He took her jibe good-naturedly.

"If your protection were in my power, then you would have it, my dear. You, yours and this fine old maid of a public house," he said, waving his hand like a conjurer. "Alas, my powers in the arena of protection were always few. If you were a vineyard or a theatre, perhaps I could have aided you. Now, such abilities as I had are non-existent. Stories are all I have."

She flicked the debris on her cloth into the fire, dipped it into a pail of water, and wrung it out. "You say stories are everything. You've been saying that to me since I was a little girl."

"I do. I have. We are all stories. You are a story. I am a story. Our minds are stories we tell ourselves. Our position in society is a story other people tell about us. When you are gone, if you are remembered, the story will remain, though the real you will be gone. Stories are immortality. Stories are magic," he said, his eyes gleaming with more than the wine.

"Then tell me a story where I'm rich, and this place lasts forever," she said.

"Alas, I cannot. I am of the story, I do not fashion it. I cannot shape that which I tell. My ability is to relay it in whatever manner seems fitting. What has happened, sometimes what is, nothing more than that. You have heard me expound on the matter often enough."

"You're full of nonsense though, aren't you?" she said fondly.

"That I am!" he said with delight. "Most stories are nonsense, and so am I." Eliturion laughed and put his fat arms onto the back of his enormous chair. It was of black wood, its carvings worn smooth with use. The chair was nearly as old as the Nelly Bold, and had been made especially for the god not long after he had started patronising the pub. "Three hundred years I have been coming here," he said. "Since before city houses replaced the flowers of the bog, and the bald heaths stretched as far as a man could see. There were Tyn in the brook now encased in stone beneath the street, and the pounding of the Great Tides on the cliffs could be heard on quiet nights in place of industry's clamour."

Ellany smiled and looked around the room. Her tired face was content. "All that's gone, but she's still here. She's a grand old girl, the best story ever told."

"She is that! She is!" Eliturion agreed. "I never tire of old Nelly. I was coming here before my brothers and sisters were sent away, and have been coming ever since."

"You're welcome to keep coming until the end of time," said Ellany. She moved into the next room to continue her cleaning. The maid would do it again in the morning, but she liked to make sure all was in its proper place and tidy before she retired. It was the right way to end the day.

"Ah, my dear, if only things would last so long as to the end of time," said Eliturion, raising his voice so that she could hear. "We are all stories in the end, and all stories have an end. Even mine. My story. It must end." He hiccuped. "Do you understand? An end," he said dolefully.

"I understand it's late," she said, walking back into the main room with the rag draped over her shoulder. "I'm tired and you're drunk."

"Not so!" he protested. "Not so," he continued more sadly. "I am a god, the god of wine at that. I cannot become intoxicated." He peered into the bottom of his giant tankard in a way that suggested his statement was not entirely true. "And so, seeing as I am immune, perhaps one last drink before bed?"

Ellany laughed and wiped her hands on her apron. "Eli! We both know that is the most outrageous dracon shit. You are as drunk as the sea. You're not having any more."

He gave her a pitiable expression. "You would heap such privation on me? The last of the gods! Woe, I am so lonely. Just one final drink before I must go."

"You're only going down the bloody hill. You're in the museum tomorrow," she said.

"I am not," he said with a mixture of smugness and sorrow. "I am having the rest of eternity off!" he proclaimed grandly, then held out his pot. "So one more won't be hurting anybody."

"No."

"By the way you laugh, I judge I have already won this contest," said the god. He pushed his tankard at her over the table with his giant fingertips and stuck out his bottom lip. "Please?"

"Oh, alright then," groaned Ellany. She dragged up the tankard and waddled out. She was broad about the beam, Ellany, with an indomitable walk.

Corks popped at the bar. Eliturion shouted, "Have one yourself, a final drink in the old girl."

"Final?" Ellany came bustling back with his tankard full to the brim. "I'll be having plenty more drinks here, so will you." She eased the giant pot onto the table, "I wish I'd have used the barrow. Bloody heavy thing. I'm not getting any younger. Three bottles of good Ellosantin red in that. Drink up, and don't you dare ask for more."

"And where is yours?"

"Give me a chance, you old slave driver." She went away, and came back again with a glass that appeared as capacious as a thimble next to his, and eased herself onto the bench by the god, satisfied at another day's work done.

"Your good health, my dear," said Eliturion. He very carefully knocked his enormous clay pot against her glass.

"Same to you, you old fraud," she said.

They drank in companionable quiet for a few moments to the crackle of the dying fire, she sipping thoughtfully, he taking enormous, breathy gulps.

"Are you alright, Eli?" asked Ellany. "You've been behaving a mite oddly these last few nights."

"Oh? How so?"

"All your blather's been about the end of stories and that. Struck me as strange. You'll not leaving us, are you?"

Eliturion took another massive pull on his pot, and wiped a human serving's worth of red wine from his moustaches.

"My dear, dear Ellany, great-great granddaughter, or thereabouts, of the original Bold Nelly."

"Nell was my great-great-gran. Bold Nelly my four times great-gran. Get it right."

"Stories don't have to be correct, only true," he said sadly. He looked at her earnestly. "I advise you, please, to find alternative accommodation for tonight."

"There is something wrong," she said. She put her glass down, suddenly afraid.

"Yes," he said sorrowfully.

The glimmer lamps lining the road outside flickered and went out, plunging the street into darkness.

Ellany got up in surprise, knocking her glass over. She peered out of the window, letting the wine drip unnoticed to the floor.

"What's going on? Why are the glimmer lamps out?"

Eliturion shrugged, took another sip of his drink. "Please Ellany, leave now. I am breaking so many unwritten laws even hinting at what might happen next, but it is not good." He was pale and his hand shook the pot.

A ferocious hammering made the door leap in its frame. The bell jingled madly on its spring.

"Leave," said Eliturion. "Now."

Ellany's hand went to her mouth, but she shook her head determinedly. "Go... go away!" she said, her voice gaining strength until it reached the volume her family were justly renowned for. "We're closed! Come back in the morning!"

"You are being brave," said Eliturion. "It won't help."

Quietly, Ellany waited, tense and frightened.

The door burst inward, slamming back against the entrance vestibule wall. Splinters of wood sprayed across the flags. The bell bounced across the flagstones. A blackness poured through the portal. The stone and wood of the Nelly Bold warped and creaked as if the whole building winced.

"Lost gods," Ellany whispered.

An immense figure pulled its way through the door, head bowed and back lowered to allow it within. First through was an enormous head. A pair of goat's horns curled down around his temples. A long queue of hair ran down his back held together by a clasp of gold, but much of the hair had come loose from the binding. The creature's coat was similarly dishevelled. The well-tailored velvet was dirty, scuffed and crusted with matter. His bronze skin smouldered with an inner heat, he had an animal's expression on a man's face, though he was neither.

The Infernal Duke entered the Nelly Bold.

Inside the main bar the Infernal Duke was able to stand upright. He looked down upon Ellany with a wicked smile and wild, glowing eyes. Remains of boots clung to his lower legs, the soles having burned away. The floor smoked under his hoofed feet.

"Closed?" said the duke. "You have one god here. You will entertain a second, surely?"

"Go! Now!" said Eliturion urgently.

Ellany let out a shriek and ran for the door.

"I think not." The duke's arm stretched like rubber, and caught her about the neck as she fled. She grabbed at his huge, taloned fingers with both her hands, but could not budge them. He ignored her struggles. "Your fondness for human creatures is a weakness, Eliturion."

"That's..." Eliturion raised his eyebrows and tilted his head, "enormously hypocritical of you."

"It is not. I seek one special companion, you love them all for their ridiculous foibles. You are a god. They made you. They expect more of their deities. Your indulgence will not do."

Eliturion snorted. "The gods. Warped stories, and a pack of bastards." He sipped his drink. "It's why I let old Res drive you all out."

"He didn't drive me out."

"Do you know why he did not?" asked Eliturion.

The duke frowned. "Fate had another role in mind for me. You know about fate."

"A story, a fate. They are the same," Eliturion agreed. "But that was not the reason why. Fate had nothing to do with it."

The duke took a step closer. Ellany squirmed in his grasp. His eyes glowed diabolically.

"Let her go," said Eliturion. "What will you gain by killing her?"

The duke licked his lips. "Enjoyment."

"Once, you would never have said such a thing. Once, you would never have killed. You are making yourself enjoy this. You lose yourself a little more. The character follows the plot, you should do otherwise, and drive it for yourself!"

"We are not what we were," said the duke, but there was a tremor of uncertainty. "We have no freedom."

"And what exactly is that? Are you a free spirit of the One, or a weakling hijacked by other people's ways of seeing? It's not her fault. Let her buy her life. Let her fetch us both a drink, then let her leave. I beg you."

"Eliturion begs. The great traitor!"

"'A man who betrays himself is a worse fiend than one who betrays his comrades,'" said Eliturion.

"You even quote the mortals now," sneered the duke.

"They speak sense, a lot of the time. If you listened, you would hear it. But you only want worship. I see you have added another skull to your collection." Eliturion pointed to the necklace of green glass beads around the duke's neck. "Eight is a lot of times to be disappointed. I'd give up, if I were you."

The duke growled.

"Drink with me, talk!" said Eliturion. "We are both of the Y Dvar. There should be no violence between us."

The duke lowered Ellany to the ground and released her. She clutched at the red fingermarks burned into her throat.

"Fetch me a drink," rumbled the duke.

Eliturion nodded at her. "This is a good red, he will enjoy that. Get my spare pot for him."

The duke yanked out one of the long benches lining Eliturion's table. It was the longest table in the Nelly Bold, so that Eliturion might entertain a large crowd, and the benches were made to match. Only Eliturion's throne would fit a god, the rest of the furniture was sized for mortal men, and the Duke hunched over when he sat down athwart the bench. The table was too low to accept his legs beneath. He drew talons across the board, scraping up curls of wood, and both bench and table smouldered under his touch.

Ellany affected the fastest service of her career. She returned with the wine immediately, pouring three bottles with shaking hands into another of Eliturion's vessels. The room had turned sweltering, and her face was pink with the heat of the duke. She handed the pot to her tormentor, and stepped back, her eyes wide with terror.

"Thank you," The duke kept yellow eyes fixed on Eliturion's face as he drank. The wine in the flagon bubbled.

"Not bad," said the duke.

"Now you can go," said Eliturion to Ellany.

"No, you stay," said the duke. He caught her wrist, making her wince. "We need service still."

"You should have gone when I told you," said Eliturion.

"You knew this was going to happen!" said Ellany.

"He always does, this old fool," said the duke, waving his claws at Eliturion. "He thinks he knows everything."

"Why didn't you warn me?"

"I tried to." Eliturion said.

"Your friend here is bound by laws he did not write," said the duke. "He goes against what he is meant to be."

Eliturion looked up sharply. "Meant to be? We are a perversion of what was meant to be. These forms we wear and destinies we tread are not those given to us! What would the One say if he saw us now?"

"I recall we had no choice in the matter," said the duke. He set his steaming flagon down.

"Choice or not, we accepted the role gladly enough," said Eliturion angrily. "We all did."

"You too?" asked the Duke.

"Me too."

"I had a visit from a shapeless thing given form. A servant of the Dark Lady who says he now serves Omnus. He brought news." The duke leaned in closely. "They are coming back. Our brothers and sisters, the gods, will return."

"So you have decided which side you are on."

"What?" said the duke. "You thought I might stand with you? I have let you be, Eliturion, for you and I are alone in the world. When I went into the wreck of the Godhome the shades there told me what you had done. I almost came to kill you then. You had no right to do what you did."

"You don't understand. None of you do," said Eliturion in anguish. "We were being changed further. We would have destroyed everything. We had no will of our own."

The duke shook his head. "You are a fool to deny what we are now. Omnus is right in wanting you dead.

We can never be what we were again. Spirits of air and light." He shook his horned head. "Never again."

"We had to go," said Eliturion, "to save those who tried to remain pure."

"None of the Y Dvar can lay claim to purity. We squandered that. It does not mean we should be extinguished." The duke tapped the table in thought. "You know I am going to kill you? If I am lucky, when Omnus returns, I will be forgiven for not having ended you earlier. You are a traitor, and the slayer of our siblings as surely as if you had cast the spells yourself. You cannot stop me."

"I have no intention of doing so," said Eliturion softly.

Ellany took her chance and scrambled for the door.

The duke lunged to his feet with a roar, grasping the table as he rose and flipping it over as if it were made of card. It broke in half with an agonised creak, half falling back down onto Eliturion's legs, the other upended and blocking the main door, stopping Ellany's escape. Eliturion lifted his drink instinctively as the table was torn away, cradling the pot to his chest.

"Pathetic," snarled the duke at Eliturion's blinking, fish-belly white face.

Fires kindled around the duke's fists, blue tongues that curled around his fingers like the brandy flame on a midwinter pudding. As they grew, the Nelly Bold's fire died down. The flames from the hearth were sucked away and stolen to garland the duke's hands. Candles guttered and the glimmer lamps, the pride of the tavern, gave out with violent bangs. In the dark, the duke was demonic. He changed, his body moving further from the human toward the animal. Floorboards combusted around him.

"I am going to hit you now," said the duke. The fires roared out banners behind his fists as he swung, and punched Eliturion on the cheek. The god of wine and drama's ample jowls rippled with the impact. He fell sprawling from his black wooden throne. His precious wine flew from his hands. The pot, a gift from an artist who was the toast of her century, shattered against the wall, leaving a dark purple stain.

"Get up," said the duke.

"Leave him be!" shouted Ellany. "He's done no harm to no one."

"Oh, he has, he has done a great deal of harm," snarled the duke.

Eliturion pulled himself onto his hands and knees. He turned his haunted expression upon the last landlady of the Nelly Bold. Blood, luminous with inner light, dripped from his lips and glowed upon the floor.

"Run!" he whispered.

"Get up!" roared the duke. He swelled in size, his fine coat splitting and falling from straining muscles. His trousers burst apart and slid from him in rags that ignited and burned as they fell. "Get up!" He said, and his voice was bestial, and full of rage.

Eiturion attempted to rise, but his efforts only angered the duke, and he kicked his fellow god hard in the ribs, flipping him over. Eliturion flailed against the legs of his seat, and pulled himself around it.

"Where are you clever stories now, you treacherous bastard?" said the duke.

"You are evil! You willingly serve the Dark Lady. How could I betray you?" Eliturion said.

The duke grabbed the throne with both hands. The smell of burnt wood and polish filled the bar as his fingers charred through its carvings, and he tore it into splintered halves that ignited violently. He cast them aside into the corners of the room where they burned with unnatural heat. Fire leapt from them, catching on everything it touched. The curtains burned. The benches burned. Ellany screamed. Gathering her wits, she made for the kitchen, and the door onto the alley round the back.

"We were the same, once. We were brothers," the duke said. "Made of the same numinous matter, sculpted from the flesh of the One."

"And what is left of those beings?" cried Eliturion. "Nothing! Do you know why we two alone remained?"

"You betrayed us, it was your price. I have never understood why I was spared."

"I was willing to go! I wanted to die. But you see, you and I are alike. We embraced our stories! We allowed ourselves to become these things," Eliturion said. "We allowed ourselves to be pulled from the air, and remade. Res Iapetus did not banish us, because he could not. Do you not see? We are more real than our brothers and sisters were. We are as we are now, Eliturion, god of wine and drama, and you, the nameless, Infernal Duke, whose need for love is a poor disguise for evil. We have become our stories! We never fought against what the mortals made us."

"The thing told me our original forms could be won again. I did not believe him."

Eliturion laughed, and it became a sob. "We are all traitors to the One, but you and I are the worst, my friend." He looked up, eyes wet. "We embraced what happened to us. I was too much of a coward to end it myself. It is time to rectify the mistake."

"Fight me!"

"No."

"You will die anyway." The duke kicked Eliturion hard in the chest, branding him with a smoking hoof mark. So powerful was the blow that the god crashed through the facade of the Nelly Bold, taking glass and stone with him into the street.

Eliturion staggered upright. The duke roared and leapt through the air, knocking him down again. He stood over his fallen brother with his flaming fists clenched.

"Magic is a story we tell the world so compelling it becomes the truth," said Eliturion. "We have no power any more. This is not our world. We've lost it. How could you bear it? How can you bear what you have become?"

"I cannot."

"Then why did you remain?"

"Why did you?"

"Because I had a story to tell," says Eliturion with a bloodied smile. "It doesn't have to end this way."

"The children of the water kin are coming back," said the duke. "The Draathis return. The Morfaan move. This is the only way if we of the air are not to die out completely."

"It is not. You can defy them all. You can defy this nature foisted upon you, go into the dark. Leave it all behind."

The duke's hands clenched and unclenched. "I do not have the courage for that. I want to live."

"Then I am sorry that we both have to die."

Five pillars of burning white light shot up around the street, illuminating the scene as mercilessly as theatre limelights. A voice boomed from the foremost.

"Raen Jalong of the Soaring Air, we name thee for thy true self."

The duke reared back and howled in pain. The spear of his ancient name sank deep into his spirit, and snagged there.

"What? *Them?* You told them I was coming!" He staggered back from Eliturion.

"I am forbidden to know what will happen next," said Eliturion, panting words through froths of glowing blood. "My gift is to know the story of everything that has been, and everything that is, but never what will be." He laughed weakly. "But I have been known to cheat. Sometimes, I skip ahead."

"They can't save you."

"I don't want them to," said Eliturion. He pushed himself upright with a groan and sat down heavily on the road. "I said I have no more stories left to tell."

"Raen Jalong, we name you!" the voice boomed from the lead pillar of light. The duke threw up his hand to shield his face and roared with pain.

"Raen Jalong! Begone from here, we command you, as the lords of the five, first children of the One."

The Infernal Duke steadied himself, and he leant hard on his knees.

"You can wound me, you can hurt me, but you can never kill me! That name is only a painful memory." The duke thrust out his chest, and clenched his fists, whose fires burned brightly again. "I am no longer Raen Jalong. I am the Infernal Duke, no other. You cannot abjure me with that naming."

"Raen Jalong, we—"

"Oh do be quiet!" The Infernal Duke held out his hand, and a lance of fire burst from his palm. It struck against an invisible shield surrounding the leftmost column of light. He leaned in and pushed, joining a second stream of flame from his other hand to the first. The pillars uttered hurried cantrips in consternation. The light of fire and the light of the stars battled in the street. The duke screamed out two centuries of frustration, loneliness and anger. His lances of fire shoved hard against the shields of light, piercing them and wreathing one of the columns in devilish flames.

A horrific scream issued from the engulfed column. The brilliant light went out. The remaining four retreated under roaring blasts of fire. The duke threw up his hands. A circle of flame walled he and Eliturion off from the street.

"You will stop!" the voice said.

"I will not! Who is the mightier now?" the Infernal Duke shouted. "You seek to arrest change to survive in the world you corrupted. I accept corruption, and so have form you cannot match!"

"You cannot beat them," said Eliturion. "They will quench your fire."

"Maybe they will," said the duke, turning on the other god, "but I will kill you before they can stop me."

Roaring, the Infernal Duke punched down hard, his burning fists knocking Eliturion's head into the paving with terrible impact. He got down on his knees and followed the first blow with a second, then a third, pummelling away and snarling incoherent curses until the god of wine and drama's head was a smoking mess.

ELLANY RAN, FLINGING open the back door onto the alley. The Off Parade had been changed greatly by Per

Allian's redesign of the city, but around such venerable buildings as the Nelly Bold a few of the old ways remained, fragments of the warrens of yesteryear.

The alley opened directly onto the main street that had cut it in half. Ellany exited via a new arch whose stonework had yet to be stained black by Karsa City's smogs.

She screamed at the sight of Eliturion's giant body lying in the road. The light from the inferno consuming the Nelly Bold danced across a hellish scene; the duke, naked and wreathed in fires of his own, the dead god, his caved in head outlined by a pool of glowing blood. Pillars of light advanced on a wall of fire surrounding the duke, their light so bright her eyes streamed when she looked at them.

Ellany tried to see what was within the columns, her vision swam and stung and she had to quickly look away, but she had a glimpse of a tall, four-armed being. Half-blinded by the light, she staggered away to raise the alarm.

The Off Parade was equipped with all modern amenities: piped water, expansive sewers and glimmer lighting among them. Her need was for the alarm post, a globe of glass encased in copper fretting atop an iron stand. Sluggish glimmer light moved within the globe. A small metal mallet hung by a chain from the side. In the fretting was a round hole that exposed a large enough portion of the glass to strike. This she did, her first blow cracking the glass, the second shattering it. Magister's marks engraved into the copper flared into life. The released glimmer light shot up with sudden intensity, making a beacon of itself that lit up the clouds. The bell on the firehouse six streets away started ringing.

There was a moment of relief. She turned back to the creatures occupying the street. There were no other people but her out. A happening of this magnitude in Karsa would ordinarily draw crowds, no matter how dangerous, but the road was like a stage; empty but for the principal players.

She saw poorly thanks to the afterimages the columns of light had imprinted on her vision. The beings of light surrounded the Infernal Duke, their harsh illumination turning him into a shadow puppet devil.

Ellany could not believe what she saw, not even after years of her association with a god. She had come to see Eliturion as a big, fat uncle. Now it was as if a myth unfolded before her.

She crept closer, realising she saw something important, something no one else was seeing. The descendants of Bold Nelly lived up to her reputation. There was not a coward among them.

A battle of fire and light raged in the street. Bursts of starlight and lashes of fire enwrapped each other. The air trembled to the snap of unleashed power. Still no one came forth from their homes.

The pillars boxed the duke in. A cage of light linked them, angled bars springing into being between the columns, until the duke was imprisoned between the four.

"You force us into this, Raen Jalong," said a thunderous, inhuman voice. "You force us to kill you, and so we of the Tyn Y Dvar become fewer, and the pure state of the World of Will is put further from recovery."

Fetters of light wrapped themselves around the duke's wrists, waist, neck and ankles.

"Purity is lost, there is only what there is. I intend to live within the constraints of reality as it is presented to me!" shouted the duke.

"When the One returns, you shall be judged."

"He will never return! And if he does, he will find me alive, and you extinct."

The duke let out a shout of tremendous effort, and yanked his limbs inward. The columns were dragged toward him, and he threw up his arms. A cloud of fire billowed around him, sending the columns spinning aside, and sundering their bars of light.

When the fire had gone, so had the duke.

A quiet snap of an iron catch saw the lead column of light extinguished, and a small, elderly creature take its place. The others followed, their lights going out, their earthly forms reimposed upon reality as they replaced the iron collars about their necks.

Ellany stifled a gasp. In place of the beings of light, were the bowed, small shapes of Greater Tyn.

Two of the Tyn went to the crumpled shape on the ground—a fifth Tyn, its clothes smoking.

"He lives," said one of the two. "Just."

The leader was a female. She adjusted her iron collar, and covered it with a colourful scarf.

"Take him. We go now, before humans come and see their god dead in the street, and Tyn all about him. They see the truth they will, and take inappropriate actions."

"We are fine, the spell holds. No one comes. We leave unnoticed," said a male.

"Never sure of that," said the female. "Always, there is a thorn beneath the berry."

"Tyn Lydar my lady, if Tyn Fruin dies she will be the second of the Five to fall in as many years."

"More can be appointed," said Tyn Lydar.

"But you are the last of the ancients. First of the Five. What if you die? You cannot be replaced like he."

"We shall pray to the One it does not come to that," she said.

The night swirled around them, concealing them in folds of dark. They snuck away unseen as the first of the fire watch arrived, and bewildered people poured out of doors and looked out of windows onto the aftermath of a conflict they had somehow missed.

Unseen, that is, by anyone but Ellany.

CHAPTER FORTY-TWO
A Difficult Decision

DAYS TURNED TO weeks. The pulse of the tide beat against the stony shores of the Sotherwinter. The Great Tide filled the bay to overtopping, further shattering the wall of ice across the sea and floating fantastically sculpted pieces of it onto the stony shore. Low Tides dropped the level dramatically, revealing the bay to be as steep as a glacial corrie, with wet, stratified cliffs full of secret caverns and odd tunnels that boomed and sang in the surf when the water was right.

A watch was set upon the top of the great rock near Antoninan's stores. Ilona took her turns upon it like the rest of the marines. Two were there at all times. One watching the sea for the *Prince Alfra*, the other staring fixedly at the column of vapour climbing from the Draathis advance. Ardovani fixed staves into the rock's top to measure their progress, and the thickness of the column. For a long while, the cloud they generated grew no nearer. Then, one day, it began to move.

Ilona watched it inch its way between two of Ardovani's measuring staves. The distance between, the magister said, was roughly equivalent to thirty miles. The marines had found that if they sat in the right place on the rock's surface, the white interior of the Sotherwinter disappeared, and the steam column seemed to make its way directly along an artificial horizon of black stone. The effect of doing so was that the progression of the steam column was more readily discerned. Over the preceding week it had moved through three sticks, and was now heading toward the last.

"They'll be here in four days, that's what the magister says," said Aretimus, who was taking watch with Ilona.

"We're going to have to leave."

"Isn't that up to you, goodlady?" Aretimus looked over the edge where preparations for the next expedition meeting were underway.

She heard the resentment in his voice. "When I'm down there, I'm a goodlady," she said. "When I'm with you, I'm just a Marine Ordinary."

"You never will be though, will you?" said Aretimus awkwardly. "I mean no offence to you goodlady."

"None taken, but please stop calling me goodlady."

"But you are a goodlady. That's what I mean."

"Ilona," she said. "Call me Ilona. Say it. Now."

"Ilona," said Aretimus reluctantly. Karsan social class was bred into the bone. His discomfort at crossing the boundary made him visibly tense. "You're too highborn to remain in the lower ranks for long. If you go back, there's no way they'll let you stay in the service, and they'd never let you be an officer. I expect

First Lieutenant Bannord is going to find himself in plenty of hot water for making you a soldier."

"Probably," she said, hating that he was right. "But we're not in Karsa now, are we Ari? So you get on with watching the sea for the ship, and I'll get on watching the snow for the Draathis, and we can argue about this if we ever, ever find ourselves back in the isles."

HALF AN HOUR before her watch was due to end, Ilona was relieved by Devall. He clambered up the ropes to the top of the rock and grinned at her apologetically. For some reason he kept forgetting she could speak Maceriyan, and mimed and gurned at her.

"Devall, I speak Maceriyan adequately," she said for the tenth time.

"Sorry medame," he said. He behaved strangely around her. Musran attitudes to women were even more backward than those in the isles, so far as she could tell. "You are wanted down in the camp. The meeting is beginning."

"Thank you, mesire," she said. He grinned again at her use of the honorific. She decided that Musrans were odd.

The camp had a febrile mood. They had been there too long, she thought. The men were restless, she was restless. Tyn Rulsy appeared from nowhere to waddle at her side.

"Don't like it," said the Tyn. What she did not like, or why, she did not elaborate.

There was the meeting tent, with its sides rolled up, site of every meeting they had had. There were the other tents, some from the ship, some from

Antoninan's stores. There were the sleds, piled high with supplies, ready to depart at a moment's notice. There were the men, who whether joking or stern were all determined. Barriers between the two groups had come down. Persin was still tolerated more than welcomed by both sides, but even he had managed to overcome resentment with some genuinely useful insights.

And there was Ilona, who, Aretimus' unwelcome reminder aside, was treated more or less as one of the men, and she liked that.

What he had said on the rock troubled her. It was no revelation, because she had been thinking exactly the same thing night in, night out.

She listened to Antoninan and Bannord arguing over what to do. He repeated his position forcefully. He wanted to wait, especially now the bay was open. Antoninan, who swore less but was more emotionally volatile, repeated his position that he wanted to leave. Every meeting, every week for the last month.

She remained silent. They would vote soon. Antoninan and Bannord's votes were a given. Ullfider always did whatever Bannord suggested. Persin waited to see the outcome.

These were matters of life and death. Such power men had over the lives of others. In Pris it was the other way around entirely, but that land was an exception regarded suspiciously by the others. In a dozen other kingdoms women had more of a voice, but though they might rule, they rarely led, and those kingdoms did not matter. They were small, or backward, sparsely populated or all three. The most powerful lands, Maceriya and its satellites, and the realms of Mohaci, Khushashia, and Karsa, were the lands of men. Women were expected to be silent.

Now she had it, she no longer welcomed the power Bannord had put in her hands. No one should have to make decisions that could lead to another's death. But as it was necessary, women had as much right to a say as any man. She wondered what had led Bannord to give her this voice so often denied her sex. Affection? The need for a willing, pliable ally? Or was it worse than that, and she was given this falsely, to protect the reputation of men at home? A shield for Arkadian Vand.

"Ilona?" Bannord was looking at her expectantly. Ullfider coughed next to him. The antiquarian was getting weaker. Good fortune smiled on the rest of them that he seemed to be suffering an ailment of age, rather than something they might all catch.

"What?" she said.

"Which way are you going to vote, stay or leave?"

"I agree with Antoninan, we should go," said Persin, who was subtle enough to see Ilona had heard none of the debate. "The choice rests with you, goodlady."

The council members waited. Antoninan's fists were clenched. The men were all staring at her. She took a deep breath.

"By Magister Ardovani's instrument upon the rock, I have watched the Draathis come closer. They will be here within a few days. I believe we have no choice. We must cease waiting, and abandon Sea Drays Bay."

Antoninan looked skyward in triumph. Bannord was right about him, he was more interested in having another attempt at finding his elusive route north than simply surviving. Well, that would serve them, if it existed.

"Are you sure?" said Bannord. "I mean, we could wait another day or two."

She fought back an angry retort. Her face burned with annoyance. "I am sure," she insisted. "I vote we leave."

THE LINE OF sleds drew away from Sea Drays Bay, heading around the back of the sea dray colony and into the hills behind, there they would loop back through wide valleys where the blue tongues of glaciers rested, and follow them north. Antoninan had mapped them extensively. That would be the easiest part of the trip, he assured them.

The men walked by the sleds. All were laden down with supplies taken from the cache, and the carcasses of slaughtered sea drays. The distance they had on the Draathis allowed them these stores, and they would be glad of them in the weeks ahead.

Antoninan stood at the side of the route from the bay as the dogs hauled their heavy loads though a notch in the hill and onto wide plains of snow and rock, whose horizons were tumorous with the cracked bodies of ice caps. Valatrice led the way. Then came the Karsan expedition's second sled, then Labarr leading the first of Persin's sleds, the other two close behind. He waited until the baying of the hounds had drawn off. The last man trudged below, his rifle at the ready. Antoninan waved down at him. The man, unrecognisable in his arctic gear, waved back.

The group would fret that he was not there. They could wait. He wanted to enjoy the peace of the Sotherwinter, without the bark of dogs and chatter of men. He wanted to hear the voice of the continent, its animal noises, the crack and boom of shifting ice, the soughing wind, the crash of water on the unyielding black stone of the shore. There was no silence in a land like that, not ever, but the peace of it even at its noisiest dwarfed any comfort Eustache Antoninan could find in a city of men. He loved that land fiercely.

He came there for that. People thought him concerned only for glory. Glory he desired, it was true, but it was not his sole motivation, nor the chief of them.

Antoninan looked back over the bay. The tide was dropping. The ice had nearly all gone, and the barrier reefs that shielded the bay were turned to sharp ridged walls by the water's retreat. There were breaches where the ocean had won out, but only one gateway in the fortress, as he fancifully thought of it, a deepwater channel to the eastern side. He remembered the discovery of the bay. He remembered the times he had been there. Each time he saw it, he thought it might be the last. This time was no different.

He closed his eyes. Warm sun bathed his face. The voice of the Sotherwinter spoke to him. It would change for the worse, if he were successful.

But by then he would be rich, and he would mourn the loss of the land's voice in style.

A faint hoot intruded into his reverie. He opened his eyes. They were momentarily dazzled by the glare of the snow and the sea. The sound came again. He searched the horizon.

Out on the ocean, far, far on the edge of human vision, a wisp of white steam, faintly luminous with the discharge of spent glimmer, threaded its way skyward.

He watched it for a few moments more. The rest of the party were well over the hill and would be heading down the other side. They would hear nothing.

He turned to follow the sleds.

He followed the disturbed snow at a jog. Without saying a word of what he had seen, he took the lead of the line of sleds heading toward the northwest.

The conquering of the Sorskian Passage, and all of its attendant wealth and prestige, would be his.

CHAPTER FORTY-THREE
The Challenge

THE MODALMEN FILLED the arena. Tribes inimical to each other stood peacefully together, swaying in time to an internal rhythm. Their singing was so low the ground shook. Clan markings shone a glorious display in the smoke of burned human corpses. Fires crackled every twenty paces around the arena's rim, fuelled by the broken wood of the cage wagons and the flesh of the dead. Surrounded by modalmen on every side, the remaining men waited in terror for their fate.

Rel watched from behind bars, alone. Thirteen cages of men remained. The survivors of the escape were crammed into six of them so tightly it seemed the cages sprouted waving hair made of human limbs, but the density in the wains was misleading. Many men had been killed. Weakened by months of starvation, they were easy prey to Brauctha's hounds. The lucky ones had died instantly, many of the rest had endured things no man should ever see, let alone feel. The corpses of those brought down had been roasted by the man eaters, as had many of the living. The stink of fat off the cooking fires clung to Rel's filthy clothes; the screaming of the dying echoed still in his ears. For days he had endured hell.

He had the cage to himself. Brauctha had made a great show of placing the wagon at the centre of the thirteen, so that Rel had a clear view of the arena floor and the fates of the men he had failed to save.

The elders of the modalmen tribes stood in a circle a few paces from Rel. Their humming set the music for the others to follow. They stood motionless, their wordless drone reverberating off the ancient stones and into the desert.

In the course of his short military career, Rel had witnessed more bloodshed than many Kingdoms soldiers saw in a lifetime. But his current situation was so profoundly unsettling it wore his courage out. He felt brittle, like an old pan corroded through, which though holding its shape awaited the final knock that would see it disintegrate into flakes of rust. The world had the contradictory, hyperreal nonsensicality of a nightmare, only he was wide awake.

Images of what the man eaters had done to their captives pushed themselves into his mind. He tapped his temple with the heel of his hand. The memories would not be dislodged. They changed, and the blood streaked, screaming faces became his own.

He could not decide whether the anticipation of what they might do to him or the guilt for causing so many men to suffer was worse. The question was academic. He would either be transformed, or tortured to death himself. He did not think he could be brave either way.

He stared at the elders until his eyes blurred with tears.

"I have so thoroughly fucked up," he said.

He kicked the bars and dropped his head onto his knees.

A whir and metallic clink sounded from above his head. He looked upward, and caught sight of a large insect. It disappeared onto the far side of a bar, its feet tapping on the metal. A moment later it crawled back around, reappearing on the nearside of the bar at eye level. At that distance it was obvious it was no living insect, but a tiny machine similar to Onder in miniature, with a body made of brass and wing casings of iridescent silver. Tiny rubies made its eyes. Segmented antennae, delicate as curls of fine swarf, stroked the bars. It stopped, rearing up on its back legs. Rel jumped as its wing cases snapped open, and it flew noisily to land on his leg. Its sharp feet pricked his skin.

"Ow," he said.

"Do not be alarmed," said the beetle. Though the voice was high pitched it was undoubtedly Qurunad's.

"I'm not alarmed by you," Rel said. "That out there alarms me." He pointed through the bars.

"I am Qurunad," it said.

"Of course it's you!" said Rel angrily. "I don't see anyone else capable of making such a thing."

"Very clever," said the god.

"We have things like this in the Kingdoms, only they can't talk. They're toys."

"From toys great science comes," said the beetle. It vibrated, tickling Rel. The back legs blurred when it spoke, rubbing against the metal thorax faster than the eye could see.

"Speaking legs, how novel," said Rel.

"You are in no position to be flippant. I have come to you now in your hour of need. You should have departed when I said. You achieved nothing but the deaths of men who might have been transformed and bolstered the army that will win this war."

"Thanks," said Rel. "I'm glad you are here, talking to me. Speaking with a false god through the medium of a metal beetle is brightening my day up no end."

"Be silent!" squeaked the beetle. "Brauctha has been waiting for you to make a mistake. He will use your actions now as a pretext for challenging Shkarauthir. He is the better warrior, and will probably win. When a challenger defeats another, he is entitled to all the defeated party's chattels, and in modalmen terms that means Shkarauthir's tribe. He will then challenge me. You have given him the perfect opportunity to avoid a vote at the moot. He will invade the Hundred Kingdoms. This will be your fault."

"I retract my previous comment about feeling better."

"You should not feel anything but remorse. Brauctha is free to act because of you. He told the moot that you should never have been brought into the camp before the horde's course of action was decided, and that your attempt to free his slaves was an insult that Shkarauthir must pay for. Brauctha is every bit as dangerous as I thought."

"You know him well."

"He is over one thousand years old," said Qurunad. "Our paths have crossed frequently."

"Masters rarely have a care for the personalities of their slaves," said Rel bitterly.

"Something you as a Karsan should understand. Your nation's treatment of the Tyn is worse than my treatment of the modalmen. You are horrified by slavery, yet you practise it."

"Are you going to get me out of here?"

"I regret that I cannot. This device lacks the appropriate tools. I cannot intervene in person. If I provoke Brauctha, he will certainly destroy me."

"As opposed to probably."

"I must take the risk. I have to survive. Apart from my knowledge's usefulness to the world, which is of incalculable worth, I am reluctant to die."

"You've certainly gone to lengths to save your own hide, that's for sure."

"My hide, as you have it, long ago turned to dust. I admit I am self-interested. Survival is the imperative of all life. I am not ashamed. I work to save the world, but I save the world so I will live."

"If your beetle can't get me out, and you won't come down from your fortress, I can infer that you've basically come here to say 'I told you so'?"

"Notwithstanding the fact that I did tell you so, not entirely," stridulated the beetle. "You may survive this if you can escape from this cage. When Brauctha triumphs over Shkarauthir, he will invoke my name, and request that I release to him the Machineries of Change. This I will do."

"That is so noble, the way you're standing up to him," said Rel sarcastically.

"More modalmen to face the Draathis is to be desired, whatever you may think of their creation. You have no right to judge. You gave up your best chance to influence these events in your favour. You are ruled by sentiment. It will be your downfall."

"Thanks," said Rel. "I guess I'll come and thank you when I've got four arms and illuminated skin."

"That will not happen. They will not put you through the machines."

"I guess they don't want me to be in a position to kill them."

"It is not that," said Qurunad. "It is because you are of a mageborn family. In the ancient days we would enhance the ability of the mageborn. As living weapons they served us. They were also changed by the machines."

"Why are you telling me this now?"

"Because now is the time," said the beetle smugly. "What good would it have done before, except to tempt you?"

"I would not have been tempted."

"Well, now you have no choice. The purity of mageborn blood is diluted in modern times, hence your lack of ability. But you still carry the magic, wrapped up in the words of the book of life that is inside every man. Putting a mageborn through the Machineries of Change grants them enormous power. The modal form will not support the use of magic, we created them that way. Humans have an innate ability to effect the world through the application of their will. We took it from the modalmen, we intensified it in the mageborn. It is simple, actually. All the most complicated things are."

"I beg to differ," said Rel.

"There is a chance," continued the beetle, "if you can get yourself through the Machineries of Change, that you will activate your dormant talent for magic and you will become as the living weapons of old."

"Seriously?" said Rel. "What happens when it doesn't work?"

"Then you will die."

"How the fuck is that supposed to help me?"

"It is a small chance. The mageblood in you is weak. There is no guarantee of success. If it works, your body will most likely become unstable. Your life will be shortened. In return you will have access to immeasurable power."

"So I will die anyway?"

"Not immediately. Dying later is always preferable to dying now. It is the tenet by which I have lived my entire life. It has worked for me so far."

Rel looked through the bars. The elders showed no sign of stopping their music.

"All I have to do is to escape from this cage, make my way past ten thousand monsters, avoid their leader, then jump into a magical device that may very well tear me to pieces?"

"That is about the measure of it, yes."

"Fine. I've had better odds, but I accept." He held up his manacled hands. "First, I have to get these off, and get out of the cage."

"I cannot help you," said the beetle.

"Oh yes you can." Rel seized the brass god's device. He gripped it tightly in his hand, ignoring the stabbing of its needled legs as it struggled to get free. He relaxed his grip enough so that it could speak.

"Do you need to tell me anything else?"

"Kill Brauctha," said the beetle. "That is our only chance to avert disaster. You have set in train events that may end the world. Put them right."

"I'll do my best." Rel wrenched the beetle's large rear legs off. The damaged machine thumped to the floor and crawled off pathetically. Rel paid it no attention. He had what he needed. He held the limbs up to his eyes, and started to twist the legs into shape.

REL WAS WORKING at the manacles with his improvised lockpicks when the humming of the elders cut out. Movement rustled throughout the arena. Rel glanced up, afraid he would be noticed, but the doings of a mere human were below the modalmen's attention. All eyes were on the arena floor.

Brauctha strode out from the edge of the arena, draped in a cloak of shining feathers. The circle of elders parted to let him through. Rel watched him warily, hiding his tools in his lap, but although Brauctha had put Rel centre stage, he spared no glance for him.

Brauctha raised his arms and made a barking cry. He began to speak, passionately laying out whatever claim he had against Shkarauthir. He gestured toward Rel's cage a couple of times, but did not once look at him. Rel backed away until he was in the corner, where he would be most obscured from view. Trying not to rush, he jiggled the picks in the manacle's lock. The keys had been very simple, long shafts with a blank bit.

Rel had picked locks before. He was a rich man, so did it for the thrill when he was a boy. The man he had learned it from needed the ability to survive. He had been caught, and expected to be punished. Instead his father had encouraged him. No skill, his father had said, was ever wasted.

His father had given him an easier time than his siblings. He supposed it was because he was the youngest. He had no predetermined role to fulfil. He was a spare. Their father could afford to be indulgent with him.

The pick bit. The lock clicked. His manacles were heavy and fell off his hands loudly. Brauctha was still speaking, and the modalmen were staring at only at him.

Rel looked down the cage. The beetle had gone, leaving the filthy boards empty. The cage's gate was twenty feet distant, as far as the other side of the world. If he went for it now, he would be spotted and killed.

He could not make his attempt while Brauctha spoke. That would be seen.

When he did make his move, he was going to have to unlock the door pretty much instantly. The lock was as simple as that on the manacles. It was possible to get it open, the question was, could he do it quickly enough?

There was a sudden thunder of stamping feet. Brauctha was holding his arms high, basking in the adulation of his people. For the first time since Rel had been dragged into the arena earlier in the evening, the crowd was not acting in concert. Sections occupied by the men eaters bellowed out approbation, but many others hissed their disapproval.

Brauctha started to speak again, ending his last pronouncement on a single shouted word.

"Shkarauthir!" he roared.

A gong boomed.

Shkarauthir entered the stadium. He carried his long spear in his right upper hand, a shield in the left. His lower arms carried paired daggers. Two swords hung from his belt. Upon his chest he wore a bronze breastplate, softer than iron, but the modalman's great strength meant the metal could be thick. Matching greaves and vambraces covered his lower arms and legs. The upper parts of his arms and shoulders were protected by leather spaulders. A helm of iron covered his head, with an iron grille for the visor.

He strode toward Brauctha. His eyes met Rel's for a second. Rel hoped Shkarauthir knew he was sorry.

Brauctha laughed and shouted out a challenge. The words were repeated by the elders. Shkarauthir replied quietly. Rel struggled to pick out words he understood, but Shkarauthir's agreement to the contest was clear. Rel's actions had given him no choice.

Brauctha raised his arms again. His followers roared. Two of his tribesmen came to his side and removed his feathered cloak. He was naked beneath, without armour. A warrior brought him a pair of mail gloves. A second carried out his immense sword. Brauctha stared at Shkarauthir as pulled on the gloves, took the hilt of the sword and drew the blade. He held it vertically before his face. The warrior took away the scabbard.

The modalmen hooted and trilled their tongues while the elders solemnly pronounced something else Rel did not understand, though it must have been along the lines of honour and death and all the associated pomposity men proclaim when they are serious about killing each other.

Rel looked at the door again. If Shkarauthir won, then maybe he wouldn't have to endure a nerve wracking attempt to get it open. His bowels were watery. It was the fear of failure that terrified him now, rather than dying.

A chorus of vocal booming began the fight.

Brauctha smirked at Shkarauthir. The king of the Gulu Thek circled his opponent. He held his spear overarm, point aimed at Brauctha's heart. His shield covered his left side. His lower arms held their daggers loosely. In contrast to the rest of Shkarauthir's posture, which was totally still, his lower arms were constantly in motion, daggers weaving back and forth like a serpent about to strike.

"You will die for the little one in the cage," said Brauctha, surprising Rel with his use of Maceriyan. "You can thank him that the aims of this horde will be decided, and that I shall be its overlord." He smiled at Rel and licked his lips. "I am going to eat him alive when this is done."

Shkarauthir maintained his steady, crosswise pacing, one leg placed over the other, legs bent, spear arm poised. A chant built in the crowd comprised of two main components sung by Brauctha's and Shkarauthir's supporters. The two songs met, and intertwined. The modalmen were wild beings of opposing temperaments, but their actions nevertheless ended in accordance. The noise they made together was a shushing, thumping similar to the mechanical pounding of a glimmer engine.

They are machines, built for war, thought Rel.

The two modalmen moved out from their starting positions, their feet marking out a spiral in the sand. The manoeuvring looked as if it would never end, until an explosive movement from Shkarauthir opened the duel in earnest.

Shkarauthir leapt across the space separating him from his opponent, spear darting out an instant before his feet moved. He made no cry, and gave no motion that betrayed his intention. One moment he was stalking his prey, the next he was arrowing across the sand.

Brauctha gave a joyous shout. He bent backward, out of the spear's way. Shkarauthir ran past him, the dagger in his lower arm cutting across Brauctha's torso. Blood, red as that of any man, spilled onto the sand. Brauctha's markings flared intensely, and he laughed.

"A good start, a good cut. It will be your last. I will enjoy your friend's flesh all the more for the pain." Again Brauctha spoke in Maceriyan for Rel's benefit.

Rel crept into himself in a show of fear. He did not have to act particularly hard.

Shkarauthir made a lightning-fast feint. He whipped the spearhead back at the last moment, spinning the shaft in his hand, cracking Brauctha across the jaw. The spear whirled about, coming to rest clamped under Shkarauthir's arm, the head singing as it pointed at his enemy. The king of the Giev En spat blood and laughed. He let the end of his giant sword drop into the sand and pointed at Shkarauthir. The crowd cheered and howled.

"Now it is my turn."

Brauctha's weapon was not made for speed, but he wielded it quickly, and in a diverse range of movements that took Rel by surprise. He jabbed with the point like a spear. He grasped the blade with his armoured hands and used the length to catch blows, he reversed the weapon, using the quillions as a pick. All the while the serrations and fluting of the sword sang with a shrieking voice that echoed around the arena.

Its unearthly calls made it seem possessed of a life of its own. The sound of it quietened the crowd, until the humming screams of Brauctha's greatsword, the bang of blade on shield, the whisper of Shkarauthir's spear point and the grunts of the combatants were all that could be heard.

The pair of them were sweating heavily, their clan marks flashed out sharp, staccato patterns that Rel read as unbridled aggression. Blood dripped from Brauctha's cut and from his mouth. Shkarauthir had yet to be hit, though his shield was cleaved deeply in three places. The king of the Gulu Thek looked to have the upper hand, but Rel reckoned that to be deceptive. Shkarauthir's quicker weapons might cut Brauctha many times. It would take only one good blow from Brauctha's murderous blade to slay Shkarauthir.

They wheeled and leapt. Brauctha's weapon was large and heavy. He wore no armour and carried no weapons in his secondary arms to compensate, so although his blows were necessarily slower than Shkarauthir's, he was capable of acrobatic feats that the other could not match—running and leaping, striking down with his blade as he arched over the head of Shkarauthir. Rel saw his friend's armour as a mistake. It slowed him, but would not stop a clean strike from so heavy a blade. The threat to his own life receded from his mind as he fixated on the duel. He had no desire to see Shkarauthir die.

Another charge from Shkarauthir, another swipe from spear, dagger, dagger, and Brauctha was behind his foe. He turned with awesome grace upon the ball of his foot, repositioning his body as Shkarauthir was recovering from his own attack. Brauctha swung his sword at Shkarauthir in a savage, overhand strike that shattered the shaft of Shkarauthir's spear. Howling madly, Brauctha span around again, his arms fully outstretched with the weight of his sword. Shkarauthir leaned backward, avoiding by a hair's breadth a blow that would have cut him in half, and swayed aside, turning the move into a roll that brought him to his feet some yards away.

Panting, the two modalmen circled each other again. Shkarauthir discarded his shield, and cast down the stump of his spear. Brauctha charged again. Shkarauthir drew his paired swords and struck at Brauctha as he came running past. Brauctha executed a deft parry. Sparks fountained from the blades as they scraped together. By the merest twist of his wrists, Brauctha sent the edge of his sword sliding down between Shkarauthir's weapons, the length and angulation of his sword granting him slightly more leverage. In fencing terms, that was a deadly advantage. Shkarauthir barely recovered. His daggers came up to catch the sword's tip before it could gut him. It glanced from his armour, and scored a deep groove across his chest above the breastplate, and he grunted with the pain. Shkarauthir shoved the weapon away with all four of his blades. Brauctha let him, used his opponent's momentum to slip a hooked notch near the end of his blade over one of Shkarauthir's swords, ran it down to the hilt, and with a savage twist, snapped it.

Shkarauthir threw the broken blade down. Brauctha taunted him in the modalman language, then shouted at Rel.

"Your champion is running out of weapons!"

He used this last utterance as a cover for his attack. Shkarauthir anticipated it, but he was weakening. The cut to his chest, while not deep, was bleeding profusely. His arms were tiring from the repeated parrying of Brauctha's heavy sword. He deflected high, but did not command the blade as he intended. Brauctha's sword skidded past the quillions of Shkarauthir's weapon, and bit deep into his thigh.

Shkarauthir collapsed to one knee. Thick blood pumped from the wound in his leg, running into the whorls of his tribal marks, drowning their light.

Brauctha levelled his blade at Shkarauthir's neck. He spoke a single word. Their language came hard to Rel, a word could have a half dozen meanings according to the pitch applied to its syllables, but the modalmen were above all a warrior race, and Rel knew this one.

"Yield," Brauctha said.

Shkarauthir threw a dagger by way of reply. A blur of steel buried itself in Brauctha's shoulder. The lord of the Giev En howled in outrage and he swung his great blade with all his might.

Shkarauthir had provoked this attack purposefully. As Brauctha struck, Shkarauthir's sword sank into Brauctha's gut, but the man eater did not fall, and his huge blade sliced through Shkarauthir's neck as if it were a fruit upon a table struck by an axe.

The king of the Gulu Thek's head toppled to the sand. His lifeblood jetted skyward in a crimson fountain. His body followed his head to the ground.

"Brauctha! Brauctha! Brauctha!" bellowed the crowd. More than half of them shouted out their new lord's name. Only the Gulu Thek did not. They stood and wailed, clapping their hands repeatedly to their heads in grief.

Rel searched the crowds for his friends. He found Drauthek, staring at him. He looked to him in apology, but Drauthek turned away in disgust.

CHAPTER FORTY-FOUR
Lord of the Modalmen

THE ELDERS CAME out, and in the prolix manner of all modalmen ritual, proclaimed Brauctha the winner. They spent several minutes singing out streams of information which Rel could not comprehend. At the end of every musical phrase, the modalmen sang a long, wordless note that started so low the earth trembled, and rose to a moderate pitch before dropping back even lower than it had begun.

A part of the incomprehensible ritual was done. The elders spoke many tribal names. The wailing of the newly subjugated grew louder, as did the cheers of Brauctha's clan.

The modalmen were beating their chests and slapping their cheeks with their mouths open, so that a tocking noise underpinned by a slapping rumble took the place of the cheers and cries, a sound similar to heavy rain on a metal roof.

To this strange, clacking storm, the elders of the Gulu Thek paid homage to Brauctha, kneeling in the blood of their dead king. Other lords among the giants who had been of Shkarauthir's party came and pledged allegiance thereafter. Those who withheld alliance were few.

Rel looked at the cage gate. Soon, he would have to make his move.

Brauctha spoke. He pointed west, he pointed to the captives, he pointed to the Twin. The back and forth debate of the first moot day was gone. Two thirds of the modalmen in the arena got to their feet and shouted out, "Yes! Yes! Yes!"

Brauctha looked at Rel triumphantly. "You see that? The vote is made, we march to the Kingdoms as warriors. There will be no peace with the Forgetful."

The elders sang another proclamation. Horns blew. Gongs boomed. The stone door at the end of the arena ground open, and from the subterranean space revealed were brought forth a number of strange machines.

Chief among them was a wide lens floating between a pair of curved brass arms very much like the horns upon the silver reader. It was mounted on a cart of gold, with golden wheels. A series of nested spheres followed that, and other, smaller devices.

More readily explicable was a circular table made of curved bars of Morfaan steel, and equipped with chains that corresponded with a man's throat, wrists and ankles. The machines were arrayed around the arena, the table at the centre.

Brauctha swaggered toward the cages. His shoulder bled where Shkarauthir's dagger had pierced him, and his lower left hand was pressed against the wound in his belly. He was in pain but gloated in his triumph.

Rel hid his open manacles as best as he could.

Brauctha went to stand before the row of cages to Rel's left. The modalman called a warrior from the arena floor's edge. He brought a bloody sack forward, and tipped the contents out where Rel could see them.

Aramaz's corpse thudded onto the ground. His legs and arms were curled inward, his tail wrapped round them. His tongue hung out of one side of his mouth. Bloodied like that, he seemed far smaller than he had in life.

"When you are changed, you will dine on this beast and its master, you will not care," Brauctha said to the men in the cages. "Rejoice! You will be modalman. You will join me as brothers, and follow me as king."

Rel stared at his dead mount. He was unprepared for the sorrow that brought him.

The new king of the horde nodded at the men in the cages, and limped toward Rel. He pushed his face against the bars, bringing himself as close to Rel as he could get. Brauctha's solitary, yellow eye peered at him, and he broke into a cruel smile.

"You watch me change them, you watch them eat your lizard, then you die screaming. Modalmen not make friends with unmen, never again."

He hooted through two cupped hands, clapping the others. The door to the first cage was pulled open, and a man hauled out by his ankles.

The modalmen shouted excitedly. Those who disapproved were in a minority.

The man was taken to the table, the chains looped about his neck and spread limbs. An elder pinned the man in place with a single, enormous hand. The table was rotated into an upright position and the five chains drawn taut by five modalmen. The man's screams for mercy were ignored.

The elders turned to face the Fallen Citadel, their hands raised, begging the Brass God for his aid in replenishing their population.

The Brass God obliged.

The nested spheres rotated within each other, the patterned, silver metal whispering on itself. Glimmer light built in the hollow, central space, visible when holes in the spheres were aligned. The machine shook; a deep thrum perturbed the air. The elders sang droning chants in accompaniment.

The shaking grew violent, so that Rel thought the machine would break apart. As it seemed that could be the only outcome, it boomed, and its running became smooth. Glimmer light shone from its markings. The light at the centre was too bright to look at. The turning of the spheres dragged at the world, deadening sound and inducing a leaden malaise in Rel's soul. Colour drained from its vicinity.

The elders' song changed. They shifted their hand positions in perfect unison, the sleeves of their robes snapping with the motion. An arc of power cracked out from the spheres and rooted itself to the lens. Motes of light danced inside the glass, and the apparatus swivelled down to point at the chained man. He howled in terror. The motes merged with one another, glaring brightly as a forge fire. A blade of light moved as slow as a sadist's knife out from the centre. The modalmen turned away, their eyes closed.

Rel couldn't stop watching, though the light burned his eyes. A shaft of boiling radiance stabbed into the man. It hit his chest, and spread through his body, illuminating his circulatory system from within. Light burned from his eyes and mouth. His screams changed to choking whimpers that grew deeper, then petered out into pained grunts.

Before Rel's eyes, the man swelled in size. His torso rippled with new muscle. His bones cracked as they broke and lengthened. His head ballooned, his features became liquid. His eyes swam around his face like fish in a bowl. His ragged clothes split from his body, falling to the ground. The light inside him shone brighter, turning him into a pink lantern decorated with branching patterns of backlit nerves. His ribcage cracked open, the skin on his chest tore. Exposed insides writhed with eager growth, budding new organs so rapidly they overfilled him and welled from his broken chest and his mouth.

As the man grew, the modalmen gently let out the chains. Links rattled through the table one by one, pulled through by his swelling body. The man's grunts became moans as his body rearranged itself and his throat was unstopped. His struggles lessened, and his head lolled. His eyes closed, his features stabilised, taking on the broad set of the modalman's faces even while his head continued to grow. Blotches of charcoal grey appeared over his body, spreading like blots of ink, until they had joined together, and the man's original dusky brown hue was swallowed.

Chains slackened. The man approached the towering height of the modalmen. His ribs closed over vigorously beating organs. A final snapping of bone, and new, tiny arms budded from his side, skinless and wet. They pushed outward like gory shoots. The space under his armpits shifted and changed with the growth of a second set of shoulders. Skin rippled up over exposed muscle, covering it in sleeves of black.

The ray of light snapped off. Where a man of the west had been, a naked, new born modalman hung unconscious from the chains. His flesh steamed. The metal of the table creaked as it cooled. Though he had the physique of a modalman, he lacked their clan markings.

An elder advanced with slow, deliberate steps. He placed a finger upon the new modalman's head. The light of the elder's markings pulsed and shone silver. The patterns crept up from the elder's finger, and drew itself upon the new modalman's body. His skin opened as if cut. Light flowed along the channels, stemming the blood before it could flow.

The channels curled all over the modalman. When they reached his ankles, the elder removed his finger, and stepped back.

"Awake!" the elder commanded in the modalman tongue.

Groggily, the modalman came around. He looked about him in complete confusion. His legs gave under him. Were it not for the chains he would have fallen. The new modalman looked at his feet. Tentatively, he stood.

The giants holding the chains relaxed their grip completely. The chains fell in loops at their new kinsman's feet.

Modalmen with the same clan markings came to his side, and welcomed him, clothing him in the harness and kilt worn by their race. Speaking soothing words they led him away.

The modalmen sang and stamped in greeting, all of them.

And then the process began again.

THEY TOOK RAFOZO before Tuvacs. He screamed in terror as they bound him to the table. Tuvacs watched as Rafozo was changed, changed by sorcery into the very things that had tormented them. The pain on Rafozo's face as they remade him was terrible to see, and soon it would happen to Tuvacs. He could not shake that thought. The pain, and the change.

"Fucking hell, fucking hell," said Dunets over and over. Finally, his spirit had broken, and he was as scared as all the rest.

The next man was taken. As the door opened, all the men within screamed unashamedly. A few bellowed insults, but most were thoroughly cowed by their long ordeal, and cried like babes. Tuvacs was no exception, when his turn came.

He came close to losing his mind when they pulled him out. He could not think. Sheer terror grasped him. He was helpless in the modalmen's grip, unable even to struggle as they placed him against the table and yanked the chains tight. The spheres screamed with pent up sorcerous power. The lens tilted down to point at him.

A peculiar calm came over him as he stared at the shining glass. Acceptance of his fate, maybe, or a realisation that it would all soon be over. The magic built within the lens, the blade of light extended. Before it slammed into his body, he spoke.

"Lavinia."

Light burned through him. Every mote of his being was set ablaze. In this universe of pain he clung onto his memories, snatching for them like a man chasing sheets of paper blowing away down a street. His childhood was ripped from him, his memories of Travnic were plucked out from the library of his mind one by one. Mohacs-Gravo disintegrated. His time in Karsa melted away. But he held on hard to the memory of his sister, and he clutched tighter still to an image of Suala, heavy with his child. He would never see the child, not if he forgot. Light and pain became his world. His mental struggles lessened. His soul unravelled, but he held fast to his sister and his lover, focussing all his will on remembering their faces.

An eternity passed. The light faded. A newly made modalman lay steaming upon the table. Through half-closed eyes, the modalman who had been Tuvacs saw the elder approach to take him into his clan.

"Suala," the modalman whispered. "Lavinia."

The elder drew with a burning touch upon his remade flesh, and Tuvacs' vision went black.

REL MOVED TO the cage door as cautiously as was possible. The glaring light of the Machinery of Change obscured his actions. It flooded the arena, brighter than the sun itself. The modalmen were focussed on the birth of their new clansmen, but if only one looked his way at the wrong time, he would be dead.

"I'm going to be dead anyway," he said to himself as he rattled his makeshift pick in the lock. "It will be sooner rather than later. They can't see through the light. They can't see like you can," he told himself. In all that effulgence, the modalmen's vision would work against them.

The cage lock was unwilling to cooperate. He had to scurry back to his chains repeatedly as the light died. An hour passed. Fifteen more men were turned into bewildered modalmen before Rel heard the telltale click of the lever turning. The lock would not open.

He looked nervously around. No one could see him through the glare. His hands were sweating profusely. He wiped them on his clothes. A few more jiggles, and the lock snapped wide.

The latest new modalman was made. The light died. Rel hurried back to the other end of the cage. He was forced to leave the door ajar, its padlock hanging from the hasp.

He had to wait. Another man must be altered for him to escape.

Rel looked at the cage. He wondered who it would be. He wondered who would die so that he would have a chance to live. He tried to frame it in the context of saving the world rather than himself, but the end of the world was an abstract. His own life was in immediate danger. A man would die in exchange for his life, there was no other way to see it.

The latest modalman was led, weak-limbed, to his clan mates. At the climax of each transformation, a new elder came forward, claiming the warrior for his tribe, until every clan had been apportioned a fresh recruit. Once all had taken a turn, the elder of the Giev En took a second.

Rel waited with his heart in his mouth. He forced himself not to look at the door. He could not help but be conscious that it was open, clearly so.

Modalmen walked within a couple of yards of his cage to fetch a prisoner. They pulled out another terrified man. Many of them were crying. Others screamed insults at their captors. Their profanities fell on deaf ears. The modalmen took off their latest victim's manacles, and carried him to the table.

Rel didn't know the man. By his sacrifice would Rel be free, if he survived.

The apparatus was engaged. The light built, the chanting began. When the beam of change forced itself into the man's very being and began its reforging, Rel threw himself at the cage door and jumped out.

Dazzling light shone from every part of the arena, whiting out the details of the ancient carvings. Odd shadows collected in sheltered places, throwing off the geometry of the building.

Rel sprinted headlong for the beam of light. For half the distance he was not seen. As he closed upon the machine, his world drew in, wrapping him in radiance and exaggerated sound. His breathed rushed in his ears. The sand kicked up by his feet pattered down like hailstones. Then uproar chased him.

He had been seen.

A giant's spear slashed the sand yards from where he ran, cutting up a furrow and skidding across the arena floor. More followed. Modalmen broke from their duties guarding the cages or attending the elders and ran after him, but their eyes, sensitive in the dark, were virtually blind as the Machineries of Change did their work, and Rel dodged their lumbering attempts to grab him.

Then Brauctha was there in front of him.

"No," he said.

Rel skidded to a halt, and turned quickly. Brauctha's fists thudded into the sand after him. He expected the end. Brauctha reached for him, but another modalman slammed into the side of the king and bore him to the ground.

Drauthek's voice chased Rel.

"Run!"

Rel glanced back. Drauthek had the bigger modalman in a headlock, the fingers of his lower left hand buried in the wound Shkarauthir had inflicted upon Brauctha's belly.

Rel dodged a final clumsy swipe, and leapt for the beam of light. It was further than he had ever jumped in his life.

Time took on the treacly slowness it had before he had ridden the Road of Fire. His hand slipped into the light, jolting him with power. He wished to turn back, but he could not, and he landed in front of the table. There he took the full brunt of the beam.

The Machinery of Change called to something inside him, something that had always been there that he had never noticed, but now it was shown to him, he realised it had been there all along.

Rel was slammed sideways from his body. His soul compressed to a tiny point, hard as diamond. The sky opened, filled with shifting vistas and screaming, tortured faces. He looked away from them, terrified, only to find himself staring downward into infinity. Pillars of black and red smoke turned complex dances, lightning stabbing between them. Streams of light intersected with each other, turned inside out, and became dark. He hung nowhere for an endless moment, then the dark burst apart in kaleidoscopic explosions. With a sickening lurch, he was turned on his head. His lips were numb. His arms lost their form. His skin inflated, encompassing the camp, the modalmen, the mountains, desert, the Earth, the Twin, the sun, and on, past the cold ice that warmed itself at the very last extent of the sun's rays, out into the void between stars, until his soul brushed the edges of eternity, and galaxies rotated within his mind.

He burst into fragments. There were a billion of him, an infinity, all living different lives. Reality fractured like a scene blurred by a trick lens. Rel fell down through a shattering, coalescing myriad of images.

He landed hard on nothing, found himself swooping over strange lands where men and women lived strange lives. Primitives in fur, warriors in armour, cities of vertical slabs with a thousand windows, undersea villages, glittering palaces of metal and stone that floated in the black void. Mankind everywhere, on every sort of world. He was slammed sideways into another place, another time, where Morfaan stood as gods before savage tribes, and took them through gates of light. Another place, and another. A lonely woman sat upon a bed in a strange room lit by lamps that were not fire but were not glimmer. A visitor offered her a different life. On and on, people taken from all across the endless variations of time and space and brought there, to this Earth.

He fell further, tumbling down the twisting ways of fate and time. He watched reality come apart and reshape itself under the influence of living minds, some deliberately exerted, most change unconsciously done. Finally, he arrived in a blackness of a compact sort, where an incomprehensible being as large as the forever moulded two worlds from nothing, one light and ever changing, one dark and eternal.

The spell broke, Rel slammed into the arena sand.

Shouts were coming from everywhere. Human and modalman. Rel attempted to stand. On his first try, he could not, on his second, he went from prone to standing upright without passing through the stages between. His feet drifted over the ground. Power poured from him in torrents, magic coursed through his being. He experienced reality around him not as a concrete actuality, but a series of choices that were now his alone to make.

Brauctha was shouting in the modalman tongue. Rel fervently wished he understood it. As soon as he had the thought, he could.

"Kill him! Destroy him!" raged the king of the Giev En. Spears and arrows raced at Rel from every side. They vanished as soon as he was aware of them. Warriors ran at him with their weapons drawn. He threw out his hand and scattered them, blasting apart their bodies into showers of meat.

"Brauctha," said Rel. His voice roared around the arena. "The horde will ride to the Kingdoms in friendship. You will cease your transformation of these men. Your day as king has come and passed. Submit, and all will be well."

The modalmen were sent into confusion by Rel's use of their language. His words boomed from him like cannon fire, reverberating from the mountains.

"You will die, and I will eat you," said Brauctha. He snatched his sword from an attendant, and charged at Rel.

Rel looked at Brauctha's wound. He imagined it opening wide, spreading around his body and splitting his skin in a neat line up over his shoulders and down his back. As he imagined it, so it was.

Brauctha fell to pieces under Rel's will. His guts unraveled upon the floor. His skin fell off. His remaining eye dropped from his skull. The impetus of his charge propelled him a few more yards. Within three steps he was a walking pile of gristle and steaming bone. He did not stop, but pressed on until he collapsed into a wet mound of fats and unravelling flesh that bubbled, liquefied, and sank into the sand.

Rel spread his arms, and commanded the world to let him fly. Meekly, reality hoisted him skyward.

"Release these men!" he shouted.

Silence fell. The man on the table screamed, halfway transformed, condemned to a choking death by malformed organs bursting in his chest. Rel looked upon him, and attempted to undo the change. That he could not do. All that resulted was more screaming.

"Release them!" he shouted. His voice broke and stuttered. The fire in his blood went from empowering to burning. His belief in his own power wavered. Flight was seen as the impossibility it was, and he fell to the ground. A modalman moved on him, sword up. Rel removed his head with a thought, but still his power faltered. The energy streaming from him stuttered.

Drauthek was being held on his knees by four other modalmen. The men shouted from their cages. Rel stood.

"This horde is mine by right of conquest," he said.

The modalmen milled about, their unity gone. The elders argued around him, then one pointed toward the citadel, and the others looked and cried out.

Lights ran around the broken fortress. A glowing cloud detached itself from the summit and flew unerringly for the moot ground. It descended and touched down between Rel and the dying, half-transformed man, where it solidified into the machine body of Qurunad, the Brass God.

"And lo, so came unto them the God of Brass!" Qurunad said.

The modalmen fell to their knees, prostrating themselves before their deity. A panicked song of worship arose from all quarters.

"You, Rel Kressind, cease to exert yourself or you will die. Your abilities are unstable. Stop now. Let me finish the business of tonight."

Rel held his hands up. They sparkled with fitful power, but his thoughts were unformed. The sand flowed around him, half alive. Flowers sprang up and died. Tiny armies made of dirt fought a battle by his feet. He tried to regain control, but the more he strived, the more slippery reality became, and he had the sudden fear he would wish himself from existence.

"Modalmen!" said the Brass God. "The Endless War continues. Your might at arms is needed again." He pointed at the cages. "End what you began! Add these men to your ranks, swell your numbers. The war demands it! I demand it!"

"What are you doing?" said Rel. He felt sick. He was incredibly thirsty and hungry but the thought of consuming anything nauseated him.

"I said you that you could not save them," said Qurunad. "This war cannot be won without sacrifice. They are needed, but not as men. Be thankful that you live."

"You did this on purpose," said Rel. "You knew what would happen. You used me to remove Brauctha."

"Now you catch on," said the Brass God. "Shkarauthir also had to go. He would not have pursued the correct course of action either. All was necessary, and all was ordained. I told you I had limited powers of foresight. You did not listen. If it makes you feel better, I am sorry it has to be this way, and I am sorry it has to be you, but this war cannot be lost."

Rel's body was failing, he was dissipating on the wind. He could see through his own skin to the bones and blood vessels beneath, and the sandy floor behind that.

"You fucking bastard!" whispered Rel. "I'm dying."

"You are," said the Brass God. "Your gifts will kill you, but not tonight. I am not done with you yet. I did not lie when I said I cannot leave this place. This is my army, but I require you to lead it."

The Brass God came limping to his side and clamped his metal hand against Rel's head. Coldness spread through Rel's body. Darkness took away the tyranny of choice, and Rel's ability to force his will upon the fabric of being faded along with his consciousness.

CHAPTER FORTY-FIVE
The Darkling Remembers

UNDER A CEILING of stone hundreds toiled. The Darkling watched them from atop a boulder hidden away in the mouth of an abandoned side gallery.

There had been no need to cajole the population of Perus to work in the excavation of the caverna. The word of the gods' will had spread quickly. The growing Church of the Returned was swelled by thousands of fresh converts. Many of them toiled gladly in the dark underworld of Perus, driving a hundred yard wide diagonal shaft downward into the city's hidden depths, where the last functioning World Gate on the continent lay hidden.

Through Guis Kressind's stolen eyes the Darkling observed goodfellows and peasants alike hacking away at the stone. Miners had been brought in from all over the kingdom, but they were in a minority. Engineers fought a losing battle to impose order on the enthusiastic hordes of citizens tunnelling their way downward. Few of them had real tools. Many employed the uprights torn from iron railings as crude picks, ramming them home with little more than devotion to their gods to sustain them. Women and children carried water to the masses, and a few distributed food. But in their fervour most wanted to be at the rock face themselves. Bishop Rousinteau's priests shouted sermons, promising life eternal at the right hand of the gods if only they could breach the walls, take out the rock, and expose the means of their deities' access to the world anew. They worked themselves into exhaustion, falling where they dug. Some of them would not rise, their lives expended in the most profound form of worship.

"Can you see that?" whispered the Darkling. There was no one with it. An observer would see a man on the edge of physical dissolution speaking with himself, insane, perhaps. But the Darkling was never alone. Imprisoned deep inside his own body languished the spirit of Guis Kressind, and he could hear every word. "Your species changes the world again. Their zeal," he sketched his gloved black hand through the air, "it reinforces itself. It makes the return of the gods more likely. I do not like Shrane. The taint of iron in her magic sickens me, but though she is skillful, I am craftier than she. Her beloved iron lords will not inherit this Earth."

The Darkling smirked at Guis' wordless anguish. The Darkling felt it inside himself, as piquant an emotion as new love.

"Shhhh," it said. "You witness a great event. You are privileged. You will see the restoration of the true masters of this Earth. You shall see the renaissance of the Children of the Five. The Tyn Y Dvar will be born again."

Explosions trembled the rock as magisters let off charges of glimmer and iron. Clouds of rockdust billowed up the shaft. A cheer went up that turned quickly to shouts of terror as a secondary collapse occurred. Rock cracked. Screams echoed out from an unauthorised side gallery. Boulders tumbled free, bouncing down the steep incline of the shaft, crushing the devout. The dust cleared. The dead were carried away. Blessings were sung to those who had sacrificed themselves doing the gods' work, and the frantic industry was set in motion again. The Darkling watched it all.

"See how willingly they die? This is primal exultation, the act of worship in blood and sweat. Such focus warps reality. Your kind has such a gift for that.

"Before the god driving, when I served the Dark Lady proudly in immortal form, these spaces under Perus were avoided by humanity. The poor, the dispossessed, the insane lived here, wretches hiding in the palaces of the mighty past. But I remember further back, to this place as it was before the destruction wrought by the Children's War. I remember gleaming spires, and mighty temples to the One. I remember the days my arrogant kin raised up the Morfaan from the beasts of the Earth to fawn after them, and moulded life into iron to make their Draathis slaves. I remember the days the Morfaan opened the first of their gates, simpering for the approval of their masters, breaking through the walls of this world as these labouring citizens break through this rock, without care or understanding of what they did. And then they brought you here." He growled. "I was once a free being, a creature who dwelled in the air, beyond the hubris of other Y Dvar. You think me evil, but I was above such notions, until your kind trapped me in this shape and pushed the fathers of the Morfaan to the edge of your world. As the poor fouled the palaces, so your species has fouled this Earth. No more. These fools will fling open the roads of fire. The iron children will come and wipe away the stain of your existence. The Draathis shall destroy the last of the Morfaan, and then, when their role is done, my masters will cast off the prisons your worship put upon them, and they will destroy our wayward brothers and sisters, and smash the iron abominations, and sweep this place clean of all contamination. Then all shall return to the way it was, before Morfaan and Draathis and men. The worlds of Form and Will shall be restored to the designs of the One. And you, dear Guis Kressind, shall have the pleasure of knowing you were instrumental in the extinction of your species upon this world before I devour your soul."

Running feet cut their way through the clattering of iron on stone. A youth approached the Darkling's hiding place. The Darkling smiled at the expression on his wan features. Dread and awe mixed meant worship, and worship meant power. The Darkling hissed in pleasure at the strength given him by the boy's belief in his divinity.

"My lord," said the boy. He dropped to his knees and abased himself. The Darkling slid off the boulder he squatted upon and landed softly on dusty rubble.

"Rise," he commanded. "Look upon me."

The boy did as ordered. His eyes widened further as he looked into Guis Kressind's unhealthy features, the sallow skin, the greasy hair coming away in clumps, the red-rimmed eyes. A sick-sweet stench of spiritual decay enveloped him.

"My lord god," said the boy. "Adamanka Shrane, most blessed prophet of the returning gods, requests your presence. The final wall before the chamber of the gate is to be breached. She desires your presence."

"Then she shall have it," said the Darkling. He made to go, but paused, and smiled. "Tell me boy, do you wish my benediction? Do you wish the blessing of your gods?"

"Yes, your holiness. More than anything!" He clasped his hands beneath his chin.

"Then stand."

The boy stood, shaking with anticipation. The Darkling reached out, and caressed his cheek with stinking fingers. The boy whimpered in rapture.

"Accept the blessing of your gods," it said. The Darkling grabbed the boy at the back of the neck, and drove the fingers of its right hand deep into his eyes. The Darkling inhaled the boy's screams, until the youth's gaping mouth let out little more than a squeak. Holding the thrashing youth fast, the Darkling squirmed his fingers through the jelly of the boy's eyes, pushing until orbital bones cracked, and through into the soft meat of the brain. The boy jerked hard twice, and died.

The Darkling let him drop, his slick fingers slipping free of the boy's ruined face as he fell.

Guis Kressind's face smiled horribly widely. The Darkling licked humours, blood and brain matter from its hands, and wiped the remainder upon his filthy coat.

"You are blessed," said the Darkling. Whistling to itself, it sauntered out from the hollow and into the tunnel, heading for the end of the world.

CHAPTER FORTY-SIX
An Admission of Expertise

AUTUMN CONTINUED AS it began—colder, darker and wetter than in previous years. The countess was increasingly preoccupied with the idea that the Twin had an effect on the weather. In search of inspiration, she prepared to set her orrery going again. The experiment required a little adaptation to the machine before she activated it. The sun at the centre of the device was a decorative bronze sphere. She required something that gave out light and heat that she could measure. Nothing absolutely relative to the real sun, but enough to allow extrapolative modelling. She removed large parts of the bronze with a magister's saw, another fabulously expensive device, to open the sun up so that it would take a glimmer lamp.

She spent many contented hours absorbed in the work. During this time she sought no one out, and anyone who disturbed her was sent running by bellowed invective. Her mechanical skills were more than adequate and she enjoyed employing them. She had all she needed within the hall. The annoying noises of renovation outside the keep receded from her attention. Her fretting about the events in Perus subsided. Days of peaceful effort were hers, interrupted only by Astred or Hovernia's half-hearted attempts to get her to stop and eat or get a little sleep. She neglected both. Indeed, the countess could barely bring herself to toilet when inspiration had a hold of her, allowing herself to go only when her bladder felt it would burst.

After she installed lamps in the sun, she spent hours tending to the rest of the machine, oiling workings and freeing up parts that had stuck. The salt nature of Mogawn's air spared nothing and she was forced to disassemble the entirety of Bolsun's complicated subsystem and clean rust off dozens of parts to get all the little moons working again.

Impatience urged her to damn it all and set the thing running in the hope it would simply work. She refrained for fear of damaging it.

As a child she had been whipped three times a week at least for lack of consideration before acting. It was one lesson she was glad her father had taught her. There was a sort of delicious frustration to be experienced in doing it all right, even if she was tired and irritable by the time Bolsun's little flock of children were orbiting their father properly.

It was early morning of the 13th of Takcrop when she set the machine going again. The sun had not yet risen. She could have slept, she probably should have, but she could not until the task was done. The glimmer engine complained at being restarted. The arms supporting the planets wobbled and bounced as they commenced their movement, only settling into smooth motion as they picked up speed. Soon enough model worlds were whirling about at several hundred times real speed. She had forgotten to reset the velocity parameters. Clucking her tongue, she went to the ornate pillar that held the workings and power motivation, ducking past speeding metalwork that could have caused serious injury. She flipped open the access panel hidden underneath the maker's plate, and adjusted the speed to match that of the celestial spheres the machine modelled. They ground to a near stop, or so it seemed.

She doused the fire despite the cold, so that the harsh blue-white glimmer lamp in the altered sun was the sole source of light in the room. With the ersatz sun burning, she felt she watched the procession of the spheres from some secret place out in the dark of the sky. There was no air up there, she was sure of that. Understanding the insulating qualities of air, she wondered if it would be hot or if it would be cold in the direct face of the sun, and if a human body could survive the vacuum, if given a sufficient supply of air. She had done experiments on the expansion of dissolved gasses in liquids at low pressures, and she thought there was a good chance one's blood would boil.

How could she explain that? Say "boil" and people think heat. So few people understood what she did. When she was forced to explain things it aggravated her. But she persisted. She wanted them to understand. She wanted not to be alone in her wisdom.

Engrossed in her experiment and her own thoughts, it was with annoyance that she greeted the opening of the hall's door and the arrival, along with Captain Qurion, of a great deal of predawn light.

"Oh shut the door!" she snapped.

"My apologies, goodlady," said the captain. "You are working?"

"No, I am at embroidery and watercolours like any noble goodlady, what do you think?"

He had the decency to appear apologetic. There was a boyish quality to his face when he looked like that. He was an odd one, she thought. He was obviously quite well respected by his men. He was manly in that way a soldier should be, but he had an impudent streak to him. They were all boys at heart, men. They did not have to undergo the pain of growing up properly, she thought. This was their world.

"Your orrery. You have your sun." He frowned. "I expected the planets to move."

She sighed, annoyed at the intrusion of yet another man who though an explanation was owed him. "They are moving, only very slowly. It is adjustable. At the moment, I have this set to a true representation of their orbital speeds. It will take the Earth one year to orbit the sun atop the pillar at this setting. It is also a matter of scale. This is a model, whose bounds are determined by this room. In reality, the system of worlds around our sun is many thousand million miles across, and the planets move at thousands of miles an hour, faster than anything you can imagine. Scaled down, it is not so exciting, but it is accurate."

"You can prove all this, I assume?"

"By mathematics," said the countess. "The same mathematics that allow an artillerist to determine where his shot will land enable me to accurately calculate the precise size, trajectory and speed of the celestial bodies. Yes, I can prove it. I have."

"I am impressed."

"You do not need to be impressed, and you certainly do not need to patronise me."

"I meant no offence, I am impressed. I was quite successful at mathematics at school, and then modestly so at the lyceum. I could never have matched this though."

"You have a degree?" she asked, surprised.

"In mathematics, yes. I was very keen on becoming an empiricist. But my father insisted on the army, for the money, he said. I'll grant you that an academic can earn nothing if he finds no station, but a soldier's wage is not so large. I think he wanted an officer son for the prestige. It is good to have a hero in the family," he said ironically.

"I am sorry," she said, and meant it.

"Don't be. We are all trapped by birth. There's plenty of time. I won't be a soldier forever. If you would indulge me a little?"

"Yes," she said sharply, though not sharply enough to put him off.

"I take it the spheres themselves are not to scale. Bolsun, in particular."

"If they were, Bolsun," she pointed at the largest planet, which she had spent a day laboriously repairing, "would either have to be the size of a grain of sand, or, if rendered at that size, situated somewhere out over Mogawn-On-Land, which is ten miles away. The other planets would either be too small or too far away to see. So the model is a fancy, the relative speeds are, however, correct. And, as a model for testing theories, should we assume that these model worlds are a genuine system in themselves, which I am forced to, then it works quite well. The mathematics is sound. I can show you, if you wish." She shouldn't have to be so insistent on her own competence. If she were a man, she would not have to be.

"Do you know, I would genuinely like to see that," he said.

"Really?" she asked, taken aback.

"Really. The work behind this is astounding. I have seen orreries before, naturally, but they are curiosities. Not one takes into account the variables you have. None of them are much use."

"You have an understanding of my work then. Why did you not say?"

"I thought it might be a bit crass," said Qurion. "Barrelling in here, announcing to the best mind in Karsa that I know all about her work when I don't. I'd be trying a little too hard. Besides, I'm here to refortify and garrison this castle, until such time as the threat of the drowned passes, not foolishly try to equal you."

"You are a hidden dracon's claw," she said thoughtfully.

"I prefer circumspect and tactful."

"But you do understand what I am doing."

Qurion shook his head. "Oh no no, not at all. If they taught your brand of mathematics in the lyceums, then maybe I would, but they didn't."

"One day they shall," she said fiercely.

"I hope they will. You are respected for your work, you know that."

Lucinia shrugged. She did and she didn't.

"What are you doing now? Why did you install the lamp in the sun?"

"Oh," she said absentmindedly. "I am testing my new theory, again very approximate, that the Twin's unusual proximity is directly affecting the weather. I expect it is simply because of the deflection of solar radiation from our world. It can't dim the light by much to represent this, but the passage of my model Twin over the model Earth will have an effect. I'm curious to see exactly what. I doubt I could work out all the variables without long term observational data, and I don't have four thousand years in me. But, it is precisely this kind of tiny change I find fascinating."

"So, precluding the end of the world, you will next commence an exploration of meteorology?"

"I am drawn to complex systems and complex people." She gave him a sidelong look. "It is a personal failing." Her eyes were gritty with fatigue, and she rubbed them with her wrist as her hands were covered with rust. She realised she must look frightful. Her hair was everywhere, and she smelled terrible even to herself. "I apologise if I am being rude, captain, but what is it you wanted?"

"Yes, that," he said. "I came to ask you a question." He gave her an impudent smile that made her heart skip a beat.

"Well, what?"

"Have you ever ridden a dracon before?"

"MISTRESS, MISTRESS, ARE you sure this is a good idea? They are dangerous!" said Hovernia.

"I can get the dray carriage ready for you, countess," said Holless. He shot a mistrustful look at Qurion. "The dogs would appreciate the run."

"Do stop flapping." The countess slapped her gloves into her bare palm. The creature she was to ride did look dangerous. It was man-high at the shoulder, with long legs that though slender at the bottom were bunched with muscle at the thigh. Its forelimbs were powerfully developed, with short, triangular claws tipping three fingers and a rudimentary thumb on each hand. The mid-limbs were underdeveloped, and folded close into the thing's— she had no idea if it were male or female—greasy coat of feathers. The real danger came from its mouth, which was lined with razor sharp teeth, its feet, whose upraised big toe sported a killing claw as big as a sickle, and the tail. There was no knobbed club or spikes as one found on some wild draconic species, but it was long and muscular. One flick would smash a human ribcage. So the claws were sheathed with leather, the mouth muzzled, and the tail's movement restricted by a brake, a harness that ran lines through hoops to the rear of the tall saddle. These were long enough to allow the tail to be carried straight or curved, as the animal needed it to balance, but too short to allow it to be swung.

"I am sure I will be fine," she said. "Look at it, the poor thing is covered over in leather. It must be uncomfortable. It probably can't breathe, never mind bite me!"

Qurion was already mounted on his own dracon.

"I assure you Femis can't tell. The dracons are raised to the brakes and sheaths. She's perfectly happy, as is Donda." He scratched his dracon's neck affectionately. It chirruped happily and shook out its head crest. Now it was dry, its plumage was deep green. Her own's was a dull brown with white patches.

"I have been promising to visit the village for a while and look over affairs there. Arriving on the back of a dracon will certainly set tongues wagging." She grinned wickedly. She was feeling herself again. "We will be back as soon as the captain has posted his orders, and I have spoken with Ullvis."

"Yes mistress," said Hovernia.

Qurion's second-in-command, Druvion, held the dracon steady for her. The beast was his, and he advised her where to place her feet and how to haul herself onto the saddle. She mounted on the third attempt, flinging her left leg over its back and settling gingerly onto the saddle ridge. Her wounded leg twinged with the effort, but small pains were all she suffered. The injury was nearly healed. The dracon felt remarkably delicate underneath her. It moved suddenly and she gave out a little cry of delight.

"Steady there goodlady," said Druvion, who was a good-natured sort. "Femis here has eaten today, so she is at her least dangerous. She'll follow Captain Qurion, you won't have to do much at all. Hold on, and try to match her movements with your hips." He thrust in and out with his own by way of demonstration, though it looked like he were showing her something else.

She laughed. "If that is all there is to it, I should be a natural," she said. Being outdoors after so long secluded in the keep was an unexpected pleasure. The soldiers and her servants had been hard at work. Mogawn's bailey looked better than it had for years. Much of the rubbish had been gathered up into a bonfire on the northern shore, where the island's small birch wood filled in the space between wall and cliff. The barracks had a new roof, the gates had been replaced, and the soldiers had set themselves to many other improvements. She felt giddy for a moment, swept up in the notion that she were a warrior woman of ancient days about to sally from her castle.

"Are you ready?" asked Qurion.

She nodded.

"Then let's go."

With a kick of his heels, Qurion set his own dracon running. Hers followed without any encouragement.

The dracons accelerated from a dead stop into a fast run. The gatehouse whipped by, and then the stone bridge beyond, then they were into the spiral tunnel carved through Mogawn's bubbled rock that led down to the mudflats. The dracons' croaks echoed from the walls. Light let in by holes in the stone strobed by. They were through quickly, running out over the drawbridge at the island's base and onto the slippery plaza that terminated the causeway linking Mogawn to dry land. The dracons managed the change in terrain easily, and galloped out onto the road.

Lucinia glanced behind her. Mogawn rose up, huge and imposing, far bigger than it felt when she was in the castle. The lower parts of the island were black from submersion in the sea, the upper white with the sun. The rock was full of trapped bubbles of gas that gave floatstone its buoyancy and the isle was covered in hemispherical cavities and sword-sharp ridges of stone where they had eroded through. She caught a glimpse of the towers rising over the edge of the cliffs before her twisting in the saddle upset the dracon's stride, and she turned herself to look forward.

For half its length, the road ran on a mole of heaped stone that kept them high off the mud. Iron posts, carved with warding marks and linked with chain, deterred the drowned and the ghosts that haunted many foreshores. The metal was heavily corroded, and caked with shellfish. Bright orange and blue oxides painted the cobbles around the base of each.

The mudflats either side of the causeway shone like silver. A small tide was due that night, and already sheets of water were pouring themselves in slicks of silver over the mud. Temporary sand dunes fronted the low hills that marked the end of the beach. Behind were tumbled hills marching arduously up to her estates on the land; gradual elevation defeated the great tides at Mogawn rather than bastion cliffs.

Cold, southerly winds blasted at the countess, buffeting her as they intersected with the draughts caused by the dracon's progress.

The countess had never ridden anything before.

History taught her that there had once been animals called horses, who were kin to the goats who provided meat, milk and hides to the peoples of Ruthnia. Not much was known about the creatures in modern times, though their skeletons were often unearthed, sometimes in vast numbers. A manual on horsemanship had survived the violent eras since the fall of Maceriya. By this one account, it was known horses were herbivores who were difficult to care for, being easily poisoned by common plants, and were not at all the fantastical beasts of folklore. Their fate had been sealed by the adoption of the predatory riding dracon by Ruthnia's armies, for the horse had no claws or sharp teeth, and was no match in battle for the reptiles. Too expensive and difficult for commoners to keep, too weak for war, the horse had died out thousands of years ago.

As the larger species of dracon used for food were too large and ponderous to ride, and the lesser dracons were too dangerous, all transport before the advent of glimmer engines in the western Hundred was by dog drawn conveyance. Dracons were ridden commonly in the eastern Kingdoms, where the open plains and sparse population limited the potential for fatal accident, and giant dracon cattle were employed to draw vehicles in other lands. But in Ruthnia, the dog ruled supreme, and dogs could not be ridden.

Had they not been moving so quickly the countess would have shared this information with Qurion. She didn't try. The streaming wind snatched her words from her mouth. Her clumsy attempts to match the surging motion of her mount made her breathless. Actually sitting on a creature bearing her was more exhilarating than being drawn behind one, and though she judged they were not moving any faster than her dray coach, it felt like she were running as fast as the wind.

She was grateful for the complex saddle. That, more than her own efforts, kept her seated.

A coat of salt-tolerant grasses and spiky, semi-aquatic bushes covered over the flats as they drew nearer to land. The broken shoreline of Mogawn approached. The rock there was weak with faulting, and broken into huge blocks as regular as tumbled bricks.

Birds wheeled screeching into the sky. They too differed to the draconic species, even to the dracon-birds they shared the skies with. Thinking on the horse and the dracon, the countess idly considered how such differing animals came to be living cheek-by-jowl. The creatures of fur and feather such as birds, or the goats, or the rodents that plagued mankind's settlements were taken to be simply animals, bracketed with and no different from the reptilian creatures. But there were obvious differences in their anatomies.

Another thing to explore. There were possibilities for study wherever she looked. If only life were longer!

The road remained level while the land rose up. Mud was replaced by a pleasant sandy beach marked by lines of debris from the dance of the tides. Drifts of sand built up in the wind around the debris, becoming dunes that were erased next time the sea came in.

A bastion ridge of permanent sand hills marked the beginning of land proper. By the time Lucinia and Qurion were a half mile out from the dune wall the causeway was level with the sand, which there was scarred by deep, short-lived creeks. This was the furthest extent of all but the greatest tides. Pale sand sifted down from the dune wall onto the flats. Mogawn's road acted as an artificial inlet, its verges crunchy with dried seaweeds and shells. Upon meeting the shore it rose up, lost its straightness, and switched back upon itself a couple of times, rising sharply up mature dunes dark with young soils and hairy with marram.

Qurion reigned his dracon in at the summit of the ridge. The dune wall held back the sea on one side, and a maze of shifting hills and half-buried stone blocks on the other. Wind blasted off the Tiriatic Ocean at a constant speed, its passage blocked by nothing until it hit the Karsan Isles. Curls of sand blew up from the beach, snaking their way into the labyrinth. Patches of dark cloud broke up the blue sky. Sunbeams turned like the spokes of a wheel, rolling over the land and foreshore in golden procession. Five miles across the flats Mogawn occupied the centre of the vista, its castle a model atop stone luminous in the sun. At the edge of vision beyond Mogawn the white line of the sea advanced for its modest raid on the shore.

"A good view made better from dracon back!" laughed the countess. Her mount paced on the spot, scraping long furrows in the sand blowing over the road.

"Now you can say you have ridden a dragon, more or less," shouted Qurion, who was as exhilarated by the ride as she. He turned his dracon from the view, toward the rattling grass. The hills of Mogawn stepped their way up to the interior, becoming thick with wind-stunted trees and yellow grasses away from the dunes. The road was a line shaved into the landscape.

"Not far now," said the countess. "We should press on before we lose too much of the day."

She turned reluctantly from the view. Copying Qurion's technique, she spurred her mount into a loping trot ahead of him, eliciting shouts of approval.

CHAPTER FORTY-SEVEN
A New Development

THEY WENT TO the railway station first, where the sending office was located. Qurion filled in a confidential military message form and passed it on to the magister who manned the sending desk, a minor talent whose sole gift had been trained to serve the machines.

"I've asked for stone and more lumber," said Qurion to the countess outside. "I'll be lucky to get half of what I ask for. Incompetence takes a half of everything in the army, corruption a quarter more." He looked up at the sending tower projecting from the top of the office, a bronze pole covered with mysterious spheres and delicate arrays of metal. "I can't get used to this modern world. When I was a boy, if you had an urgent message you had get someone to do this with their mind alone. Cost a fortune."

"The science of magic changes everything," said the countess. "Man is the author of change. Our species alters everything."

"You approve then. Sometimes, I wish for a simpler life." He remounted his dracon.

"I don't approve of every advancement," said the countess. "No change is without price."

"Where's your man then?"

"Ullvis. His name is Ullvis. He lives this way, on the way out of the village."

They rode down narrow lanes bordered with hedgerows so dense the wind was a feeble sigh through the leaves, and a permanent green twilight shaded the way.

"These roads are ancient," the countess said. "Older than mankind's presence on the islands. They were carved into the landscape by the passage of Tyn feet, so they say."

"Are there Tyn in these parts?" said Qurion.

"Not any more, no. Although the villagers would disagree. They say everything that goes wrong here is the fault of the Tyn, and any pile of stones is said to be an abandoned Tyn house. The villagers believe the Tyn dwell still further out on the peninsula, towards the end where there are only grasses, goats and seagulls. But I do not know if they are really there still, or a figment of overactive imaginations. The land is mine, and I never saw a living soul, Tyn or otherwise out there. But I used to enjoy the stories when I was a child."

The road opened out a little, winding its way over a landscape of gentle downs divided by more hedgerows. Worn outcrops watched over cornfields and pasturelands grazed short by herds of goats and dracon-cattle, who shook their horned heads and grumbled as the riders pranced by. The people they saw were even more wary of the carnivorous reptiles than Lucinia's servants had been, most removing themselves from the road with such haste they almost forgot to doff their hats to their mistress.

Ullvis dwelled in the mill by Mogawn brook, a half mile from the village's diffuse heart. He was a solid, uncomplicated man with little sense of humour and a dedication to the village that bordered on the pathological. He was also the miller as well as the mayor, both jobs he'd inherited from his father. The former because the mill had been in his family since the time of King Brannon, the latter because nobody else wanted to do it.

If he was surprised to see his lady, he hid it well, and gave the dracon no more than a second glance. He greeted Lucinia with respect before launching into a long list of what he called concerns, but which might more accurately have been named complaints. Qurion stood aside quietly as the miller went through the various issues facing the villagers. The countess's smalltalk dried up as he went on. It was clear to her that she had neglected her estate quite badly. She apologised, which mollified him somewhat.

Lucinia sincerely promised to make good on her responsibilities, and bade Ullvis goodnight. The meeting took longer than she had expected. As they rode back down the country lane from the mill to the village centre, she broke her silence.

"I am sorry, captain. I have been a bad landlord. There appears to be as much work to do here as there is at the castle." She pulled a thoughtful face. "I had a servant who left my employ last year. He took care of most of this for me. I did not know how much he did. Ullvis was right to keep me so long, but we will now have to stay here overnight. Today's tide is a small one that will not cover the causeway, but there is the issue of the unghosted dead, even so far out in the country."

"I am glad you recommended it, goodlady," said Qurion. "If the drowned do have designs on Mogawn, then they may be scouting the castle as we speak. I cannot rule out an opportunistic attempt on your life. If we stay over at the inn, then I can take a further look around tomorrow. It may do us well to ensure the villagers are prepared as well as we."

"You think the drowned will strike this far inland?"

"At the highest of tides, the village is only five miles from the water, so it is possible, yes. On most days, the drowned will not be able to come so far from the sea, but on the night of a great or a major tide? I think they could, if sufficiently motivated."

MOGAWN-ON-LAND'S CENTRE WAS eighty houses and other buildings around a derelict temple. There was a store, and a physic had his practise there, as did an animal doctor, Guider and the other professionals necessary to service a rural community. Dusk ushered in a cold autumnal night. Warm rectangles of candlelight broke up the blue dark. The largest building after the temple ruins was the Old Count, Mogawn-On-Land's tavern. From the sound emanating from within, most of the village's population were patronising it.

Qurion handed off the dracons to a terrified kennel maid, with strict instructions on their care. When they entered the smoky common room quiet dropped like a stone. The inhabitants mumbled greetings to the countess as she strode to the bar.

"Umi! Umi!" she banged on the wood, summoning the surprised proprietor from a back room. "Give us two rooms for tonight, would you? It's too late to go back to the castle."

"What a pleasure! The countess visits us!" said Umi. "I shall have rooms prepared immediately for you goodlady. I am glad you are here. There's talk of strangers around. I wouldn't want you riding back at this hour."

"The captain will protect me," said Lucinia.

Umi gave him a beady stare. "I'm sure he will," he said. He was suspicious of all outsiders, as is the habit of country folk. "Will you be dining with us? I only have the usual simple food, but I can find something good for you..."

She leaned over the bar and slapped him playfully on the shoulder in a breach of etiquette. None of the villagers batted an eyelid. They were used to their mistress's ways. "Your usual food is fine enough for me, Umi, just put us in the private dining room would you? The captain and I have things to discuss. It's not what you think, before any of your silly tongues get away from you. He's here to keep us all safe, not keep me warm."

Umi pulled a face at her forwardness. "Really, goodlady."

She turned to face the quiet barroom. "My lovely people, I apologise that I have neglected you these last months. In part I have avoided tackling the situation here as I realised how much I had shirked my duties, and was daunted. No more. This very day, I have spoken at length with Mayor Ullvis, and I have heard some of what needs to be done. Of course, the word of one man, even so fine a goodman as Ullvis, is never the whole story. I promise you that I shall hold a village meeting at the hall next week where all of you may bring to my attention anything that troubles you."

She was forced to shout over the hubbub this generated. "Please! If you would keep your questions and complaints until then, I would appreciate it." She turned to Umi, but spoke loud enough for everyone to hear. "Until then, two drinks a piece for everyone here tonight, to be charged to the castle. Holless will sort it out, next time he comes through."

A cheer went up, followed by a surge toward the bar. The press of people caught the countess in a web of doffed caps and modest bows as they expressed their gratitude.

"Free booze," she whispered to Qurion once she had extricated herself, "will put a smile on the face of the most disgruntled man."

THEY ATE IN the dining room off the main bar. There was not much call for private dining in Mogawn, and Umi had to rapidly clear the table of baskets waiting to be mended. A crooked window looked out on the wind rippled leaves of an alder. Those that had not yet turned yellow switched from silver to green in the last light of the evening.

"I did say the food was good, did I not?" she said.

Qurion nodded around a mouthful of goat stew. "It's much better than what the army gives us," he said.

"As good as that, eh?"

"I admit, it is poor praise. It is delicious."

Umi, who was making a clumsy attempt to serve wine the refined way, dipped his head in pleasure. He poured two glasses, then departed, pulling the door quietly closed behind him.

"A shame you can't say the same for the wine!" whispered the countess. She grinned. "I love this place," she said. "When my father was away, my mother used to come here on her own and I was allowed to play with the other children. It has fond memories for me. That all stopped when my mother died."

"He did not let you come here after your mother passed over?"

"Oh gods no! Father did not approve. 'A goodlady should be engaged in improving pursuits, not brawling in the mud with farm brats,' he'd say. He would never speak to the people like that directly, they all thought he was marvellous. He was a two-faced Ellosantin bastard. Married my mother for her money, then hounded her to death."

"Is that why you have never married?"

"What!" she snorted. "Me being my age, a terrible spinster, I should have married years ago, is that it? I'm disappointed in you," she said. She had meant it as a joke, but found herself actually offended.

"I genuinely meant no offence. Having got to know you a little, I am surprised."

"If you are trying to seduce me again, just ask. I can't abide hollow flattery."

"It is not hollow."

She sipped the wine. It was bad, and she pulled a face. "I am not married because I hate being responsible for other people. All this, the village and the castle, it has accreted around me like mortar. It drags at me. I love Mogawn, and I adore most of these people, do not think I am careless of them, but I wish to be free. They treat me like their mother. Marriage would be more of the same. It is the worst kind of imprisonment for a woman. Even if it goes well, and the man does not steal your fortune, or beat you, or ignore you, or fuck all the maids yet grow outraged when you speak to another man. Even if there is love in the relationship, you are responsible for someone else's happiness. That is the greatest responsibility of all, I cannot take that on. I simply cannot."

"You might be surprised, if you met someone who you felt similarly for. Then the burden would feel like a blessing."

"I hadn't expected such mawkish sentiment from you." She quirked her eyebrow. "You captain, are married. I can tell. You are also flirtatious, and unfaithful to your wife. I suspect frequently. You are not a suitable role model, nor are you in a position to be giving me advice on marital affairs."

Qurion nodded. "I am not a good husband. But there are good husbands. And there are good marriages that make good husbands even out of bad men."

The countess laughed uncomfortably. "This is all hypothetical. Who would marry a woman with a countenance like this?" She drew a circle around her face in the air. "It is the greatest irony of my life that I hated my father so much, but look just like him. I am truly a hag."

"Goodlady," said Qurion. "You are no hag."

"That is what they call me, though. My father thought so too. He ridiculed me about my face. He called me an ugly young witch. He wanted a son, and I was not one. I was lucky he died before he could marry me off." She took a shaky drink. "I know nothing about these good marriages you speak of, but I know there are bad marriages, and they make bad men worse."

The door creaked.

"Umi!" She said before looking to see who was there. "Please knock next time. We have sensitive matters to talk over."

"You should not speak of your father that way, Lucinella, he was a good man, and he did love you whether you believe it or not."

Cold shivers ran up the countess's spine. At the sound of the voice she turned her head as slowly as if it were a mechanical novelty mounted upon a child's saving bank.

Stood in the doorway was Mansanio, her disgraced manservant.

"Goodlady!" he said, half pleadingly, half longingly. His clothes were torn. Scratches marked his face, many deep and weeping.

Her shock turned to anger. Her face twisted savagely, and she pulled a single shot pistol from a pouch at her belt with the fluidity of someone who has practised the move a great many times.

"You have five seconds to tell me what you are doing here, before I put a hole in your heart, you little shit," she said.

"You have a gun?" said Qurion.

"What self-respecting woman does not?" she replied, stony faced. She looked Mansanio dead in the eye.

"Five," she began.

"Please goodlady, let me explain, I come here contrite," blustered Mansanio.

"Four."

"Take me back home, back to the castle. I will explain everything." He looked over his shoulder nervously. "I cannot stay here. I need to be on the sea! It is the only place I shall be safe."

Mansanio's entire manner had changed. The assured castellan of Mogawn was gone; in its place was a cringing, malnourished creature. He flung himself to the floor, hands writhing over his head. "I beg you! I must have forgiveness, or they shall kill me."

"What the hells are you talking about?" said Qurion. "Who is this creature, goodlady?"

"Three!" said Lucinia. She stood abruptly, knocking her chair back, pulled back the hammer on her pistol, and aimed it at Mansanio's head. "Explain yourself, or I will kill you."

"Wait a minute," said Qurion powerlessly. He got up slowly, fearful of provoking murder.

A tapping came at the window, too soft and insistent to be the branches of the tree. Qurion whirled around in time to see a tiny face snarling at the glass, eyes glowing. "Lost gods!" He snatched up his sword belt from where it hung on the back of his chair, and drew his sabre. "We have company."

Lucinia gave him a questioning look.

"Tyn," he said.

"I told you, there are no Tyn here, and no stories of them off the peninsula for generations," she said.

"You were talking of the lesser sort, because that is what was tapping on the window!"

"No. We've never had those at all," she said, puzzled. "What have you done, Mansanio?"

"Stop them, please!" sobbed Mansanio.

Umi came running to the door. "Goodlady, goodfellow, what is happening?"

"Get the doors shut!" said Qurion urgently.

"What is going on?"

The countess held up her hand to silence the innkeeper.

"Two," she said, her voice barely more than a whisper.

Feathery wings batted at the window. Small creatures, most no bigger than Qurion's thumb, fluttered against the glass, their ugly faces contorted in hate. Larger things without wings pulled themselves onto the sill to pluck at the transoms of the glass. The smallest were mounted upon the back of nocturnal insects, brandishing miniature lances in parody of the dragon knights of old. Filthy fingernails squeaked on the glazing.

"By the hundred hells!" swore Qurion. "They're picking the glass out."

"Please, please," whimpered Mansanio. "Take me away from here, get me away from them, and I'll tell you everything. I promise."

"One," said the countess. She bent down, and pressed her gun against his head.

"I killed a Tyn!" Mansanio shrieked hysterically. "I tore it off that bastard Kressind's shoulder, and I broke its gods-damned neck. I killed it, I killed it!" he wept.

"What... wait... Guis' Tyn, you killed Guis Kressind's Tyn?" said Qurion, torn between watching the window and dragging the cowering Mansanio from the floor.

Mansanio was past listening. "I'm sorry, I'm so sorry, they won't let me be."

"They're coming through!" shouted Qurion. A long-fingered hand, its owner hidden below the level of the wall, picked apart the old wood holding the glass in place with black nails that were closer to talons. The pane fell with a soft tinkle, and the Tyn burst in.

Qurion swiped his sword through the swarm of tynfolk. The countess discharged her gun. They boiled around blade and bullet, and dived onto Mansanio. Some of them played horrible, shrill instruments, and they sang as they plucked and tore at Mansanio's flesh and clothes.

"Confess, confess, confess!" they sang, their voices discordant. "Speak the truth of your crime, lie not, and die not, confess, confess, confess!"

The countess screamed. Qurion yanked her back, but the Tyn had intentions only on Mansanio, who they tormented until a burly villager came rushing in, and uncapped the lens of a powerful bulls-eye glimmer lamp. The cone of light sent the Tyn screeching toward the window.

From the common room came the shouts of people as they crowded the windows to see this phenomenon. Qurion shooed away straggling Tyn. He did so gently for he had no wish to earn their ire also, and hauled the shaking Mansanio to his feet.

"Every night! Every night!" wailed Mansanio. "Please help me. I confess, it was me, it was me. I killed the Tyn. I killed it!" he wept. "They said confess. I have! I have, and they still torment me." He fell to his knees, his bloodied face in his hands. "What do they want? What do they want?"

The countess and the captain shared a glance.

It had been a most eventful trip.

CHAPTER FORTY-EIGHT
A Traitor to the Realm

"GOODMAN AND GOODWIVES, goodfellows, please!" shouted Demion Morthrock.

The meeting hall at the Morthrocksey Mill echoed to shouting. Men of the lower orders stood and wagged their fingers at goodfellows of much higher social standing. Goodfellows shouted back.

"Please!" Demion said again.

A shot stopped the uproar in its tracks. Goodfellow Brask held a pistol in the air, barrel smoking.

"Sorry," Brask said. "I will pay for the damage to the ceiling."

Katriona sat upon the stage at the front with several of her key supporters. A long table with a white cloth divided them from their audience. Mill workers from all over the district, as well as several mill owners, filled the hall so densely there was standing room only.

"Goodfellows, goodmen," she said. There were a scattering of women in the audience. She didn't like to exclude them, but she could feel calm slipping from her and had to be quick. Besides, it was not they who were making all the noise. "We have come here to work in amity, not argue."

"Arguing's all you get if you keep on talking down to us like that!" shouted one man.

"Please brother, let the goodlady speak," said Monimus. "Just for a moment. Hear her out."

"It appears unlikely that my proposals will make their way through the Third House. We are here to find a solution to that, not to fight. The conditions in the mills of Karsa must be improved they—"

"They'll be improved when the rich stops making a pretty living off the backs of the poor!" shouted a man. "When our children can breathe air as clean as that on the Spires."

"You impudent scoundrel," said a richly dressed man. "That is what she is trying to achieve. Why don't you let her speak?"

"She's a Tyn-lover, and a woman!" shouted someone else. Katriona fixed the man's face in her mind. State-sponsored agitators were the bane of labour and trade association meetings.

"Let her talk!" shouted another.

The room descended into furious, bellowing argument again. Demion shared a look with his wife, then leant in to speak into her ear above the bluster.

"Do not lose heart, my love," he said. "They're here talking. That would never have happened only a few months ago."

He grasped her hand and squeezed it tightly. His smile was enough for her to know that he was proud of her, and that he loved her.

She drew in a deep breath, and stood. Her speech went undelivered.

The double doors to the meeting room burst inward. Soldiers in the bright yellow uniforms of the Karsan infantry ran inside in two files, weapons at the ready. They ran around the outside of the room, clubbing those who would not move out of the way with the butts of their rifles. They took up their positions smoothly. The crowd got to their feet, retreating from the guard, knocking chairs over and shoving each other out of the way. The shouts of raucous debate turned to calls of alarm. A decorated sergeant blew a whistle, and the guards slammed their guns down, butt first, onto the floor with a noise that caused more panic. Then the soldiers presented their arms and levelled them at the meeting.

The whistle peeped twice more, and Eduwin Grostiman walked into the room, flanked by more soldiers. With a dramatic flourish, he unfurled a piece of paper.

"I have here a warrant for the arrest of Katriona Kressinda-Morthrocksa and her co-conspirators: Goodfellow Brask, Goodfellow Martenion and Goodman Monimus."

"What is the meaning of this?" said Brask. "Under what charges?"

"High treason against the state of Karsa," said Grostiman triumphantly. "Take them," he ordered. "Break this meeting up. And then find the Tyn."

Every other soldier in the cordon slung their weapons onto their back, drew wooden truncheons, and pushed their way into the crowd. Any man or woman that stood in their way was struck hard, as were many that did not.

"Leave the building! Disperse, in the name of Prince Alfra!" bellowed their sergeant. "Out, out!"

Slowly at first, then all in a rush, the people fled the room, goodman and goodfellow alike struggling past each other to be out of the doors. Grostiman and his soldiers stood aside to allow them to leave. Those who were reluctant or who simply found themselves at the back of the pack were hit repeatedly. Blood flowed. Several men were set upon, beaten down by soldiers who set about their work with stolid efficiency.

"What the hells has happened?" said Brask. Two soldiers grabbed him by the elbows, and hustled him toward the exit. Though arrogant in his position as an aristocrat, he was wise enough in the ways of the world not to struggle.

"Playing innocent?" said Grostiman. "We shall see about that when you are incarcerated in the Drum. A few nights of discomfort is enough to loosen the tongue of a popinjay like you."

"I've no idea what the hells you are talking about!" snapped Brask.

"Nor have I," said Katriona. Her escort did not manhandle her, but stood close enough to ensure escape was impossible. She walked down from the stage with them at her side. Martenion was treated with less cordiality.

"Gods man!" shouted Brask. "Careful with Martenion. Have you no shame?" The soldiers hauled him in front of Grostiman. Katriona came next. The lower ranked men were treated with less respect. Grunts echoed around the hall as Monimus was beaten senseless.

"None whatsoever," said Grostiman. "Not when it comes to prosecuting traitors." He smirked.

"You don't believe a word of it," said Demion.

"The god was slain in the Off Parade twelve days gone," said Grostiman.

"What's that got to do with us?" snapped Demion.

"Your Tyn had something to do with it," said Grostiman with relish.

"What?" said Katriona.

Grostiman sighed. "I expect your husband to protest his innocence, but really goodlady. Eliturion is dead, as full well you know. After a stringent investigation I found that Tyn, your Tyn, took part in this foul murder, aiding the Maceriyan devil in his foul work. This news in not yet public. When it is, the populace will become unruly. This I think is part of your plan to destabilise our society so you might seize control of the state at the head of some kind of communitarian revolution."

"This is outrageous! You can't prove any of this!" said Demion Morthrock. "You always were a little snake, Grostiman. I see the poor opinion held of you is a gross underestimation of your perfidious nature. You cannot arrest my wife! She has cost you a few pennies, but enriched your moral standing. You should thank her, you little lackwit."

Grostiman held up a gloved hand. "Careful there goodfellow, or I shall have you arrested too. Now then," he said to his soldiers, "Take them away."

"I should—" began Demion.

"Demion, say nothing more to him. Do not add to our woes," said Katriona. "I shall go with him. They will release me, because I have done nothing."

The soldiers marched their prisoners out of the door. Two crossed rifles in front of Demion. Three more carried the unconscious Monimus from the room. Blood streamed from a cut to his head.

"I will hire an army of lawyers!" Demion called after his wife. "I will not allow this. I will not! Be steadfast, my dear. Be steadfast!"

Katriona was escorted from the room. The soldiers exited.

"You are out of your depth, Goodfellow Morthrock," Grostiman said. "You should keep your woman under better control. If you can exercise a husband's authority over her, then you may have her back. And when she is returned to you, keep her at home, and you can go back to your cards and your racing. The world is a dangerous place for those who upset the floatstone."

Grostiman left. The two soldiers barring Demion were last out. He ran after them. Soldiers glared at him from the back of dray wagons. An enclosed carriage, with a sole barred window in its rear-facing door, was already racing away to the mill's north entrance.

From the south, Tyn were being marched en masse to a group of wagons. Lights were coming on in the workers' housing.

Helplessly, Demion Morthrock watched his wife and his unborn child being taken away.

FILDEN OBSERVED THE commotion around the main offices of the Morthrocksey mill. Soldiers escorted out the Kressind woman and several others. *What is it,* he thought, *about that family?*

He kept himself out of sight in the loft door of a foundry. A braced I-beam dangled a pulley and hook for lifting materials into the building, and he blended into the shadow it cast as if he were part of it. The building was shut down for the night. It was getting dark, although not late. The nights were drawing in.

He waited for the occurrence at the offices to be done. Demion Morthrock stood impotently in the doorway.

Filden snorted. Morthrock was a well-known weakling. Well regarded as a nice fellow, but "nice" was a huge disability in Filden's world. Contempt was the least negative emotion he felt for Morthrock.

The arrest of Katriona and the rest provided the perfect distraction. Filden vanished into the building, and made his way silently through the mill complex. Locked doors posed no barrier to him. He sped down empty staircases. The few people he encountered saw nothing but a Morthrocksey worker's uniform. They would never recall the face beneath the peak of his cap.

He took back ways between the buildings. Unlike some mills, the Morthrocksey shut down all production for the night. Another of Katriona's reforms that benefitted Filden greatly.

Tracking a single Mohaci urchin across Karsa city would have taxed most men, but not Filden. Money opened mouths. Violence worked on those it did not. From an ex-employee of the Lemio mill he had got a description of the constable who had closed down the Lemio mill's orphanage. From him, he had found the dray wagon drivers. They in turn told him where they had dropped the children in the Aranthaddua stews. A boy he found there had given him a name and a description. He had been lucky that Lavinia was the only Mohaci girl at the Lemio mill. Tracking her to Golden Lane south of the North Gate had been harder, but once there it wasn't difficult to find someone who had seen her be taken. He pressed the local watchmen for information, discovered that a Renian by the name of Donati had rounded up children, including a Mohaci, under license of the Morthrocks to the Morthrocksey mill. A little more digging around the mill had uncovered the Renian's interest in very young women, and that his eye had fallen upon this Lavinia. A handful of coins was enough to discover the location of his apartments within the mill, and his shift patterns. Everything about the Renian that could be known, Filden knew.

Easy work for a man like him, though he admitted without following the Sniffer he would never have found her. Vand's aims would be achieved. The Sniffer would be cheated, Vand's daughter would be safe from its attentions—though Filden cared neither one way or the other about that. Killing the Sniffer would be Filden's reward. As he did not like to be afraid of anything, he looked forward to removing the source of his fear. His disquiet at the Sniffer only fuelled his hate of it, and his desire to kill.

He reached the Renian's quarters. Donati had set himself up in an out of the way part of the factory in order to hide his proclivities. As Filden had discovered them easily enough, it had not worked. The remoteness was, however, useful to Filden. He would not be disturbed.

Filden kicked the door in. In an instant he had taken in the surroundings. A double bed, wash stand, chamber pot. A few clay flasks of wine. The room was built into the eaves. The ceiling slanted with the roof above, a single, dirty skylight let in mottled light. It stank of sex and sweat.

The girl was naked in the bed with the Renian. She came awake far quicker than he did. They always did that, women. Filden supposed they were more often prey creatures, at greater risk than men. She scrambled up, dragging the bed clothes with her to cover her small breasts. She was most of the way to womanhood, but not quite there. Filden felt the barest iota of pity.

"You, over there," he said, waving her into the corner with his gun.

Donati came round only a fraction of a second after her. He did not move, but smiled cockily at him.

"What are you, her old pimp? She's mine. I bought her fair and square, more or less. Fuck off."

"You interferers with little girls are all the same," said Filden, and he shot the Ronian. The bullet was trapped in his skull, and he fell dead, a neat round hole drilled in his forehead. The gun he had been hiding under the sheets thumped to the floor. "You aren't used to dealing with adults," he said.

The girl screamed.

"It's your lucky day," Filden said. "I'm taking you from this place and this man's hands."

"Where?"

"Somewhere better. I'm not going to hurt you. I could be lying, I could say what I want with this gun in my hand, but I am not. Get dressed. Now."

The girl was smart enough to do as he asked. The sheet she covered herself with snagged and half fell. Whatever Vand had planned for her, Filden hoped it was not terminal. She would be a fine looking woman in a few years' time. If she survived Vand's machine, he thought about revisiting her when she matured.

The girl pulled on her dress and shoes. She got a short, factory issue coat, and went to stuff things into a linen bag.

"Leave it. You'll be given all you need." He jerked the gun toward the door. "Let's go."

She headed to the door with minimum encouragement.

"You first," he said, poking the gun into the small of her back. But she stopped dead.

"Get on!" He said. He repeated himself. She twisted round.

"I can't..." she said in a voice of utter dread. "I cannot move. I—" She froze completely, lifeless as a stick of wood.

Filden's survival instinct kicked in. He threw himself to the side of the girl and opened fire with his gun, aiming three bullets two feet above the floor.

The height of the Sniffer's head.

Filden's bullets sped at the creature. It stood there, a mild expression on its face. The bullets slowed to a dead stop an inch from its face, spinning still from the rifling of his gun barrel. The Tyn blew on them, and they fell to the floor with a trio of tinkles.

"Filden, Filden! How I have benefitted you. Is this my repayment, being cheated by your master? Attempted murder? I am so disappointed."

Filden raised his gun to fire again. The Tyn waved a finger and the weapon flew from his grasp into the wall, where it remained stuck, jiggling against the brickwork as if it would escape.

Filden went for his other gun, but he could not move. The various amulets he wore burned so hot with counterspells that they scalded his skin. He hissed with the pain.

The Sniffer waved another hand. Lavinia floated up from her spot in the corridor and hovered in the air.

"Vand should never have considered reneging on our deal." The Sniffer knelt, placed his carpet bag on the bare boards of the corridor, and opened its neck up wide. Sickly light poured from it. "Now what he wants will carry a steeper price. Two nights? A week? I shall make a thing of delight from his daughter, and he will have no choice but to agree." He grinned horribly at Filden.

The Tyn snapped his fingers. The girl floated light as a cloud over the bag, rotated about her waist until she was head down, and descended within. The bag swallowed her whole. When she was gone the Tyn closed the bag and snapped shut the clasps. He stood up, and dusted his crooked knees off.

"Now you. Vand will suffer a father's anguish, but you will not be so fortunate."

Filden struggled helplessly against the Tyn's magic. The Sniffer and the room seemed to be growing. The corridor became cavernous. Strange smells filled Filden's nose. Air currents caressed his face. To his horror, he saw the means by which he felt these unnoticed draughts were long whiskers springing from his cheeks. His nose grew, merging with his mouth, becoming a pink snout. Dense grey-brown fur sprouted all over his face. His teeth fell out. He squealed in pain as new, long incisors forced themselves out of his gums. His clothes pooled around him, become mountains of cloth trapping him. His amulets, weapons and other equipment fell from his body. No Tyn made magic or iron blade was any use against his foe.

The Tyn was by now a giant. He stood over Filden, hands on his hips, and peered down.

"These trinkets cannot foil the power I possess. Stupid little man. Stupid little mouse!"

Sharp nails nipped at Filden's freshly grown tail. The Sniffer hoisted the mouse the assassin had become high up into the air. Filden shouted at him, but his voice was a powerless squeak.

"No bag for you, my friend."

The Sniffer tilted his head back, opened his jaws wide, and lowered the struggling mouse into his mouth, whereupon he swallowed it whole.

Humming to himself, the Sniffer plucked his carpet bag from the floor. He capered off down the corridor. That night he would deliver Lavinia to Arkadian Vand.

Then he would claim his reward.

CHAPTER FORTY-NINE
The Coming of the Drowned King

"Do you think he's telling the truth about Guis?" asked Qurion.

Mansanio sat in the centre of the cell, his chin on his drawn up knees and his arms wrapped around his legs. He had arranged dozens of iron nails in concentric circles around himself, their points outwards. More nails hung from the ceiling on threads. His skin was painted with black paint made of ground iron.

"We saw the lesser Tyn. I can think of no other reason why they might attack him."

"Fuck it," said Qurion. "No wonder no one's heard from Guis for so long. I thought he was having one of his artistic sulks. We have to get word to his family. Gods alone know what's happened to him. Do you think a mage could help him? Or a Guider?"

"I appreciate that Guis Kressind is your friend, but he hurt me deeply," said the countess.

"No one deserves what's happened to him."

"No. I suppose they don't." She turned away from the viewing slit in the door.

"Please goodlady!" called Mansanio from inside. "Shut it, please!"

She slid the cover closed. "No one has been down here in years. I can't remember the last time Mogawn had a prisoner. Not even my father used this place."

The cell was one of three leading off a large room. Iron hooks hung from walls wet with damp. Rust streaked the stone.

"When I was young, my father used to threaten me with this place; that he would lock me away here if I did not do as he commanded," she said. "He told me this room was used for torture in the days when the pirate lords of Mogawn ruled." She shuddered. "Even he was never cruel enough to act on his word and put me here. Sometimes, you can hear noises down in the cells, late at night."

"The unghosted?"

"Worse, I fear. Mansanio must be terrified to want to stay here."

"There's plenty of iron," said Qurion. "No kind of Tyn likes much of that. Do you think the iron and sea will keep the Tyn away?"

"Since when did I become an expert on the Lesser Tyn?" said the countess. "Mansanio thinks it will work, or he would not ask to be put here. I doubt it makes much difference. Horrifying. I feel sorry for both Guis and him. And to be the cause of it..."

"Goodlady," said Qurion earnestly, "a woman should never blame herself for a man's actions in her name."

"I still feel responsible. I was blind to Mansanio's affection. I could have let him down more gently. I could have been less lascivious in my behaviour. To think, he was watching all the time!"

"You have done no wrong."

"I am surprised to hear a man say something like that."

"I am celebrated by my peers for my exploits with women. You are censured for the same activities with men. It is not right."

"The world is not fair," she said. "I learned that a long time ago."

They looked into each other's eyes. The invisible thread that draws lips together tugged at her. She resisted it, but she could not look away.

The clatter of boots on stairs interrupted them.

A soldier came into the room and saluted smartly.

"Sir, goodlady. I have news. A rider approaches."

"The tide is coming in, isn't it, Morian?" said Qurion.

"Yes sir. He's not natural sir," said the soldier. "We think he's one of them."

THE CASTLE LOOKED more impressive than Lucinia could remember. Soldiers with ironlocks patrolled the wall walks. The hoarding roofs over the parapets had been repaired. Windows were blocked with smart new masonry, walls shored up by buttresses. The repaired gates gleamed with fresh dark green paint. The cannons had been taken apart, the guns and the carriages winched laboriously up to the walls and reassembled in situ. Guns topped every tower. Qurion led the way into the gatehouse inner tower. He took the narrow spiral stairs three steps at a time. He, the countess and Morian emerged onto the flat roof mounting two light cannon. Between them an artillerist peered through a telescope toward land.

A light drizzle fell, shrouding the land in grey. That night the tide was due to drown the causeway, though not lift the castle. The road was yet uncovered, and from the landward side of Mogawn a single rider came down the road upon the back of a stiffly moving dracon.

"This looks like an official visit," said Qurion. "From the kind of official no one wants."

His man stepped back from the telescope. Qurion took his place.

"Gods," Qurion breathed. "You're not wrong, infantryman. He is not natural."

"What is it?" asked Lucinia.

"Take a look," Qurion said, and offered her his place. The countess pressed her eye to the piece, and recoiled.

"By the gods," she said. She looked back through the telescope. The telescope was almost as good as her own observatory pieces, and the magnification so powerful the face of the approaching rider seemed close enough to kiss.

The creature riding toward them had once been a man. He was no longer. He had the shape of a man, and he was dressed as one, but the telescope's unflinching eye revealed his true nature. Upon the dracon rode a corpse, his leathery skin brown with preserving fluid. Black lips framed shockingly white teeth. Moist, living eyeballs sat unblinking in an angular face. The eyelids were dried back to scabs. He was garbed like a goodfellow of high standing. His clothes were new, followed the latest fashions and were well made. But they were not the sole tailored thing about him. Stitching of silk ribbon peeked out from under his ostentatious collar, holding the skin of his neck to his chest.

The dracon was also dead, and more obviously so than its rider. Bone was visible through holes in its hide. A large area of its skin had been cut away, and its internal organs removed. There were no eyes in its head. Wood and iron lent the skeleton support. A living dracon moved with a pleasing strut. This waddled like a clockwork, wholly unlovely.

"What the hells is he?" said the countess.

"I'd guess he's the emissary of the Drowned King, the ambassador to the isles of Karsa and the Hundred Kingdoms," said Quiron.

"He is a horror, sir," said Morian.

The rider came to a halt where they could still see him from the tower, a few hundred yards out from the castle, and retrieved a crisp, white handkerchief from the breast pocket of his suit. He held this up over his head. Every movement was a stiff contortion.

"He wants to talk," said Qurion. "What do you think?"

"You're in command of the military here, captain."

"It's your castle goodlady, while the situation is calm I am happier to have your input."

"We should speak with him," she said.

"We should."

"But I don't want him in the castle."

The emissary of the drowned stood stock still, a macabre anatomist's model on the causeway.

"Agreed. I advise on meeting him outside. I don't want him reporting on our strength to his master." The water washed against the causeway mole. It was an ordinary scene made sinister. Every wavelet held menace.

"Let us meet him in front of the gatehouse. He needs to see we are serious."

"Let's do that," said Qurion. He turned to the few men atop the tower. "I need a volunteer to convey the message."

Nobody stepped forward.

"Fine. Morian, you're volunteering. Go fetch him, and be quick about it. The rest of you, it's happening. To your positions. I want the picket in place and the drawbridge to the plaza up as soon as this monster's off the island, is that clear?"

"Yes captain," the soldiers said, and ran off to their positions. The small bell in the gable tower of the great hall rang a few moments later. Lucinia imagined the consternation that would cause among her servants. She hoped they would keep their heads and not embarrass her.

Qurion and the countess watched from atop the tower. Morian ran out onto the causeway, a white flag in his hand. He noticeably slowed as he caught full sight of the drowned man.

"Come on Morian," muttered Qurion, peering through the scope. "Keep yourself together. If he frightens you, you'll be useless in the fight."

The dead man and the live man conversed a moment. Morian gestured back up at the castle. The emissary nodded. A moment later Morian turned back. The emissary of the drowned followed him.

"Well then, goodlady," said Qurion. "To business."

LUCINIA AND QURION awaited the emissary under the shelter of the outer gateway. The first gates were open, the inner gates closed. The smaller, outer bailey was pristine, cleared of junk, accreted soil dug away, the paving swept by the soldiers, and the walls cleaned of years of grime and whitewashed. The countess wished that there'd been time to get the pointing redone, not that she'd been able to see the walls for the last fifteen years.

She would have been mortified to receive the emissary into the mess that was there before.

The rain fell heavily. The hiss of it on the flat sea rising around the island reached as high as the castle.

They waited in the damp silence. Sheets of falling water shortened the horizons. The land retreated into the gloom.

Morian came out of the tunnel through the rock with parade ground dignity, though his face was as white as his flag, and his eyes so firmly held forward his expression resembled that of the dead man he escorted.

The leaden click of the unliving dracon's claws echoed up the passageway long before he emerged onto the low stone bridge leading to the gates. The emissary brought his mount to a halt before the countess and the captain.

Morian stamped twice upon the bridge. "Sir, goodlady," he said in a clear voice. "His Excellency the Emissary of the Drowned King."

"You are dismissed, infantryman," said Qurion.

The merest suggestion of relief quirked the edge of Morian's eyes and he marched into the outer bailey.

"Captain, goodlady," said the emissary courteously. He bowed his head. Dried sinews snapped and crackled in his neck. His skin folded stiffly, threatening to crack. "Forgive me if I do not dismount. I find the movement awkward."

Leather bindings enwrapped his legs, fastening him to the dracon's saddle. The dead animal stood as still as a child's wooden toy, as a neglected museum exhibit.

"I see that your government have taken the threats of my master seriously," said the emissary. He looked up at the gatehouse towers, where several ironlocks were trained upon him. "You have repaired the fortifications. There are soldiers here where there have been none for years. See the benefits peace between our kingdoms brought. It is a pity the Three Houses did not take the rest of my master's message to heart." The rain wet his skin, making it glisten like seaweed. A melange of smells rose from his preserved corpse, heavy perfume failed to mask smoked meat. A chemical tang stung Lucinia's eyes, but most prevalent was the potent smell of brine.

"The message you delivered to the mission in Perus?" said Garten. "You chose to speak with Garten Kressind, and not the ambassador."

"It was his brother who caused the original offence," said the emissary. He moved like a badly made puppet. His black lips, drawn back over shining white teeth, precluded any meaningful expression, but he managed to convey an urbane air. He spoke reasonably, and with good humour. "Who the message was delivered to is a detail. The message was delivered. Your government was slow in responding, and you gave an answer that was unsatisfactory. The Drowned King is offended."

"The ambassador died," said Qurion. "The continent is in uproar. If you were to contact the Ministry of Karsa-in-the-Hundred here, your concerns would have been addressed more quickly."

"You say this, captain. But we have had our answer. You are the leader of an armed force stationed here, in the sea, the territory of my master. That is a further provocation."

"Mogawn is part of the sovereign territory of Karsa, and is the property of Lucinia Vertisa, Countess of Mogawn," said Qurion. "We are a token force, here to oversee the renovation of this castle as part of a general programme of works to overhaul Karsa's fortifications."

The emissary managed to stretch his brittle lips wider over his perfect teeth in a hideous smile.

"You dissemble, captain. We both know this is at best a bending of the truth."

"Do you call me a liar, goodfellow?"

"I intend no slur against your honour, captain. If it is a lie, it is not yours. You and I are but servants of greater powers. I will not insult you."

"You are willing to insult our nation," said Lucinia. "That is an insult to me."

"Goodlady, you nation has insulted ours. I agree these are trying times, but the Drowned King is not the ruler of some minor kingdom to be fobbed off with excuses and insincere apologies, and he will certainly not accept a simple reiteration of arguments he has already stated he regards as non-valid. The Drowned King is the lord of the ocean. He has been trespassed against, and his reasonable complaints have been ignored. I will speak with the Minister of Karsa-in-the-Hundred, naturally. But only to say to him what I am telling you. The demands of the Drowned King have changed. He will uphold the peace, and forgive the insult of Trassan Kressind's illegal crossing of the Drowning Sea in the

Tiriatic Ocean, and the further insult of governmental inaction, upon the surrender of Mogawn Island and castle to his nation, to be garrisoned by his soldiers, and to be an inalienable part of his realm for all time."

"Never!" said Lucinia. "This island is my home."

"That is why I am asking you, goodlady. You could surrender this island and save a lot of bloodshed, for if it is not given freely, the Drowned King will declare war upon the isles and take it."

"It is impossible," said Qurion. "You know that. She can't. It is a part of the realm."

"I admit, this meeting is more of a formality than a genuine attempt at negotiation." The emissary scratched his sunken nose in a ghoulish imitation of life. "But one can always hope that cooler heads will prevail, and sense will out. Alas, it is not to be. Perhaps my master will be more convincing."

"The Drowned King is coming here?" said Lucinia.

"Why do you think your dashing young captain has been sent to you? Of course he is coming here. His superiors are well aware that the Drowned King covets this place. Before the king's coming to us, it was the great bastion against our people. After his arrival, and the creation of our kingdom from so many disparate bands of lost souls, it was Karsa's bulwark against the sea. It is a place of neither land nor water. He desires it. Give it to him."

"No," said Lucinia.

"So be it. Then I regret to inform you that the kingdom of the Drowned is now at war with the kingdom of Karsa." The emissary bowed his head to the awful creak and pop of dry muscle. "Goodlady, it has been a pleasure to meet you, having missed you in Perus. I would speak with you further, for I hear many good things regarding your science. When this altercation is over, maybe we shall have the chance. I shall see to it that you are not harmed.

"Captain, may victory go to the noblest cause." He turned his dead mount around. "Now, if you will excuse me. The tide is rising, and although I can tolerate a little rain, the changes made to me to enable my presence on dry land mean I can no longer allow myself to get soaking wet. I am leaving. I trust you will not shoot me in the back. It would do you little good, in any case."

He headed over the drawbridge back into the tunnel. Qurion looked upward and shook his head. Guns were withdrawn from the parapets and through loops in the tower wall.

"Sir!" shouted one of the men. "Out to sea! The drowned are here."

"They are here already?" said the countess.

"They never expected us to hand it over. They're cutting us off before I can get a message out. Come on, we better get inside. I need to see what I am up against." Qurion guided the countess back into the inner bailey. Men shouted orders. The inner gates opened. A squad of soldiers ran out, running a light cannon between them, and headed off into the tunnel. "Get the drawbridges shut and the gates closed!" shouted Qurion. "Let's show these dead bastards we're ready for them."

"Lieutenant! There's more of them, west and north."

"Shit," said Qurion. "Come on."

"You knew this would happen!"

"It was likely," he said. "We're in a bit of a bind. We couldn't have too many soldiers here, for fear of provoking the drowned. Too few, and they could walk right in. We just need to hold out a while until reinforcements arrive."

"How will you summon them."

"There are scouts on the foreshore. They'll get the message back."

"The strangers Umi mentioned?"

"Those are the ones. Idiots weren't supposed to be seen. All this subterfuge is part of war, I'm afraid."

From the inner bailey, they went into the gatehouse and ran up the narrow stairs to the top of the tower to where the telescope was.

Around the castle, men were moving.

Qurion reached the telescope first. Lucinia waited as he panned the glass back and forth across the horizon. She decided to go to her observatory later, and train her own equipment upon her enemy.

"Take a look," said Qurion.

The countess bent to the glass, and drew in a sharp, short breath.

The drowned were rising from the ocean all around the castle. Armoured knights upon the backs of juvenile anguillons cut sharp wakes in the water. Ramshackle siege engines bobbed to the surface upon boiling waters, rocking to stillness on beds of floatstone. Waist deep in the shallows was the Drowned King himself, a behemoth composed of rotten corpses and shattered sea wrack. Qurion's men shouted and pointed in consternation at the arrival of the giant king. The countess put a hand to her mouth.

"Be calm," said Qurion. "They'll not take this place, I swear."

"Sir, I have a small group within range of the forward battery," called one of Qurion's men.

"Give fire at will," said Qurion. "Let's show these dead bastards that this island belongs to Karsa!"

Three cannon boomed, their discharge rocking the ancient stones of the castle.

Mogawn knew war again.

CHAPTER FIFTY

A Temporary Farewell to an Ersatz God

REL FACED THE Brass God across a carpet of woven gold. Qurunad's soulless glass eyes stared unblinkingly back. The god sat immobile. Perhaps he was not present in his brass body, or perhaps the tics he had exhibited the first time they had met were part of his elaborate deception.

No longer did the Brass God lurk in his citadel. A great pavilion had been erected at the centre of the lake bed. Its fabric was of metal, stronger than steel but lighter than air, and provided the same directionless illumination as the citadel walls. For six days the god had sat enthroned within, surrounded by machines like him, all bearing weapons. For several days the elders came and went, bringing him tribute and asking his counsel. They were all gone now. Rel had demanded that he speak with the god alone, and his request had been granted. When their king and their god commanded, the modalmen were eager to obey.

"You needn't look at me like that," said the Brass God. "I saved you from certain death, gave you a power not known since Res Iapetus walked the earth, and made you a king."

"Is that what you did?" said Rel. "I'd say you tricked me, manipulated me into risking my life and afterlife, and killed the men I came here to save to suit your own agenda."

"There is truth in that," admitted the Brass God. "But it is not the whole of the truth. You came here of your own free will. Every choice you made was your own. I would go so far as to say that the other options open to you were not optimal for your survival. You did what you had to do. You made the right choices. You will return to your kingdoms with a powerful asset against the enemy. Your civilisation will survive, if fortune smiles on you."

"And so will you."

"Naturally. I have been honest with you, Captain Kressind. Your kind were employed by mine as warriors, little better than slaves to begin with. I could have been far more ruthless in my use of you."

"Could you? I do not think I am the only one who had limited choices."

The Brass God tapped the arms of his throne. "That is true. Look at yourself." He lifted his hand to gesture at Rel's new raiment. Rel wore a full suit of armour of Morfaan steel, its plates inset with black panels bearing glowing script. He bore a sword that hummed with magic when it was drawn from its scabbard. It was broad bladed but lighter than a small sword. "These armaments are of ancient make. No mortal man has borne such tools of war for millennia. You are honoured."

"Honoured for a slave."

"Your kind began as slaves. At the end, you were anything but. I was sincere in my hopes for the future. We can build a new world together."

"How can I trust you, I—" Rel twitched. A sharp pain threaded itself through his innards. Agonising while it lasted, but quickly gone.

"The pains will worsen. The armour will help."

"How long do I have?" Rel said.

The Brass God was annoyed that Rel was not more grateful for his gifts. "I cannot say. The mageblood in you was weak. The machine had to change you greatly, and so your book of life has too many pages, parts of it are written upon one another, and it has become illegible in others. The book of life contains the spells, if you will, that are read by a mage who determines your fate, he—"

"You are the most condescending person I have ever met in my entire life," interrupted Rel. "Wizards reading my fate from material written in my flesh?"

Qurunad made a mechanical noise. "Yes, well. The concepts are somewhat beyond you."

"Try," said Rel. "Please."

"If you insist." Qurunad thought a moment, and once again adopted the schoolmaster's tone he favoured. "Your body is made up a variety of chemicals, some of which would be recognisable to your alchemists, if they were isolated. Four of these chemicals combine in a certain way within you. These are letters in what I refer to as the book of life. Their various combinations determines the synthesis and employment of other chemicals, which in turn influence the creation and catalysation of further chemicals. In essence, your body is a factory for chemicals, where everything it requires to function is created from the raw materials you ingest—your food and drink. All this meat," he gestured at Rel, "is the product of chemical reaction upon chemical reaction. Where it becomes very complicated, instead of simply complicated, is the way in which the life spirit of the world interacts with said chemicals. It is the interface between the universal soul of all creation and the base chemical reactions of your organism that makes you you, rather than merely a very clever wet machine. Were it not for that, you would have no soul, and there would be no ghost to go on from this place, and no will to exert upon reality."

"See? I understood that."

"Greatly simplified," reiterated the Brass God.

"There is no need for imaginary, miniature wizards reading books in my bowels," said Rel.

The Brass God continued, ignoring Rel's jibe. "We Morfaan changed the way these chemicals express themselves by modulating the effect of the world spirit. Magic, in essence, is the disregarding of natural law in favour of an artificial weighting of spiritual influence. Nature and magic are complementary to each other, they arise symbiotically from each other. The former is an expression of Form, the latter of Will. Life could not exist without both. The universe creates life, life changes the universe. By altering the balance, we alter reality in our favour. There is the empiricist's approach, used by our scientists and your magisters, and the brute approach, which you are now capable of; the changing of the universe by exercise of thought alone. You are a mage.

"In your case, the functioning of these chemicals—and we really do refer to them as letters in the book of life, before you become completely unreasonable—has been disrupted by a surfeit of magic. You are out of balance. The disruption will spread. In time, the informational content of your body will become too corrupt for you to live."

"Magic will not keep me alive?"

"It could, but ironically only while accelerating the process. The armour you wear will help you keep your form. You possess great power Rel, but wielding it will hasten your death."

"How long do I have?"

"If you do not exert your gift, you may live twenty more years. At the other extreme, if you rely upon your new talents, you will be dead before the end of next winter. If you are careful, you will function for a good while yet."

"So much effort to secure a straight answer," said Rel.

"You must think of the larger situation," said the Brass God. "You are not alone in this. Many people are going to die. If you use your gift wisely, it will be fewer than if you do not. You may think yourself unlucky, but truthfully I do not think it could have been anyone else but you who came here. These events, though exploited by myself, were set in motion by a higher power. We are all the pawns of fate. No one is free, least of all myself."

Rel's head drooped. He was dismayed by the transformation of his fellow men into the giants, and although he attempted to see a noble purpose in it, upset by his shortened lifespan.

"You make a lot of assumptions about me," said Rel. "You assumed I would not abandon my countrymen. What if I had gone, and taken the message?"

"Either outcome would have been useful. This is more so. I like to make sure my schemes bring me benefit, whichever plan is realised."

"Like your brass body."

"Just so."

"You also assumed I would help you once you were rid of Brauctha. I could have killed you. I still could."

The Brass God tilted his head equivocally. "You could try. Are you going to? Either of our deaths would be a terrible waste."

Rel shook his head angrily. "No, but your need for my acceptance and forgiveness is the only reason I do not ram this sword you have given me right through your mechanical guts."

"Why?" said the Brass God.

"Because it means you are flawed, and that means you are human," said Rel. "So most of what you are saying is probably true."

"I am not human."

"So you would like to think. Don't worry, it is not a compliment."

The Brass God laughed. "You have a fine spirit."

"It's all I have left." Rel looked down at the alien armour. He felt powerful; simultaneously, he felt weak. The unseen threads that made him were unravelling. "Tell me. Will I succeed? Can the Draathis be stopped?"

"I do not know."

Rel smiled bitterly. "So much for the powers of foresight."

REL WALKED OUT into the glaring desert day where the modalmen mustered. He wondered who was luckier, the newly made modalmen, who might live ten thousand years but would never recall themselves, or himself, who wielded the power of a minor god at the cost of his life.

The camp was mostly disassembled. The modalmen were as thorough in the valley as they had been in the desert and left little evidence of their presence. Refuse was burned to fine ash, from excrement to bones, and raked into the sand. Campfires were turned over so the char was hidden. Their innumerable footprints would be wiped away by the next sandstorm. Only the palisade remained as evidence, but the fence of ancient stone would appear like everything else in the Black Sands; a relic of a past most men could not begin to conceive of.

Outside the Brass God's tent, Drauthek waited, holding the bridle of Rel's new mount.

The dragon snorted and looked down at him disdainfully, but though its claws were bare and its mouth unmuzzled, it made no move against the lesser creatures around it. Rel could feel its mighty spirit, he experienced the furnace of its beating heart. To say he controlled it would not be correct, but he influenced it. In him, it recognised something more dangerous than itself, and so gave its fealty.

Drauthek knelt as Rel approached.

"Do you really need to do that?"

"You are our king," said Drauthek. "I must kneel. The ways of the True Men must be observed."

Rel wished he could get them to give up some of their traditions. Not one was alterable, whether it be the greeting of the sun, or the disgusting trophies the man eater clans bore.

Using the dragon's forearm as a step, Rel climbed to the base of the saddle on its back. The saddle had been made for him, but it was still so big it was more throne than riding seat, and could only be accessed by short ladders hanging either side.

Once he was seated, the dragon got up and let out a roaring croak, similar to Aramaz's, thought Rel. Once, he would have been terrified to be near the thing, but he felt nothing. He had yet to discover how deeply the changes went into him. Drauthek leapt onto his garau. Mounted, his head was roughly level with Rel's knees.

"It's good to be bigger than you for once," said Rel.

"Don't get used to it," said Drauthek. The modalman had an easy humour and confidence Rel had not appreciated before he could speak the modalman language. "Great one, if I may advise you, the Gates of the World, as you call the border fort, is that way." He pointed. "Five weeks march, and we shall be there."

"How quickly if we took the Road of Fire?"

"Seven minutes, but we cannot take that route, great one. There are too many of us, and the way is closed, and so we must march across the desert."

"Fine," said Rel. He looked out at the horde. Before he had to estimate; now, when he looked at them, he knew their number exactly. Twelve thousand, three hundred and twenty one, including the seven hundred and fifty six newly made modalmen. They were ready, mounted on their garau, all looking to him for guidance. A coterie of young modalmen rode at his side. One bore his banner, a new creation featuring the Kressind dragonling rampant, but its serpentine body wove its way through a brass cog that was certainly not present on the family arms, nor were the three sigils of the greatest modal tribes that formed a triangle around it.

Staring at the banner, he noticed that the modalman bearing the flag looked familiar. Rel leaned down from in his monstrous mount, and looked at him carefully. "You, what is your name?" he said.

Though Rel had asked the question in the modalman's language, the modalman replied in fluent Karsarin, gently softened by the accent of the eastern kingdoms. As soon as he spoke, Rel knew who he had been.

"My name?" The young modalman frowned. "I have yet to be given my name, great one."

Rel looked at him sadly. There were traces of the man he had spoken to in the cage, and who he had seen around the towns at the Gates, but they were only echoes, no more than that.

"Then I shall give you one," he said. "I will call you Tuvacs."

"Tuvacs," repeated the modalman. A look of recognition briefly crossed his face. "Tuvacs." Then it was gone.

Rel sat back in his saddle. "Forward," he ordered. "To the Appin Mountains, the Gates of the World, and the Hundred Kingdoms of Ruthnia."

A dozen clan leaders riding at his side repeated the orders as booming calls.

Horns blowing, the horde moved out. Rel let the dragon plod along on foot, though he sensed its urge to fly.

"I want to too," he whispered, more with his mind than his voice. "We cannot, because I fear I shall never come back, but fly the skies forevermore."

He liked the idea.

The dragon looked back at him, its yellow eyes alive with fearsome intelligence.

"You understand," said Rel.

As the army departed, the Brass God remained in his tent. Rel thought it likely the wily Morfaan was watching them leave by some means.

In long train, the modalman horde wound its way out through the narrow gate. Rel kept his eyes forward, not for any reasons of resolution, or the appearance of command, but because a little way behind him rolled great wagons which he did not wish to see. Their cages had been removed, the iron of their bars used to reinforce the flatbeds for the great weight they now supported.

Upon the wagons were the Machineries of Change.

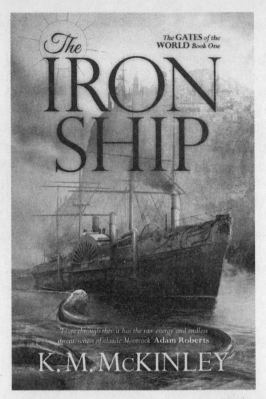

The GATES of the WORLD Book One

The IRON SHIP

'Tear through this: it has the raw energy and endless inventiveness of classic Moorcock' **Adam Roberts**

K. M. McKINLEY

Merchant, industrialist and explorer Trassan Kressind has an audacious plan – combining the might of magic and iron in the heart of a great ship to navigate an uncrossed ocean, seeking the city of the extinct Morfaan to uncover the secrets of their lost sciences.

Ambition runs strongly in the Kressind family, and for each of Trassan's siblings fate beckons. Soldier Rel is banished to a vital frontier, bureaucrat Garten balances responsibility with family loyalty, sister Katriona is determined to carve herself a place in a world of men, outcast Guis struggles to contain the energies of his soul, while priest Aarin dabbles in forbidden sorcery. The world is in turmoil as new money brings new power, and the old social order crumbles. And as mankind's arts grow stronger, a terror from the ancient past awakens...

This highly original fantasy depicts a unique world, where tired gods walk industrial streets and the tide's rise and fall is extreme enough to swamp continents. Magic collides with science to create a rich backdrop for intrigue and adventure in the opening book of this epic saga.